More praise for
The Monarchies of God Series

"One of the best fantasy works in ages . . . Tough, muscular realism . . . Kearney paints the gore, the sex, and the lust for power in vivid color."

—*SFX*

"Impressive for its human insights, its unusual take on the use of magic and its fine blending of historical elements with sheer invention."

—*Locus*

**Be sure to discover
the first book of The Monarchies of God . . .**

HAWKWOOD'S VOYAGE

Also by Paul Kearney

HAWKWOOD'S VOYAGE
Book One of The Monarchies of God

THE HERETIC
KINGS

BOOK TWO OF THE MONARCHIES OF GOD

PAUL KEARNEY

ACE BOOKS, NEW YORK

This is a work of fiction. Names, characters, places, and incidents either are the product of the author's imagination or are used fictitiously, and any resemblance to actual persons, living or dead, business establishments, events, or locales is entirely coincidental.

THE HERETIC KINGS

An Ace Book / published by arrangement with
Orion Publishing Group

PRINTING HISTORY
Victor Gollancz edition / 1996
Vista mass-market edition / 1997
Ace mass-market edition / February 2002

Visit our website at
www.penguinputnam.com
Check out the ACE Science Fiction & Fantasy newsletter!

ISBN: 0-441-00908-5

ACE®
Ace Books are published by The Berkley Publishing Group,
a division of Penguin Putnam Inc.,
375 Hudson Street, New York, New York 10014.
ACE and the "A" design
are trademarks belonging to Penguin Putnam Inc.

PRINTED IN THE UNITED STATES OF AMERICA

10 9 8 7 6 5 4 3 2 1

For my brothers,
Sean and James Kearney

Acknowledgments to:

*John McLaughlin, Richard Evans and
Jo Fletcher, for their patience and
hard work on my behalf*

WHAT WENT BEFORE...

IT is over half a millennium since the birth of the Blessed Saint Ramusio, the man who brought the light of true belief into the western world. The empire of the Fimbrians, which once spanned the wide continent of Normannia, is only a dim memory. Their empire has been transformed into a series of powerful kingdoms, and the Fimbrian Electorates have remained isolated within their borders for over four centuries, indifferent to events beyond them.

But now things are taking place which cannot be ignored. Aekir, the Holy City on the eastern frontier and seat of the High Pontiff Macrobius, head of the Church, has fallen to the teeming armies of the heathen Merduks, who have been pressing on the eastern frontier of the Ramusian kingdoms for decades.

Caught up in the fury of its fall, Corfe Cear-Inaf flees westwards, one of the few of its defenders who has survived. On the refugee-choked road he befriends an old man the Merduks have blinded, and finds out that he is none other than Macrobius himself, who escaped unrecognized by the troops of Shahr Baraz, the Merduk general. Corfe is nursing his own private grief: he left his wife in Aekir, and believes her dead. Unknown to him, however, she survived the assault and was captured and sent to the court of the Sultan as spoils of war to join his harem. Corfe and Macrobius trek westwards along with thousands of others, seeking sanctuary in the impregnable fortress of Ormann Dyke, the west's last line of defence after Aekir.

In the meantime, across the continent, the mariner Richard Hawkwood returns from a voyage to find that in this time of fear and uncertainty the militant Churchmen of the Inceptine Order are cracking down on anyone in the great port-capital of Abrusio, first city of the kingdom of Hebrion, who is either a user of magic, or a foreigner. Since half of Hawkwood's crew are not native to Hebrion, they are hauled off to await the pyre. Hebrion's king, Abeleyn, tries to do what he can to limit the scale of the purge in the raucous old port, and at the same time is involved in a battle of wills with his senior Churchman, Himerius, who has instigated it, and who has also asked the Church to send him aid in the form of two thousand Knights Militant, the fanatical military arm of the Church.

The wizard Bardolin is also affected by this purge. He befriends a young female shape-shifter, rescuing her from one of the city patrols, but it seems likely to be only a temporary reprieve. Then his old teacher, the King's wizardly (and proscribed) advisor, the mage Golophin, tells him of a possible way out. The Hebrian King is sponsoring a westward voyage of exploration and colonization, and its ships will have room for a sizable contingent of the Dweomer-folk who at this moment are being hunted down across the kingdom.

The captain of the expedition is none other than Richard Hawkwood, who has been blackmailed into taking on the mission by an ambitious minor noble, Murad of Galiapeno. Murad is after a kingdom of his own, and he believes that there is a lost continent somewhere across the expanse of the Great Western Ocean. He possesses an ancient rutter recording a long-ago voyage to such a continent. He does not tell King Abeleyn, or Hawkwood, that the earlier westward voyage ended in death and madness, with a werewolf aboard ship.

The expedition sets sail, Hawkwood having said good-bye to his volatile, nobly born mistress, the lady Jemilla, and to his wan, hysterical wife Estrella. But the ships are burdened with one last, unwelcome passenger. The Inceptine cleric Ortelius takes ship with the explorers, no doubt so that the Church can keep an eye on this unorthodox voyage.

MEANWHILE; in the east, events are proceeding apace. Corfe and Macrobius finally arrive at Ormann Dyke, where Macrobius is recognized and welcomed and Corfe is once more an officer in the Torunnan army. The Merduk Sultan, Aurungzeb, orders an immediate assault on the dyke against the better judgement of the old general, Shahr Baraz. Two successive attacks fail, the second in large part due to the efforts of Corfe himself. When the Sultan orders a third attack, his orders communicated via a homonculus, Shahr Baraz refuses outright and kills the homonculus, thus crippling and disfiguring Aurungzeb's court mage, Orkh. Shahr Baraz then flees into the steppes of the east, and campaigning comes to an end for the winter. Ormann Dyke is safe, for the present. Promoted to colonel by the dyke's commander, Martellus the Lion, Corfe is to escort Macrobius to the Torunnan capital, Torunn, where the old Pontiff has now taken on new stature.

For the Church has split down the middle. In Macrobius' absence the Prelates of the Five Kingdoms have elected the hardline Prelate of Hebrion, Himerius, as the

new Pontiff, and he refuses to accept that Macrobius is
alive. Matters come to a head at the Conclave of Kings
in Vol Ephrir, which all the monarchs of Ramusian Normannia attend. At this conference, three kings—Abeleyn
of Hebrion, Mark of Astarac (who is Abeleyn's ally and
soon to be his brother-in-law) and Lofantyr of embattled
Torunna—recognize Macrobius as the rightful Pontiff,
whereas every other Ramusian ruler on the continent
sides with Himerius. This produces a religious schism of
vast proportions, and the prospect of fratricidal war
amongst the Ramusian states at a time when the Merduk
threat has never been worse. But that is not the only event
of the moment which occurs at the conclave.

The Fimbrians, so long isolated, have sent envoys to
the meeting to offer their troops to any state which needs
them—for a price. The hard-pressed Lofantyr of Torunna
immediately takes the envoys up on their offer, and re-
quests that a Fimbrian force be sent to aid his fought-out
troops at Ormann Dyke. But Abeleyn is uneasy, sure that
the Fimbrians have a secret agenda of their own; dreams
of rekindling their empire, perhaps.

As the conclave breaks up in acrimony and hostility,
Abeleyn receives another notable piece of information.
His newly acquired mistress, the lady Jemilla, is, she in-
forms him, pregnant with his child. Abeleyn sets out for
home knowing that the Church has done its best to take
over his kingdom in his absence, and that he has a bastard
heir on the way.

WHILE Normannia is riven by war and religious dis-
cord, Hawkwood's two ships are sailing steadily
westwards. Murad, to Hawkwood's annoyance, takes a
couple of the female passengers as servants and bed-
mates. One of the pair is Bardolin's ward, the young
shape-shifter, Griella. She hates Murad, but something in
her responds to his cruelty as he responds to the strange
feral nature he senses within her. Bardolin is both jealous

and afraid of the consequences of their liaison, but there
is nothing he can do.

The ship survives a terrible storm but is blown far off
course. When a calm ensues, Hawkwood calls upon the
talents of Pernicus, a weather-worker, to bring them a
wind, despite the objections of the Inceptine, Ortelius,
who insists that the voyage is cursed. The wind comes,
but not for long. Pernicus is found butchered in the hold,
his wounds inflicted by what seems to be some sort of
beast.

As the ships crawl westwards they lose contact with
each other, and Hawkwood does not know if his other
vessel is still afloat or sunk. There is enough trouble to
occupy him on his own ship, however. His first mate is
killed next, and a cabin-boy disappears. Bardolin, sure
that Griella is behind the killings, confronts her, but becomes convinced that she is innocent of them, leaving
him baffled. The ship comes to resemble a prison, with
guards everywhere and a mutinous, terrified crew. Only
Hawkwood's authority and Murad's savage discipline
keep passengers and crew in line.

But one dark night the beast on board strikes at Hawkwood, Murad and Bardolin themselves. There are two
werewolves in the attack: one turns out to be Ortelius,
the other the missing cabin-boy, nursing his grievances
ever since Hawkwood cast him aside. In the ensuing battle Griella shifts into her beast form to protect her lover,
Murad, and Bardolin dispatches the other lycanthrope
with a bolt of Dweomer. Griella dies of her wounds,
however, leaving Murad horrified and grief-stricken.

The unhappy ship sails on, and finally the lookouts
sight land. They have reached the Western Continent at
last, but they are the only ones to have done so. The
wreck of Hawkwood's other ship is visible on the reef
which rings the strange coast, and there is no sign of
survivors.

Hawkwood's Voyage ends with the explorers finally

setting foot on the shores of this new land. They have no idea what to expect but they know that Ortelius was trying to prevent them from getting here, as something has prevented ships from surviving the westward voyage for three centuries and more. They suspect that this new world is inhabited. But by whom, or what?

PROLOGUE

ALWAYS, men move west. Is it something to do with the path of the sun? They are drawn to it like moths to the flame of a taper.

Many long turning years have slipped by, and still I remain: the last of the founders, my body scarcely my own at the end. I have seen four centuries of the waking world trickle past, their passage scarcely marked by any change in the land I have made my home. Men change, and they like to think that the world changes with them. It does not; it merely tolerates them, and continues to follow its own, arcane revolutions.

And yet there is something in the air, like a whisper of winter in this country which knows no seasons. I feel a change coming.

THEY came treading the saffron and scarlet course of the sinking sun, as we had always known they would, with their tall ships trailing streamers of weed from worm-eaten hulls.

We watched them from the jungle. Men in salt-encrusted armour with scurvy-swollen faces bearing swords and pikes, and, later, reeking arquebuses, the slow-match glowing and hissing in the wind. Gaunt men of Hebrion, or Astarac, or Gabrion; the sea-rovers of the Old World. Hard-handed buccaneers with the greed dazzling their eyes.

We had come here fleeing something; they had come seeking. We gave them fear to fill their bellies and night-dark terror to plump out their purses. We made of them the hunted, and took from them whatever we desired.

Their ships rotted slowly at their moorings, untenanted and filled with ghosts. A few, a very few, we let live, to take the tale of us back east to the Monarchies of God. In this way, the myth was created. We hid our country behind a curtain of tall tales and dark rumours. We laced the truth with the hyperbole of madness; we beat out a legend as though it were the blade of a sword on a smith's anvil. And we quenched it in blood.

But the change is coming. Four centuries have we lingered here, and our people have slowly filtered back to the east in accordance with the plan. They are everywhere now in Normannia. They command soldiers, they preach to multitudes, they watch over cradles. Some of them have the ear of kings.

The time is come for our keels to recross the Western Ocean, and claim what is ours. The beast will out, in the end. Every wolf will have its day.

PART ONE

SCHISM

ONE

YEAR OF THE SAINT 551

VESPERS had long since been rung, but Brother Albrec had affected not to hear. He chewed the end of his quill so that damp bits of feather dropped on to the bench, but he did not notice. His face, squinting in the dim light of the dip, was akin to that of a near-sighted vole, pointed and inquisitive. His hand shook as he turned the page of an ancient parchment which lay before him. When once a corner crumbled at the touch of his nimble fingers he whined a little back in his throat, for all the world like a dog seeing its master leave the room without it.

The words on the parchment were beautifully inscribed, but the ink had faded. It was a strange document, he thought. There were none of the illuminations which had always been thought so necessary an adornment to the holy texts of Ramusio. Only words, stark and bare and elegantly written, but fading under the weight of so many years.

The parchment itself was poor quality. Had the scribe

of the time possessed no vellum? he wondered, for this was hand-enscribed, not churned out on one of the famous presses of Charibon. This was old.

And yet it was almost as though the author had not wanted to draw too much attention to the work. And indeed the manuscript had been found, a rolled-up wad of untidy fragments, stuffed into a crack in the wall of one of the lowest of the library levels. Brother Columbar had brought it to Albrec. He had thought perhaps to use the parchment as blotting for the scriptorium, for Charibon still produced hand-written books, even now. But the faint, perfect writing visible upon it had made him hesitate, and bring it to the attention of the Assistant Librarian. Albrec's natural curiosity had done the rest.

Almost he halted, rose from his seat to tell the Chief Librarian, Brother Commodius. But something kept the little monk rooted there, reading on in fascination while the other brothers were no doubt sitting down to their evening meal.

The scrap of parchment was five centuries old. Almost as old as Charibon itself, holiest of all the university-monasteries on the continent now that Aekir was gone. When the unknown author had been writing, the Blessed Ramusio had only just been assumed into heaven—conceivably, that great event had happened within the lifetime of the writer.

Albrec held his breath as the petal-thin parchment stuck to his sweating fingers. He was afraid to breathe on it for fear that the ancient, irreplaceable text might somehow blur and run, or blow away like sand under some sudden zephyr.

. . . and we begged him not to leave us alone and bereft in such a darkening world. But the Blessed Saint only smiled. "I am an old man now," he said. "What I have begun I leave to you to continue; my time here is finished. You are all men of faith; if you believe in the things

which I have taught you and place your lives in the hand of God, then there is no need to be afraid. The world is a darkening place, yes, but it darkens because of the will of man, not of God. It is possible to turn the tide of history—we have proved that. Remember, in the years ahead, that we do not merely suffer history, we create it. Every man has in him the ability to change the world. Every man has a voice to speak out with; and if that voice is silenced by those who will not listen, then another will speak out, and another. The truth can be silenced for a time, yes, but not for ever . . .

The rest of the page was missing, torn away. Albrec leafed through the indecipherable fragments that followed. Tears rose in his eyes and he blinked them away as he realized that the parts which were missing were indeed lost beyond recall. It was as if someone had given a thirsting man in a desert a drop of water to soothe his parched mouth, and then poured away a quart into the sand.

Finally, the little cleric got off his hard bench and knelt on the stone floor to pray.

The life of the Saint, an original text which had never been seen before. It told the story of a man named Ramusio, who had been born and who had lived and grown old; who had laughed and wept and spent sleepless nights awake. The story of the central figure in the faith of the western world, written by a contemporary—possibly even someone who had known him personally . . .

Even if so much of it had been lost, there was still so much gained. It was a miracle, and it had been granted to him. He thanked God there on his knees for revealing it to him. And he prayed to Ramusio, the Blessed Saint whom he was now beginning to see as a man, a human being like himself—though infinitely superior, of course. Not the iconic image the Church had made him out to be, but a man. And it was thanks to this incredibly precious document before him.

He regained his seat, blowing his nose on the sleeve of his habit, kissing his humble Saint's symbol of bog-oak. The tattered text was beyond price; it was comparable to the *Book Of Deeds* compiled by St. Bonneval in the first century. But how much of it was here? How much was legible?

He bent over it again, ignoring the pains that were shooting through his cramped neck and shoulders.

No title page or covering, nothing that might hint at the identity of the author or his patron. Five centuries ago, Albrec knew, the Church had not possessed the virtual monopoly on learning that it did now. In those days many parts of the world had not yet been converted to the True Faith, and rich noblemen had sponsored scribes and artists in a hundred cities to copy old pagan texts or even invent new ones. Literacy had been more widespread. It was only with the rise to prominence of the Inceptines in the last two hundred years or so that literacy had declined again, becoming a preserve of professionals. It was said that all the Fimbrian emperors could both read and write, whereas until recently no western king could so much as spell his own name. That had changed with the new generation of kings that was coming to the fore, but the older rulers still preferred a seal to a signature.

His eyes stung, and Albrec rubbed them, sparking lights out of the darkness under their closed lids. His friend Avila would have missed him at dinner, and might even try to seek him out. He often scolded Albrec for missing meals. No matter. Once he saw this rediscovered jewel . . .

The quiet thump of a door shutting. Albrec blinked, looking about him. One hand pulled a sheaf of loose papers over the old document while the other reached for the lamp.

"Hello?"

No answer. The archive room was long and cluttered, shelves piled high with books and scrolls dividing it up into compartments. It was also utterly dark, save where Albrec's trembling lamp flame flickered in a warm circle of yellow light.

Nothing.

The library had its share of ghosts, of course; what ancient building did not? Working late sometimes, clerics had felt cold breath on their cheeks, or sensed a watching presence. Once the Senior Librarian, Commodius, had spent a night in vigil in the library praying to Garaso, the saint for whom it was named, because some novices had become terrified by the shadows they swore gathered there after dark. Nothing had come of it, and the novices had been ribbed for weeks afterwards.

A sliding scrape in the blackness beyond the light of the lamp. Albrec got to his feet, gripping his A-shaped Saint's symbol.

> *Sweet Saint that watches over me*
> *In all the lightless spaces of the night*

he prayed the ancient prayer of travellers and pilgrims.

> *Be thou my lamp and guide and staff,*
> *And keep me from the anger of the beast.*

Two yellow lights blinked in the darkness. Albrec received a momentary impression of something huge hulking in the shadow. The hint of an animal stink which lasted only a second, and then was gone.

Someone sneezed, and Albrec's start rocked the table behind him. The lamplight fluttered and the wick hissed as oil spilled upon it. Shadows swooped in as the illumination guttered. Albrec felt the hard oak of the symbol creak under the white bones of his fingers. He could not speak.

A door again, and the pad of naked feet on the bare stone of the floor. A shape loomed up out of the darkness.

"You've missed dinner again, Brother Albrec," a voice said.

The figure came into the light. A tall, gaunt, almost hairless head with huge ears and fantastically winged eyebrows on either side of a drooping nose. The eyes were bright and kindly.

Albrec let out a shuddering breath. "Brother Commodius!"

One eyebrow quirked upward. "Who else were you expecting? Brother Avila asked me if I would look in on you. He is doing penance again—the Vicar-General will tolerate only so many bread fights of an evening, and Avila's aim is none so good. Have you been digging in the dust for gold, Albrec?"

The Senior Librarian approached the table. He always walked barefoot, winter and summer, and his feet, splayed and black-nailed, were in proportion to his nose.

Albrec's breathing was under control again.

"Yes, Brother." Suddenly the idea of telling the Senior Librarian about the rediscovered text did not appeal to Albrec. He began to babble.

"One day I hope to find something wonderful down here. Do you know that almost half the texts in the lower archives have never been catalogued? Who knows what may await me?"

Commodius smiled, becoming a tall, comical goblin. "I applaud your industry, Albrec. You have a true love of the written word. But do not forget that books are only the thoughts of men made visible, and not all those thoughts are to be tolerated. Many of the uncatalogued works of which you speak are no doubt heretical; thousands of scrolls and books were brought here from all over Normannia in the days of the Religious Wars so that the Inceptines might appraise them. Most were burned, but it is said that a good number were laid in corners and forgotten. So you must be careful what you read, Albrec. The merest whiff of unorthodoxy in a text, and you must bring it to me. Is that clear?"

Albrec nodded. He was sweating. Somewhere in his mind he was wondering if withholding facts would be construed as a sin. He remembered his own private store of scrolls and manuscripts that he had hoarded away to save from the fire, and his unease deepened.

"You look as white as paper, Albrec. What's wrong?"

"I—I thought there was something else in here, before you came."

This time both eyebrows shot up the hairless head. "The library has been playing its tricks again, eh? What was it this time, a whisper in your ear? A hand on your shoulder?"

"It was . . . a feeling, no more."

Commodius laid a massive, knot-knuckled fist on Albrec's shoulder and shook him affectionately. "The faith is strong in you. Albrec. You have nothing to worry about. Whatever ghosts this library is home to cannot touch you. You are girded with the armour of true belief; your faith is both a beacon to light the darkness and a sword to cleave the beasts which lurk therein. Fear cannot conquer the heart of a true believer in the Saint. Now come: I mean to rescue you for a while from the dust and the prowling ghosts. Avila has saved some supper for you and insists you be made to eat it."

One great hand propelled Albrec irresistibly away from his work table, whilst the other scooped up the lamp. Brother Commodius paused to sneeze again. "Ah, the unsettled dust of the years. It settles in the chest you know."

When they had exited the darkened room Commodius produced a key from his habit and locked the door behind them. Then the pair continued up through the library to the light and noise of the refectories beyond.

● ● ●

FAR to the west of Charibon's cloisters, across the ice-glittering heights of the Malvennor Mountains. There is a broad land there between the mountains and the sea beyond, an ancient land: the birthplace of an empire.

The city of Fimbir had been built without walls. The Electors had said that their capital was fortified by the shields of the Fimbrian soldiery; they needed no other defence.

And there was truth in their boast. Almost uniquely among the capitals of Normannia, Fimbir had never been besieged. No foreign warrior had ever entered the massively constructed City of the Electors unless he came bearing tribute, or seeking aid. The Hegemony of the Fimbrians had ended centuries before, but their city still bore the marks of empire. Abrusio was more populous, Vol Ephrir more beautiful, but Fimbir had been built to impress. Were it ever to become deserted, the poets said, men of later generations might suppose that it had been reared up by the hands of giants.

East of the city were the parade grounds and training fields of the Fimbrian army. Hundreds of acres had been cleared and flattened to provide a gaming board of war upon which the Electors might learn to move their pieces. A hill south of the fields had been artificially heightened to provide a vantage point for generals to regard the results of their tactics and strategy. Nothing that ever occurred in battle, it was said, had not already been replicated and studied upon the training fields of Fimbir. Such were the tales that the tercios of the conquerors had engendered over the years and across the continent.

A cluster of men stood now on the vantage point of the hill overlooking the fields. Generals and junior officers alike, they were clad in black half-armour, their rank marked only by the scarlet sashes that some wore wrapped beneath their sword belts. A stone table that was a permanent fixture here stood in their midst, covered with maps and counters. Coprenius Kuln himself, the first

Fimbrian emperor, had set it here eight hundred years previously.

Horses were hobbled off to one side, to mount order-bearing couriers. The Fimbrians did not believe in cavalry, and this was the only use they had for the animals.

On the training fields below, formations of men marched and counter-marched. Fifteen thousand of them, perhaps, their feet a deep thunder on the ground that had hardened with the first frosts. A cold early morning sunlight sparked off the glinting heads of their pikes and the barrels of shouldered arquebuses. They looked like the massed playthings of a god left lying on a nursery floor and come to sudden, beetling life.

Two men strolled away from the cluster of officers on the hill and stood apart, looking down on the panoply and magnificence of the formations below. They were in middle age, of medium height, broad-shouldered, hollow-cheeked. They might have been brothers save that one wore a black hole where his left eye should have been, and the hair on that side of his head had become silver.

"The courier, Caehir, died at his own hand last night," the one-eyed man said.

The other nodded. "His legs?"

"They took them off at the knee; there was no saving them. The rot had gone too far, and he had no wish to live as a cripple."

"A good man. Pity to lose one's life because of frostbite, no more."

"He did his duty. The message got through. By now, Jonakait and Merkus will be in the passes of the mountains also. We must hope they meet with better luck."

"Indeed. So the Five Kingdoms have split. We have two Pontiffs and a religious war in the offing. And all this while the Merduks howl at the gates of the west."

"The men at Ormann Dyke; they must be soldiers."

"Yes. That was a fight. The Torunnans are no mean warriors."

"But they are not Fimbrians."

"No, they are not Fimbrians. How many of our people are we to send to their aid?"

"A grand tercio, no more. We must be cautious, and see how this division of the kingdoms goes."

The Fimbrian with the unmutilated face nodded fractionally. A grand tercio comprised some five thousand men: three thousand pike and two thousand arquebusiers, plus the assorted gunsmiths, armourers, cooks, muleteers, pioneers and staff officers who went with them. Perhaps six thousand in all.

"Will that be enough to save the dyke?"

"Possibly. But our priority is not so much to save Ormann Dyke as to establish a military presence in Torunna, remember."

"I find I am in danger of thinking like a general instead of a politician, Briscus."

The one-eyed man named Briscus grinned, showing a range of teeth with smashed gaps between them. "Kyriel, you are an old soldier who sniffs powder-smoke in the wind. I am the same. For the first time in living memory our people will leave the bounds of the electorates to do battle with the heathen. It is an event to quicken the blood, but we must not let it cloud our judgement."

"I do not altogether like farming our men out as mercenaries."

"Neither do I; but when a state has seventy thousand unemployed soldiers on hand, what else can one do with them? If Marshal Barbius and his contingent impress the Torunnans sufficiently, then we will have all the Ramusian kingdoms crying out for our tercios. The time will come when every capital will have its contingent of Fimbrian troops, and then—"

"And then?"

"We will see what we can make out of it, if it happens."

They turned to look down on the training fields once

more. The pair were dressed no differently from the other senior officers on the hill, but they were Fimbrian Electors and represented half the ruling body of their peculiar country. A word from them, and this army of thousands would march off the training fields and into the cauldron of war wherever they saw fit to wage it.

"We live in an age where everything will change," one-eyed Briscus said quietly. "The world of our forefathers is on the brink of dissolution. I feel it in my bones."

"An age of opportunity, also," Kyriel reminded him.

"Of course. But I think that before the end all the politicians will have to think like soldiers and the soldiers like politicians. It reminds me of the last battle by the Habrir river. The army knew the Electors had already signed away the Duchy of Imerdon, and yet we deployed that morning and fought for it nonetheless. We won, and threw the Hebrians in disorder back across the fords. Then we gathered up our dead and marched away from Imerdon for ever. It is the same feeling: that our armies can win any battle they choose to fight, and yet in the end it will make no difference to the outcome of things."

"You wax philosophical this morning, Briscus. That is unlike you."

"You must forgive me. It is a hazard of advancing years."

From the formations below, lines of smoke puffed out and seconds later the clattering rumble of arquebus fire reached them on the hill. Regiments of arquebusiers were competing against each other to see who could reload the fastest, shooting down lines of straw figures that had been set up on the plain. Volley followed volley, until it seemed that a high-pitched thunder was being generated by the very earth and was clawing up to heaven. The plain below became obscured by toiling clouds of powder-smoke, the fog of war in its most literal sense. The heady smell of it drifted up to the two Electors on the hillside and they snuffed it in like hounds scenting a hare on a winter's morning.

A third figure left the gaggle of officers around the stone table and stood to attention behind the Electors until the pair had noticed him. He was a square man; what he lacked in height he made up for in width. Even his chin was as regular as the blade of a shovel, his mouth a lipless gash above it partially obscured by a thick red moustache. His hair was cut so short as to stand up like the cropped mane of a horse; the mark of a man who often wore a helm.

"Well, Barbius?" Briscus asked the man. "How do they fare?"

Barbius stared straight ahead. "They're about as handy as a bunch of seamstresses on a cold morning, sir."

Briscus snorted with laughter. "But will they pass?"

"I'll work them up a little more before we go, sir. Three rounds a minute, that's our goal."

"The Torunnans think themselves well-drilled if they can get off two in that time," Kyriel said quietly.

"They're not Torunnans, sir—with respect."

"Damn right, by God!" Briscus said fervently. His one eye flashed. "I want your command to be as perfect as you can make it, Barbius. This will be the first Fimbrian army the rest of the kingdoms have seen in action for twenty-five years. We want to impress."

"Yes, sir." Barbius' face had all the animation of a closed helm.

"Your baggage train?"

"Fifty carts, eight hundred mules. We travel light, sir."

"And you're happy with the route?"

Here Barbius allowed himself the merest sliver of a smile. "Through the Narian Hills by way of Tulm, and so to Charibon for the Pontifical blessing. Along the south-eastern shore of the Sea of Tor and down into Torunna by way of the Torrin Gap."

"And another Pontifical blessing from the other Pontiff," Kyriel added, his eyes dancing.

"You've been briefed on your behaviour and that of your men?" Briscus said, serious now.

"Yes, sir. We are to be as respectful as possible to the Pontiff and the Church authorities, but we are not to be deflected from our line of march."

"There is nothing on that line which has the remotest chance of stopping a Fimbrian grand tercio," Briscus said, his eye narrowing. "But you are to avoid the slightest friction with anyone, especially Almarkans. That is clear, Marshal? You are a nameless functionary; you are obeying orders. All complaints, protests and similar are to be directed to Fimbir, and you are not to delay your march for anything."

"Of course, sir."

"Let them think you are a mindless soldier whose job is to do as he is told. If you pause to argue with them just once, then they will wrap you up in coils of Inceptine law and hamstring you. This army must get through, Marshal."

Barbius looked the Elector in the eye for the first time. "I know, sir."

"Very well. Good luck. You are dismissed."

Barbius slapped a forearm against his cuirass and left them. Kyriel watched him go, pulling at his lower lip with one restless hand.

"We are walking a rope here, Briscus."

"Don't I know it. Himerius must accept that we are going to help Torunna, heretic king or no; but we cannot afford to alienate him completely."

"I see what you mean, about soldiers and politicians."

"Yes. We live in a complicated world, Kyriel, but of late it's become even more interesting than it was before."

TWO

THE King was gone, and there were those who said that he would never be coming back.

Abrusio.

Capital of the Kingdom of Hebrion, greatest port of the western world—indeed, some would say of the entire world. Only ancient Nalbeni might vie with Abrusio for the title.

For centuries the Royal House of the Hibrusids had ruled in Hebrion and their palace had frowned down over the raucous old port. There had of course been dynastic squabbles, internecine warfare, obscure marital entanglements; but in all that time the Royal house had never relaxed its grip on the throne.

Things had changed.

Winter had come to the west, propelled on the wings of war. The armies that battled on the eastern frontiers of the continent had withdrawn to their winter quarters and it seemed that the ships which plied the western seas had followed their example. The trade lanes of nations grew emptier as the waning year grew colder.

In Abrusio the Great Harbour, the Inner and Outer Roads as the other harbours were named, the sea itself, were whipped into a broken swell of tumultuous waves, white-tops gilding their tips. A steady roar of surf pounded the huge man-made moles that sheltered the harbours from the worst of the winter storms, and the beacon towers were lit along their length, gleaming flames battling the wind to warn approaching ships of the shallows and mark the harbour entrances.

The wind had backed as it freshened; the season for the Hebrian Trade had long ended, and now it howled in from the south-west, shoving Hebrion-bound vessels landwards and making the teeth of ship-masters grate as they fought to avoid that worst nightmare of any mariner, a lee shore.

Abrusio was not at its best at this time of year. It was not a city that relished winter. It housed too many pavement taverns, open-air markets and the like. It was a place which needed sunshine. In the summer its inhabitants might curse the unwavering heat that set the buildings shimmering and brought almost to an art form the stink of the sewers and tanneries, but the city was more alive, more crowded—like a termite-mound with a broken shell. In winter it closed in on itself; the harbours saw only a tithe of the trade they were accustomed to, and the waterside inns and brothels and ships suffered as a result. In winter the city tightened its belt, turned its face from the sea and grumbled to itself, awaiting spring.

A spring without a king, perhaps. For months King Abeleyn of Hebrion had been absent from his capital, away at the Conclave of Kings in Perigraine. In his absence the new High Pontiff of the west, Himerius—onetime Prelate of Hebrion—had ordered an army of the Church's secular arm, the Knights Militant, into Abrusio to check the rising tide of sorcery and heresy in the old city. The King no longer ruled in Hebrion. Some said he would pick up the reins as soon as he returned from his travels. Others said that when the Church manages to worm its way into the chambers of government, it is not so easy to eject it.

SASTRO di Carrera let the wind water his eyes and stood with his doublet billowing about him on the wide balcony. A tall man, his black beard oiled to a curling point and a ruby the size of a caper set in one ear, he had the hands of a lutist and the easy carriage of one accustomed to having his own way. And that was only natural, for he was the head of one of the great houses of Hebrion and, at present, one of the de facto rulers of the kingdom.

He stared out and down across the city. Below were the prosperous quarters of the merchants and the lesser nobility, the halls of some of the more prestigious guilds, the gardens of the rich denizens of the Upper City. Farther down the hills, the teeming slums and tenements of the poorer, low-born people; thousands of ochre-tiled roofs with hardly a gap between them. A sea of humble dwellings that bloomed out in the drizzle and wind of the day down to the harbours and the waterfronts, what some called the bowels of Hebrion. He could pick out the looming, stone-built massiveness of the arsenals and barracks in the western arm of the Lower City. Down there were the sinews of war, the culverins and powder and laid-up arquebuses and swords of the Crown. And the men: the soldiers who comprised the Hebrian tercios, some eight thousand of them. The mailed fist of Abrusio.

Looking farther out still, he fixed his gaze where the city ended in a maze of quays and jetties and warehouses, and a huge tangled forest of masts. Three enormous harbours crammed with miles of ship berths, an uncountable myriad of vessels from every port and kingdom in the known world. The bloodstream of trade, which kept Abrusio's leathery old heart beating.

And there, over half a league away, Admiral's Tower with its scarlet pennant snaking and snapping in the wind, hardly to be seen but for the glint of gold upon it. In the state shipyards rested galleys, galleasses, caravels and war-carracks by the hundred. The fleet of the most powerful seafaring nation west of the Cimbric Mountains. There, that was what power looked like. It was a gleam of iron on the barrel of a cannon; the glitter of steel at the head of a lance. It was the oak of a warship's hull. These things were not the trappings, but the essence of power, and those who thought themselves in positions of authority often forgot that, to their lasting regret. Power in this day and age was in the muzzle of a gun.

"Sastro, for the Saint's sake close the screen, will you? We'll perish in here of the cold before we're done."

The tall nobleman smiled out at the wintry metropolis, cast his glance left, to the east, and he saw there something to brighten the dullness of the day. On a cleared patch of ground near the summit of the city, perhaps some four acres in extent, was what appeared to be a conflagration, a carpet of fire which lit up the afternoon. On closer inspection it might be seen that the inferno was not one single blaze, but a huge number of lesser bonfires grouped closely together. They were silent; the wind carried the hungry roar of the flames away from him. But he could just make out the dark stick-figure at the heart of every tiny, discrete fire. Every one a heretic, yielding up his spirit in a saffron halo of unimaginable agony. Over six hundred of them.

That, Sastro thought, is power also. The ability to withhold life.

He stepped in off the balcony and shut the intricately carved screen behind him. He found himself in a tall stone room, the walls hung with tapestries depicting scenes from the lives of various saints. Braziers burned everywhere, generating a warm fug, a charcoal smell. Only above the long table where the others sat did oil lamps burn, hanging from the ceiling on silver chains. The day outside, with the screen closed, was dark enough to make it seem nocturnal in here. The three men seated around the table, elbow-deep in papers and decanters, did not seem to notice, however. Sastro took his seat among them again. The headache which had occasioned his stepping out on to the balcony was still with him and he rubbed his throbbing temples as he regarded the others in silence.

The rulers of the kingdom, no less. The dispatchrunner had put in only that afternoon, a sleek galleass which had almost foundered in its haste to reach Abrusio. It had set out from Touron a scant nineteen days ago, spent a fortnight pulling against the wind to get clear of the Tulmian Gulf, and then had spread its wings before the wind all the way south along the Hebrian coast, running off eighty leagues a day at times. It bore a messenger from Vol Ephrir who was now a month on the road, who had hurtled north through Perigraine killing a dozen horses on the way, who had stopped at Charibon a night and then had hurtled on again until he had taken ship with the galleass in Touron. The messenger bore news of the excommunication of the Hebrian monarch.

Quirion of Fulk, Presbyter of the Knights Militant, an Inceptine cleric who bore a sword, leaned back from the table with a sigh. The chair cracked under his weight. He was a corpulent man, the muscle of youth melting into fat, but still formidable. His head was shaved in the fashion of the Knights, and his fingernails were broken by years of donning mail gauntlets. His eyes were like two gimlets set deep within a furrowed pink crag, and his cheekbones thrust out farther than his oft-broken nose. Sastro had seen prize-fighters with less brutal countenances.

The Presbyter gestured with one large hand towards the document they had been perusing.

"There you have it. Abeleyn is finished. The letter is signed by the High Pontiff himself."

"It is hastily written, and the seal is blurred," one of the other men said, the same one who had complained of the cold. Astolvo di Sequero was perhaps the most nobly born man in the kingdom after King Abeleyn himself. The Sequeros had once been candidates for the throne, way back in the murky past which followed the fall of the Fimbrian Hegemony some four centuries ago, but the Hibrusids had won that particular battle. Astolvo was an old man with lungs that wheezed like a punctured wineskin. His ambitions had been extinguished by age and infirmity. He did not want to be a player in the game, not at this stage of his life; all he wanted of the world now were a few tranquil years and a good death.

Which suited Sastro perfectly.

. The third man at the table was hewn out of the same rock as Presbyter Quirion, though younger and with violence written less obviously across his face. Colonel Jochen Freiss was adjutant of the City Tercios of Abrusio. He was a Finnmarkan, a native of that far northern country whose ruler, Skarpathin, called himself a king though he was not counted among the Five Monarchs of the West. Freiss had lived thirty years in Hebrion and his accent was no different from Sastro's own, but the shock of straw-coloured hair which topped his burly frame would always mark him out as a foreigner.

"His Holiness the High Pontiff was obviously pressed for time," Presbyter Quirion said. He had a voice like a saw. "What is important is that the seal and signature are genuine. What say you, Sastro?"

"Undoubtedly," Sastro agreed, playing with the hooked end of his beard. His temples throbbed damnably, but his face was impassive. "Abeleyn is king no more; every law of Church and State militates against him. Gentlemen, we have just been recognized by the holy Church as the legitimate rulers of Hebrion, and a heavy burden it is—but we must endeavour to bear it as best we may."

"Indeed," Quirion said approvingly. "This changes matters entirely. We must get this document to General Mercado and Admiral Rovero at once; they will see the legitimacy of our position and the untenable nature of their own. The army and the fleet will finally repent of this foolish stubbornness, this misplaced loyalty to a king who is no more. Do you agree, Freiss?"

Colonel Freiss grimaced. "In principle, yes. But these two men, Mercado and Rovero, are of the old school. They are pious, no doubt of that, but they have a soldier's loyalty towards their sovereign, as have the common troops. I think it will be no easy task to overturn that attachment, Pontifical bull or no."

"And what happened to your soldier's loyalty, Freiss?" Sastro asked, smiling unpleasantly.

The Finnmarkan flushed. "My faith and my eternal soul are more important. I swore an oath to the King of Hebrion, but that king is no more my sovereign now than a Merduk shahr. My conscience is clear, my lord."

Sastro bowed slightly in his chair, still smiling. Quirion flapped one blunt hand impatiently.

"We are not here to spar with one another. Colonel Freiss, your convictions do you credit. Lord Carrera, I suggest you could exercise your wit more profitably in consideration of our changed circumstances."

Sastro raised an eyebrow. "Our circumstances have changed? I thought the bull merely confirmed what was already reality. This council rules Hebrion."

"For the moment, yes, but the legal position is unclear."

"What do you mean?" Astolvo asked, wheezing. He seemed faintly alarmed.

"What I mean," Quirion said carefully, "is that the situation is without precedent. We rule here, in the name of the Blessed Saint and the High Pontiff, but is that a permanent state of affairs? Now that Abeleyn is finished, and is without issue, who wears the Hebrian crown? Do we continue to rule as we have done these past weeks, or are we to cast about for a legitimate claimant to the throne, one nearest the Royal line?"

The man has a conscience, Sastro marvelled to himself. He had never heard an Inceptine cleric talk about legality before when it might undermine his own authority. It was a revelation which did away with his headache and set the wheels turning furiously in his skull.

"Is it one of our tasks, then, to hunt out a successor to our heretical monarch?" he asked incredulously.

"Perhaps," Quirion grunted. "It depends on what my superiors in the order have to say. No doubt the High Pontiff will have a more detailed set of commands on its way to us already."

"If we put it that way, it may make clerical rule easier to swallow for the soldiery," Freiss said. "The men are not happy at the thought of being ruled by priests."

Quirion's gimlet eyes flashed deep in their sockets. "The soldiery will do as they are told, or they will find pyres awaiting them on Abrusio Hill along with the Dweomer-folk."

"Of course," Freiss went on hastily. "I only point out that fighting men prefer to see a king at their head. It is what they are used to, after all, and soldiers are nothing if not conservative."

Quirion rapped the table, setting the decanters dancing. "Very well then," he barked. "Two things. First, we present this Pontifical bull to the admiral and the general. If they choose to ignore it, then they are guilty of heresy themselves. As Presbyter I am endowed with prelatial authority here, since the office is vacant; I can thus excommunicate these men if I have to. Charibon will support me.

"Two. We begin enquiries among the noble houses of the kingdom. Who is of the most Royal blood and untainted by any hint of heresy? Who, in fact, is next in line to the throne?"

As far as Sastro knew that privilege was old Astolvo's, but the head of the Sequero family, if he knew it himself, was saying nothing. Whoever ruled would be a puppet of the Church. With two thousand Knights Militant in the city and the regular tercios hamstrung into impotence by the delicate consciences of their commanders, the new king of Hebrion, whoever he might turn out to be, would have no real power—whatever appearances might suggest. Power as Sastro had defined it to himself earlier. The kingship was not necessarily to be coveted, whatever prestige it might bring with it. Not unless the king were a man of remarkable abilities, at any rate. Clearly, the High Pontiff meant the Church to control Hebrion.

"The situation requires much thought," Sastro said aloud with perfect honesty. "The Royal scribes will have to look through the genealogical archives to trace the bloodlines. It may take some time."

Astolvo stared at him. The old nobleman's eyes were watering. He did not want to be king and thus said nothing; but no doubt there were young bloods aplenty in his house who would jump at the chance. Could Astolvo keep them in check? It was doubtful. Sastro did not have much time. He must arrange a private meeting with this Finnmarkan mercenary, Freiss. He needed power. He needed the muzzles of guns.

A true northerly, one that the old salts liked to call the Candelan Heave, had blown down as steady and pure as an arrow's flight to take them out of the gulf of the Ephron estuary and into the Levangore. South-south-east had been their course, the mizzen brailed up and the square courses bonneted and full before the stiff stern wind.

On reaching the latitude of Azbakir, they had turned to the west, taking the wind on the starboard beam.

Slower going after that, as they forged through the Malacar Straits with their guns run out and the soldiers lining the ship's side in case the Macassians cared to indulge in a little piracy. But the straits had been quiet, the shallow-bellied galleys and feluccas of the corsairs beached for the winter. The northerly had veered after that, and they had had it on their starboard quarter ever since: the best point of sail for a square-rigged vessel like a carrack. They had entered the Hebrian Sea without incident, passing the winter fishing yawls of Astarac and pointing their bows towards the Fimbrian Gulf and the coast of Hebrion beyond, three quarters of their homeward voyage safely behind them. The northerly had failed them then, and a succession of lesser breezes had veered round to east-south-east, right aft. Now the wind showed signs of backing again, and the ship's company were kept busy trying to anticipate its next move.

Forgist had begun, that dark month which heralded the ending of the year. One month, followed by the five Saint's Days which were for the purification of the old year and the welcoming in of the new, and then the year 551 would have slipped irrevocably into the annals of history. The unreachable past would have claimed it.

King Abeleyn of Hebrion, excommunicate, stood on the windward side of the quarterdeck and let the following spray settle rime on the fur collar of his cloak. Dietl, the master of the swift carrack beneath his feet, kept to the leeward rail, studying his mariners as they braced the yards round and occasionally barking out an order which was relayed by the mates. The northerly was showing signs of reappearing as the wind continued to back; soon they would have it broad on the starboard beam.

A young man, his curly black hair unspeckled with grey as yet, the Hebrian King had been five years on his throne. Five years which had seen the fall of Aekir, the imminent ruin of the west at the hands of the Merduk hordes and the schism of the holy Church of God. He was a heretic: when he died his soul would howl away the eons in the uttermost reaches of hell. He was as damned as any heathen Merduk, though he had done what he had done for the good of his country—indeed, for the good of the western kingdoms as a whole.

Abeleyn was no simpleton, but the faith of his rigidly pious father had settled deep in his marrow and he felt the thin, cold fear of what he had done worming there. Not fear for his kingdom, or for the west. He would always do what was best for them and let no qualm of conscience tug at the hem of his cloak. No—fear for himself. He felt a sudden terror at the thought of his deathbed, the demons which would gather round the spent body to drag away his screaming spirit when the time came for him to quit the world at last . . .

"Grim thoughts, sire?"

Abeleyn turned, seeing again the bright swells of the Hebrian Sea, feeling the rhythm of the living ship under his feet. There was no one near him, but a tattered-looking gyrfalcon sat perched on the ship's weather-rail regarding him with one yellow, inhuman eye.

"Grim enough, Golophin."

"No regrets, I trust."

"None of any import."

"How is the lady Jemilla?"

Abeleyn scowled. His mistress was pregnant, scheming, and very seasick. His early departure from the Conclave of Kings had meant that she could take ship with him back to Hebrion instead of finding her own way.

"She is below, no doubt still puking."

"Good enough. It will occupy her mind wonderfully."

"Indeed. What news, old friend? Your bird looks more battered than ever. His errands are wearing him out."

"I know. I will grow a new one soon. For now, I can tell you that your fellow heretics are both well on their way back to their respective kingdoms. Mark is headed south, to cross the Malvennors in southern Astarac where they are passable. Lofantyr is in the Cimbrics, having a hard time of it, it seems. I fear it will be a bitter winter, sire."

"I could have told you that, Golophin."

"Perhaps. The Fimbrian marshals are made of sterner stuff. Their party is forcing the Narboskim passes of the Malvennors. They are waist deep already, but I think they will do it. They have no horses."

Abeleyn grunted. "The Fimbrians were never an equestrian people. Sometimes I think that is why they have never bred an aristocracy. They walk everywhere. Even their emperors tramped about the provinces as though they were infantrymen. What else? What news of home?"

There was a pause. The bird preened one wing for several seconds before the old wizard's voice issued eerily from its beak once more.

"They burned six hundred today, lad. The Knights Militant have more or less purged Abrusio of the Dweomerfolk now. They are sending parties out into the surrounding fiefs to hunt for more."

Abeleyn went very still.

"Who rules in Abrusio?"

"The Presbyter Quirion, formerly Bishop of Fulk."

"And the lay leaders?"

"Sastro di Carrera for one. The Sequeros, of course. Between them they have carved up the kingdom very nicely, with the Church in overall authority, naturally."

"And the diocesan bishops? I always thought Lembian of Feramuno was a reasonable man."

"A reasonable man, but still a cleric. No, lad: their faces are all set against you."

"What of the army, the fleet?"

"Ah, there you have the bright spot. General Mercado has refused to put his men at the disposal of the council, as these usurpers style themselves. The tercios are confined to barracks, and Admiral Rovero has the fleet well

in hand also. The Lower City of Abrusio, the barracks
and the harbours are no-go areas for the Knights."

Abeleyn let out a long breath. "So we can make landfall. There is hope, Golophin."

"Yes, sire. But Mercado is an old man, and a pious
one. The Inceptines are working on him. He is as loyal
as a hound, but he is also intolerant of heresy. We cannot
afford to lose any time, or we may find the army ar-
raigned against us when we reach Hebrion."

"You think a Pontifical bull could have arrived there
already?"

"I do. Himerius will waste no time once he hears the
news from Vol Ephrir. And therein lies your danger, sire.
Refusing to obey the will of a few trumped-up, would-
be princes is one thing, but remaining loyal to an absent
heretic is quite another. The bull may be enough to sway
the army and the fleet. You must prepare yourself for
that."

"If that happens I am finished, Golophin."

"Nearly, but not quite. You will still have your own
lands, your own personal retainers. With Astarac's help
you could reclaim the throne."

"Plunging Hebrion into civil war while I do."

"No one ever said this course would be an easy one,
sire. I could wish that we had made better time in our
journey, though."

"I need agitators, Golophin. I need trusted men who
will enter the city before me and spread the truth of the
matter. Abrusio is not cut out to be ruled by priests.
When the city hears that Macrobius is alive and well,
that Himerius is an imposter and that Astarac and Torunna are with me in this thing, then it will be different."

"I will see what I can do, lad, but my contacts in the
city are growing thinner on the ground day by day. Most
of them are ashes, friends of fifty years. May the lord
God rest their souls. They died good men, whatever the
Ravens might think."

"And you, Golophin. Are you safe?"

Something in the yellow gleam of the bird's eye chilled Abeleyn as it replied in the old mage's voice.

"I will be all right, Abeleyn. The day they try to take me will be one to remember, I promise you."

Abeleyn turned and stared back over the taffrail. Astarac was out of sight over the brim of the horizon, but he could just make out the white glimmer of the Hebros Mountains ahead, to the north-west.

Astarac, far astern of them: the kingdom of King Mark, soon to be his brother-in-law. If there were ever time for weddings again after all this. What was waiting for Mark in Astarac? More of the same, perhaps. Ambitious clerics, nobles leaping at the opportunity to rule. War.

A sea mile astern of Abeleyn's vessel two wide-bellied *nefs*, the old-fashioned trading ships of the Levangore, were making heavy going of the swell. Within them was the bulk of Abeleyn's entourage, four hundred strong; the only subjects whose obedience he still commanded. It was because of them he had taken the longer sea route home instead of trying to chance the snowbound passes of the mountains. He would need every loyal sword in the months to come; he could not afford to abandon them.

"Golophin, I want you to do something."

The gyrfalcon cocked its head to one side. "I am yours to command, my boy."

"You must procure a meeting with Rovero and Mercado. You must let the army and the fleet know the truth of things. If the Hebrian navy is against me, then we will never get to within fifty leagues of Abrusio."

"It will not be easy, sire."

"Nothing ever is, my friend. Nothing ever is."

"I will do my best. Rovero, being a mariner, has always had a more open mind than Mercado."

"If you must choose one, then let it be Rovero. The fleet is the most important."

"Very well, sire."

"Sail ho!" the lookout cried from the maintop. "I see five—no, six—sail abaft the larboard beam!"

Dietl, the master, squinted up at the maintop.

"What are they, Tasso?"

"Lateen-rigged, sir. Galleasses by my bet. Corsairs maybe."

Dietl blinked, then turned to Abeleyn.

"Corsairs, sire. A whole squadron, perhaps. Shall I put her about?"

"Let me see for myself," Abeleyn snapped. He clambered over the ship's rail and began climbing the shrouds. In seconds he was up in the maintop with Tasso, the lookout. The sailor looked both amazed and terrified at finding himself on such close terms with a king.

"Point them out to me," Abeleyn commanded.

"There, sire. They're almost hull up now. They have the wind on the starboard beam, but you can see their oars are out too. There's a flash of foam along every hull, regular as a waterclock."

Abeleyn peered across the unending expanse of white-streaked sea while the maintop described lazy arcs under him with the pitch and roll of the carrack. There: six sails like the wings of great waterborne birds, and the regular splash of the oars as well.

"How do you know they're corsairs?" he asked Tasso.

"Lateen-rigged on all three masts, sir, like a xebec. Astaran and Perigrainian galleasses are square-rigged on fore and main. Those are corsairs, sir, no doubt about it, and they're on a closing course."

Abeleyn studied the oncoming ships in silence. It was too much of a coincidence. These vessels knew what they were after.

He slapped Tasso on the shoulder and sidled down the backstay to the deck. The whole crew was standing staring, even the Hebrian soldiers and marines of his entourage. He joined Dietl on the quarterdeck, smiling.

"You had best beat to quarters, Captain. I believe we have a fight on our hands."

THREE

AT times it seemed as though the whole world were on the move.

From Ormann Dyke the road curved round to arrow almost due south through the low hills of northern Torunna. A fine road, built by the Fimbrians in the days when Aekir had been the easternmost trading post of their empire. The Torunnan kings had kept it in good repair, but in their own road-building they had never been able to match the stubborn Fimbrian disregard for natural obstacles, and thus the secondary roads which branched off it curved and wound their way about the shoulders of the hills like rivulets of water finding their natural level.

All the roads were clogged with people.

Corfe had seen it before, on the retreat from Aekir, but the other troopers of the escort had not. They were shocked by the scale of the thing.

The troop had passed through empty villages, deserted hamlets, and even a couple of towns where the doors of the houses had been left ajar by their fleeing occupants.

And now the occupants of all northern Torunna were on the move, it seemed.

Most of them were actually from Aekir. With the onset of winter, General Martellus of Ormann Dyke had ordered the refugee camps about the fortress broken up. Those living there had been told to go south, to Torunn itself. They were too big a drain on the meagre resources of the dyke's defenders, and with winter swooping in— a hard winter too, by the looks of it—they would not survive long in the shanty towns which had sprung up in the shadow of the dyke. Hundreds of thousands of them were moving south, trekking along the roads in the teeth of the bitter wind. Their passage had had a catastrophic effect on the inhabitants of the region. There had been looting, killing, even pitched battles between Aekirians and Torunnans. The panic had spread, and now the natives of the country were heading south also. A rumour had begun that the Merduks would not remain long in winter quarters, but were planning a sudden onslaught on the dyke, a swift sweep south to the Torunnan capital before the heaviest of the snows set in. There was no truth to it. Corfe had reconnoitred the Merduk winter camps himself, and he knew that the enemy was regrouping and resupplying, and would be for months. But reason was not something a terrified mob hearkened to very easily, hence the exodus.

The troop of thirty Torunnan heavy cavalry were escorting a clumsy, springless carriage over the crowded roads, battering a way through the crowds with the armoured bodies of their warhorses and warning shots from their matchlocks. Inside the carriage Macrobius III, High Pontiff of the Western World, sat with blind patience clutching the Saint's symbol of silver and lapis lazuli General Martellus had given him. Nowhere in Ormann Dyke could there be found material of the right shade to clothe a Pontiff, so instead of purple Macrobius wore robes of black. Perhaps it was an omen, Corfe thought.

Perhaps he would not be recognized as Pontiff again, now that Himerius had been elected to the position by the Prelates and the Colleges of Bishops in Charibon. Macrobius himself did not seem to care whether he was Pontiff or not. The Merduks had carved something vital out of his spirit when they gouged the eyes from his head in Aekir.

Unbidden, her face was in Corfe's mind again, as clear as lamplight. That raven-dark hair, and the way one corner of her mouth had tilted upward when she smiled. His Heria was dead, a burnt corpse in Aekir. That part of him, the part which had loved her, was nothing but ash now also. Perhaps the Merduks had carved something out of his own spirit when they had taken the Holy City: something of the capacity for laughter and loving. But that hardly mattered now.

And yet, and yet. He found himself scanning the face of every woman in the teeming multitude, hoping and praying despite himself that he might see her. That she might have survived by some miracle. He knew it was the merest foolishness; the Merduks had snatched the youngest and most presentable of Aekir's female population on the city's fall to be reserved for their field brothels. Corfe's Heria had died in the great conflagration which had engulfed the stricken city.

Sweet blood of the holy Saint, he hoped she had died.

The outrider Corfe had dispatched an hour before came cantering back up the side of the road, scattering trudging refugees like a wolf exploding a flock of sheep. He reined in his exhausted horse and flung a hurried salute, his vambrace clanging against the breast of his cuirass in the age-old gesture.

"Torunn is just over the hill, Colonel. Barely a league to the outskirts."

"Are we expected?" Corfe asked.

"Yes. There is a small reception party outside the

walls, though they're having a hell of a time with the refugees."

"Very good," Corfe said curtly. "Get back in the ranks, Surian, and go easier on your mount next time."

"Yes, sir." Abashed, the youthful trooper rode on down the line. Corfe followed him until he had reached the bumping carriage.

"Holiness."

The curtains twitched back. "Yes, my son?"

"We'll be in Torunn within the hour. I thought you might like to know."

The mutilated face of Macrobius stared blindly up at Corfe. He did not seem to relish the prospect.

"It starts again, then," he said, his voice barely audible over the creak and thump of the moving carriage, the hoofbeats of horses on the paved road.

"What do you mean?"

Macrobius smiled. "The great game, Corfe. For a time I was off the board, but now I find myself being moved on it again."

"Then it is God's will, Father."

"No. God does not move the pieces; the game is an invention of man alone."

Corfe straightened in the saddle. "We do what we must, Holy Father. We do our duty."

"Which means that we do as we are told, my son."

The wreck of a smile once more. Then the curtain fell back into place.

TORUNNA was one of the later-founded provinces of the Fimbrian Empire. Six centuries previously, it had consisted of a string of fortified towns along the western coast of the Kardian Sea, all of them virtually isolated from one another by the wild Felimbric tribesmen of the interior. As the tribes became pacified Torunn itself, built athwart the Torrin river, became an important port and a major fortress against the marauding steppe nomads who

infested the lands about the Kardian Gulf. Eventually the
Fimbrians settled the land between the Torrin and Searil
rivers by planting eighty tercios of retired soldiers there
with their families to provide a tough buffer state between the prospering province to the south and the savages beyond.

Marshal Kaile Ormann, commander of the Eastern
Field Army, dug a huge dyke at the only crossing point
of the swift, gorge-cutting Searil river and for forty years
it was the easternmost outpost of the Fimbrians, until the
founding of Aekir on the Ostian river still farther east.
The Torunnans themselves were thus direct descendants
of the first Fimbrian soldier-settlers, and the great families of the kingdom all traced their origins back to the
most senior officers from among those first tercios. The
Royal family of Torunn was descended from the house
of Kaile Ormann, the builder of Ormann Dyke.

It was one of the ironies of the world that Torunna was
the first province to rebel against Fimbria and declare its
independence from the Electors. It snatched Aekir for
itself and was recognized by the then High Pontiff, Am-
mianus, as a legitimate state in return for four thousand
volunteer troops, who were to become the forerunners of
the Knights Militant.

Torunna was thus a cockpit of momentous history in
the west, and during the long years of Fimbrian isolation
following the empire's collapse it had become the foremost military power among the new monarchies, the
guardian-state both of the Pontiff and the eastern frontier.

A man coming upon Torunn for the first time—
especially from the north—might see in it uncanny sim-
ilarities to the layout and construction of Fimbir. The old
city walls had long ago been enlarged and changed so
that they bristled with ravelins, bastions, crownworks and
hornworks designed for a later age of warfare, when gunpowder counted for more than sword blades; but there

was a certain brutal massiveness about the place which was wholly Fimbrian.

It brought back memories for Corfe as his troop of horsemen and their trundling charge came over the final slopes before the city. A tangled riot of later building meant that Torunn was surrounded by unwalled suburbs beyond which the grey stone of the walls could be seen lying like the flanks of a great snake amid the roofs and towers of the Outer City. This was the place where he had joined the tercios, where he had been trained, where his adolescence had been roughly hewn into manhood. He was a native of Staed, one of the southern coastal cities of the kingdom. To him, Torunn had seemed like a miracle when first he had seen it. But he had seen Aekir since, and knew what a truly huge city looked like. Torunn housed some fifth of a million people, and that same number were now on the roads leading towards it, seeking sanctuary. The enormity of the problem defeated his imagination.

In the suburbs the press of people was worse. There were Torunnan cavalry there, struggling to keep order, and open-air kitchens had been set up in all the market places. The noise and the stink were incredible. Torunn had the aspect of one of those apocalyptic religious paintings which depicted the last days of the world. Though Aekir at its fall, Corfe thought bitterly, had been even closer.

Before the new, low-built city gates a tercio of pikemen had been drawn up in ranks and a pair of demi-culverins flanked them. Slow-match burned in lazy blue streamers. Corfe was not sure if the show of force was to receive the High Pontiff or to keep the teeming refugees out of the Inner City, but as the carriage was spotted the culverins went off in salute, blank charges roaring out in clouds of smoke and spitting flame. From the towers above, other guns began to fire until the walls seemed to ripple with smoke and the thunderous sound recalled for Corfe the Merduk bombardment at Ormann Dyke.

The Torunnans presented arms, an officer flourished his sabre, and the High Pontiff was welcomed through the gates of Torunn.

KING Lofantyr heard the salute echoing across the city, and paused in his pacing to look out of the tower windows. He pushed aside the iron grilles and stepped out on to the broad balcony. The city was a serried sea of roofs reaching out to the north, but he could glimpse the puffing smoke clouds from the casemates on the walls.

"Here at last," he said. The relief in his voice was a palpable thing.

"Perhaps now you will sit a while," a woman's voice said.

"Sit! How can I sit? How will I ever take my ease again, mother? I should never have listened to Abeleyn; his tongue is too renowned for its persuasiveness. The kingdom is on the brink of ruin, and I brought it there."

"Pah! You have your father's gift for drama, Lofantyr. Was it you who brought the Merduks to the gates of Aekir?" the woman retorted sharply behind him. "The kingdom won a great battle of late and is holding the line of the east. You are Torunnan, and a king. It is not seemly to voice the doubts of your heart so."

Lofantyr turned with a twisted smile. "If I cannot voice them to you, then where shall I utter them?"

The woman was seated at the far end of the tall tower chamber in a cloud of lace and brocade. An embroidery board was perched on a stand before her, and her nimble hands worked upon it without pause, the needle flashing busily. Her eyes flicked up at her son the King and down to her work, up and down. Her fingers never hesitated.

Her face was surrounded by a deviously worked halo of hair that was stabbed through with pearl-headed pins and hung with jewels. Golden hair, shot through with silver. Earrings of the brightest lapis lazuli. Her face was fine-boned, but somehow drawn; it was possible to see that she had been a beautiful woman in her youth, and even now her charms were not to be lightly dismissed, but there was a fragility to the flesh which clothed those beautiful bones, a system of tiny lines which proclaimed her age despite the stunning green magnificence of her eyes.

"You have won the battle, my lord King—the fight against time. Now you have a Pontiff to parade before the council and quell these murmurings of heresy." She caught her tongue between her teeth for a second as the needle bored in a particularly fine stitch. "Unlike the other kings, you can show your people that Macrobius truly lives. That, and the storm which approaches from the east, should suffice to unite most of them under you."

She set aside her needle at last. "Enough for today. I am tired."

She stared keenly at Lofantyr. "You look tired also, son. The journey from Vol Ephrir was a hard one."

Lofantyr shrugged. "Snow and bandit tribesmen—the usual irritants. There is more to my tiredness than the aftermath of a journey, mother. Macrobius is here, yes; but beyond the city walls thousands upon thousands of Aekirians and northern Torunnans are screaming for succour, and I cannot give it to them. Martellus wants the city garrisons moved to the dyke, and the Knights Militant promised to me will now never arrive. I need every man I can spare across the country to hold down the nobles. They are straining at the leash despite the fact that I promised them the true Pontiff. Already there are reports of minor rebellions in Rone and Gebrar. I need trusted commanders who do not see opportunity in the monarch's difficulties."

"Loyalty and ambition: those two irreconcilable qualities without which a man is nothing. It is a rare individual who can balance both of them in his breast," the woman said.

"John Mogen could."

"John Mogen is dead, may God keep him. You need another war leader, Lofantyr, someone who can lead men like Mogen did. Martellus may be a good general, but he does not inspire his men in the right way."

"And neither do I," Lofantyr added with bitter humour.

"No, you do not. You will never be a general, my son; but then you do not have to be. Being King is trial enough."

Lofantyr nodded, still with a sour smile upon his face. He was a young man like his fellow heretics, Abeleyn of Hebrion and Mark of Astarac. His wife, a Perigrainian princess and niece of King Cadamost, had already left for Vol Ephrir, vowing never to lie with a heretic. But then she was only thirteen years old. There were no children, and a severed dynastic tie meant little at the moment with the west struck asunder by religious schism.

His mother, the Queen Dowager Odelia, pushed aside her embroidery board and rose to her feet, ignoring her son's hurriedly proffered arm.

"The day I cannot rise from a chair unaided you can bury me in it," she snapped, and then: "Arach!"

Lofantyr flinched as a black spider dropped from the rafters on a shining thread and landed on his mother's shoulder. It was thickly furred, and bigger than his hand. Its ruby eyes glistened. Odelia petted it for a moment and it uttered a sound like a cat's purr.

"Be discreet, Arach. We go to meet a Pontiff," the woman said.

At once, the spider disappeared into the mass of lace that rose up at the back of Odelia's neck. It could barely be glimpsed there, a dark hump nestled in the fabric which transformed her upright carriage into something of a stoop. The purring settled into a barely audible hum.

"He is getting old," the Queen Dowager said, smiling.

"He likes the warmth." She took her son's arm now, and they proceeded to the doors in the rear of the chamber.

"As well I became a heretic," Lofantyr said.

"Why is that, son?"

"Because otherwise I'd have to burn my own mother as a witch."

THE audience chambers were filling rapidly. In his eagerness to show the living Macrobius to the world, Lofantyr had allowed His Holiness only a few hours to recover from his journey before requesting humbly that he bestow his blessing upon a gathering of the foremost nobles of the kingdom. There were hundreds of people congregating in the palace, all clad in the brightest finery they possessed. The ladies of the court had emulated Perigrainian fashions with the King's marriage to the young Balsia of Vol Ephrir, and they looked like a cloud of marvellous butterflies with wings of stiff lace and shimmering jewels, their faces painted and their fans fluttering —for the audience chambers were hot with the press of people and the huge logs blazing merrily in the fireplaces. It was a far cry from the austere days of Lofantyr's father, Vanatyr, when the nobles wore only the black and scarlet of the military and the ladies simple, form-fitting gowns without headdresses.

Corfe and his troop had quartered their mounts in the palace stables and tried to spruce themselves up as best they could, but they were muddy and worn from the travelling and many of them wore the armour they had spent weeks fighting in during the battles at the dyke. His men made a dismal showing, Corfe admitted to himself, but every one of them was a veteran, a survivor. That made a difference.

The court chamberlain had hurriedly procured a set of purple robes for Macrobius, but the old man had refused them. He had also refused to be carried into the audience chamber in a sedan-chair, and to let anyone but Corfe

take his arm and guide him up the long length of the
crowded hall.

"You have guided me on a harder road than this," he
said as they waited in an antechamber for the trumpet
blasts that would announce their entry. "I would ask you
one last time to be my eyes for me, Corfe."

The doors were swung open by liveried attendants, and
the vast, gleaming length of marble that was the floor of
the audience chamber shone before them, whilst on either
side hundreds of people—nobles, retainers, courtiers,
hangers-on—craned their necks to see the Pontiff they
had thought dead. At the end of the hall, hundreds of
yards away it seemed to Corfe, the thrones of Torunna
glittered with silver and gilt. Lofantyr the King and his
mother the Queen Dowager sat there. A third throne, that
of the young Queen, was empty.

The trumpet notes died away. Macrobius smiled.
"Come, Corfe. Our audience awaits."

The tramp of his military boots and the slap of Macrobius' sandals were the only sound. Perhaps there was
a faint murmuring as the crowd took in the soldier in the
battered armour and the hideously mutilated old man. Out
of the corner of his eye, Corfe glimpsed some of the
spectators looking hopefully back at the end of the hall,
as if they expected the real Pontiff and his guide to come
issuing out of the end doors in a sweep of state and ceremony.

They walked on. Corfe was sweating. He took in the
immense height of the building, the arched roof with its
buttresses of stone and rafters of black cedar, the huge
hanging lamps . . . then he saw the galleries there, packed
with watching faces, brilliant with liveries of every rain-
bow hue. He cursed to himself. This was not his province, this august ceremonial, this painted game of politics
and etiquette.

Macrobius squeezed his arm. The old man seemed
amused by something, which unsettled Corfe even more.

His hand slithered round the hilt of his sabre, the one he had taken off a dead Torunnan trooper on the Western Road.

And he remembered. He remembered the inferno of Aekir, a roaring chaos like the very end of the world. He remembered the long, vicious nights in the retreat west. He remembered the battles at Ormann Dyke, the desperate fury of the Merduk assaults, the ear-numbing roar of the enemy guns. He remembered the endless killing, the thousands of corpses which had clogged the Searil river.

He remembered his wife's face as she left him for the last time.

They had reached the end of the hall. On the dais before them the King of Torunna regarded them with mild astonishment. His mother's gaze was a calculating green appraisal. Corfe saluted them. Macrobius stood silent.

There was a cough somewhere, and then the chamberlain banged his staff on the floor three times and called out in a practised, ringing voice which filled the entire hall.

"His Holiness the High Pontiff of the Western Kingdoms and Prelate of Aekir, the head of the holy Church, Macrobius the Third..." The chamberlain looked at Corfe then with incipient panic. Obviously he had no idea who the Pontiff's battered companion might be.

"Corfe Cear-Inaf, colonel in the garrison at Ormann Dyke, formerly under the command of John Mogen at Aekir." It was Macrobius, in a voice clearer and stronger than Corfe had ever heard him use before, even when he had preached at the dyke.

"Greetings, my son." This was to Lofantyr.

The Torunnan King hesitated a moment, and then descended from the dais in a sweep of scarlet and sable, his circlet catching the light of the overhead lamps. He knelt before Macrobius, and kissed the old man's ring—another gift from Martellus; the Pontifical ring had been lost long before.

"You are welcome to Torunna, Holiness," he said, a little stiffly, Corfe thought. Then he recalled his own manners, and as Lofantyr straightened he bowed. "Your majesty."

Lofantyr nodded briefly to him and then took Macrobius' arm. He led the blind old man up to the dais and placed him on the vacant Queen's throne. Corfe stood alone and uncertain until he caught the eye of the chamberlain, who was beckoning discreetly to him. He marched over into the whispering press of people who were gathered on either side of the dais.

"Stay out of the way," the chamberlain hissed into his ear, and he banged his staff on the floor again.

Lofantyr had risen from his throne to speak. A hush fell on the hall once more. The King's voice was less impressive than his chamberlain's but it carried well enough.

"We welcome here at our court today the living embodiment of the faith that sustains us all. The rightful High Pontiff of the world has been delivered by a miracle out of the cauldron of war in the east. Macrobius the Third lives and is well in Torunn, and with his presence here this city of ours has become the buckler of the Church—the true Church. With the Holy Father's prayers to sustain us, and the knowledge that right is on our side and God watches over our ranks, we are sure that the armies of Torunna, greatest and most disciplined in the world, will continue the work begun in the past few weeks at Ormann Dyke. Other victories will be stitched upon the battle flags of our tercios, and it will not be long ere our standard is reared up once again on the battlements of Aekir and the heathen foe is flung back across the Ostian river into the wilderness of unbelief and savagery from whence he came . . ."

There was more of this. It passed over Corfe's head unheeded. He was tired, and the rush of adrenalin which had carried him up the hall had washed out of him, leaving him as drained as a flaccid wineskin. Why had Martellus insisted he come here?

"So I say to the usurper in Charibon," Lofantyr went on, "there is no heresy in recognizing the true spiritual head of the Church, in fighting to hold the eastern frontier safe for the kingdoms behind us. Torunna and Hebrion and Astarac represent the kingdoms of the True Faith, not the diocese of an imposter who must in his turn be branded heretic."

The speech ended at last, and the hall boiled with talk. The people within began to spread out across the bare central space in knots of conversation, whilst from side doors up and down the chamber attendants came bearing silver salvers upon which decanters of wine and spirits gleamed. The King poured for Macrobius, and the hall hushed again as the Pontiff stood up with the wineglass blood-full in his hand.

"I am blind."

And the silence became absolute.

"Yes, I am Macrobius. I escaped from the ruin of Aekir when so many did not. But I am not the man I once was. I stand before you—" He paused and looked sightlessly to one side, where the Queen Dowager had risen from her seat and taken his arm.

"In our haste to welcome the Holy Father into the city, we did not take account of his weariness. He must rest. But before he leaves us for the chambers we have appointed for him, we would beg him for his blessing, the blessing of the true head of the Church."

Some of the people near the dais took up the cry.

"A blessing! A blessing, Your Holiness!"

Macrobius stood irresolute for a moment, and Corfe had the weirdest feeling that the old man was somehow in danger. He pushed through the clots of people towards the dais, but when he got to its foot he found his way blocked by a line of halberd-bearing guards. The chamberlain appeared at his elbow as if by magic. "No farther, soldier."

Corfe looked up at the figures on the dais. Macrobius stood stock still for several moments, whilst the smile on the Queen Dowager's face grew ever thinner. Finally, he raised his hand in the well-known gesture, and everyone in the hall bowed their heads.

Except for the flint-eyed guards facing Corfe.

The blessing took a matter of seconds, and then attendants in scarlet doublets helped the Pontiff off the dais by a door at the rear of the thrones. Lofantyr and Odelia resumed their seats, and the room seemed to relax. Talk blossomed, punctuated by the clink of glasses. From the galleries floated the soft sounds of lutes and mandolins. A woman's alto began singing a song of the Levangore, about tall ships and lost islands or some other romantic rubbish.

A tray-bearing attendant offered Corfe wine, but he shook his head. The air was thick with perfume; it seemed to rise from the white throats of the ladies like incense. Everyone was talking with unusual animation; obviously Macrobius' appearance had ramifications beyond Corfe's guessing.

"What am I to do?" he asked the chamberlain harshly. A red anger was building in him, and he was not sure as to its source.

The chamberlain gazed at him as though surprised to see he was still there. He was a tall man, but thin as a reed. Corfe could have snapped him in two over his knee.

"Drink some wine, talk to the ladies. Enjoy a taste of civilization, soldier."

"I am colonel, to you."

The chamberlain blinked, then smiled with no trace of humour. He looked Corfe in the eye, an unflinching stare which seemed to be memorizing his features. Then he turned away and became lost in the mingling crowd. Corfe swore under his breath.

"Did you dress especially for the audience, or are you always so trim?" a woman's voice asked.

Corfe turned to find a foursome at his elbow. Two young men in dandified versions of Torunnan military dress, and two ladies on their arms. The men seemed a curious mixture of condescension and wariness; the women were merely amused.

"We travelled in haste," the remnants of politeness made Corfe say.

"I think it made for a very touching scene." The other woman giggled. "The ageing Pontiff in the garb of a beggar and his travelworn bodyguard, neither sure as to who should lean on whom."

"Or who was leading whom," the first woman added, and the four of them laughed together.

"But it is a relief to know our king is no longer a heretic," the first woman went on. "I imagine the nobles of the kingdom are thanking God while we speak." This also produced a tinkle of laughter.

"We forget our manners," one of the men said. He bowed. "I am Ensign Ebro of His Majesty's guard, and this is Ensign Callan. Our fair companions are the ladies Moriale and Brienne of the court."

"Colonel Corfe Cear-Inaf," Corfe grated. "You may call me 'sir.'"

Something in his tone cut short the mirth. The two young officers snapped to attention. "I beg pardon, sir," Callan said. "We meant no offence. It is just that, within the court, one becomes rather informal."

"I am not of the court," Corfe told him coldly.

A sixth person joined the group, an older man with the sabres of a colonel on his cuirass and a huge moustache which fell past his chin. His scalp was as bald as a cannonball and he carried a staff officer's baton under one arm.

"Fresh from Ormann Dyke, eh?" he barked in a voice better suited to a parade ground than a palace. "Rather stiff up there at times, was it not? Let's hear of it, man. Don't be shy. About time these palace heroes heard news of a real war."

"Colonel Menin, also of the palace," Ebro said, jerking his head towards the newcomer.

It seemed suddenly that there was a crowd of faces about Corfe, a horde of expectant eyes awaiting entertainment. The sweat was soaking his armpits, and he was absurdly conscious of the mud on his clothing, the dints and scrapes on his armour. The very toes of his boots were dark with old blood where he had splashed in it during the height of the fighting.

"And you were at Aekir, too, it seems," Menin went on. "How is that? I thought that none of Mogen's men survived. Rather odd, wouldn't you say?"

They waited. Corfe could almost feel their gazes crawl up and down his face.

"Excuse me," he said, and he turned away, leaving them. He elbowed his way through the crowd feeling their stares shift, astonished, to his back, and then he left the hall.

Kitchens, startled attendants with laden trays. A courtier who tried to redirect him and was brushed aside. And then the fresh air of an early evening, and the blue dark of a star-spattered twilit sky. Corfe found himself on one of the bewildering series of long balconies which circled the central towers of the palace. He could hear the clatter of the kitchens behind him, the humming din of a multitude. Below him all of Torunn fanned out in a carpet of lights to the north. To the east the unbroken darkness of the Kardian Sea. Somewhere far to the north Ormann Dyke with its weary garrison, and beyond that the sprawling winter camps of the enemy.

The starlit world seemed vast and cold and somehow alien. The only home that Corfe had ever truly known was a blackened shell lost in that darkness. Utterly gone. Strangely enough, the only person he thought he might have spoken to of it was Macrobius. He, too, knew something of loss and shame.

"Sweet Lord," Corfe whispered, and the hot tears scalded his throat and seared his eyes though he would not let them fall. "Sweet Lord, I wish I had died in Aekir."

The music started up again from within. Tabors and flutes joined the mandolins to produce a lively military march, one for soldiers to swing their arms to.

Corfe bent his head to the cold iron of the balcony rail, and squeezed shut his burning eyes on the memories.

FOUR

THE first shot sent the seabirds of the gulf wailing in distracted circles about the ships and puffed up a plume of spray barely a cable from the larboard bow.

"Good practice," Dietl, the carrack's master, admitted grudgingly, "but then we are broadside-on to them, as plump a target as you could wish, and the galleasses of the corsairs carry nothing but chasers. No broadside guns, see, because of the oars. They'll close and board soon, I shouldn't wonder."

"We can't outrun them then?" Abeleyn asked. He was a competent enough sailor, as Hebrion's king should be, but this was Dietl's ship and the master knew her like no one else ever could.

"No, sire. With those oars of theirs, they effectively have the weather gauge of us. They can close any time they wish, even into the wind if they have to. And as for those pig-slow *nefs* your men are in, a one-armed man in a rowboat could overtake them. No, it's a fight they're looking for, and that's what they're going to get." Dietl's earlier diffidence to the King on his quarterdeck seemed to have evaporated with the proximity of action. He spoke now as one professional to another.

All along the decks of the carrack the guns had been run out and their crews were stationed about them holding sponges, wads, wormers and lint-stocks—the paraphernalia of artillery, whether land or naval. The thin crew of the merchant carrack which Abeleyn had hired in Candelaria was supplemented by the soldiers of his retinue, most of them well used to gunnery of one sort or another. The deck had been strewn with sand so the men would not slip in their own blood once the action began, and the coiled slow-match was burning away happily to itself in the tub beside every gun. Already the more responsible of the gun captains were sighting down the barrels of the metal monsters, eyeing the slender profiles of the approaching vessels. Six sleek galleasses with lateen sails as full and white as the wings of a flock of swans.

The carrack was heavily armed, one of the reasons why Abeleyn had hired her. On the main deck were a dozen demiculverins, bronze guns whose slim barrels were eleven feet long and which fired a nine-pound shot. On the poop deck were six sakers, five-pounders with nine-foot barrels, and ranged about the forecastle and up in the tops were a series of falconets, two-pounder swivel guns which were to be used against enemy boarders.

The sluggish *nefs* a mile behind on the choppy sea were less well armed, but they carried the bulk of Abeleyn's men: over a hundred and fifty trained Hebrian soldiers in each. It would take a stubborn enemy to board them with any hope of success. Abeleyn knew that a galleass might have a crew of three hundred, but they were not of the same calibre as his men. And besides, he knew that he was the prize the enemy vessels were after. The corsairs were out king-hunting this bright morning in the Fimbrian Gulf, that was certain. He would have given a lot to know who had hired them.

Another shot ploughed into the sea just short of the carrack, and then another. Then one clipped the waves like a stone sent skimming by a boy at play and crashed into the side of the ship with a rending of timbers. Dietl went purple. He turned to Abeleyn.

"By your leave, sire, I believe it's time we heated up the guns."

Abeleyn grinned. "By all means, Captain."

Dietl leaned over the quarterdeck rail. "Fire as they bear!" he shouted.

The culverins leaped back on their carriages with explosions of smoke and flame erupting from their muzzles. The main-deck almost disappeared in a tower of smoke, but the northerly sent it forward over the forecastle. The crews were already reloading, not waiting to see the fall of shot. Some of the more experienced gunners clambered over the side of the ship to gauge their aim. Abeleyn stared eastwards. The six galleasses appeared unhurt by the broadside. Even as he watched, little globes of smoke appeared on their bows as the chasers fired again. A moment later came the retorts, and the high whine of shot cutting the air overhead. The King saw holes appear in the maincourse and foretopsail. A few fragments of rigging fell to the deck.

"They have us bracketed," Dietl said grimly. "There's hot work approaching, sire."

Abeleyn's reply was cut off by the roar of the carrack's second broadside. He glimpsed a storm of pulverized water about the enemy vessels and the flap of white canvas gone mad as the topmast of one galleass went by the board and crashed over her bow. The carrack's crew cheered hoarsely, but did not pause in their reloading for an instant.

From the maintop the lookout yelled down: "Deck

there! The northerly squadron is veering off. They're going after the *nefs*!"

Abeleyn bounded to the taffrail. Sure enough, the farther squadron of vessels was turning into the wind. They already had their sails in. Under oar power alone, they changed course to west-nor'-west on an intercept course with the two *nefs*. At the same time, the remaining three galleasses seemed to put on a spurt of speed and their oars dipped and rose at a fantastic rate. All three of their bows were pointed at the carrack.

Another broadside. The galleasses were half a mile off the larboard bow and closing rapidly. Abeleyn saw an oarbank burst to pieces as some of the carrack's shots went home. The injured galleass at once went before the wind. There were men struggling like ants on the lateen yards, trying to brace them round.

The whine of shot again, some of it going home. The fight seemed to intensify within minutes. The crew of the carrack laboured at the guns like acolytes serving the needs of brutal gods. Broadside after broadside stabbed out from the hull of the great ship until it seemed that the noise and flame and sour smoke were intrinsic to some alien atmosphere, an unholy storm which they had blundered blindly into. The deck shook and canted below Abeleyn's feet as the guns leapt inboard and then were loaded and run out again. The regular broadsides disintegrated as the crews found their own rhythms, and the battle became one unending tempest of light and tumult as the vessels of the corsairs closed in to arquebus range and, closer still, to pistol range.

But then a series of enemy rounds struck home in quick succession. There were crashes and screams from the waist of the carrack and in the smoking chaos Abeleyn saw the monster shape of one of the culverins upended and hurled away from the ship's side. It tumbled across the deck and the entire ship shuddered. There was a shriek of overburdened wood, and then a portion of the deck gave way and the metal beast plunged out of sight, dragging several screaming men with it. The deck was a shattered wreck that glistened with blood and was littered with fragments of wood and hemp. But still the gun crews hauled their charges into position and stabbed the glowing match into the touch-holes. A continuous thunder, ear-aching, a hellish flickering light. Some fool had discharged his culverin without hauling it tight up to the bulwark, and the detonation of the gun had set the shrouds on fire. Teams of fire-fighters were instantly at work hauling up wooden tubs of seawater to douse the flames.

The ship's carpenter staggered to the quarterdeck.

"How does she swim, Burian?" Dietl asked out of a powder-grimed face.

"We've plugged two holes below the waterline and we've secured that rogue gun, but we've four feet in the well and it's gaining on us. There must be a leak in the hold that I can't get at. I need men, Captain, to shift the cargo and come at it, otherwise she'll go down in half a watch."

Dietl nodded. "You shall have them. Take half the crews from the poop guns—but work fast, Burian; we'll need those men back on deck soon enough. I'm thinking they're closing to try and board."

"You're sure they won't try ramming?" Abeleyn asked him, surprised.

Another broadside. They had to howl in one another's ears to be heard.

"No, sire. If you're the prize they're after, they'll try and take you alive, and a rammed ship can go to the bottom in seconds. And besides, they're a mite too close to get up the speed for ramming. They'll board, all right. They have the men for it. There's damn near a thousand of the bastards in those three galleasses; we can muster maybe a tenth of that. They'll board, by God."

"Then I must have my men from your gun crews, Captain."

"Sire, I—"

"Now, Captain. There's no time to lose."

Abeleyn went round the guns in person collecting the soldiers who had taken ship with him. The men dropped their gun tools, picked up their arquebuses and began priming them, ready to repel boarders. Abeleyn glimpsed the enemy vessels over the ship's side, incredibly close now, their decks black with men, the sails taken in and the chase-guns roaring. Some of the sailors had left their culverins and were also reaching for arquebuses and cutlasses and boarding-pikes. From the tops a heavy fire came from the falconets and swivels, knocking figures off the bows of the galleasses.

A crash from aft which knocked Abeleyn off his feet. One of the galleasses had grappled alongside and corsairs were climbing up the side of the carrack from the lower enemy vessel, scores of them clinging to the wales and waving cutlasses, shrieking as they came. Abeleyn got up and ran to a deserted culverin.

"Here!" he yelled. "To me! Give me a hand here!"

A dozen men ran to help him, some of them canvas-clad mariners, others in the gambesons of his own soldiers.

"Heave her up, depress the muzzle! Quick there! Don't bother worming her out—load her."

A crowd of faces at the gunport, one broken open by the thrust of a soldier's halberd. A press of men wriggling over the ship's side to be met by a hedge of flailing blades. The carrack's crew defended her as though they were the garrison of a castle standing siege. There was another shuddering crash as a second galleass grappled with the tall ship. Men on the enemy vessel's yards cast lines and grappling irons, entangling the rigging of the struggling vessels, binding them together, whilst in the carrack's top the falconets fired hails of smallshot and fought to cut the connecting lines.

"Lift her—lift her, you bastards!" Abeleyn shouted, and the men with him lifted the rear of the culverin's barrel whilst he wedged it clear of its carriage with bits of wood and discarded cutlasses.

A wave of enemy boarders overwhelmed the carrack's defenders in the waist. The men around Abeleyn found themselves in a vicious mêlée with scarcely room to swing their swords. When men went down they were trampled and stabbed on the deck. A few arquebus shots were fired but most of the fighting was with steel alone. Abeleyn ignored it. He grasped the slow-match that lay smouldering on the deck, was knocked to his knees in the slaughterous scrum, stabbed his rapier into a howling face and had the weapon wrenched out of his hand as the man fell backwards. Then he thumped the slow-match into the culverin's touch-hole.

A flash, and a frenzied roar as it went off, flying back off its precarious perch. It fell over, crushing half a dozen of the enemy boarders. Abeleyn's own men surged forward, cheering hoarsely. A hellish cacophony of shouts and screams came from over the ship's side. Abeleyn struggled to the carrack's larboard rail and looked down.

The galleass had been directly below and the heavy shot had struck home. The deck was closer to the water already, and men were diving off it into the foam-ripped sea. The vessel was finished; the cannonball must have blasted clear through her hull.

But the boarders from the second galleass were clambering into the waist in droves. Abeleyn's defenders were outnumbered five to one. He seized a broken pike, raising it into the air.

"To the castles!" he shouted, waving his pike. "Fall back to the castles. Leave the waist!"

His men understood, and began to fight their way inch by murderous inch towards the high fore- and sterncastles of the carrack which dominated the waist like the towers of a fortress. A bloody rearguard action was fought on the ladders there as the corsairs sought to follow them, but they were held. Abeleyn found himself back on the quarterdeck. Dietl was standing there holding a rope tourniquet about one elbow. His hand had been lopped off at the wrist.

"Arquebusiers, form ranks!" Abeleyn screamed. He could see none of his officers present and shoved his men about as though he were the merest sergeant. "Come on, you God-damned whoresons! Present your pieces! You sailors—get a couple of those guns pointing down into the waist; load them with canister. Quickly now!"

The Hebrian soldiers formed up in two ragged ranks at the break of the quarterdeck and aimed their arquebuses into the raging press of men below.

"Give fire!"

A line of stabbing flames staggered the front ranks of the boarders down below. Men were flung back off the ladders, tumbling down on those behind them. The waist was a toiling mass of limbs and faces.

"Fire!" Dietl yelled, and the two canister-loaded sakers which his mariners had manhandled round erupted a few seconds later. Two groups of shrieking corsairs were levelled where they stood, and the bulwarks of the carrack were intagliated with gore and viscera as the thousands of balls in the canister shot tore through their bodies. On the forecastle, another rank of arquebusiers was firing, dropping more of the enemy, whilst the men in the tops were blasting almost vertically downwards with the little falconets. The corsairs who had boarded were thus surrounded on all sides by a murderous fire. Some of them ducked into the shattered hatches of the carrack, seeking shelter in the hold below, but most of them dived overboard. Scores of them left their bodies, or what was left of them, strewn across the reeking deck.

The gunfire petered out. Farther to the north they could

hear broadsides booming as the *nefs* fought for their lives
against the other squadron, but here the corsairs were
drawing off. One galleass was already awash, the sea up
to her scuppers and her bow half submerged. Another
was drifting slowly away from the carrack, the men in
the tops having cut her grappling lines. The third was
circling just out of arquebus range like a wary hound
padding round a cornered stag. The water about the four
vessels was crammed with swimming men and limp bodies, pieces of wreckage and fragments of yards.

"They'll ram us now, if they can," Dietl panted, his
face as white as paper under the blood and filth that
streaked it. He was holding his stump upright with his
good hand. Bone glinted there, and thin jets of blood spat
from the severed arteries despite the tourniquet. "They'll
draw off to gain speed and pick up their men. We have
to hit them while they're at close range."

"Stand by the starboard guns!" Abeleyn shouted. "Sergeant Orsini, take six men and secure any enemy still on
board. Load the starboard culverins, lads, and we'll give
them something to remember us by!" He bent to speak
through the connecting hatch to the tillermen below, who
all this time had been at their station keeping the carrack
on course through the storm of the fighting. "Bring us
round to due south."

"Aye, sir! I mean Majesty."

Abeleyn laughed. He was strangely happy. Happy to
be alive, to be in command of men, to hold his life in
the palm of his own hand and tackle problems that were
immediate, visible, final.

The gun crews had rushed back down into the waist
and were loading the starboard batteries, unfired as yet.
The enemy galleass was struggling to brace round the
huge lateen yards; both vessels had the wind right aft
now, but the square-rigged carrack was better built to
take advantage of it than the fore-and-aft yards of the
galleass. She was overtaking her foe.

"Tiller there!" Dietl shouted, somehow making his failing voice carry. "Wait for my word and then bring her round to sou'-west."

"Aye, sir!"

Dietl was going to cut around the bow of the galleass and then rake her from stem to stern with his full broadside. Abeleyn spared a look for the other enemy vessels. One was visible only as a solitary mast sticking above the packed sea. The other was taking on survivors of the failed boarding action and reducing sail at the same time. The sea was still stubbled with the bobbing heads of men.

The carrack gained on her enemy, sliding ahead. The gun crews, or what was left of them, crouched like statues by their weapons, the slow-match smoke drifting from the hands of the gun captains as they awaited the order to fire.

"If we bow-rake her, can't she ram us amidships?" Abeleyn asked Dietl.

"Aye, sire, but she hasn't enough way on her yet to do us any real damage. Her oarbanks are shot to hell and she's not too happy with this stern wind. We'll rake her until she strikes."

The galleass was on the starboard quarter now. A few arquebus shots came cracking overhead from her, but mostly she seemed intent on putting her oarsmen and her yards in order.

"Bring her round to sou'-west!" Dietl shouted down the tiller-hatch.

The carrack curved to starboard in a beautiful arc, turning so her starboard broadside faced the beakhead of the oncoming galleass. Abeleyn glimpsed the wicked-looking ram on the enemy vessel, only just awash, and then Dietl screamed *"Fire!"* with what seemed to be the last of his strength.

The air was shattered as the unholy noise began again and the culverins resumed their deadly dance. The crews had depressed the muzzles of the guns as much as they could to compensate for the larboard roll of the ship as she turned. At this range and angle the heavy balls would hit the bow and rip through the length of the enemy vessel. The carnage on her would be unbelievable. Abeleyn saw heavy timbers blasted from her hull and flung high in the air. The mainmast swayed as shot punched through its base, and then toppled into the sea, smashing a gap in the galleass' side. The vessel lurched to larboard, but kept coming, her ram gleaming like a spearhead.

And struck. She collided amidships with the carrack and the concussion of the impact staggered Abeleyn and toppled Dietl off his feet. The gun crews of the carrack were still reloading and firing, pouring shot into the helpless hull of the galleass at point-blank range. The decks of the enemy vessel were running with blood and it poured from her scuppers in scarlet streams. Men were leaping overboard to escape the murderous barrage, and a desperate party of them came swarming up the carrack's side but were beaten back and flung into the sea.

"Port your helm!" Abeleyn yelled to the tillermen. Dietl was unconscious in a pool of his own blood on the deck.

There was a grating noise, a deep, grinding shudder as the wind worked on the carrack and tore her free of the stricken galleass. She was sluggish, like a tired prizefighter who knows he has thrown his best punch, but finally she was free of the wrecked enemy vessel. There were half a dozen fires raging on board the corsairs' craft and she was no longer under command. She drifted downwind, burning steadily as the carrack edged away.

The third galleass was already in flight, having picked up as many of the corsairs as she could. She spread her sails and set off to the south-east like a startled bird, leaving scores of helpless men struggling in the water behind her.

An explosion that sent timbers and yards a hundred feet into the air as the crippled galleass which remained burned unchecked. Abeleyn had to shout himself even hoarser as flaming wreckage fell among the carrack's rigging and started minor fires. The exhausted crew climbed the shrouds and doused the flames. The carpenter, Burian, appeared on the quarterdeck looking like a dripping rat.

"Sire, where's the master?"

"He's indisposed," Abeleyn told him in a croak. "Make your report to me."

"We've six feet of water in the hold and it's still gaining on us. She'll settle in a watch or two; the breach the ram made is too big to plug."

Abeleyn nodded. "Very well. Get back below and do what you can. I'll set a course for the Hebrian coast. We might just make it."

Suddenly Dietl was there, staggering like a drunk man but upright. Abeleyn helped him keep his feet.

"Set a course for the Habrir river. West-sou'-west. We'll be there in half a watch. She'll bring us to shore, by God. She's not done yet, and neither am I."

"Take him below," Abeleyn said to the carpenter as the master's eyes rolled back in his head. Burian threw Dietl over his shoulder as though he were a sack, and disappeared down the companionway to his task of keeping the ship afloat.

"Sire," a voice said. Sergeant Orsini, looking like some bloody harbinger of war.

"Yes, Sergeant?"

"The *nefs*, sire—the bloody bastards sank them both."

"*What?*" Abeleyn ran to the starboard rail. Up to the north he made out the smoke and cloud of the other action. He could see two galleasses and two burning hulks, one unrecognizable, the other definitely one of the wide-bellied *nefs* of his retinue. As he watched, a globe of flame rose from it and seconds later the boom of the explosion drifted down the wind.

"They're lost then," he said. The weariness and grief were slipping into place now. The battle joy had faded.

Three hundred of his best men gone. Even if the carrack had been undamaged, they would take hours to beat up to windwards and look for survivors, and the two galleasses that remained would find her easy prey. It was time for flight. The monarch in Abeleyn accepted that, but the soldier loathed it.

"Someone will pay for this," he said, his voice low and calm. But the tone of it set the hair crawling on Orsini's head. Then the King turned back to the task in hand.

"Come," he said in a more human voice. "We have a ship to get to shore."

FIVE

BROTHER Columbar coughed again and wiped his mouth on the sleeve of his habit. "Saint's blood, Albrec, to think you've been thirteen years down in these warrens. How can you bear it?"

Albrec ignored him and raised the dip higher so that it illuminated the rough stone of the wall. Columbar was an Antillian like himself, clad in brown. His usual station was with Brother Philip in the herb gardens, but a cold had laid him low this past week and he was on lighter duties in the scriptorium. He had come down here two days ago, hunting old manuscript or parchment that might serve as blotting for the scribes above. And had found the precious document which had been consuming most of Albrec's time ever since.

"There have been shelves here at one time," Albrec said, running his fingers across the deep grooves in the wall. "And the stonework is rough, as though built in haste or without regard for appearances."

"Who's going to see it down here?" Columbar asked.

He had a pendulous nose that was red and dripping and his tonsure had left him with black feathers of hair about his ears and little else. He was a man of the soil, he was proud of saying, a farmer's son from the little duchy of Touron. He could grow anything given the right plot, and thus had ended up in Charibon producing thyme and mint and parsley for the table of the Vicar-General and the poultices of the infirmary. Albrec had a suspicion that he was unable to read anything beyond a few well-worn phrases of the Clerical Catechism and his own name, but that was not uncommon among the lesser orders of the Church.

"And where's the gap where you found it?" Albrec asked.

"Here—no, over here, with the mortar crumbling. A wonder the library hasn't tumbled to the ground if the foundations are in this state."

"We're far below the library's foundations," Albrec said absently, poking into the crevice like a rabbit enlarging a burrow. "These chambers have been hewn from solid rock; those buttresses were left standing while the rest was cleared away. The place is all of a piece. So why do we have mortared blocks here?"

"It was the Fimbrians built Charibon, like they built everything else," Columbar said, as if to prove that he was not entirely ignorant.

"Yes. And it was a secular fortress at first. These catacombs were most probably used for the stores of the garrison."

"I wish you would not call them catacombs, Albrec. They're grim enough as it is." Columbar's breath was a pale fog about his face as he spoke.

Albrec straightened. "What was that?"

"What? I heard nothing."

They paused to listen in the little sanctuary of light maintained by the dip.

To call the chambers they were in catacombs was not

such a bad description. The place was low, the roof uneven, the floor, walls and roof sculpted out of raw granite by some unimaginable labour of the long-ago empire. One stairway led down here from the lower levels of the library above, also hewn out of the living gutrock. Charibon had been built on the bones of the mountains, it was said.

These subterranean chambers seemed to have been used to house the accumulated junk of several centuries. Old furniture, mouldering drapes and tapestries, even the rusted remains of weapons and armour, quietly decayed in the dark peace. Few of the inhabitants of the monastery-city came down here; there were two levels of rooms above them and then the stolid magnificence of the Library of St. Garaso. The bottom levels of the monastery had not been fully explored since the days of the emperors; there might even be levels below the one on which the two men now stood.

"If you hate the dark so much, I'm blessed if I know what you were doing down here in the first place," Albrec whispered, his head still cocked to listen.

"When Monsignor Gambio wants something you find it quick, no matter where you have to look," Columbar said in the same low tone. "There wasn't a scrap of blotting left in the whole scriptorium, and he told me not to poke my scarlet proboscis back round the door until I had found some."

Albrec smiled. Monsignor Gambio was a Finnmarkan, a crusty, bearded old man who looked as though he would have been more at home on the deck of a longship than in the calm industry of a scriptorium. But he had been one of the finest scribes Charibon possessed until the lengthening years had made crooked mockeries of his hands.

"I should be grateful you put scholarly curiosity over the needs of the moment," Albrec said.

"I suffered for it, believe me."

"There! There it is again. Do you hear it?"

They paused again to listen. Somewhere off in the cluttered darkness there was a crash, the sound of things striking the stone floor, a clink of metal. Then they heard someone cursing in a low, irritated and very unclerical manner.

"Avila," Albrec said with relief. He cupped a hand about his mouth. "Avila! We're over here, by the north wall!"

"And which way is north in this lightless pit? I swear, Albrec . . ."

A light came into view, flickering and bobbing over the piles of rubbish. Gradually it neared their own until Brother Avila stood before them, his face smeared with dust, his black Inceptine habit grimed with mould.

"This had better be good, Albrec. I'm supposed to be face-down in the Penitential Chapel, as I was all yesterday. Never throw a roll at the Vicar-General if you've buttered it first. Hello, Columbar. Still running errands for Gambio?"

Avila was tall, slim and fair-haired, an aristocrat to his fingertips. Naturally, he was an Inceptine, and if he refrained from flinging too many more bread rolls he could be assured of a high place in the order ere he died. He was the best friend, perhaps the only one, that Albrec had ever known.

"Did anyone see you come down here?" Albrec asked him.

"What's this? Are we a conspiracy then?"

"We are discreet. Think about that concept, Avila."

"Discretion—there's a novel quality. I'll have to consider it. What have you dragged me down here for, my diminutive friend? Poor Columbar looks on the verge of a seizure. Have the ghosts been leaning over his shoulder?"

"Don't say such things, Avila," Columbar said with a shiver.

"We're looking for more of the document that Columbar unearthed, as you know very well," Albrec put in.

"Ah, *that* document: the precious papers you've been so secretive about."

"I must be going," Columbar said. He seemed more uneasy by the moment. "Gambio will be looking for me. Albrec, you know that if—"

"If the thing turns out to be heretical you had nothing to do with it, whereas if it is as rare and wonderful as Albrec hopes you'll be clamouring for your sliver of fame. We know, Columbar." Avila smiled sweetly.

Brother Columbar glared at him. *"Inceptines,"* he said, a wealth of comment in the word. Then he stomped away into the darkness taking one of the dips with him. They heard him blundering through the tumbled rubbish as his light grew ever fainter and then disappeared.

"You had no call to be so hard on him, Avila," Albrec said.

"He's an ignorant peasant who wouldn't know the value of literature if it sat up and winked at him. I'm surprised he didn't take your discovery to the latrines and wipe his arse with it."

"He has a good heart. He ran a risk for my sake."

"Indeed? So what is this thing that has got you so excited, Albrec?"

"I'll tell you later. For now, I want to see if we can find any more of it down here."

"A man might think you had discovered gold."

"Perhaps I have. Hold the lamp."

Albrec began to poke and pry at the crevice wherein Columbar had discovered the document. There were a few scraps of parchment left in it, as broken and brittle as dried autumn leaves. Almost as fragile was the mortar which held the rough stones surrounding it together. Albrec was able to lever some of them loose and widen the gap. He pushed his hand in farther, trying to feel for the back of the crevice. It seemed to run deep into the stonework. When he had pushed and scraped his arm in as far as his elbow, he found to his shock that his hand was in an empty space beyond. He flapped his fingers about, but the space seemed large. Another room?

"Avila!"

But Avila's strong hand was across his mouth, silencing him, and the dip was blown out to leave them in utter night.

Something was moving on the other side of the subterranean chamber.

The two clerics froze, Albrec still with one arm disappearing into the gap in the wall.

A light flickered as it was held aloft and under its radiance the pair could see the grotesque shadow-etched features of Brother Commodius scanning the contents of the chamber. The knuckles which were wrapped about the lamp handle brushed the stone ceiling; the light and dark of its effulgence made his form seem distorted and huge, his ears almost pointed; and his eyes shone weirdly, almost as though they possessed a light of their own. Albrec had worked under Commodius for over a dozen years, but this night he was almost unrecognizable, and there was something about his appearance which filled Albrec with terror. He suddenly knew that it was vitally important he and Avila should not be seen.

The Senior Librarian glared around for a few moments more, then lowered his lamp. The pair of quaking clerics by the north wall heard his bare feet slapping on the stone, diminishing into silence. They were left in impenetrable pitch-blackness.

"Sweet Saint!" Avila breathed, and Albrec knew that he, too, had sensed the difference in Commodius, the menace which had been in the chamber with his presence.

"Did you see that? Did you feel it?" Albrec whispered to his companion.

"I—What was he doing here? Albrec, he looked like—"

"They say that great evil can be sensed, like the smell of death," Albrec said in a rush.

"I don't—I don't know, Albrec. Commodius, he's a *priest*, in the name of God! It was the lamplight. The shadows tricked us."

"It was more than shadows," Albrec said. He withdrew his hand from the wall crevice, and as he did something came out along with it and clinked as it struck the stone floor below.

"Can you rekindle the light, Avila? We'll be here all night else, and he's gone now. The place feels different."

"I know. Hold on."

There was a rustling of robes, and then the click and flare of sparks as Avila struck flint and steel on the floor. The spark caught the dry lichen of the tinder almost at once and with infinite care he transferred the minute leaf of flame to the lamp wick. He picked up the object that had fallen and straightened.

"What is this?"

It soaked up the light, black metal curiously wrought. Avila wiped the dust and dirt from it and suddenly it was shining silver.

"What in the world—?" the young Inceptine murmured, turning it over in his slender fingers.

A dagger of silver barely six inches long. The tiny hilt had at its base a wrought pentagram within a circle.

"God's blood, Albrec, look at this thing!"

"Let me see." The blade was covered in runes which meant nothing to Albrec. Within the pentagram was the likeness of a beast's face, the ears filling two horns of the star, the long muzzle in the centre.

"This is an unholy thing," Avila said quietly. "We should go to the Vicar-General with it."

"What would it be doing down here?" Albrec asked.

Avila put the lamp against the black hole in the wall.

"This has been blocked off. There's a room beyond these stones, Albrec, and the Saint only knows what kind of horrors have been walled up in it."

"Avila, the document I found."

"What about it? Is it a treatise on witchery?"

"No, nothing like that." Briefly Albrec told his friend about the precious manuscript, the only copy in the world perhaps of the Saint's life, written by a contemporary.

"That was here?" Avila asked incredulously.

"Yes. And there may be more of it, perhaps other man-uscripts—all behind this wall, Avila."

"What was it doing lying hidden with this?" Avila held up the dagger by the blade. The beast's face was uncan-nily lifelike, the dirt rubbed into the crevices in its fea-tures giving it an extra dimension.

"I don't know, but I intend to find out. I can't take this to the Vicar-General, Avila, not yet. I haven't finished reading the document for one thing. What if they deem it heretical and have it burned?"

"Then it's heretical, and for the best. Your curiosity is overcoming rationality, Albrec."

"No! I have seen too many books burned. This one I intend to save, Avila, whatever it takes."

"You're a damn fool. You'll get yourself burned along with it."

"I'm asking you as a friend: say nothing to anyone of this."

"What about Commodius? Obviously he suspects something, else he would not have been here."

They were both silent, remembering the unnerving as-pect of the Senior Librarian's appearance a few minutes ago. Taken together with the artefact they had found, it seemed to shake their knowledge of the everyday ordi-nariness of things.

"Something is wrong," Avila murmured. "Something is most definitely wrong in Charibon. I think you are right. We were not frightened by shadows alone, Albrec.

I think Commodius was . . . different, somehow."

"I agree. So give me a chance to see if I can get to the bottom of this. If there is indeed something wrong, and Commodius has something to do with it, then part of it is here, behind this wall."

"What are you going to do, knock it down?"

"If I have to."

"And to think I likened you to a mouse when first I met you. You have the heart of a lion, Albrec. And the stubbornness of a goat. And I am a fool for listening to you."

"Come, Avila, you are not an Inceptine completely— at least not yet."

"I am starting to share the Inceptine fear of the unknown, though. If we're caught there will be a host of questions asked, and the wrong answers could send us both to the pyre."

"Give me the dagger, then. I have no wish to see you embroiled in my mischief."

"Mischief! Mischief is throwing rolls at the Vicar-General's table. You are flirting with heresy, Albrec. And worse, perhaps."

"I am only preserving knowledge, and seeking after more."

"Whatever. In any case, I am loath to let an ugly misshapen little Antillian upstage me, an Inceptine of noble birth. I'll join you in your private crusade, Brother Conspiracy. But what of Columbar?"

"He knows only that he found a manuscript of interest to me. I'll have a talk with him and secure his discretion."

"There are more brains in the turnips he raises. I hope he knows the value of the word."

"I'll impress it upon him."

They paused as if by common consent to listen again. Nothing but the soundlessness of the deep earth, the drip of water from ancient bedrock.

"This place predates the faith," Avila said in an undertone. "The Horned One had a shrine on the site of Charibon until the Fimbrians tore it down, it is said."

"Time to go," Albrec told him. "We'll be missed. You have your penance to finish. We'll come back some other time, and we'll have that wall down if I have to scrape it away with a spoon."

Avila tucked the pentagram dagger into the pocket of his habit without a word. They set off through the dark together towards the stairs beyond, the tall Inceptine and the squat Antillian. In a few short minutes it seemed that their world had become less knowable, full of sudden shadows.

The lightless spaces of the catacombs watched them go in silence.

TWELVE thousand of the Knights Militant had died fighting at Aekir, almost half of their total strength throughout Normannia. Their institution was a strange one; some said a sinister, anachronistic one also. They were the secular arm of the Church, at least in theory, but their senior officers were clerics, Inceptines to a man. The "Ravens' Beaks" they were sometimes called.

They were feared across the continent by the commoners of every kingdom, their actions sanctioned by the Pontiff, their authority vaguely defined but indisputable. Kings disliked them for what they represented: the all-pervading power and influence of the Church. The nobility saw in them a threat to their own authority, for the word of a Knight Presbyter might not be gainsaid by any man of lower rank than a duke. Across the breadth of the continent, men with their noses in their beer might jocularly lament the fact that Macrobius had gathered only half of the Knights in Aekir before its fall, but they did so with one eye cocked at the door, and in undertones.

Golophin hated them. He loathed the very sight of their sombre cavalcades as they trooped through the streets of Abrusio on their destriers. They wore three-quarter armour, and over it the long sable surcoats with the triangular Saint's symbol worked in malachite green at breast and back. They bore poniards, longswords and lances, having disdained the new technology of gunpowder. More often than not, folk muttered, the only weapon they needed or utilized was the torch.

The pyres were still ablaze up on the hill. Two hundred today for the Knights were beginning to run short of victims. All the Dweomer-folk of the city and the surrounding districts had fled—those who survived. Most of them were freezing in the snowbound heights of the Hebros. Some Golophin and his friends had procured berths for on outbound ships. The Thaumaturgists' Guild had been decimated by the purges; most of its members were too prominent, too well known in the city to have had any chance of escaping. But a few, including Golophin, survived, scuttling like vermin in the underbelly of Abrusio, doing what they could for their people.

His face was a blurred shadow under his wide-brimmed hat. Anyone who looked at him would find it strangely difficult to remember any of its features. A simple spell, but one hard to maintain in the bustle of the Lower City. Speech negated it, and anyone who looked long and hard enough might just see through it. So Golophin moved quickly, a tall, incredibly lean figure of economic movements in a long winter mantle with a bag slung over one bony shoulder. He looked like a pilgrim journeying in haste to the site of a shrine.

The Lower City was still virtually off-limits to the Knights Militant, the common people bolstered in their defiance by the stand that General Mercado and Admiral Rovero were making. But already whispers were abroad that a messenger had brought news of the King's excommunication to the newly established Theocratic Council which technically ruled Abrusio. Abeleyn had been named a heretic, it was said, and his kingship was annulled. The general and the admiral must soon acknowledge the rule of the council or face the same fate themselves. And after that, the pyres would be kept stocked for years as the Knights went through the Lower City cleansing it of all who had defied them.

Admiral's Tower reared up over the rooftops ahead like a brooding megalith. It housed the headquarters of Hebrion's navy, the administrative offices of the State Shipyards and the halls of the fleet nobility. Golophin knew the place well, an outdated, labyrinthine fortress which butted on to the waters of the Inner Roads. The masts of the fleet rose like a forest in the docks at its foot and the old walls were whitened by the guano of a hundred generations of seabirds.

It was busy down here. The ships of the fleet required constant overhaul and their crews were kept eternally occupied by vigilant officers. Between eight and ten thousand mariners in all, they were volunteers to a man. Less than half their vessels were in port at the moment, however.

Ships of the Hebrian fleet were continually occupied with guarding the sea lanes which constituted the life's blood of Abrusio, even in winter. There were squadrons maintained in the Malacar Straits, the Hebrionese, even as far north as the Tulmian Gulf. They kept the trade routes free of the corsairs and the northern Reivers, and often exacted a discreet toll from passing merchantmen in return.

The sentries at the gates of Admiral's Tower never noticed the man in dun robes and wide-brimmed hat. Momentarily they both found the flight of a gull overhead utterly engrossing, and when they had blinked and looked at each other in mild puzzlement, he was past them, wending his undisturbed way through the darkened passages of the old fortress.

"YOU came then," Admiral Jaime Rovero said. "I was not sure if you would, especially in daylight, but then I suppose a man like you has his ways and means."

Golophin swept off his hat and rubbed an entirely bald scalp that gleamed with perspiration despite the raw coldness of the day.

"I came, Admiral, as I said I would. Is Mercado here yet?"

"He awaits us within. He is not happy, Golophin, and neither am I." Admiral Rovero was a burly, heavily bearded man whose face spoke of long years of exposure to the elements. His eyes seemed permanently slitted against some contrary wind and when he spoke only one corner of his mouth opened, the lips remaining obstinately shut on the other side. It was as if he were making some sardonic aside to an invisible listener at his elbow. The voice which issued from his lopsided mouth was deep enough to rattle glass.

"Who is happy in these times, Jaime? Come, let's go in."

They left the small anteroom and went through a pair of thick double doors which led to the state apartments of the Admiral of the Fleet. The short day was already winding down towards a winter twilight, as grey and cheerless as a northern sea, but there was a fire burning in the vast fireplace which occupied one wall. It made the daylight beyond the balcony screens seem blue and threw the far end of the long room into shadow.

The rams from fourteen Astaran galleys were set in the stone near the ceiling like the trophy heads of a hunter; they testified to the years of naval rivalry with Astarac. The curved scimitars of corsairs and Sea-Merduks crisscrossed the walls in patterns of flickering steel, and immensely detailed models of ships stood on stone pedestals below them. On the walls also, vellum maps of the Hebrian coast, the Malacar Straits and the Levangore hung like pale tapestries between the weapons. The room was a lesson in Hebrian naval history.

Another man stood with his back to the fire so that the

flames threw his shadow across the flagged floor like a
cape. He turned his head as Admiral Rovero and the old
mage entered and Golophin saw the familiar shine of
silver from the battered face.

"Good to see you again, General," he said.

General Mercado bowed. His visage was something of
a marvel, created by Golophin himself. As a colonel in
the bodyguard of Bleyn the Pious, he had taken a scimitar
blow in the face. The blade had slashed away his nose,
his cheekbone and part of his temple. Golophin had been
on hand to save his sight and his life, and he had grafted
a mask of silver on the injury. One half of Mercado's
face was thus the bearded countenance of a veteran soldier, the other was an inhuman façade of glittering metal
from which a bloodshot eye glared, lidless and tearless,
but sustained by pure theurgy, a spell of permanence
whose casting had cost Golophin the last of the scanty
hair on his scalp. That had been twenty years ago.

"Have a seat, Golophin," the General said. The metal
half of his face made his voice resound oddly, as though
he were speaking from out of a tin cup.

"You've heard the rumours, I suppose," the old mage
said, seating himself comfortably not far from the fire
and rummaging through his robes for his tobacco pouch.

"Not rumours, not any more. The Papal bull of excommunication arrived two days ago. Rovero and I have been
summoned to the palace tomorrow to view it and recon-
sider our positions."

"So the pair of you will walk tamely into the palace."

The human part of Mercado's face quirked upwards in
a smile. "Not tamely, no. I intend to take an honour guard
of two hundred arquebusiers, and Rovero will have a
hundred marines. It will be public, no chance of a dagger
in the back."

Golophin thumbed leaf into the bowl of his long-
stemmed pipe. "It is not my place to preach to you about

security," he conceded. "What will you do if you are satisfied the bull is genuine?"

Mercado paused. He and Rovero looked at one another. "First tell us what you have to say on the matter."

"Then your minds are not made up?"

"Damn it, Golophin, stop playing games!" Admiral Rovero burst out. "What of Abeleyn? Where is he and how does he fare?"

The old wizard lit his pipe with a spill caught from the flames of the fire. He puffed in silence for a few seconds, filling the room with the scents of Calmar and Ridawan.

"Abeleyn has just fought a battle," he said calmly at last.

"*What*?" Mercado cried, horrified. "Where? With whom?"

"Two squadrons of corsairs ambushed his ships as they were sailing south through the Fimbrian Gulf. He beat them off, but lost three-quarters of his men and two of his own vessels. He had to beach his remaining ship on the coast of Imerdon. He is intending to march overland the rest of the way to Hebrion."

Rovero was grinding one fist into a palm, striding back and forth restlessly and spitting words out of the corner of his mouth as though he were unwilling to let them go.

"Corsairs that far north. In the gulf! Two squadrons, you say. Now there's a happy chance, a synchronicity of fate. Someone tried to take the King, that's clear. But who? Who hired them?"

"Why Admiral," Golophin said with mild surprise, "you almost sound as though you care about the fate of our heretical ex-monarch."

Rovero stopped his pacing and glared at Golophin. "Beat them off, eh? Then at least he hasn't forgotten all I've taught him. Ex-monarch, my arse! Assault the person of the King, would they, the Goddamned heathen piratical dastards . . ."

"He sank three of them," Golophin went on. "They

were in galleasses, the older sort with no broadsides, only chasers."

"How were the King's vessels armed?" Rovero demanded, his face alight with professional interest.

"Culverins, sakers. But that was only on the carrack. The two *nefs* had falcons alone. The corsairs sank one and burned the other to the waterline."

"Abeleyn's bodyguard?" Mercado asked abruptly.

"Almost all lost. Most were in the *nefs*. They gave a good account of themselves, though. Abeleyn has barely a hundred men left to him."

"They were good men," Mercado murmured. "The best of the Abrusio garrison."

"Where has he beached? How long will he take to get here?" Admiral Rovero asked, his eyes as narrow as the edge of a blade.

"That I don't know for sure, alas, and neither did the King when . . . when I communicated with him last. He is in the coastal marshes, close to the border with Imerdon, south-west of the mouth of the Habrir river. That is all I know."

The admiral and the general were silent, conflicting emotions flitting across their faces. "Is Abeleyn still your liege-lord, gentlemen?" Golophin asked. "He needs you now as he never has before."

Rovero grimaced as though he had bitten into a lemon. "God forgive me if I do wrong, but I am the King's man, Golophin. The lad is a fighter, always has been. He is a worthy successor to his father, whatever the Ravens might say."

Only someone watching Golophin with particular care could have seen the tiny whistle of breath that escaped his lips, the imperceptible sag of relief which relaxed his hitherto rigid shoulder blades.

"General," he said quietly to Mercado, "it would seem that Admiral Rovero still has a king. What say you in this matter?"

Mercado turned his face from Golophin so that the mage could see only the expressionless metal side.

"Abeleyn is my king too, Golophin, God knows. But can a king rule if his soul is damned? Who would gainsay the word of the Pontiff, the successor to Ramusio? Maybe the Inceptines are right. The Merduk War is God's punishment. We all have a penance to do before the world can be set to rights."

"The innocent are burning, Albio," Golophin said, using the general's first name. "A heretic sits on the throne of the Pontiff whilst its true occupant is in the east. Macrobius lives, and he is aiding the Torunnans in their battles to maintain the frontier. He helped them save Ormann Dyke when the world thought it irredeemably lost. The faith is with him. He is our spiritual head, not this usurper who sits in Charibon."

Mercado twisted to meet Golophin's eyes. "Are you so sure?"

Golophin raised an eyebrow. "I have my ways. How else do you think I stay abreast of Abeleyn's adventures?"

The fire cracked and spat. A gun began to boom out the evening salute somewhere on the battlements beyond. They would be lighting the ship beacons along the harbours of the city. The men of the ships would be changing watch, half of them trooping into the messes for the evening meal.

Faint and far-off amid the nearer noises, Golophin thought he could hear the cathedral bells tolling Vespers up on Abrusio Hill, nearly two miles away. He knew that if he stepped outside and looked that way he would be able to make out the dying glow of the pyres, finally fading. The dwindling reminder of another day's genocide. He stifled the bitter fury which always arose when he thought of it.

"We must play for time," Mercado said at last. "Rovero and I must not see this bull of theirs. We must hold

them off as long as we are able, and get Abeleyn into
the city safely. Once he is back in Abrusio, the task is
simpler."

Golophin rose and gripped the general's hand. "Thank
you, Albio. You have done the right thing. With you and
Rovero behind him, Abeleyn can retake Abrusio with
ease."

Mercado did not seem to share Golophin's happiness.

"There is something else," he said. He sounded troubled, almost embarrassed.

"What?"

"I cannot be sure of all my men."

Golophin was shocked. "What do you mean?"

"I mean that my adjutant, Colonel Jochen Freiss, has
been conducting secret negotiations with a member of the
council, Sastro di Carrera. I believe he has suborned a
significant number of the garrison."

"Can you not relieve him of his post?" Golophin demanded.

"That would be tipping our hand too soon. I have yet
to plumb the depths of his support, but I believe some
of the junior officers may have joined him in conspiracy."

"It will mean war," Admiral Rovero said ominously.
His voice sounded like the rumble of surf on a far-off
strand.

"How can you sound out the loyalty of your men?"
Golophin asked sharply.

"I have my ways and means, even as you have, Mage,"
Mercado retorted. "But I need time. For now we will
continue to hold the Lower City. Some of the lesser
guilds are on our side, though the Merchants' Guild is
waiting to see which way the wind blows before committing itself."

"Merchants," Rovero said with all the contempt of the
nobility for those in trade.

"We need the merchants on our side," Golophin told
them. "The council is sitting on the treasury. If we are

to finance a war then the merchants are our best source of money. Abeleyn will grant them any concessions they wish, within reason, in return for a regular flow of gold."

"No doubt the council will be putting the same proposition to them," Mercado said.

"Then we must be sure it is our proposition they accept!" Golophin snapped. He stared into the ashen bowl of his pipe. "My apologies, gentlemen. I am a little tired."

"No matter," Rovero assured him. "My ships may tip the scales. If the worst comes to the worst I can threaten them with a naval blockade of the city. That'll soon loosen their purse-strings."

Golophin nodded. He tucked his pipe back into a pocket which was scorched from similar use. "I must be going. I have some people to see."

"Tell the King, when next you speak to him, that we are his men—that we always have been, Golophin," Mercado said haltingly.

"I will, though he has always known it," the wizard replied with a smile.

SIX

THE chamber was small and circular. Its roof was domed and in the dome was a bewildering array of small beams, too slender to provide any architectural support. Corfe could not guess at their purpose, unless it were mere ornamentation. They were hung with cobwebs.

Large windows covered half the circumference of the walls, some of stained glass, predominantly Torunnan scarlet which lent a rosy hue to the place despite the greyness of the weather outside. Inside, the furnishings were rich and comfortable. Velvet-upholstered divans whose lines curved with the walls. Intricately embroidered cushions. A miniature library, the shelves untidy with added scrolls and papers. A tiny desk with a quill springing out of an inkwell. A bronze figurine of a young woman, nude, the face laughing exquisitely. An embroidery stand with rolls of thread tumbled about its foot. The room of an educated, affluent woman.

Corfe had no idea why he was here.

A palace flunkey, all lace cuffs and buckled shoes, had shown him the way soon after he had received the summons. He stood alone now in the private tower of the Queen Dowager, utterly at a loss.

There was a click, and a part of the wall opened to admit the Queen Dowager Odelia. It shut behind her and she stood serenely looking Corfe up and down, a slight smile on her face.

Corfe remembered his manners and bowed hurriedly; he was not of sufficient rank to kiss her hand. Odelia inclined her head graciously in response.

"Sit, Colonel."

He found himself a stool, absurdly conscious of the contrast between his appearance and the lady's. He still looked rather as though he had just trudged off a battlefield, though he had been in Torunn for two days. He had no money, no way to improve his wardrobe, and no one had offered him any advice or help in the matter. Macrobius had been borne away on wings of policy and state, and Corfe had had it brought home to him exactly how insignificant he was. He longed to be back at the dyke with his men doing the only job he had ever been fit for, but could not leave until he had the King's permission, and getting to see the King was well-nigh impossible. He was baffled, therefore, by the Queen Dowager's summons; he had thought himself entirely forgotten.

She was watching him patiently, a glint of what might have been humour in the marvellous green eyes. Carnelian pins secured her golden hair in a stately column atop her head, emphasizing the fine line of her neck. Corfe had heard the rumours; the Queen Dowager was a sorceress who preserved her looks through judicious use of thaumaturgy, sacrifices of new-born babes and the like. It was true she looked a good deal younger than her years. She might have been Lofantyr's elder sister rather than his mother, but Corfe could see the blue veins on the backs of her hands, the slightly swollen knuckles, the faint creases at the corners of her eyes and on her brow. She was attractive, but the signs were there.

"Do you believe me a witch, Colonel?" she asked, startling him. It was almost as though she had followed his train of thought.

"No," he said. "At least, not as the rumours have it. I don't believe you slay black cockerels at midnight or some such nonsense . . . your majesty." He was not sure of the right way to address her.

Something black scuttled along one of the beams above his head, too quickly for him to catch more than a glimpse of it. So they have rats even in palaces, he thought.

"Lofantyr is 'Majesty,' " the Queen Dowager said. "To you I am just 'lady,' unless there is some other epithet you would prefer."

She seemed to be deliberately trying to disconcert him. The realization irritated him. He had no time for the games of the Torunnan court.

"Why did you summon me here?" he asked bluntly.

She cocked her head to one side. "Ah, directness. I like that. You would be amazed how little of it there is in Torunn. Or perhaps you would not. You are a soldier pure and simple, are you not, Colonel? You are not at ease here in the intricacies of the court. You would rather be hip-deep in gore at Ormann Dyke."

"Yes," he said, "I would." There was nothing else he could say. He had never been any use at dissembling, and he sensed it would do him no good here.

"Would you like some wine?"

He nodded, totally at sea.

She clapped her hands and the door through which Corfe had entered opened. A willowy girl with the almond-shaped eyes and high cheekbones of the steppe peoples—a household slave—entered bearing a tray. She set out a decanter and two glasses in silence and then left as noiselessly as she had come. The Queen Dowager poured two generous glassfuls of ruby liquid.

"Ronian," she said. "Little known, but as good as Gaderian if it is well cared for. Our southern fiefs have fine vineyards, but they don't export much."

Corfe sipped at the wine. It might have been gun oil for all he tasted it.

"General Pieter Martellus thinks highly of you, Colonel. In his dispatches he says you made an excellent defence of Ormann Dyke's eastern bastion ere it fell. He also adds that you seem to work best as an independent commander."

"The general flatters me," Corfe said. He had not known that the dispatches he carried from the dyke had included a report on himself.

"You are also the only Torunnan officer to have survived Aekir's fall. You must be a man of luck."

Corfe's face became a stiff mask. "I don't much believe in luck, my lady."

"But it exists. It is that indefinable element which in war or peace—but especially in war—sets a man apart from his fellows."

"If you say so."

She smiled. "Aekir has marked you, Corfe. Before the siege you were an ensign, a junior officer. In the months since you have soared to the rank of colonel purely on merit. Aekir's fall may have been the counterweight to your ascent."

"I would give all my rank, and more besides, to have Aekir back again," Corfe said with some heat. And to have Heria again, his soul cried out.

"Of course," she said soothingly. "But now you are here in Torunn, friendless and penniless, an officer without a command. Merit is not always enough in this world. You must have something else."

"What?"

"A . . . sponsor, perhaps. A patron."

Corfe paused, frowning. At last he said: "Is that why I am here? Am I to become your client, lady?"

She sipped her wine. "Loyalty is more precious than gold at court, for if it is to be real it cannot be bought. I want a man whom gold cannot buy."

"Why? For what purpose?"

"For my own purposes, and those of the state. You know that Lofantyr has been excommunicated by the rival Pontiff Himerius. His nobles know Macrobius is alive—they have seen him with their own eyes. But some do not choose to believe what they see, because it suits them. Torunna is boiling with rebellion; men of rank never need much in the way of an excuse to repudiate their liege-lord. If nothing else, Corfe, I think Aekir and Ormann Dyke have burnt loyalty into you, whether you like it or not. That kind of loyalty, when it is accompanied with real ability, is a rare thing."

"There must be some men loyal to the King in the kingdom," Corfe growled.

"Men tend to have families; they put that loyalty first. If they serve the crown well, it is because they want advancement not only for themselves but for their families also. Thus are the great houses of the nobility created. It is a necessary but dangerous exchange."

"What do you want of me, lady?" Corfe asked wearily.

"I have spoken to the Pontiff of you, Corfe. He also thinks highly of you. He tells me you have no family, no roots now that the Holy City is no more."

Corfe bent his head. "Perhaps."

She rose from her chair and came over to him. Her hands encircled his face, the fingertips just touching his cheekbones. He could smell the lavender her dress had been stored in, the more subtle perfume that rose off her skin. The brilliant eyes held his.

"There is pain in you, a rawness that may never scab over entirely," she said in a low voice. "It is this which drives you on. You are a man without peace, Corfe, without hope of peace. Was it Aekir?"

"My wife," he said, his voice half strangled in his throat. "She died."

The fingertips brushed his face as lightly as a bee nuzzling a flower. Her eyes seemed enormous: viridian orbs with utter black at their core.

"I will help you," she said.

"Why?"

She leaned down. Her face seemed almost to glow. Her breath stirred his forelock.

"Because I am only a woman, and I need a soldier to do my killing for me." Her voice was as low as the bass note of a lute, dark as heather honey. Her lips brushed his temple and the hair on the back of his neck rose like the pelt of a cat caught in a thunderstorm. They remained like that for an endless second, breathing each other's breath.

Then she straightened, releasing him.

"I will procure a command for you," she said, suddenly brisk. "A flying column. You will take it wherever I wish to send it. You will do whatever it is I want you to do. In return—" She hesitated and her smile made her seem much younger. "In return, I will protect you, and I will see that the intrigues of the court do not hamstring your every move."

Corfe looked up at her from his stool. He was not tall; even had he been standing their eyes would just have been level with each other.

"I still don't understand."

"You will. One day you will. Go to the court chamberlain. Tell him you have need of funds; if he objects, tell him to come to me. Procure for yourself a more fitting wardrobe."

"What of the King?" Corfe asked.

"The King will do as he is told," she snapped, and he

saw the iron in her, the hidden strength. "That is all, Colonel. You may go."

Corfe was bewildered. As he stood up she did not move away at once and he brushed against her. Then she turned away from him.

He bowed to her slender backbone, and left the chamber without another word.

IT was a featureless, windswept land. Flat salt marshes spread out for miles in every direction but the sea. The only sounds were the piping of marsh birds and the hissing of the wind in the reeds. Off to the north-west the Hebros Mountains loomed, their knees already pale with snow.

The longboats were ferrying the last of the stores from the ship. The soldiers had lit fires on the firmer of the reed islands and were busy constructing shelters to keep out the searching wind. Abeleyn stood by one of the fires and stared out at the skewed hulk of the beached carrack. Dietl was beside him, his eyes red-rimmed with grief and pain. They had sealed his stump with boiling pitch, but the agony of seeing his ship in such a pass seemed to have affected him more than the loss of his hand.

"When I come into my kingdom again, you shall have the best carrack in the state fleet, Captain," Abeleyn told him gently.

Dietl shook his head. "Never was there such a ship. She broke my heart, faithful to the last."

They had heaved the guns overboard as the ship took on more and more water, then the heavier of the stores and finally the fresh water casks. The carrack had grounded upon a sandbar with the sea swirling around her hatches, and there had settled, canting to one side as the tide went out. It was a narrow bar, and as the supporting water withdrew her back had broken with an agonized screeching and groaning that seemed almost sentient.

Abeleyn clapped Dietl on his good shoulder and walked away from the fire. "Orsini!"

"Yes, sire." Sergeant Orsini was immediately on hand. He was the only soldier of any rank remaining with Abeleyn's company: the officers had gone down fighting in the two *nefs*.

"What have we got, Sergeant? How many and how much?"

Orsini blinked, his mind turning it over.

"Some sixty soldiers, sire, maybe a dozen of your own household attendants, and the remaining crew of the carrack numbers near thirty. But of that total, maybe twenty are wounded. There's two or three won't last out the night."

"Horses?" Abeleyn asked tersely.

"Drowned in the hold, most of 'em, sire, or shot through with splinters in the battle. We managed to get out your own gelding and three mules. It's all there is."

"Stores?"

Orsini looked at the mounds of waterlogged sacks, crates and casks that were piling up on the little island and its neighbours, half hidden in the yellow reed beds.

"Not much, sire, not for a hundred men. Supplies for a week if we're easy on 'em. Ten days at a pinch."

"Thank you, Sergeant. You'll have a guard rota set up, of course."

"Yes, sire. Nearly every man salvaged his arquebus, though the powder'll take a while to dry."

"Good work, Orsini. That's all."

The sergeant went back to his work. Abeleyn's mouth tightened as he watched the parties of soaked, bloodied and exhausted men setting up their makeshift camp on the soggy reed islands. They had fought a battle, struggled to bring a dying ship to shore, and now they would have to scrabble for survival on this remote coast. He had heard not a word of dissension or complaint. It humbled him.

He knew that they had beached somewhere south of the Habrir river; technically they were in Hebrion, the river marking the border between the kingdom and its attached duchy. This was a desolate portion of Abeleyn's dominions though, an extensive marshland which reached far inland and was crossed by only one or two causeway-raised Royal roads. There would be villages within a day's march, but no town of any significance for fifteen leagues—and that the city of Pontifidad, back to the north-east. Abrusio was over fifty leagues away, and to get to it overland they would have to cross the lower passes of the Hebros, where the mountains that were the backbone of Hebrion plunged precipitously into the sea.

A swoop of wings, and he turned to find Golophin's gyrfalcon perched on a thick reed behind him.

"Where have you been?" he asked shortly.

"The bird or I, sire? The bird has been resting, and well-earned the rest has been. I have been busy, though."

"Well?"

"Rovero and Mercado are ours, thank the Blessed Saints."

Abeleyn muttered a quiet prayer of thanks himself. "Then I can do it."

"Yes. There are other ramifications, though—"

"Talking to birds again, sire?" a woman's voice said. Golophin's familiar took off at once, leaving a barred feather circling in the air behind it.

The lady Jemilla was dressed in a long, fur-trimmed mantle of wool the colour of a cooling ember. She had let her thick mane of ebony hair tumble down about her face, emphasizing the paleness of her skin, and her lips were rouged. Of her pregnancy, some three months gone, there was as yet no visible sign.

Abeleyn's temper flickered a moment, but he mastered it. "You look well, lady."

"Last time you saw me, sire, I was prostrate, retching and green in the face. I should hope that I look well now, by contrast if nothing else." She came closer.

"I trust my men have made you comfortable?"

"Oh, yes," she replied, smiling. "They are such gallants at heart, your soldiers. They have built me a lovely shelter of canvas and driftwood, with a fire to warm it. I feel like the Queen of the Beachcombers."

"And the—the child?"

One hand went immediately to her still-flat belly. "Yet within me, as far as I can tell. My maid was convinced that the seasickness would put paid to it, but the child seems to be a fighter. As a king's child should be."

She was verging on insolence and Abeleyn knew it, but he had ignored her lately and the last few days must have been hard on her. So he merely bowed slightly in acknowledgement, not quite trusting himself to retort with civility.

Her voice changed; it lost its hard edge. "Sire, I apologize if I disturbed you in your . . . meditations. It is only that I have missed your company of late. My maid has set a skillet of wine on the fire to heat. Will you not join me in a glass?"

There were a million and one things he should be doing, and he was with child himself to hear Golophin's news; but the offer of hot wine was tempting, as was the other, unspoken offer in her eyes. Abeleyn was exhausted to the marrow. The thought of relaxing for a little while decided him. His men could do without him for an hour.

"Very well," he said, and he took the slim hand she extended and let himself be led away.

From its perch on a nearby bulrush, the gyrfalcon watched with cold, unblinking eyes.

HER shelter was cosy indeed, if a timber-framed canvas hut could be cosy. She had salvaged a couple of chests and some cloaks from the wreck; these did duty as furnishings.

She dismissed the maid and hauled off Abeleyn's

bloody, salt-cracked boots with her own hands, tipping a
trickle of water out of each; then she ladled out a pewter
tankard of the steaming wine. Abeleyn sat and watched
the flames of the fire turn from pale transparency to solid
saffron as the day darkened. So short, the daylight hours
at this time of year. A reminder that this was not the
campaigning season, not the proper season for war.

The wine was good. He could almost feel it coursing
through his veins and warming his chilled flesh. He recalled Jemilla's maid and ordered her to take the rest of
it to the tents of the wounded. He saw Jemilla's lips thin
as he did, and smiled to himself. The lady had her own
ideas of worthy and unworthy, expendable and indispen-
sable.

"Are you hurt, sire?" she asked. "Your doublet is be-
spattered with gore."

"Other men's, not mine," Abeleyn told her, sipping his
wine.

"It was magnificent—all the soldiers say so. A battle
worthy of Myrnius Kuln himself. Of course, I only heard
it. Consuella and I were crouched in the stink of the
lower hold under sacks; hardly a good post to observe
the ebb and flow, the glory of it."

"It was a skirmish, no more," Abeleyn said. "I was
careless to think we would get away so easily from Perigraine."

"The corsairs were in league with the other kings,
then?" she asked, shocked.

"Yes, lady. I am a heretic. They want me dead—it is
that simple. Using corsairs to kidnap or assassinate me
rather than national troops was merely to utilize a certain
discretion."

"Discretion!"

"Diplomacy has always been a mixture of cunning,
courtesy and murder."

She placed a hand on her stomach, seemingly unaware

of the gesture. "What of King Mark and King Lofantyr? Were attempts made on their lives?"

"I don't know. Possibly. In any case, when they arrive home they will face men of power who intend to take advantage of the situation. As I will."

"It is rumoured that Abrusio is in the control of the Church and the nobles," Jemilla said.

"Is it? Rumours are unreliable things."

"Are we still travelling to Abrusio, sire?"

"Of course. Where else?"

"I—I had thought—" She collected herself, squaring her shoulders like a woman determined to face bad news. "Are you to be married, sire?"

Abeleyn rubbed his eyes with one hand. "One day I hope to be, yes."

"To the sister of King Mark of Astarac?"

"More rumours?"

"It was the talk of Vol Ephrir when we left."

Abeleyn stared at her. "That rumour happens to be true, yes."

She dropped her eyes. There were also rumours that the lady Jemilla had had a low-born lover ere Abeleyn had taken her into his bed. She was not sure if the King had heard them.

"Then what of . . . what of the child I bear?" she asked pitifully.

Abeleyn knew his mistress to be one of the most calculating and accomplished women of his court, the widow of one of his father's best generals; but with his death, she was unrelated to any of the great families of Hebrion. That was one reason why he had allowed himself to be seduced by her: she was alone in this world, and did not belong to any of the power blocs which wrangled in the shadow of the Hebrian throne. She rose or fell on Abeleyn's whim. He could call in Orsini and have her run through here and now, and no one would raise a hand to defend her.

"The child will be looked after," he said. "If it happens to be a boy, and shows promise, then the lad will never lack for anything, I swear to you."

Her eyes were fixed on his, black stabs of colour in her ivory-pale face. Her hand alighted upon his knee.

"Thank you, sire. I have never been blessed with a child before. I hope only that he will grow up to serve you."

"Or she," Abeleyn added.

"It is a boy." She smiled, the first genuine smile Abeleyn had seen from her since leaving Hebrion. "He feels like a boy. I see him curled in my womb with his fists clenched, growing."

Abeleyn did not reply. He stared into the fire again, remembering the flame and wreck of the battle lately fought. A skirmish, he had called it, honestly enough. There was worse awaiting them in Abrusio. The Knights Militant would not vacate the city without a fight, and no doubt the personal retainers of the Sequeros and Carreras would stand shoulder to shoulder with them. But he would win, in the end. He had the army and the fleet at his back.

Jemilla's hand slid slowly upwards from the King's knee, bringing him out of his reverie. It began to stroke him intimately.

"I thought in your condition . . ." he began.

She smiled. "There are many things a man and a woman can do together, your majesty, even in my condition, and I have not taught you a tithe of them yet."

It was this quality in her that both pricked his pride and fascinated him. She was older, experienced, the tutor of his bed. But he was too weary. He lifted her hand away gently.

"There are things to do, lady. I do not have the time, even if the inclination is there."

Her eyes flared for a second: another thing about her which aroused him; she was unaccustomed to not getting her own way—even with a king, it seemed. It took an effort of will for Abeleyn to stand up. Her hand caressed his ankle, the fish-white skin which had not been wholly dry for days.

"Later, perhaps," she said.

"Perhaps. There will not be much time for it in the days to come, however."

He hauled on the clammy boots and kissed her.

She turned her cheek aside so his lips met her mouth. Then her tongue was questing like a warm snake over his teeth. She drew away with an arch smile. Abeleyn stumbled out of the hut into the firelit darkness beyond, feeling that once again she had somehow had the last word.

SEVEN

THE barricades had gone up overnight.

When the deacon led his demi-troop out on their regular patrol of the city in the blue murk of the dawn, they found that the streets were occupied. Carts had been overturned, sacks and crates from the docks piled up and roped together. Even the narrowest of alleys had its obstacle, manned by citizens who had lit braziers against the cold and were standing round them rubbing their hands and chatting good-naturedly. Every street, roadway, avenue and alley which led down into the western half of the Lower City of Abrusio had been blocked off. The place had been sealed as tight as the neck of a stoppered bottle.

The deacon of the Knights Militant and his nine serving brethren sat their heavy horses and watched the Abrusian citizens and their makeshift fortifications with a mixture of anger and uncertainty. True, over the past weeks the Lower City had been an unfriendly place and any Knight who ventured down there was liable to have a chamber pot emptied over his head from an upper window. The Presbyter, Quirion, had ordered his men to stay away from the region whilst the delicate negotiations went on with the Abrusio garrison commanders. But this, this was different. This was open rebellion against the powers which had been ordained by the High Pontiff to rule the city.

The quiet horses with their heavy loads of steel and flesh stood their ground on the cobbles of the street, breathing out spumes of steam into the cold dawn air. It was a narrow place, the closely packed timber-framed houses of this part of the city leaning together overhead so that it seemed their terracotta tiles almost met to form an arch over the thoroughfare below. The citizens behind the barricade left their braziers to stare at the Knights. They were of both sexes, old and young. They carried makeshift weapons fashioned from agricultural implements, or simply hefted the tools of their trades: hammers and picks, scythes, pitchforks, butcher's cleavers. A weaponry as diverse as the colourful citizenry of Abrusio.

The shape of the city was like a horseshoe, within which was the trefoil outline of a cloverleaf. The horseshoe represented the confining outer walls, curving round to end on the northern and southern shores of the Southern Gulf, or the Gulf of Hebrion as it was sometimes called. The cloverleaf represented the three harbours within the walls. The northernmost blade of the leaf was the Inner Roads which extended into the heart of the city, the wharves and docks lapping at the very foot of Abrusio Hill. To left and right of it, and not so far inland, were the Outer Roads, two later-built harbours which had been improved by the addition of man-made moles. The western Inner Roads housed the shipyards and dry docks of the Hebrian navy and were frowned over by the bulk of Admiral's Tower. On a promontory to their north, another ageing fortress stood. This was the Arsenal, the barracks and magazines of Abrusio's garrison. Both fleet and army were therefore quartered in the western arm of the Lower City, and it was this area which had been blocked off by the barricades of the citizens.

But the earnest young deacon was not deliberating on that as he sat his horse in the early morning and wondered what to do. He knew only that a group of rabble had seen fit to deny passage to a demi-troop of the Knights Militant, the secular defenders of the Church on earth. It was an insult to the authority of the Pontiff himself.

"Out swords!" he ordered his men. They obeyed at once. Their lances had been left in their billets as they were inconveniently long to carry when traversing the narrow, packed streets of Lower Abrusio.

"Charge!"

The ten horsemen burst into a trot, then worked into a canter, the shoes of their mounts striking sparks off the cobbles. Two abreast, they thundered down the narrow street like avenging angels, if angels might be so laden with iron and mounted on steaming, wide-nostrilled warhorses.

The citizens stared at the approaching apocalypse for one moment, and then scattered. The barricades were deserted as people took to their heels, fleeing down the street or shouldering in the closed doors of houses on either side.

The deacon's mount struck the piled oddments which blocked the street and reared up, armour, rider and all, then scrambled over the barricade, tearing half of it down as it did so. The other Knights followed suit. The street became full of the din of nickering animals and the clang of steel. The up-ended cart fell back on to its wheels with a crash. They were through, urging their gasping mounts into a trot again, screaming "Ramusio!" at the top of their purpling lungs.

They clattered onwards. People were trying to dodge the heavy swords and the hooves of the destriers. The deacon clipped one fellow on the back of the head and took a chunk out of the base of his skull. When he went down, the horses trampled him into a steaming pulp.

Others too slow to hide or get away were smashed off their feet and suffered the same fate. There were no side alleyways, no way out. Several men and women were hacked as they thumped closed doors frantically with their fists, seeking sanctuary in the adjoining houses. The horses reared as they were trained to do, splintering bone and rending flesh with their iron-shod forehooves. The street became a charnel house.

But it opened out. The streams of survivors scattered as the street became one arm of a three-way junction. There was a little square there.

The deacon was hoarse from yelling the Knights' battlecry, grinning as he swung and hacked at the fleeing mob. Sweat dripped off his nose and slicked his young body inside his armour. This was sport indeed.

But there was something in the air. An odd smell. He paused in his slaughter, puzzled. His men gathered about him panting, the gore dripping from their swords in viscous ribbons. The clattering chaos of a few moments before stilled.

Powder-smoke.

The end of the street had emptied of people. Standing there now were two ranks of Hebrian soldiers with streams of smoke eddying from the lighted match in their arquebuses.

Still the deacon did not fully understand. He kicked his mouth forward, meaning to have a word with these fellows. They were in the way.

An officer at the end of the front rank lifted his sword. A pale winter sun was rising over the rooftops of the houses. It caught the steel of his rapier and turned it into a blaze.

"Ready your pieces!"

The arquebusiers cocked back the wheel-locks which held the glowing match.

"Front rank, kneel!"

The front rank did so.

"Wait!" the deacon shouted angrily. What did these men think they were doing? Behind him, his brother Knights looked on in alarm. One or two began kicking their tired horses into life.

"Front rank, give fire!"

"*No!*" the deacon yelled.

An eruption of flame and smoke, a furious rolling crackle. The deacon was blasted off his horse. His men staggered in the saddle. Horses were screaming as the balls ripped through their iron armour and into their flesh. The massive animals tumbled to the ground, crushing their riders beneath them. A fog of smoke toiled in the air, filling the breadth of the street.

In the powder-smoke, the surviving Knights heard the officer's voice again.

"Rear rank, present your pieces."

The surviving Knights turned as one to the enemy and savagely urged their terrified horses into a canter. Shrieking like fiends they charged down the street into the smoke, determined to avenge their fallen brethren.

They were met by a second storm of gunfire.

All of them went down. The momentum of the two lead riders carried them into the ranks of the arquebusiers, and the horses collapsed through the formation scattering the Hebrian soldiers like skittles. One of the Knights was flung clear, clanging across the cobbles. As he struggled to his feet in the heavy armour that the Knights wore, two Hebrian soldiers flipped him on his back again, as though he were a monstrous beetle. They stood on his wrists, pinioning him, then ripped off his casque and cut his throat.

A final shot as a moaning horse was put out of its pain. From the doors of the houses the people emerged. A ragged cheer went up as they saw the riddled corpses which littered the roadway, though some went to their knees in the clotted gore, cradling the head of a butchered friend or relative. The keening cries of women replaced the cheering.

The citizens of Abrusio rebuilt their barricades whilst the Hebrian soldiers methodically reloaded their weapons and resumed their hidden stations once more.

"I don't believe it!" Presbyter Quirion said. Abrusio stretched out mist-shrouded and sun-gilded in the morning light. He blinked as the sound of arquebus fire came again, echoing over the packed rooftops to the monastery-tower wherein he stood.

"So far three of our patrols have been ambushed," the Knight-Abbot said. "Skirmishing goes on even as we speak. Our casualties have been serious. We are cavalry, without firearms. We are not equipped to fight street battles with foes who possess arquebuses."

"And you are sure it is the Hebrian soldiery who are involved, not civilians with guns?"

"Yes, your excellency. All our brothers report the same thing: when they try to force the barricades, they are met with disciplined gunnery. It has to be the garrison troops; there can be no other explanation."

Quirion's eyes were two blue fires.

"Recall our brethren. There is no profit in them throwing themselves under the guns of rebels and heretics."

"Yes, your excellency."

"And have all officers above the rank of deacon assemble in the speechhall at noon. I'll address them myself."

"At once, your excellency." The Knight-Abbot made the Sign of the Saint on his armoured breast and left.

"What does this mean?" the Presbyter asked.

"Would you like me to find out for you?" Sastro di

Carrera said, one hand fiddling with the ruby set in his earlobe.

Quirion turned to face his companion squarely. They were the only occupants of the high-ceilinged room.

"No."

"You don't like me, your excellency. Why is that?"

"You are a man without much faith, Lord Carrera. You care only for your own advantage."

"Doesn't everyone?" Sastro asked smiling.

"Not everyone. Not my brothers . . . *Do* you know anything about these developments then?"

Sastro yawned, stretching out his long arms. "I can deduce as well or better than the next man. My bet is that Rovero and Mercado have somehow had a communication from our ex-King Abeleyn. They have come down on his side at last—another reason why they postponed the viewing of the Pontifical bull scheduled yesterday. The army and the fleet will hold the Lower City against us until Abeleyn arrives in person, then go over on to the offensive. It is also my guess that your Knights were not meant to be slain; they pressed too hard. Obviously the general and the admiral meant this to look like a popular uprising, but they had to use national troops to defend their perimeter when your brethren tested it."

"Then we know where we stand," Quirion snarled. His face looked as though invisible strings had pulled chin and forehead towards each other; fury had clenched it as it might a fist. "They will be excommunicated," he went on. "I will see them burn. But first we must crush this uprising."

"That may not be so easy."

"What of your friend Freiss?" And when Sastro seemed genuinely surprised, Quirion's bass gravelled out a harsh laugh. "You think I did not know of your meetings with him? I will not let you play a private game in this city, my Lord Carrera. You will pull alongside the rest of us, or you will not be a player at all."

Sastro regained his composure, shrugging. His hand toyed now with the gleaming, scented point of his beard. He needed to toy with his features constantly, it seemed to Quirion. An irritating habit. The man was probably a pederast; he smelled like a sultan's harem. But he was the most effective of the nobles, and a necessary ally.

"Very well," Sastro said casually. "My friend Freiss, as you put it, says he has won over several hundred men of the garrison, men who cannot stomach heresy and who expect to be rewarded for their loyalty once the Church has assumed full control of Abrusio."

"Where are they?"

"In barracks. Mercado has his suspicions and has segregated them from the other tercios. He is probably having them watched also."

"Then they are of little use to us."

"They could stage a diversion while your brethren assault these absurd barricades."

"My brethren are not equipped for street fighting, as you have already heard. No, there must be another way."

Sastro regarded the ornate plasterwork of the ceiling with some interest. "There are, of course, my personal retainers . . ."

"How many?"

"I could muster maybe eight hundred if I called out some of the lesser client houses as well."

"Their arms?"

"Arquebuses and sword-and-buckler men. No pikes, but then pikes are no better at street fighting than cavalry."

"That would be ideal. They could cover an assault by my brethren. How long would it take to muster them?"

"A few days."

The two men looked at each other like a pair of prize-fighters weighing up each other's strengths and weaknesses in the ring.

"You realize I would be risking my house, my followers, ultimately my fortune," Sastro drawled.

"The Hebrian treasury is in the possession of the council. You would be amply compensated," Quirion growled.

"That is not what I was thinking of," Sastro said. "No, money is not my main concern. It is just that my men like to fight for the betterment of their lord's situation as well as their own."

"They would be defending the True Faith of the Ramusian kingdoms. Is that not reward enough?"

"It should be, I know, my dear Presbyter. But not all men are as . . . single-minded, you might say, as your brethren."

"What do you want, Lord Carrera?" Quirion asked, though he thought he already knew.

"You are looking through the archives, are you not, trying to establish who should take the throne now that the Hibrusid line is finished?"

"I have Inceptine archivists working on it, yes."

"You will find, I think, that Astolvo di Sequero is the most eligible candidate. But he is an old man. He does not want the kingship with all that it entails. He will refuse it."

"Are you so sure?"

"Oh, yes. And his sons are flighty, vicious young things. Hardly Royal material. You will need the next king of Hebrion to be a mature man, a man of abilities, a man who is happy to work hand in gauntlet with the holy Church. Otherwise the other noble houses might get restless, mutinous even, at the idea of one of Astolvo's brats ruling."

"Where might we find such a man?" Quirion asked guardedly. He had not missed the threat in Sastro's words.

"I am not sure, but if your archivists delve deep

enough I believe they may find the house of Carrera closer to the throne than you think."

Quirion laughed his coarse laugh—the guffaw of a commoner, Sastro thought with disgust, though nothing of his feelings showed on his face.

"The kingship in return for your men, my lord?" the Presbyter said.

Sastro raised his carefully trimmed eyebrows. "Why not? No one else will make you a similar offer, I'll warrant."

"Not even the Sequeros?"

"Astolvo will not. He knows that were he to do so his life would be hanging by a thread. His sons are champing at the bit beneath him; he would not last a year. How would that look? The Church-sponsored monarchy of Hebrion embroiled in murderous intrigue, perhaps even parricide, within months of its establishment."

Quirion looked thoughtful, gauging. "Such decisions of moment must be referred to Himerius in Charibon. The Pontiff will have the final word."

"The Pontiff, may the Saints be good to him, will no doubt follow the recommendations of his representative on the spot."

Quirion repaired to the table on which sat a host of decanters. He poured himself a dribble of wine and drank it off, grimacing. He did not imbibe as a rule, but he felt the need of the warming liquid; there was a chill in the room.

"Get word to your co-conspirator, Freiss," he said. "Tell him to prepare his men for action. And start gathering your own followers together, Lord Carrera. We must work on a combined plan."

"Will there then be a messenger sent to Charibon with your recommendations?" Sastro asked.

"There will. I will . . . advise my archivists to look into the genealogy of your house."

"A wise decision, Presbyter. You are obviously a man of sagacity."

"Perhaps. Now that the bargaining is done, can we attend to the more mundane details? I want rosters, equipment lists."

The man had no style, Sastro thought. No sense of the moment. But that was by-the-by. He had secured the kingship for himself; that was the main thing. He had negotiated a path to power. But he had not arrived at its threshold, not yet. There remained much to be done.

"I will have everything ready for you to peruse this afternoon," he said smoothly. "And I will have couriers sent to my estates and those of my vassals. The men will begin assembling directly."

"Good. This thing must be done quickly. If we cannot storm the Lower City before Abeleyn arrives, it will be the work of several campaigns to secure Abrusio, with all the destruction that entails."

"Indeed. I have no wish to rule over a hill of ashes."

Quirion stared at his aristocratic companion. "The new king will rule in conjunction with the Church. I have no doubt that the Pontiff will wish to maintain a garrison of the Knights here, even after the rebels are extinguished."

"They will be an inestimable help, a valued adjunct to Royal authority."

Quirion nodded. "Just so we understand each other. Now if you will excuse me, my Lord Carrera, I must prepare to address my brethren. And there are wounded to visit."

"By all means. Will you give me your blessing before I go, excellency?"

Sastro rose, then knelt before the Presbyter with his head bowed. Quirion's face spasmed. He grated out the words of the blessing as though they were a curse. The nobleman regained his feet, made the Sign of the Saint with mocking flamboyance and left the room.

● ● ●

OVER five hundred leagues away, the Thurian Mountains were thick and white with midwinter snows. The last of the passes had been closed and the sultanate of Ostrabar was sealed off to the west and the south by the mountain barrier, itself merely an outlying range of the fearsome Jafrar Mountains farther east.

The tower had once been part of the upland castle of a Ramusian noble, one of the hundreds which had dotted the rich vales of Ostiber in the days when it had been a Ramusian kingdom. But it was different now. For sixty years the Merduk overlords had possessed the rich eastern region. Its ruler was Aurungzeb the Golden, the Stormer of Aekir, and the people he ruled had come to accept the Merduk yoke, as it was called in the west. They tilled their fields as they had always done and by and large they were no worse off under their Merduk lords than they had been under the Ramusian ones.

True, their sons must serve a stint in the Sultan's armies, but for the most talented of them there was no bar to ambition. If a man had ability, he might rise very high in the service of the Sultan no matter how low his birth. It was one of the cunning ways in which the Merduks had reconciled the people to their rule, and it brought continual new blood into the army and the administration. The grandfathers of the men who had fought under the banners of Ahrimuz the Prophet at Aekir and Ormann Dyke had struggled against those same banners two generations before. For the peasantry it was a pragmatic choice. They were tied to their land and when it changed owners they would change masters as a matter of course.

Most of the upland castle was in ruins, but one wing with its tall tower remained intact and it gave a fine view of the valleys below. On a clear day it was even possible to see Orkhan, the capital of the Sultan, glittering with minarets in the distance. But the castle was isolated. Built too high in the Thurian foothills, it had been deserted

even before the Merduks came, its occupants forced out
by the severity of the upland winters.

Sometimes the local inhabitants lower in the valley
would remark upon the dark tower standing alone on the
wintry heights above. It was rumoured that strange lights
could be seen flashing in its windows after dark, and
there were tales of inhuman beasts which roamed the fells
around it in nights of moon. Sheep had gone missing,
and a boy herder had disappeared. No one dared to approach the old ruin, though, and it was left to its malig-
nant contemplation of the dales below.

THE beast turned from the window and its monochrome world of white snow and black trees and distant lights. It shuffled across the circular tower chamber
and sank into a padded chair before the fire with a sigh.
The endless wind was moaning about the gaps in the roof
and occasional confettis of snow would flutter in the
glassless window.

A beast was dressed in human robes, and its head was
like some grotesque marriage of humanity and reptile.
The body was awkward and bent, and talons scraped the
flagged floor in place of toes. Only the hands remained
recognizably human, though they were treble-jointed and
slightly scaled, reflecting back the firelight with a green
tint.

Other things reflected back the firelight also. Arranged
around the walls on shelves were great glass carboys full
of liquid, the light of the flames kindling answering
shines from their depths. In some floated the small grey
corpses of newborn babies, eyes shut as though they were
still dreaming in the womb. In others were the coiled
bodies of large snakes, their sides flattened against the
glass. And in three of the fat-bellied jars, dark bipedal
shapes stood gazing down into the room with eyes that
were the merest gleeds of bright incarnadine. They

moved restlessly in the surrounding liquid, as though impatient at their confinement.

The room was full of a sour smell, like clothes left lying out in the rain. On a small table in front of the hearth was a silver salver upon which smoked the dying ashes of a tiny fire. There were small bones in the ashes, the miniature egg-sized remnant of a fanged skull.

The thing in the chair leaned forward and poked at the ashes with one long forefinger. Its eyes glittered. With a furious gesture it sent ashes, salver and all flying into the fire. Then it leaned back in the chair, hissing.

From a niche near the ceiling the winged shape of a homonculus fluttered down like a gargoyle in miniature. It settled on the beast's shoulder and nuzzled the wattled neck.

"Easy, Olov. It is no matter," the beast said, patting the distressed little creature. And then: "Batak!"

A door opened at the rear of the chamber and a man dressed in travelling clothes of fur-lined cape and high boots entered. He was young, his eyes coal-black, earlobes heavy with gold rings. His face was as pale as plaster and he was sweating despite the season.

"Master?"

"It failed again—as you can see. I merely destroyed another homonculus."

The young man came forward. "I am sorry."

"Yes, you are. Pour me some wine, will you, Batak?"

The young man did so silently. His hand was shaking and he mopped spilt liquid with one corner of his sleeve, darting frightened glances at the thing in the chair as he did so.

The beast took the proffered wine and threw it back, tilting its head like a chicken to drink. The crystal of the goblet cracked within its digits. The beast regarded the object with a weary irritation, then threw the flawed thing to shatter in the fire.

"The whole world is new to me," it muttered.

"What will you do now, master? Are you going to undertake the journey?"

The beast looked at him with bright, fulvid eyes. The air around it seemed to shimmer for a second and the homunculus took off for the rafters with a squeak. When the air steadied once more there was a man sitting there in place of the beast, a lean, dark-skinned man with a face as fine-boned as that of a woman. Only the eyes remained of the former monster, lemon-bright and astonishing in the handsome visage.

"Does this make you less nervous, Batak?"

"It is good to see your face again, master."

"I can only hold this form for a few hours at a time, and the eyes resist any change. Perhaps because they are the windows of the soul, it is said." The man smiled without the slightest trace of humour. "But in answer to your question: yes, I will undertake the journey. The Sultan's agents are already in Alcaras hiring ships—big, ocean-going ships, not the galleys of the Levangore. I have an escort and a carriage billeted down in the village; the Sultan means to be sure I go where I say I am going."

"Into the uttermost west. Why?"

The man stood up and put his back to the fire, splaying his hands out against the heat. There was a flickering blur, like a ripple of shadow around his silhouette. Dweomer-born illusions were always unstable in bright light.

"There is something out there, in the west. I know it. In my research I have come across legends, myths, rumours. They all point to the same conclusion: there is land in the west, and something else. Someone, perhaps. Besides, I am little use to the Sultan as I am. When Shahr Baraz—may he rot in a Ramusian hell—destroyed the homunculus which was my conductor he not only warped my body, he crippled the Dweomer within me. I am still powerful, still Orkh the master-mage, but my powers are

not what they were. I would not have that come to light,
Batak."

"Of course. I—"

"You will be discreet. I know. You are a good apprentice. In a few years you will have mastered the
Fourth Discipline and you will be a mage yourself. I have
left you enough of my library and materials for you to
continue your studies even without my guidance."

"It is the court, master, the harem. They unsettle me.
There is more to being the Sultan's sorcerer than Dweomer."

Orkh smiled, this time with some real warmth. "I
know, but that is something else you must learn. Do not
cross the vizier, Akran. And court the eunuchs of the
harem. They know everything. And never reveal to the
Sultan the limits of your power—never say you cannot
do something. Prevaricate, obfuscate, but do not admit to
any weakness. Men think mages all-powerful. We want
to keep it that way."

"Yes, master. I will miss you. You have been a good
teacher."

"And you a good pupil."

"Do you hope to be healed in the west? Is that it? Or
are you merely removing yourself from the sight of
men?"

"Aurungzeb asked me the same thing. I do not know,
Batak. I weary of being a monster, that much I do know.
Even a leper does not know the isolation I have suffered,
the loneliness. Olov has been my only companion; he is
the only creature which looks upon me without fear or
disgust."

"Master, I—"

"It is all right, Batak. There is no need to pretend. In
my research, I have discovered that several times in the
past centuries ships have sailed for the west and have not
returned. They carried passengers—sorcerers fleeing persecution in the Ramusian states. I do not believe that all

those ships were lost. I believe there may be survivors
or descendants of survivors out there still."

Batak's eyes grew round. "And you think they will be
able to heal you?"

"I don't know. But I weary of the intrigues at court. I
want to see a new horizon appear with every dawn. And
it suits Aurungzeb's policies. The Ramusians have already sent a flotilla westwards; it left Abrusio months ago
under a Gabrionese captain named Richard Hawkwood.
They should be in the west now. The Merduk sultanates
cannot allow this new world to be claimed by our enemies. I concur with Aurungzeb in that."

"You know that Shahr Baraz is not dead? He disappeared along with his pasha, Mughal. It is said they rode
off eastwards, back into the steppes."

"I know. My revenge may never happen. He will leave
his pious old bones in the Jafrar, or on the endless plains
of Kambaksk. It matters not. Other things concern me
now."

Orkh left the fire and strode over to a nearby table
which supported an iron-bound chest. He opened the lid,
looked in, nodded, then turned to his apprentice once
more.

"In here you will find the details of my intelligence
network. Names of agents, cyphers, dates of payments—
everything. It is up to you to run it, Batak. I have men
in every kingdom in the west, most of them risking their
lives each day. That is a responsibility which I do not
hand over lightly. No one else must ever see the contents
of this chest. You will secure it with your most potent
spells, and destroy it if there is a possibility of it falling
into any other hands except your own—even Aurungzeb's. Do you understand?"

Batak nodded dumbly.

"There is also a more select network of homonculi,
some dormant, some active. I have them planted everywhere, even in the harem. They are the eyes and ears you

can trust most, for they are without bias or self-interest. When their bellies are full, at any rate. Use them well; and be discreet. They can be a useful cross-reference to back up the reports of your agents. When you are ready for a familiar, I would advise you to choose a homonculus. They can be wayward, but the ability to fly is always a help and their night vision is invaluable." Here Orkh's mouth tilted upwards. "Olov has shown me some rare sights in his nocturnal patrols of the harem. The most recent Ramusian concubine is a delight to behold. Aurungzeb takes her twice nightly, as eagerly as a boy. He has little notion of subtlety, though."

The mage collected himself.

"At any rate, there is amusement to be had if you use your resources properly, but if you gain information which you should not know I do not have to tell you to keep it to yourself, no matter how useful it might prove. The network must be safe-guarded at all costs."

"Yes, master."

Orkh stepped away from the chest. "It is yours, then. Use it wisely."

Batak took the chest in his arms as though it were made of glass.   •

"You may go. I find the maintenance of this appearance wearisome. When you ride through the village, tell the escort rissaldar that I will be ready to leave at moonrise tomorrow night. I have some final packing to do."

Batak bowed awkwardly. As he went out of the door he turned. "Thank you, master."

"When you see me again—if you do—it will be as a mage, a master of four of the Seven Disciplines. On that day you shall take me by the hand and call me Orkh."

Batak smiled uncertainly. "I shall look forward to that."

Then he left.

• • •

THE snow was as crisp as biscuit underfoot and the taloned feet of the beast cracked the surface crust, but the widespread toes stopped it from sinking any deeper. Naked and scaled, its tail whipping back and forth restlessly, it prowled the streets of the sleeping village. The moon glittered from its skin as though it were armoured in many-faceted silver. The glowing eyes blinked as it eased open the shutter of a cottage with inhuman, silent strength. A dark room within, a tiny shape blanket-wrapped in the cradle.

It took the bundle out into the hills, and there it fed, dipping its snout into the steaming, broken body. Sated at last, it raised its head and stared up at the savage, snow-gleaming peaks of the encircling mountains. West, where the sun had set. Where a new life awaited it, perhaps.

It cleaned its snout in the snow. With a bestial form came bestial appetites. But it saved a morsel of the child for Olov.

EIGHT

THEY were intoning the Glory to God, the *terdiel* which brought Matins to a close. For centuries, the monks and clerics of Charibon had sung it in the early hours of every new day, and the simple yet infinitely beautiful melody was taken up by half a thousand voices to echo into the beams and rafters of the cathedral.

The benches of the monks lined the walls of the triangular cathedral's base. Monsignors, presbyters and bishops had their own individual seats at the back with ornately carved armrests and kneeling boards. The Inceptines assembled on the right, the other orders—mostly Antillian, but with a few Mercurians—on the left. As the monks sang an old Inceptine with a candle lantern went up and down the rows, nudging any of the brethren who had nodded off. If they happened to wear the white hoods of novices they would receive a kick and a glare rather than a shake of their shoulder.

Himerius the High Pontiff had joined his fellow clerics for Matins this morning, something he rarely did. He was

seated facing his brethren, his Saint's symbol glittering
in the light of a thousand beeswax candles. His hawk's
profile was clearly picked out by the candlelight as he
sang.

Elsewhere in Charibon, the thousands of other clerics
were also awake and paying homage to their God. At this
time in the morning Charibon was a city of voices, it was
said, and fishermen in their boats out on the Sea of Tor
would hear the ghostly plainchant drifting out from shore,
a massed prayer which was rumoured to still the waves
and bring the fish to the surface to listen.

Matins ended, and there was a clamour of scraping
benches and shuffling feet as the singers rose to their feet
row by row. The High Pontiff left the cathedral first in
the company of the Inceptine Vicar-General, Betanza.
Then the senior churchmen filed out, and then the Inceptines. Last in the orderly throng to leave would be the
novices, their stomachs rumbling, their noses red with
early morning chill. The crowds would splinter as the
clerics made their way to the various refectories of the
orders for bread and buttermilk, the unchanging breakfast
of Charibon's inhabitants.

HIMERIUS and Betanza had not far to go to the Pontifical apartments, but they took a turn around the
cloisters first, their hands tucked in their habits, their
hoods pulled up over their heads. The cloisters were deserted at this time of the morning as everyone trooped
into the refectories for breakfast.

It was dark, the winter morning some time away as
yet. The moon had set, though, and the predawn stars
were bright as pins in a sky of unsullied aquamarine. The
breath of the two senior clerics was a white mist about
their hoods as they walked the serene, arched circuit of
the cloisters. There was snow in the air; it was thick in
the mountains but Charibon had as yet received only a
tithe of its usual share. The heavy falls would come

within days, and the shores of the Sea of Tor would grow beards of ice upon which the novices would skate and skylark in the little free time they had. It was a ritual, a routine as old as the monastery-city itself, and absurdly comforting to both the men who now walked in slow silence about the empty cloisters.

Betanza, the bluff ex-duke from Astarac, threw back his hood and paused to stare out across the starlit gardens within the cloisters. Trees there, ungainly oaks purportedly planted before the empire fell. In the spring the brown grass would explode with snowdrops, then daffodils and primroses as the year turned. They were dormant now, sleeping out the winter under the frozen earth.

"The purges have begun across the continent," he said quietly. "In Almark and Perigraine and Finnmark. In the duchies and the principalities they are herding them by the thousand."

"A new beginning," the High Pontiff said, his nose protruding like a raptor's beak from his hood. "The faith has been in need of this. A rejuvenation. Sometimes it takes an upheaval, a crisis, to breathe new life into our beliefs. We are never so sure of them as we are when they are threatened."

Betanza smiled sourly. "We have our crisis. Religious schism on a vast scale, and a war with the unbelievers of the east which threatens the very existence of the Ramusian kingdoms."

"Torunna is no longer Ramusian," Himerius corrected him quickly. "Nor is Astarac. They have heretics on their thrones. Hebrion, thank God, is coming under the sway of the true Church once more. The bull will have reached Abrusio by now—unlike its heretical king. Abeleyn is finished. Hebrion is ours."

"And Fimbria?" Betanza asked.

"What of it?"

"More rumours. It is said that a Fimbrian army is on the march eastwards to the relief of Ormann Dyke."

Himerius waved a hand. "Talk is a farthing a yard. Have we any more word of the Almarkan king's condition?"

Haukir, the aged and irascible monarch of Almark, was laid low by a fever. The winter journey homewards from the Conclave of Kings had started it. He was bedridden, without issue, and more foul-tempered than ever.

"The commander of the Almarkan garrisons here received word yesterday. He is dying. By now he may even be dead."

"We have people on hand?"

"Prelate Marat is at his bedside; the two are said to be natural brothers on the father's side."

"Whatever. Marat must be present at the end, and the will with him."

"You truly believe that Haukir may leave his kingdom to the Church?"

"He has no one else save a clutch of sister-sons who amount to nothing. And he has always been a staunch ally of the Inceptine Order. He would have entered it himself had he not been born Royal; he said as much to Marat before the conclave."

Betanza was silent, thoughtful. Were the Church to inherit the resources of Almark, one of the most powerful kingdoms in the west, it would be unassailable. The anti-Pontiff, or imposter rather, Macrobius, and those monarchs who had recognized him, would face a Church which had become overnight a great secular state.

"Quite an empire we are building up for ourselves," Betanza said mildly.

"The empire of Ramusio on earth. We are witnessing the symmetry of history, Betanza. The Fimbrian empire was secular, and was brought down by religious wars which established the True Faith across the continent. Now is the time of the second empire, a religious hegemony which will rear up the Kingdom of God on earth. That is my mission. It is why I became Pontiff."

Himerius' eyes were shining in the depths of his hood. Betanza remembered the wheeling and dealing which had secured Himerius the Pontiffship, the bargaining. Perhaps he was naïve. Though head of the Inceptine Order, he had been a lay nobleman until quite late in life. It gave him a different outlook on things which at times made him oddly uncomfortable.

"Dawn comes," he said, watching the glow of the approaching sun in the east. He felt an obscure urge to throw himself face down on the ground and pray; a dread and apprehension the like of which he had never experienced before rose in him like a breeding darkness.

"Do you recall *The Book of Honorius*, Holy Father? How does it go?

" 'And the Beast shall come upon the earth in the days of the second empire of the world. And he shall rise up out of the west, the light in his eyes terrible to behold. With him shall come the Age of the Wolf, when brother will slay brother. And all men shall fall down and worship him.' "

"Honorius was a crazed hermit, a Friar Mendicant. His ravings verge on the heretical."

"And yet he knew Ramusio, and was one of his closest followers."

"The Blessed Saint had many followers, Betanza, among them a proportion of lunatics and mystics. Keep your mind on the present. We go to meet the Arch-Presbyter of the Knights Militant this morning to talk to him about recruiting. The Church needs a strong right arm, not a perusal of ancient apocalyptic hallucinations."

"Yes, Holy Father," Betanza said.

The two resumed their walk around the quiet cloisters of Charibon while the silent dawn broke open the sky above them.

ALBREC had missed Matins, and he did not go down to breakfast. His stomach was as closed as a stone and he was kneeling in prayer on the hard stone floor of his frigid little cell. The dawn light was slanting in through the narrow window making the lit candle he had been reading by seem dim and yellow. On the table before him the pages of the old document had been laid out in orderly piles.

He rose at last, his pointed face deeply troubled, and sat before the table where he had spent most of the night. One hand snuffed out the candle as the rising sunlight stole into the room, and the smoke from the extinguished wick writhed back and forth in front of his eyes in grey wires and strings. The eyes were rimmed in scarlet.

He turned over the leaves of the document yet again, and his movement was as gingerly as if he expected them to explode into flame at any second.

"The winter of a man's life," said the Saint, "is the time when all those around him take the measure of all he has done and sought to do. And all that he has failed to accomplish. My brothers, I have set in this soil a garden, a thing which is pleasing in the sight of God. It is yours to tend now. Nothing can uproot it, for it grows in men's hearts also: that one place where a tyrant's fist can never reach. The Empire is failing and a New Order begins, one based on the truth of things, and the compassion of God's own plans.

"But for myself, my work here is done. Others will do the teaching and the preaching now. I am only a man, and an old one at that."

"What will you do?" we asked him.

The Saint lifted his head in the morning light which was breaking over this hillside in the province of Ostiber; for we had talked and prayed the night away.

"I go to plant the garden elsewhere."

"But the faith is spread across all Normannia," we said. "Even the Emperor has begun to see that it can no longer be suppressed. Where else is there to go?" And

we begged him to remain with us and live in peace and honour among his followers, who would revere him all the remaining days of his life.

"That is the way of pride," he said, shaking his head. And then he laughed. "Would you set me up as a wrinkled idol to be venerated as the tribes of old worshipped their gods? No, friends. I must go. I have seen the road stretching ahead of me. It goes on a long way from here yet."

"There is nowhere to go," we protested, for we were afraid of losing his leadership in the great trials which still awaited us. But also we loved this old man. Ramusio had become father to us and the world without him would seem a drear and empty place.

"There is a far country which the truth has not yet reached," he told us. And then he pointed eastwards, to where the Ostian river foamed sunlit and brilliant between its banks, and farther away the black heights of the Jafrar which mark the beginning of the wilderness beyond. "Out there it is night still, but I may yet use the years remaining to me to usher in the morning in the land beyond yon mountains."

A teardrop dripped off Albrec's nose to land on the precious page below, and he blotted it at once, angry with himself.

He could see the sunshine of that long-ago morning, when the Blessed Saint had stood in the twilight of his life on a hillside in Ostiber—or Ostrabar as it was now— and had talked with the closest of his followers, themselves grown old in their travels with him. St. Bonneval was there, who was to become the first Pontiff of the holy Church, and St. Ubaldius of Neyr, who would be the first Vicar-General of the Inceptine Order. The men who watched that sunrise break over the eastern mountains would become the founding fathers of the Ramusian faith, canonized and revered by later generations, prayed to by the common people, immortalized in a thousand statues and tapestries across the world.

But that morning, in the early light of a day gone by these five centuries and more, they were merely a group of men afraid and grieved by the thought of losing he who had been their mentor, their leader, the mainstay of their lives.

And who was the mysterious narrator? Who was the writer of this precious document? Had he really been there, one of the chosen few who had accompanied the Blessed Saint through the provinces of the empire, spreading the faith?

Albrec turned through the crumbling pages, mourning the lost leaves, the illegible paragraphs.

That morning in Ostrabar was a day sacred to the Church and all Ramusians. It was the last day of the Saint's life on earth. He had been assumed into heaven from the hillside, his followers watching as God took to his bosom this the most faithful of his servants. Until Ostiber had fallen to the Merduks and become Ostrabar, the hilltop had been a holy place of pilgrimage for the Ramusians of the continent, and a church had been built there within a few years of the miraculous event.

At least, that was what Albrec and every other member of the Ramusian faith had been taught. But the document told an entirely different story.

He took no companion and would accept no company, and he forbade those he was to leave behind ever to follow him. On a mule he left us, his face towards the east, from whence the morning comes. And the last we saw of him, he was in the lower passes of the mountains, the mule bearing him ever higher. So he was lost to the west for ever.

It was this and the succeeding pages which had kept Albrec up all night, reading and praying until his eyes smarted and his knees were cold and sore from the flags of the floor. Nothing here of an assumption into heaven, a glorious vision of the Saint entering God's kingdom. Ramusio had last been seen as a tiny figure on a mule headed into the heights of the most terrible mountains in the world. The implications of that made Albrec tremble.

But the story did not end there. There was more.

Among the folk who went to and fro across the borders of the empire at that time, there was a merchant named Ochali, a Merduk who every year braved the passes of the Jafrar with his camel trains, bringing silks and furs and steppe ivory to trade from the lands of Kurasan and Kambaksk beyond the mountains. He was a worshipper of the Horned One, like all those who lived beyond the Ostian river. Kerunnos was the forbidden name he and his people gave to their God, and when he reached the provinces of the empire every summer he would give sacrifice at the roadside shrines of the tribes for a safe passage of the Jafrar. But one summer, some eight years after Ramusio had journeyed east, he neglected to make his usual sacrifices to the Horned One.

Men who knew him asked why, and he told them that he had found a new faith, a true faith which owed nothing to sacrifices or idols. An old man, he said, had been preaching in the camps of the steppe peoples for several years now, and his words had gained him many followers. A new religion was birthing in the far lands of the Merduks, and even the horse chieftains had taken it to heart.

When Ochali's acquaintances in the province of Ostiber pressed him further he refused to elaborate, saying only that the Merduk peoples had found a prophet, a holy leader who was taking them out of the darkness and putting an end to the interminable clan wars which had always racked his people. Merduk no longer slew Merduk in the distant steppes beyond the Jafrar, and the men who

*abode there lived in harmony and brotherhood. The
Prophet Ahrimuz had shown his people the one true path
to salvation.*

There was a thumping at Albrec's door and he jumped
like a startled hare. He had time to cover the ancient
document with his catechism before the door opened and
Brother Commodius walked in, his big bare feet slapping
on the stone floor.

"Albrec! You were missed at Matins. Is everything all
right?"

The Senior Librarian looked his normal ugly self; the
face regarding Albrec with concern and curiosity was the
same one the monk had worked with for nearly thirteen
years. The same huge beak of a nose, out-thrust ears and
unruly fringe of hair about the bald tonsure. But Albrec
would never again see it as just another face, not after
the night in the lowest levels of the library.

"I—I'm fine," he stammered. "I didn't feel well,
Brother. I have a bit of a flux so I thought it better to
stay away. I'm going to the privy every few minutes."
Lies, lies and sins. But that could not be helped. It was
in a greater cause.

"You should see the Brother Infirmiar then, Albrec.
It's no good sitting here and reading your catechism,
waiting for it to go away. Come, I'll take you."

"No, brother—it's all right. You go and open the library, I've made you late enough as it is."

"Nonsense!"

"No, truly, Brother Commodius, I can't keep you from
your duties. I'll visit him myself. Perhaps I'll see you
after Compline. I'm sure an infusion of arrowroot will
set me up."

The Senior Librarian shrugged his immense, bony
shoulders. "Very well, Albrec, have it your own way."
He turned to go, then hesitated on the threshold. "Brother

Columbar tells me that you and he were down in the catacombs beneath the library."

Albrec opened his mouth, but no sound came out.

"Seeking blotting for the scriptorium, it seems. And I dare say you were doing a little ferreting around on your own account, eh, Albrec?" Commodius' eyes twinkled. "You want to be careful down there. A man might have an accident among all that accumulated rubbish. There's a warren of tunnels and chambers that have not been disturbed since the days of the empire. They're best left that way, eh?"

Albrec nodded, still speechless.

"I know you, Albrec. You would mine knowledge as though it were gold. But the possession of knowledge is not always good; some things are better left undiscovered . . . Did you find Gambio's blotting paper?"

"Some, Brother. We found some."

"Good. Then you will not need to go down there again, will you? Well, I must go. As you say, I am late. There will be a huddle of scholar-monks congregated round the door of St. Garaso thinking uncharitable thoughts about me. I hope your bowels clear up soon, Brother. There is work to be done." And Commodius left, closing the door of Albrec's cell behind him.

Albrec was shaking, and sweat had chilled his brow. So Columbar could not keep his mouth shut. Commodius must have questioned him; he had seen Albrec and Avila that night, perhaps.

Albrec had joined the Antillian Order for many reasons: hatred of the open sea which had been his fisherman father's daily bread; a love of books; but also a desire for security, for peace. He had found it in Charibon, and had never regretted his thirteen years in the confines of the St. Garaso Library. But now he felt that the earth had shifted from under his feet. His safe world was no longer so tranquil. There was an old saying among the clerics of Charibon that it was but a short step from the pulpit to the pyre. For the first time Albrec appreciated the truth behind the dark humour of it.

He uncovered the document, glancing fearfully at the door as he did so, as though Commodius might leap out with his face a devil's mask again.

He should destroy it. He should burn it, or lose it somewhere. Let someone else discover it a hundred years hence, perhaps. Why should it be he who must shoulder this burden?

It is my belief, the narrative went on, *that the Blessed Saint did indeed succeed in crossing the Jafrar. He was a man in the seventh decade of his life, but he was still strong and vigorous, and the missionary flame burned hotly in him. He was like a captain of a ship who can never rest until he has found an uncharted shore, and then another, and another. There was a restlessness to him which I and others believed to be the spirit of God.*

As the greatest conquerors can never sit at peace and reflect upon their past victories but must always move on, fighting fresh battles, chancing their lives and their fortunes until the end of their strength, so Ramusio could never be content to cease his proselytizing, his unending work of spreading the truth. His fire was not suited to the administration of an organized church. He inspired men and then moved on, leaving it to his followers to write rules and catechisms, to make into formulas and commandments the tenets of his faith.

He was the gentlest man I have ever known, and yet his will was adamantine. There was a puissance to his determination which was not of this world, and which awed all those who knew him.

I do not doubt that he reached the steppes beyond the mountains, and that he awed the Merduks as he had the men of the west. Ramusio the Blessed Saint became Ahrimuz the Prophet, and the faith which sustains us here in the west is the same as that which inspires the Merduks who have become our mortal enemies. That is the pity of it.

There it was. Once he had read it, Albrec's world changed irrevocably. He knew the document was genuine, that the author had lived and breathed in the same long-lost world which the Blessed Saint had known, a world five hundred years distant. He spoke of Ramusio as a man, a teacher, and as a friend, and the authenticity of his recollections convinced Albrec of the truth of what he was reading. Ramusio and Ahrimuz were one and the same, and the Church, the kingdoms, the entire edifices of two civilizations which spanned the known world were founded on a misconception. On a lie.

He bent his head and prayed until the cold sweat was rolling down his temples in agonized drops. He prayed for courage, for strength, for some morsel of the determination which had possessed the holy Saint himself.

The last section of the document was missing entirely, the rotted threads which bound the work having given way to time and abuse. He did not know the name of the author or the date of the work, but there was no doubt why it had been hidden away.

He had to find out more. He had to go back to the catacombs.

NINE

CORFE hated the new clothes, but the tailor had assured him that they were typical court wear for officers of the Torunnan army. There was a narrow ruff which encircled his neck, below which glittered a tiny mock breastplate of silver suspended by a neck chain and engraved with the triple sabres of his rank. The doublet was black embroidered with gold, heavily padded in the shoulders and with voluminous slashed sleeves through which the fine cambric of his shirt fluttered. He wore tight black hose beneath, and buckled shoes. Shoes! He had not worn shoes for years. He felt ridiculous.

"You will do very well," the Queen Dowager had said to him when she had looked him over, with the tailor bowing and hovering like a blowfly behind him.

"I feel like a dressmaker's mannequin," he snapped back.

She smiled at that and, folding her fan, she chucked him under the chin with it.

"Now, now, Colonel. We must remember where we

are. The King has expressed a wish to see you in the
company of his senior officers. We cannot let you march
into their council of war looking like a serf dragged in
from the fields. And besides, this becomes you. You have
the build for it, even if your legs are a little on the short
side. It comes of being a cavalryman, I suppose."

Corfe did not reply. The Queen Dowager Odelia was
gliding round him as though she were admiring a statue,
her long skirts whispering on the marble floor.

"But this thing"—her fan rapped against Corfe's scab-
barded sabre—"this is out of place. We must find you a
more fitting weapon. Something elegant. This is a
butcher's tool."

Corfe's fist tightened on the pommel of the sword. "By
your leave, lady, I'd prefer to keep it with me."

"Why?"

She had glided in front of him. Their eyes met.

"It helps remind me of who I am."

They stared at each other for a long moment. Corfe
could sense the tailor's presence behind him, uneasy and
fascinated.

"You must be in the chambers of the war council by
the fifth hour," Odelia said, turning away abruptly. "Do
not be late. The King has something for you, I believe."

She was gone, the end of her skirts trailing round the
doorway like the tail of a departing snake.

A S the palace bells sounded the fifth hour, Corfe was
ushered into the council chambers by a haughty
footman. He was reminded a little of his arrival at Ormann Dyke, when he had walked in on General Pieter
Martellus' council of war. But that had been different.
The officers at the dyke had been dressed like soldiers
on campaign, and they had been planning for a battle
which was already at their door. What Corfe walked into
in the palace of Torunn was more like a parody, a game
of war.

A crowd of gorgeously dressed officers. Infantry in black, cavalry in burgundy, artillery in deepest blue. Silver and gold gleamed everywhere with the pale accompaniment of lace and the bobbing magnificence of feathers from the caps some of the men retained. King Lofantyr was resplendent in sable and silver slashed hose and the crimson sash of a general. The light from a dozen lamps glittered off silver-buckled shoes, rings, gem-studded badges of rank and chivalric orders. Corfe made his deepest bow. He had refused cavalry burgundy, preferring infantry black though he belonged to the mounted arm. He was glad.

"Ah, Colonel," the King said, and gestured with one hand. "Come in, come in. It is all informality here. Gentlemen, Colonel Corfe Cear-Inaf, late of John Mogen's field army and the garrison of Ormann Dyke."

There was a murmur of greetings. Corfe was subjected to a dozen stares of frank appraisal. His skin crawled.

The other officers turned back to the long table which dominated the room. It was scattered with papers, but what occupied its shining length principally was a large map of Torunna and its environs. Corfe went closer, but his way was blocked. Irritably he looked up and found himself face to face with one of the dandies of the palace audience.

"Ensign Ebro, sir," the officer said, smiling. "We've met, I believe, though one would hardly recognize you out of your fighting gear."

Corfe nodded coldly. There was an awkward pause, and then Ebro stepped aside. "Pardon me, sir."

His sabre was unwieldy, harder to handle than the slim rapiers the other officers sported. He found himself peering over shoulders to see the rolled-out map. Figurines of Torunnan pikemen cast in silver had been placed at the four corners to stop the stiff paper from curling up. There were decanters on the table, crystal glasses, a blunt dagger of intricate workmanship which King Lofantyr picked up and used as a pointer.

"This is where they are now," he said, tapping a point on the map some eighty leagues west of Charibon. "In the Narian Hills."

"How many, sire?" a voice asked. It was the crusty, mustachioed Colonel Menin, whom Corfe had also encountered the evening of the audience.

"A grand tercio, plus supporting artisans. Five thousand fighting men."

A series of whispers swept the chamber.

"They will be a great help, of course," Menin said, but the doubt was audible in his voice.

"Fimbrians on the march again across Normannia," someone muttered. "Who'd have thought it?"

"Does Martellus know yet, sire?" another officer asked.

"Couriers went off to the dyke yesterday," King Lofantyr told them. "I am sure that Martellus will be glad of five thousand reinforcements, no matter where they are from. Marshal Barbius and his command are travelling light. They intend to be at the Searil river in six weeks, if all goes well. Plenty of time for his men to settle in before the beginning of the next campaigning season."

Lofantyr turned aside so that an older man in the livery of a court official could whisper in his ear. He was holding a sheaf of papers.

"We have commanded General Martellus to send out winter scouting patrols to ascertain the state of readiness of the Merduks at all times. At the moment it seems they are secure in their winter camps, and have even detached sizable bodies of men eastwards to improve their supply lines. The elephants and cavalry, also, have been billeted further east where they will be nearer to the supply depots on the Ostian river. There is no reason to fear a winter assault."

Corfe recognized the papers in the court official's hands; they were the dispatches he had brought from the dyke.

"What of the Pontifical bull demanding Martellus's removal, sire?" Menin asked gruffly.

"We will ignore it. We do not recognize the imposter Himerius as Pontiff. Macrobius, rightful head of the Church, resides here in Torunn; you have all seen him. Edicts from Charibon will be ignored."

"Then what of the south, sire?" an officer with a general's sash about his middle, but who looked to be in his seventies, asked.

"Ah—these reports we've been getting of insurrections in the coastal cities to the south of the kingdom," Lofantyr said airily. "They are of little account. Ambitious nobles such as the Duke of Rone and the Landgrave of Staed have seen fit to recognize Himerius as Pontiff and our Royal self as a heretic. They will be dealt with."

The talk went on. Military talk, hard-edged and assured. Councils of war loved to talk, John Mogen had once said. But they hated to fight. Most of the conversations seemed to Corfe to be less about tactics and strategy and more about the winning of personal advantage, the catching of the King's eye.

He had forgotten how different the Torunnan military of the capital and the home fiefs was from the field armies which defended the frontiers. The difference depressed him. These did not seem to him to be the same kind of men with whom he had fought at Aekir and Ormann Dyke. They were not of the calibre of John Mogen's command. But perhaps that was just an impression; he had not mixed much with the rank and file of the capital. And besides, he lashed himself, he was not such a great one to judge. He had deserted his regiment in the final stages of Aekir's agony, and while his comrades had fought and died in a heroic rearguard action on the Western Road, he had been slinking away in the midst of the civilian refugees. He must never forget that.

There was no mention of the refugee problem at this meeting, however, which puzzled Corfe extremely. The camps on the outskirts of the capital were swelling by the day with the despairing survivors of Aekir who had first fled the Holy City itself and had then been moved on from Ormann Dyke in the wake of the battles there. If he were the King, he would be concerned with feeding and housing the hopeless multitudes. It was all very well for them to camp outside the walls by the hundred thousand in winter, but when the weather warmed again there would be the near certainty of disease, that enemy more deadly to an army than any Merduk host.

They were discussing the scattered risings of the nobles in the south of the kingdom again. Apparently Perigraine was giving the disaffected aristocrats surreptitious support, and there were vague tales of Nalbenic galleys landing weapons for the rebels. The risings were localized and isolated as yet, but if they could be welded together by any one leader they would pose a serious threat. Swift and severe action was called for. Some of the officers at the council volunteered to go south and bring back the heads of the rebels on platters and there were many protestations of loyalty to Lofantyr, which the King accepted graciously. Corfe remained silent. He did not like the complacent way the King and his staff regarded the situation at the dyke. They seemed to think that the main effort of the Merduks was past and the danger was over except for some minor skirmishing to come in the spring. But Corfe had been there; he had seen the teeming thousands of the Merduk formations, the massed batteries of their artillery, the living walls of war elephants. He knew that the main assault had yet to come, and it would come in the spring. Five thousand Fimbrians would be a welcome addition to the dyke's defenders—if they would fight happily alongside their old foes the Torunnans—but they would not be enough. Surely Lofantyr and his advisors realized that?

The talk was wearisome, about people whose names meant nothing to Corfe, towns to the south, far away from the Merduk war. As members of Mogen's command, Corfe and his comrades had always seen the true danger in the east. The Merduks were the only real foes the west faced. Everything else was a distraction. But it was different here. In Torunn the eastern frontier was only one among a series of other problems and priorities. The knowledge made Corfe impatient. He wanted to get back to the dyke, back to the real battlefields.

"We need an expedition to clamp down on these traitorous bastards in the south, that's plain," Colonel Menin rasped. "With your permission, sire, I'd be happy to take a few tercios and teach them some loyalty."

"Very good of you, I'm sure, Colonel Menin," Lofantyr said smoothly. "But I need your talents employed here, in the capital. No, I have another officer in mind for the mission."

The more junior officers about the table eyed each other a little askance, wondering who the lucky man would be.

"Colonel Cear-Inaf, I have decided to give you the command," the King said briskly.

Corfe was jerked out of his reverie. "What?"

The King paused, and then stated in a harder voice: "I said, Colonel, that I am giving you this command."

All eyes were on Corfe. He was both astonished and dismayed. A command that would take him south, away from the dyke? He did not want it.

But could not refuse it. This, then, was what the Queen Dowager had been referring to earlier. This was her doing.

Corfe bowed deeply whilst his mind fought free of its turmoil.

"Your majesty is very gracious. I only hope that I can justify your faith in my abilities."

Lofantyr seemed mollified, but there was something in his regard that Corfe did not like, a covert amusement, perhaps.

"Your troop awaits you in the Northern Marshalling Yard, Colonel. And you shall have an aide, of course. Ensign Ebro will be joining you—"

Corfe found Ebro at his side, bowing stiffly, his face a mask. Clearly, this was not a post he had coveted.

"—And I shall see what I can do about releasing a few more officers to you."

"My thanks, your majesty. Might I enquire as to my orders?"

"They will be forwarded to you in due course. For now I suggest, Colonel, that you and your new aide acquaint yourselves with your command."

Another pause. Corfe bowed yet again and turned and left the chamber with Ebro close behind him.

As soon as they were outside, striding along the palace corridors, Corfe reached up and savagely ripped the lace ruff from his throat, flinging it aside.

"Lead me to this Northern Marshalling Yard," he snapped to his aide. "I've never heard of it."

NO one had, it seemed. They scoured the barracks and armouries in the northern portion of the city, but none of the assorted quartermasters, sergeants and ensigns they spoke to had heard of it. Corfe was beginning to believe that it was all a monstrous joke when a fawning clerk in one of the city arsenals told them that there had been a draft of men brought in only the day before who were bivouacked in one of the city squares close to the northern wall; that might be their goal.

They set off on foot, Corfe's shiny buckled shoes becoming spattered with the filth of the winter streets. Ebro followed him in dumb misery, picking his way through

the puddles and mudslimed cobbles. It began to rain, and
his court finery took on a resemblance to the sodden
plumage of a brilliant bird. Corfe was grimly satisfied by
the transformation.

They emerged at last from the stinking press and
crowd of the streets into a wide open space surrounded
on all sides by timber-framed buildings. Beyond, the
sombre heights of the battlemented city walls loomed like
a hillside in the rain-cloud. Corfe wiped water out of his
eyes, hardly able to credit what he saw.

"This can't be it—this cannot be them!" Ebro sput-
tered. But Corfe was suddenly sure it was, and he realized that the joke was indeed on him.

Torunnan sentries paced the edges of the square with
halberds resting on their shoulders. In the shop doorways
all around arquebusiers stood yawning, keeping their
weapons and powder out of the rain. As Corfe and Ebro
appeared, a young ensign with a muddy cloak about his
shoulders approached them, saluting as soon as he caught
sight of the badge on Corfe's absurd little breastplate.

"Good day, sir. Might you be Colonel Cear-Inaf, by
any chance?"

Corfe's heart sank. There was no mistake then.

"I am, Ensign. What is this we have here?"

The officer glanced back to the scene in the square.
The open space was full of men, five hundred of them,
perhaps. They were seated in crowds on the filthy cobbles
as though battered down by the chill rain. They were in
rags, and collectively they stank to high heaven. There
were manacles about every ankle, and their faces were
obscured by wild tangles of matted hair.

"Half a thousand galley slaves from the Royal fleet,"
the ensign said cheerily. "Tribesmen from the Felimbri,
most of them, worshippers of the Horned One. Black-
hearted devils, they are. I'd mind your back, sir, when
you're near them. They tried to brain one of my men last
night and we had to shoot a couple."

A dull anger began to rise in Corfe.

"This cannot be right, sir. We must be mistaken. The King must be in jest," Ebro was protesting.

"I don't think so," Corfe murmured. He stared at the packed throng of miserable humanity in the square. Many of them were staring back, glowering at him from under thatches of verminous hair. The men were brawny, well-muscled, as might be expected of galley slaves, but their skin was a sodden white, and many of them were coughing. A few had lain down on their sides, oblivious to the stone cobbles, the pouring rain.

So this was his first independent command. A crowd of mutinous slaves from the savage tribes of the interior. For a moment Corfe considered returning to the palace and refusing the command. The Queen Dowager had obtained the position for him, but clearly Lofantyr had resented her interference. He was supposed to refuse it, Corfe realized. And when he did, there would never be another. That decided him.

He stepped forward. "Are there any among you who can speak for the rest, in Normannic?"

The men muttered amongst themselves, and finally one rose and shuffled to the fore, his chains clinking.

"I speak your tongue, Torunnan."

He was huge, with hands as wide as dinner plates and the scars of old lashings about his limbs. His tawny beard fell on to his chest but two bright blue eyes glinted out of the brutish face and met Corfe's stare squarely.

"What's your name?" Corfe asked him.

"I am called the Eagle in my own tongue. You would say my name was Marsch."

"Can you speak for your fellows, Marsch?"

The slave shrugged his massive shoulders. "Perhaps."

"Do you know why you were taken from the galleys?"

"No."

"Then I will tell you. And you will translate what I

say to your comrades, without misinterpretation. Is that clear?"

Marsch glared at him, but he was obviously curious. "All right."

"All right, *sir*," Ebro hissed at him, but Corfe held up a hand. He pitched his voice to carry across the square.

"You are no longer slaves of the Torunnan state," he called out. "From this moment on you are free men." That caused a stir, when Marsch had translated it, a lifting of the apathy. But there was no lessening of the mistrust in the eyes which were fixed on him. Corfe ground on.

"But that does not yet mean that you are free to do as you please. I am Corfe. From this moment on you will obey me as you would one of your own chieftains, for it is I who have procured your freedom. You are tribesmen of the Cimbrics. You were once warriors, and now you have the chance to be so again, but only under my command."

Marsch's deep voice was following Corfe's in the guttural language of the mountain tribes. His eyes never left Corfe's face.

"I need soldiers, and you are what I have been given. You are not to fight your own peoples, but are to battle Torunnans and Merduks. I give you my word on that. Serve me faithfully, and you will have honour and employment. Betray me, and you will be killed out of hand. I do not care which God you worship or which tongue you speak as long as you fight for me. Obey my orders, and I will see that you are treated like warriors. Any who do not choose to do so can go back to the galleys."

Marsch finished translating, and the square was filled with low talk.

"Sir," Ebro said urgently, "no one gave you authority to free these men."

"They are my men," Corfe growled. "I will not be a general of slaves."

Marsch had heard the exchange. He clinked forward until he was towering over Corfe.

"You mean what you say, Torunnan?"

"I would not have said it otherwise."

"And you will give us our freedom, in exchange for our swords?"

"Yes."

"Why do you choose us as your men? To your kind we are savages and unbelievers."

"Because you are all I have got," Corfe said truthfully. "I don't take you because I want to, but because I have to. But if you will take service under me, then I swear I will speak for you in everything as though I were speaking for myself."

The hulking savage considered this a moment.

"Then I am your man." And Marsch touched his fist to his forehead in the salute of his people.

Others in the square saw the gesture. Men began to struggle to their feet and repeat it.

"If we break faith with you," Marsch said, "then may the seas rise up and drown us, may the green hills open up and swallow us, may the stars of heaven fall on us and crush us out of life for ever."

It was the old, wild oath of the tribes, the pagan pledge of fealty. Corfe blinked, and said:

"By the same oath, I bind myself to keep faith with you."

The men in the square were all on their feet now, repeating Marsch's oath in their own tongue.

Corfe heard them out. He had the oddest feeling that this was the beginning of something he could not yet grasp: something momentous that would affect the remaining course of his life.

The feeling passed, and he was facing five hundred men standing manacled in the rain.

He turned to the young ensign, who was open-mouthed. "Strike the chains from these men."

"Sir, I—"

"Do it!"

The ensign paled, saluted quickly, and ran off to get the keys. Ebro looked entirely at a loss.

"Ensign," Corfe snapped, and his aide came to attention. "You will find a warm billet for these men. If there are no military quarters available, you will procure a private warehouse. I want them out of the rain."

"Yes, sir."

Corfe addressed Marsch once more. "When did you last eat?"

The giant shrugged again. "Two, three days ago. Sir."

"Ensign Ebro, you will also procure rations for five hundred from the city stores, on my authority. If anyone questions you, refer them to—to the Queen Dowager. She will endorse my orders."

"Yes, sir. Sir, I—"

"Go. I want no more time wasted."

Ebro sped off without another word. Torunnan guards were already walking through the crowd of tribesmen unlocking their ankle chains. The arquebusiers had lit their match and were holding their firearms at the ready. As the tribesmen were freed, they trooped over to stand behind Marsch.

This is my command, Corfe thought.

They were starved, half naked, weaponless, without armour or equipment; and Corfe knew he could not hope to obtain anything for them through the regular military channels. They were on their own. But they were his men.

PART TWO

THE WESTERN CONTINENT

TEN

THE air was different, somehow heavy. It trickled down their throats and through the interstices in their armour and lodged there, a solid, unyielding presence. It ballooned their lungs and crimsoned their faces. It brought the sweat winking out in glassy beads on their foreheads. It made the soldiers pause to tug at the neck of their cuirasses as though they were trying to loosen a constricting collar.

The white sand clung to their boots. They screwed up their eyes against its brightness and slogged onwards. In a few steps, the boom of the surf out on the reef became distant, separate. The sun faded as the jungle enfolded them, and the heat became a wetter, danker thing.

The Western Continent.

Sand gave way to leaf mulch underfoot. They slashed aside creepers and the lower boughs of the trees, sharp palm fronds, huge ferns.

The noise of the sea, their universe for so long, faded away. It was as if they had entered some different king-

dom, a place which had nothing to do with anything they
had known before. It was a twilit world enshadowed by
the canopy of the immense trees which soared up on all
sides. Naked root systems like the tangled limbs of
corpses on a battlefield tripped them up and plucked at
their feet. Tree trunks two fathoms in diameter had discs
of fungi embedded in their flanks. A bewildering tangle
of living things, the very atmosphere full of buzzing, biting mites so that they drew them into their mouths when
they breathed. And the stink of decay and damp and
mould, overpowering, all-pervading.

They stumbled across a stream which must have had
its outlet on the beach. Here the vegetation was less fre-
netic and they could make a path of sorts, slashing with
cutlass and poniard.

When they halted to rest and catch their breath—so
hard to do that here, so hard to draw the thick air into
greedy lungs—they could hear the sound of this new
world all around them. Screeches and wails and twitter-
ings and warblings and hoots of human-sounding laughter off in the trees. A symphony of invisible, utterly
unknown life cackling away to itself, indifferent to their
presence or intentions.

Several of the soldiers made the Sign of the Saint.
There were things moving far up in the canopy, where
the world had light and colour and perhaps a breeze.
Half-glimpsed leaping shadows and flutterings.

"The whole place is alive," Hawkwood muttered.

They had found a tiny clearing wherein the stream bur-
bled happily to itself, clear as crystal in a shaft of sunlight
which had somehow contrived to survive to the forest
floor.

"This will do," Murad said, wiping sweat from his
face. "Sergeant Mensurado, the flag."

Mensurado stepped forward, his face half hidden in the
shade of his casque, and stabbed the flagpole he had been
bearing into the humus by the stream.

Murad produced a scroll from his belt pouch and unrolled it carefully as Mensurado's bark brought the file of soldiers to attention.

" 'In this year of the Blessed Saint five hundred and fifty-one, on this the twenty-first day of Endorion, I, Lord Murad of Galiapeno do hereby claim this land on behalf of our noble and gracious sovereign, King Abeleyn the Fourth of Hebrion and Imerdon. From this moment on it shall be known as—' " he looked up at the cackling jungle, the towering trees—' 'as New Hebrion. And henceforth as is my right, I assume the titles of viceroy and governor of this, the westernmost of the possessions of the Hebriate crown.' "

"Sergeant, the salute."

Mensurado's parade-ground bellow put the jungle cacophony to shame.

"Present your pieces! Ready your pieces! Fire!"

A thunderous volley of shots went off as one. The clearing was filled with toiling grey smoke which hung like cotton in the airless space.

The forest had gone entirely silent.

The men stood looking up at the crowded vegetation, the huge absence of sound. Instinctively, everyone stepped closer together.

A crashing of undergrowth, and Ensign di Souza appeared, scarlet face and yellow hair above his cuirass, with a pair of sailors and Bardolin the mage labouring in his wake. The wizard's imp rode on his shoulder, agog.

"Sir, we heard shooting," he panted.

"We have seen off the enemy," Murad drawled. He loosened the drawstrings on the Hebrian flag and it fell open, a limp gold and crimson rag.

"Report, Ensign," he said sharply, waving powdersmoke from in front of his face.

"The second wave of boats are ashore, and the mariners are off-loading the water casks as we speak. Sequero asks your permission, sir, to get the surviving horses ashore and start hunting up fodder for them."

"Permission denied," Murad said crisply. "The horses
are not a priority here. We must secure a campsite for
the landing party first, and investigate the surrounding
area. Who knows what may be lurking in this devil's
brush about us?"

Several of the soldiers glanced round uneasily, until
Mensurado, with shouts and kicks, got them to reloading
their arquebuses.

Murad considered the little clearing. The forest noises
had started up again. Already they were becoming used
to them, a background irritation, not a thing to fear.

"We'll throw up a camp here," he said. "It's as good
a place as any, and we'll have fresh water. Captain
Hawkwood, your men can refill their water casks here
also."

Hawkwood looked at the knee-deep stream, already
muddied by the boots of the soldiers, and said nothing.

Bardolin joined him. The old wizard mopped his
streaming face with his sleeve and gestured at the surrounding jungle.

"Have you ever seen anything like this before? Such
trees!"

Hawkwood shook his head. "I've been to Macassar,
the jungles inland from the Malacars, after ivory and
hides and river-gold, but this is different. This has never
been cleared; it is the original forest, a country where
man has never made a mark. These trees might have
stood here since the Creation."

"Dreaming their strange dreams," Bardolin said absently, caressing his imp with one hand. "There is power
in this place, Hawkwood. Dweomer, and something else.
Something to do with the very nature of the land, perhaps. It has not yet noticed us, I think, but it will, in its
slow way."

"We've always said the place might be inhabited."

"I am not talking about inhabitants, I am talking about

the land itself. Normannia has been scoured and gouged and raped for too long; we own it now. We are its blood. But here the land belongs only to itself."

"I never took you for a mystic, Bardolin," Hawkwood said with some irritation. His injured shoulder was paining him.

"Nor am I one." The mage seemed to come awake. He smiled. "Maybe I'm just getting old."

"Old! You're more hale than I am."

Two seamen appeared: Mihal and Masudi, one bearing a wooden box.

"Velasca wants to know if he can let the men have a run ashore, sir," Masudi said, his black face gleaming.

"Not yet. This isn't a blasted pleasure trip. Tell him to concentrate on getting the ship rewatered."

"Aye, sir," Masudi said. "Here's the box you wanted from the cabin."

"Put it down."

Murad joined them. "I'm taking a party on a reconnaissance of the area. I want you two to come with us. Maybe you can sniff out things for us, Mage. And Hawkwood, you said—"

"I have it here," Hawkwood interrupted him.

He bent to open the box at his feet. Inside was a brass bowl and an iron sliver which had been pasted on to a wafer of cork. Hawkwood filled the bowl from the stream. Some of the soldiers crowded round to look and he barked angrily: "Stand aside! I can't have any metal around when I do this. Give me some space."

The men retreated as he set the iron to bob on the water. He crouched for a long minute staring at it, and then said to Murad: "The stream heads off to nor'-nor'-west. If we followed it—and it's the easiest passage—then we'd be coming back east-southeast."

He poured the water off, put everything back in the box and straightened.

"A portable compass," Bardolin said. "So simple! But

then the principle remains the same. I should have realized."

"We'll move out and follow the line of the stream," Murad said. He turned to di Souza. "We'll fire three shots if there's any trouble. When you hear them, pack up and get back to the ship. Do not try to come after us, Ensign. We'll make our own way. The same procedure follows if anything occurs here while we're gone. But I intend to return well before dark anyway."

Di Souza saluted.

THE party set out: Murad, Hawkwood, Bardolin and ten of the soldiers.

They tramped through the stream, as it was the path of least resistance, and it seemed to them that they were travelling through a green tunnel lit by some radiance far above. It was dusk down here, with occasional shafts of bright sun lancing through gaps in the canopy to provide a dazzling contrast to the pervading gloom.

They ducked under hanging limbs, skirted sprawling roots as thick as a man's thigh which lolled in the water like torpid animals come to drink. They slashed aside hanging veils of moss and creeper, and staggered hurriedly away from the sudden brilliance of gem-bright snakes which slithered through the mulch of the forest floor, intent on their own business.

It grew hotter. The noise of the sea died away, the fading of a once-vivid memory. They were in a raucous cathedral whose columns were the titanic bulk of the great trees, whose roof sparkled with distant light and movement, the mocking cries of weird birdlife.

The ground rose under their feet and stones began to rear up out of the earth like the bones of the land come poking through its decaying hide. Their progress grew more laboured, the soldiers with their heads down and arquebuses on their shoulders puffing like fractured bellows. A cloud of tiny, iridescent birds swept through the

company like airborne jewels. They flickered one way
and then another, turning in unison like a shoal of twisting fish, their fleetness almost derisory. A few of the
soldiers batted at them half-heartedly with gunstock and
sword but they whispered away again in a spray of lapis
lazuli and amethyst before swooping into the canopy
overhead.

The stream disappeared into a tangle of boulders and
bush, and the forest closed in on them completely. The
ground was rising more steeply now, making every step
an effort. The men scooped up handfuls and helmetfuls
of the water, gulping it down and sluicing their faces. It
was as warm as a wet nurse's milk, and hardly seemed
to moisten their mouths. Murad led them onwards, hacking with a seaman's cutlass at the barrier of vegetation
ahead, his feet slipping and turning on the mossy stones,
boots squelching in mud.

They came across ants the size of a man's little finger
which carried bright green leaves like the mainsail of a
schooner on their backs. They found beetles busily winking in the earth, their wingcases as broad as an apple,
horns adorning their armoured heads. Wattle-necked liz-
ards regarded them silently from overhead branches, the
colours of their skin pulsing from emerald through to
turquoise.

They took a new bearing from the source of the stream
and headed north-west this time, as the way seemed easiest on that course. Murad detailed one of the soldiers to
blaze a tree every twenty yards, so thick was the undergrowth. They stumbled onwards in the wake of the gaunt
nobleman as though he were some kind of demented
prophet leading them to paradise, and Sergeant Mensurado, his voice hoarsened to a croak with overuse, hurried
the stragglers along with shoves and blows and venom-
ous whispers.

The jungle began to open out a fraction. The trees were
more widely spaced and the ground between them was

littered with rocks, some as long as a ship's culverin. The ground changed texture and became dark and gritty, almost like black sand. It filled their boots and rasped between their toes.

Then Murad stopped dead in his tracks.

Hawkwood and Bardolin were farther back in the file. He called them forward in a low hiss.

"What?" Hawkwood asked.

Murad pointed, his eyes not moving from whatever drew them.

Up in the tree, maybe forty feet off the ground. The canopy was broken there, bright with dappled sunlight. Hawkwood squinted in the unaccustomed glare.

"Holy God," Bardolin said beside him.

Then Hawkwood saw it too.

It stood on a huge level branch, and had flattened itself against the trunk which spawned its perch. It was almost the same shade as the butternut-coloured tree bark, which was why Hawkwood had not seen it at first. But then the head turned, and the movement caught his eye.

A monstrous bird of some sort. Its wings were like those of a bat, only more leathery. They hugged the tree trunk: there were claws at the end of the skeletal frame. It was hard to be precisely sure as to where they began and the skin of the tree itself ended, so good was the beast's camouflage, but the thing was big. Its wrinkled, featherless and hairless body was as tall as a man's, and the span of the wings must have been three fathoms or more. The long neck supported a skull-like head, eyes surprisingly small, both set to the front of the face like an owl, and a wicked, black beak between them.

The eyes blinked slowly. They were yellow, slitted. The creature did not appear alarmed at the sight of the party, but regarded them with grave interest; almost, they might have said, with intelligence.

Bardolin stepped forward, and with his right hand he

inscribed a little glimmer on the air. The creature stared at him, unafraid, seemingly intrigued.

There was a loud crack, a spurt of flame and billow of smoke.

"Hold your fire, God-damn you!" Murad cried.

The bird thing detached itself from the tree and seemed to fall backwards. It flipped in mid-fall with incredible speed and grace, then the great wings opened and flapped twice in huge whooshes of air which staggered the smoke and blew the plastered hair off Hawkwood's brow. The wings boomed and cracked like sails. The thing wheeled up into the canopy, and then was a shape against the blue sky beyond, dwindling to a speck and disappearing.

"Who fired?" Murad demanded. "Whose weapon was that?" He was quivering with rage. A soldier whose arquebus was leaking smoke quailed visibly as Murad advanced on him.

Sergeant Mensurado stepped between them.

"My fault, sir. I told the men to keep their wheel-locks back, the match burning. Glabrio here, he tripped, sir. Must have been the sight of that monster. It won't happen again. I'll see to him myself when we get back."

Murad glared at his sergeant, but at last only nodded. "See that you do, Mensurado. A pity the fool missed, since he had to fire a shot. I'd like to have had a closer look at that."

Several of the soldiers were making the Sign of the Saint discreetly. They did not seem to share their commander's wish.

"What was it, Bardolin?" Murad asked the wizard. "Any ideas?"

The old mage's face was unusually troubled.

"I've never seen anything remotely like it, except perhaps in the pages of a bestiary. It was a warped, unnatural thing. Did you see its eyes? There was a mind behind them, Murad. And it stank of Dweomer."

"It was a magical creature, then?" Hawkwood said.

"Yes. More than that, a created creature: not fashioned by the hand of God, but by the sorcery of men. But the power it would take to bring such a thing into the world, and then give it permanence . . . it is staggering. I had not thought that any mage living could have such power. It would kill me, were I to attempt a similar thing."

"What did you make glow in the air?" Murad demanded.

"A glyph. Feralism is one of my disciplines. I was trying to read the heart of the beast."

"And could you?"

"No . . . No, I could not."

"Blast that whoreson idiot and his itchy trigger finger!"

"No, it was not that. I could not read the thing's heart because it was not truly a beast."

"What is this you're saying, Mage?"

"I am not sure. What I think I am saying is that there was humanity there, in the beast. A soul, if you will."

Murad and Hawkwood regarded the wizard in silence. The imp looked around and then cautiously took its fingers from out of its ears. It hated loud noises.

Murad realized that the soldiers were crowded around, listening. His face hardened.

"We'll move on. We can discuss this later. Sergeant Mensurado, lead off and make sure the men have their wheels uncocked. I want no more discharges, or we will have Ensign di Souza evacuating the camp behind us."

That raised a nervous laugh. The men shook out into file again, and set off. Bardolin trudged along wordlessly, the frown lines biting deep between his brows.

THE ground continued to rise. It seemed that they were on the slopes of a hill or small mountain. It was hard going for all of them, because the black sand-like stuff of the forest floor sank under their boots. It was as if they were walking up the side of an enormous dune, their feet slipping back a yard for every yard advanced.

"What is this stuff?" Murad asked. He slapped a sucking insect off his scarred cheek, grimacing.

"Ash, I think," Hawkwood said. "There has been a great burning here. The stuff must be half a fathom deep."

There were boulders, black and almost glassy in places. The trees were slowly splitting them apart and shifting them down-slope. And such trees! Nowhere in the world, Hawkwood thought, even in Gabrion, could there be trees like these, straight as lances, hard as bronze. A shipwright might fashion a mainmast from a single trunk, or a vessel's keel from two. But the labour—the work of hewing down these forest giants. In this heat, it would kill a man.

A gasping, endless time in which they put down their heads and forgot everything but the next step in front of them. Several of the soldiers paused in their travails to vomit, their eyes popping. Murad gave them permission to take off their helmets and loosen their cuirasses, but they gave the impression that they were slowly being boiled alive inside the heavy armour.

At last there was a clear light ahead, an open space. The trees ended. There was a short stretch of bare rock and ash and gravel before them, and then nothing but blue, unclouded heaven.

They bent over to grasp their knees, their guts churning, the sunlight making them blink and scowl. Several of the soldiers collapsed on to their backs and lay there like bright, immobilized beetles, unable to do anything but suck in lungfuls of steaming air.

When Hawkwood finally straightened, the sight before them made him cry out in wonder.

They were above the jungle and on top of this world, it seemed. They had reached the summit of what proved to be a razor-backed ridge which was circular in shape, an eerily perfect symmetry.

Hawkwood could see for uncounted leagues in all directions. If he turned round he could see the Western Ocean stretching off to the horizon. There was the *Osprey* riding at anchor, distant as a child's toy. A line of white surf up and down the coast marked the reefs, and there was a series of little, conical islands off to the north, eight leagues away perhaps.

Inland, to the west, the jungle rolled in an endless viridian carpet, lurid, garish, secretive. Its mass was broken by more formations identical to the one upon which they stood: circles of bare rock amid the greenery, barren as gravestones, unnatural-looking. They pocked the forest like crusted sores, and beyond them, far off and almost invisible in the heat shimmer and haze, were high mountains as blue as woodsmoke.

To the north and west was something else. Clouds were building up there, tall thunderheads and anvils and horsetails of angry vapour, grey and heavy in the underbelly. A shadow dominated that horizon, rearing up and up until its head was lost in the cloud. A mountain, a perfect cone. It was taller than any of the granite giants in the Hebros. Fifteen thousand feet, maybe, though it was hard to tell with its summit lost in billowing vapour.

"Craters," Bardolin said, appearing beside him.

"What?"

"Saffarac of Cartigella, a friend of mine, once had a viewing device, an oracular constructed of two finely ground lenses mounted in a tube of leather. He was hoping to find evidence for his theory that the earth moved around the sun, not the other way round. He looked at the moon, the nearest body in heaven, and he saw there formations like these. Craters. He postulated two causes: one, fiery rock had erupted out of the moon in a series of vast explosions—"

"Like gunpowder, you mean?"

"Yes. Or two, they were caused by vast stones falling to the surface, like the one that fell in Fulk some ten years back. Big as a horse it was, and glowing red when it hit the ground. You see them on clear nights, streaks of light falling to earth. Dying stars giving out their last breath in a streak of light and beauty."

"And that's what made this landscape?" Murad said, coming up behind them.

"It is one theory."

"I have heard that in the southern latitudes there are mountains such as this one," Hawkwood volunteered. "Some of them leak smoke and sulphurous gases."

"Mariners' stories," Murad sneered. "You are not in some Abrusian pothouse trying to impress the lowly, Hawkwood."

Hawkwood said nothing. His gaze did not shift from the panorama before them.

"Not fifty years ago a man might be burnt at the stake for daring to venture that the world was round, and not flat like a buckler," Bardolin said mildly. "And yet now, even in Charibon, they accept that we are spinning on a sphere, as Terenius of Orfor suggests."

"I do not care what shape the world is, so long as my feet can bear me across it," Murad snapped.

They looked down into the bowl which their ridge contained. It was perfectly round, a circle of jungle. They stood at a height of some three thousand feet, Hawkwood estimated, but the air did not seem any less dense.

"*Heyeran Spinero,*" Murad said. "Circle Ridge. I will put it on the map. This is as far as we will go today. It looks like rain is coming in from the north, and I wish to be back at the camp before dark."

None of them mentioned it, but they were all thinking of the monstrous bird which had studied them so nonchalantly. The thought of a night spent away from the rest of their comrades in a forest populated by such things was not tolerable.

Mensurado's croak attracted their attention. The sergeant was pointing down at the land below.

"What is it, Sergeant?" Murad asked harshly. He

seemed to be fighting off exhaustion with bile alone.

Mensurado could only point and whisper, his parade-ground bellow hoarsened out of existence. "There, sir, to the right of that weird hill, just above its flank. You see?"

They peered whilst the rest of the soldiers sat listlessly, slugging the last of their water and mopping their faces.

"Sweet Blessed Saint!" Murad said softly. "Do you see it, gentlemen?"

A space in the jungle, a tiny clearing wherein a patch of beaten earth could be glimpsed.

"A road, or track," Bardolin said, sketching out a far-seeing cantrip to aid his tired eyes.

"Hawkwood, get out that contraption of yours and take its bearing," the nobleman said peremptorily.

Frowning, Hawkwood did as he was told, filling the bowl with some of his own drinking water. He studied it, then looked up, gauging, and said: "West-nor'-west of here. I'd put it at fifteen leagues. It's a broad road, to be seen at that distance."

"That, gentlemen, is our destination," Murad said. "Once we have ourselves organized, I am taking an expedition into the interior. You will both accompany me, naturally. We will make for that road, and see if we can't meet up with whoever built it."

Sergeant Mensurado was as motionless as a block of wood. Murad turned on him.

"The fewer folk who hear of this the better, for now. You understand me, Sergeant?"

"Yes, sir."

"Good. Rouse the men. It's time we were getting back."

"Yes, sir."

In minutes they were off again, downhill this time, trudging in the hollows their feet had made on the way up. Hawkwood and Bardolin remained behind for a few minutes, watching the gathering clouds about the shoulders of the great mountain to the north.

"I'll kill him before we leave this land," Hawkwood said. "He will goad me one time too often."

"It is his way," Bardolin said. "He knows no other. He looks to you and me for answers, and hates the necessity for it. He is as lost as any of us."

"Lost! Is that how you see us?"

"We are on a dark continent which those who were here before us did not mean us to see. There is Dweomer here, everywhere, and there is such a teeming life. I have never felt anything like it. Power, Hawkwood, the power to create warped grotesqueries such as that winged creature. I did not say so before because I was not sure, but I am now. That bird was once a man like you or me. There was the remnant of a man's mind in the beast's skull. Not as it is in a shifter, but different. Permanent. There is someone or something in this land who is committing monstrous deeds, things which offend the very fabric of nature's laws. Murad may be eager to meet them, but I am not, if only because I can to some extent understand the motive behind the act. Power allied to irresponsibility. It is the most dangerous thing in the world, the most seductive of temptations. It is evil, pure and simple."

They followed off after the last of the soldiers without another word, the jungle creatures calling out mockingly all around them.

ELEVEN

IT rained on the way back, as Murad had predicted, and, like everything else in this land, the rain was strange. The sky clouded over in minutes, and the dimness beneath the tops of the trees became a twilight they stumbled through half-blind, eyes fixed on the man in front. There was a roaring noise above, and they looked up in time to catch the first drops cascading down from the ceiling of vegetation.

The roar intensified until they could hardly hear each other's voices. The rain was torrential, maniac, awesome. It was as warm as bath water and thick as wine. The canopy broke most of its force and it tumbled in waterfalls down the trunks of the trees, creating rivers which gurgled around their boots, battering plants to the forest floor and submerging them in mud and slime. The company huddled in the shelter of one of the forest leviathans whilst their dimly lit world became a storm of smashing rain, a blinding, water-choked quagmire.

They glimpsed the dark shapes of little twisting ani-

mals fall to earth, washed off their perches higher in the
trees. The rain coming down the tree boles became a soup
of bark and insects, pouring down the necks of the soldiers' armour, soaking the arquebuses and waterlogging
the powder-horns beyond hope of drying.

An hour or more they crouched there and watched the
storming elements in fear and bewilderment. And then
the rain stopped. Within the space of a dozen heartbeats,
the roaring thunder of it faded, the torrents dwindled
and the light grew.

They stood, blinking, tipping water out of gun barrels
and helmets, wiping their faces. The forest came to life
again. The birds and other unknown fauna took up their
endless chorus once more. The water about their feet
soaked into the spongy soil and disappeared, and the last
of the rain dripped in streams from the leaves of the great
trees, lit up like tumbling gems by the sunlight above.
The jungle stank and steamed.

Murad shook his lank hair from his face, wrinkling his
nose. "The place stinks worse than a tannery in high summer. Bardolin, you're our resident expert on the world.
Was that rain normal for here, do you think?"

The wizard shrugged, dripping.

"In Macassar they have sudden rains like that, but they
come in the rainy season only," Hawkwood volunteered.

"We've arrived here in the midst of the rainy season
then?"

"I don't know," the mariner said wearily. "I've heard
merchants of Calmar say that to the south of Punt there
are jungles where it rains like this every day, and there
is no winter, no summer; no seasons at all. It never
changes from one month to the next."

"God save us," one of the soldiers muttered.

"That is ridiculous," Murad snapped. "Every country
in the world has its seasons; it must have. What is a world
without spring, or winter? When would one harvest

crops, or sow seeds? When will you cease spinning your
travellers' tales with me, Hawkwood?"

Hawkwood's face darkened, but he said nothing.

They moved on without further talk, and had it not
been for Hawkwood's compass they would never have
got their bearings again, for the little stream which they
had followed that morning had become one of many
muddy rivulets. They retraced their course like mariners
at sea, by compass bearing alone, and by the time they
heard the voices of the men back at the makeshift camp
there was a transparency, a frailty to the light in the sky
which suggested that sundown was very near.

The camp was a shambles. Murad stood with his fists
resting on his lean hips and surveyed it with skull-like
intensity. The stream which had run through it had over-
flowed its soggy banks and the men were sucking
through a veritable swamp of mud and decaying vegetation, steam rising like fog from the saturated earth.
They had chopped down a score of saplings and tried to
fashion a rude palisade, but the wood would not stand
up in the soft soil; the stakes sagged and wobbled like
rotten teeth.

Ensign di Souza forced his way over to his superior,
his boots heavy with mud.

"Sir, I mean your excellency—the rain. It washed out
the camp. We managed to keep some of the powder
dry . . ." He tailed off.

"Move off to one side, away from the stream," Murad
barked. "Get the men to it at once. There's not much
light left."

A new shape in the gathering gloom and Ensign Sequero, di Souza's more aristocratic fellow officer, appeared, amazingly clean and tidy, having just come from
the ship.

"What are you doing ashore, Ensign?" Murad asked.
He looked like a man being slowly bent into some quivering new shape, the tension in him a palpable thing. The

soldiers went to their work with a will; they knew Murad's displeasure was a thing to avoid.

"Your excellency," Sequero said with a smile, hovering just below insolence. "The passengers are wondering when they'll be let ashore, and there is the livestock also. The horses especially need a run on dry land, and fresh fodder."

"They will have to wait," Murad said with dangerous quietness. "Now get you back to the ship, Ensign."

Even as he spoke, the light died. It grew dark so quickly that some of the soldiers and sailors stared around fearfully, making the Sign of the Saint at their breasts. A twilight measured in moments followed by pitch blackness, a weight of dark which was broken only by the spatters of stars visible through gaps in the canopy overhead.

"Sweet Ramusio!" someone said. "What a country."

No one spoke for a few minutes. The men stood frozen as the jungle disappeared into the night and became one with it. The noises of the forest changed tone, but did not decrease their volume one whit. The company was in the midst of an invisible bedlam.

"Strike a light, someone, for God's sake," Murad's voice cracked, and the stillness in the camp was broken. Men fumbling in the dark, the sucking squelch of feet in mud. A rattle of sparks.

"The tinder's soaked through . . ."

"Use any dry powder you have, then," Hawkwood's voice said.

A sulphuric flare in the night, like a far-off eruption.

"Burn a couple of the stakes. They're the only things which are near-dry."

For perhaps the space of half an hour, the inhabitants of the crown's new colony in the west huddled about a single soldier who was striving to create fire. They might have been men at the dawn of the world, crouched in the terrifying and unknowable dark, their eyes craving the light to see what was coming at them out of the night.

The flames caught at last. They saw themselves; a circle of faces around a tiny fire. The jungle towered off on all sides, the night creatures laughing and croaking at their fear. They were in an alien world, as lost and alone as forgotten children.

H AWKWOOD and Bardolin sat by one of the fires later in the night. There were thirty men ashore, lying around half a dozen camp-fires which spat and hissed in the surrounding mud. A dozen men stood guard with halberd and sword whilst a few others were methodically and cautiously turning a pile of gunpowder off to one side, trying to dry it out without blowing themselves to kingdom come. The arquebuses were useless for the moment.

"We don't belong here," Hawkwood said quietly, chucking Bardolin's imp under the chin so that it gurgled and grinned at him, its eyes two little lamps in the firelight.

"Maybe the first Fimbrians to venture east of the Malvennors said the same thing," Bardolin replied. "New countries, unexplored lands, are always strange at first."

"No, Bardolin, it's more than that and you know it. This country's very nature is different. Inimical. Alien. Murad thought he could wade ashore and start building his own kingdom here, but it won't be that way."

"You wrong him there," the mage said. "After what happened on the ship, I think he knew better than to expect it to be easy. He is feeling his way, but he is hidebound by the conventions of his class and his training. He is thinking like a soldier, a nobleman."

"Are we commoners so much more flexible in our thinking, then?" Hawkwood asked, grinning weakly.

"Maybe. We do not have so much at stake."

"I have a ship—I had two ships. My life is gambled on this throw also," Hawkwood reminded him.

"And I have no other home; this continent is the only place in the world, perhaps, where I and my like can be free of prejudice, make a new beginning," Bardolin retorted. "That, at least, was the theory."

"And yet tonight you were too tired even to conjure up a glimmer of werelight. What kind of omen is that for your new beginning?"

The wizard was silent, listening to the jungle noises.

"What is out there, Bardolin?" Hawkwood persisted. "What manner of men or beasts have claimed this place before us?"

The old mage poked at the fire, then slapped his cheek suddenly, wincing. He peeled an engorged, many-legged thing from his face, eyed it with mild curiosity for a second and then threw it into the flames.

"As I said, there is Dweomer here, more than I have ever sensed in any other place," he said. "The land we saw before us today is thick with it."

"Was that truly a road? Are we to stumble across another civilization here?"

"I think so. I think something exists on this continent which we in the Ramusian west have never even guessed at. I keep thinking of Ortelius, our stowaway Inceptine and werewolf. He was charged with making sure your ships never made it this far, that much is clear. Perhaps he had a fellow on your other vessel, the one that was lost. In any case, his mission was entrusted to him by someone in this land, this strange country upon which we have made landfall. And there is Dweomer running through it all, the work of mages. Hawkwood, I do not think we will leave this continent alive, any of us."

The mariner stared at him across the fire. "Rather soon to be making such predictions of doom, isn't it?" he managed at last.

"Soothsaying is one of the Seven Disciplines, but it is not one of mine, along with weather-working and the Black Change. Yet I feel we have no future here. I know it, and for all Murad's claims and posturings, I think he knows it too."

I T was a clammy, muddy campsite that presented itself to the shore party with the dawn, but Murad began issuing orders immediately and the soldiers were harangued out of their torpor by Sergeant Mensurado. Nothing had happened during the night, though few of them had slept. Hawkwood for one had missed the lulling rock of his ship beneath him, the waves lapping at the hull. His *Osprey* now seemed to him to be the most secure place in the world.

They staggered down to the brightness of the beach, the heat already being flung at their faces from its reflected glare. The carrack rode at anchor beyond the reef, an incredibly comforting sight for soldier and sailor alike.

Breakfast was ship's biscuit and wood-hard salt pork, eaten cold on the beach. All manner of fruit was hanging within easy reach, but Murad had forbidden anyone to touch the stuff so they ate as if they were still at sea.

Throughout the morning the longboats plied the passage of the reef and brought across stores and equipment. The surviving horses were too weak to swim ashore behind the boats so they were trussed up and lowered into the larger of the vessels like carcasses. Released on dry land for the first time in months, they stood like emaciated caricatures of the fine animals they had once been and Sequero put half a dozen men to finding fodder for them.

The water casks were replenished by Hawkwood's sailors and towed back out to the carrack in bobbing skeins. Another party led by Hawkwood himself rowed out to that part of the reef upon which the wreck of the *Grace of God* rested.

The surf was too rough for them to go close, but they could see a desiccated body wedged in the timbers of the beakhead, unrecognizable, the seabirds and the elements having done their work too well.

Further up the coast there was more wreckage, fragments mostly. The caravel had been shattered by its impact on the reef as if by an explosion. Hawkwood's crew found the shredded remnants of another corpse a mile to the north and some threads of clothing, but nothing more. The caravel's crew and passengers had perished to a man, it seemed.

The passengers aboard the carrack were rowed ashore at last, over eighty of them. They stood on the beach of this new land like folk cast adrift. Which in a way was what they were.

Back in Hebrion it was winter, and the old year was almost over. There would be snow thick upon the Hebros, the winter storms thrashing the swells of the Fimbrian Gulf and the Hebrian Sea. Here the heat was relentless and choking, a miasma of humid jungle stink hanging in their throats like a fog. It sapped their strength, weighed them down like chainmail. And yet the work did not cease, the orders continued to be issued, the activity went on without let-up.

They moved in off the beach a quarter of a mile, perhaps, abandoning the campsite of the night before. Murad set soldiers, civilians and sailors alike to clearing a space between the trunks of the huge trees. Many of the younger trees were felled, and the would-be colonists burned off what vegetation they could, slashing and uprooting that which was too wet to catch fire. They erected shelters of wood and canvas and thatched leaves, and built a palisade as high as a man's head, loopholed for firearms and with crude wooden watch-towers at each corner.

Almost every afternoon the work was halted by the titanic, thunderous rainstorms which came and went like the rage of a petulant god. Some of the colonists fell sick almost at once—the older ones, mostly, and one squall-

ing toddler. Two died raving in fever, the rigours of the
voyage and this new land too much for them. Thus the
fledgling colony acquired a cemetery within its first
week.

THEY named the settlement Fort Abeleius after their
young king. One hundred and fifty-seven souls lived
within its perimeter, for Murad would allow none of the
colonists to forge off on their own in search of suitable
plots of land. For the moment, Hebrion's newest colony
was nothing more than an armed camp, ready to repel
attack at short notice. No one knew who the attackers
might be, or even what they might be, but there were no
complaints. The story of the warped bird had spread
quickly, and no one was keen to venture into the jungle
alone.

Titles were distributed like sweetmeats. Sequero became a *haptman*, military commander of the colony, now
that Murad was governor. In reality, Murad still commanded the soldiers personally, but it amused him to see
Sequero lording it over his subordinate, di Souza.

Hawkwood became head of the Merchants' Guild,
which as yet did not exist, but true to his word Murad
had procured monopolies for him and he had them in
writing, heavy with seals and ribbons, the signature at the
bottom none other than that of Abeleyn himself. They
were beginning to grow mould with the damp heat, and
he had to keep them tightly wrapped in oilskin packets.

And Hawkwood was ennobled. Plain Richard Hawkwood had become Lord Hawkwood, albeit lord of nothing and nowhere. But it was a hereditary title. Hawkwood
had ennobled his family for ever, if he managed to return
to Hebrion and raise a family. Old Johann, his rascally
father, would have been uproariously delighted, but to
Hawkwood it seemed an empty gesture, meaningless in
the midst of this steaming jungle.

He sat in his crude hut sorting through what documents

he had brought from the ship. Velasca was on the carrack with a skeleton crew. The vessel had been rewatered and they had also taken on board several hundredweight of coconuts, one of the few fruits growing here which Hawkwood recognized.

His original ship's log was gone, lost in the fire which had come close to destroying his ship, and with it the ancient rutter of Tyrenius Cobrian, the only other record of a voyage into the west. Hawkwood had started a new log, of course, but flipping through it he realized with a cold start that there was no sure way he could ever find his way back to Fort Abeleius or this anchorage were he to undertake a second voyage in the wake of the first. The storm which had driven them off course had upset his calculations, and the loss of the log had made things worse for he could not remember every change of course and tack since then. The best he might do was to hit upon the Western Continent at the approximate latitude his cross-staff told him this was and then cruise up and down until he rediscovered the place.

He thought of telling Murad, but decided against it. The scarred nobleman was like a spring being compressed too tightly these days, more haughty and savage than ever. It would do no good.

It was dimming outside, and Hawkwood immediately struck himself a light, a precious candle from their dwindling store. Scarcely had he done so when the dark came, a settling of deep shadow which at some indefinable point became true night.

He dipped his nub of a quill in the inkwell and began to write his log.

26th day of Endorion, ashore Fort Abeleius, year of the Saint 551—though only a few sennights remain of the old year, and soon we will be into the Saint's days which denote the turning of the calendar.

The palisade was finished today, and we have begun

the task of felling some of the huge trees which stand within its perimeter. Murad's plan is to lop them a little at a time and use them for construction and firewood. He will never uproot them; I think such trees must have roots running to the core of the earth.

The building work proceeds apace. We have a governor's residence—the only building with a floor, though it has an old topsail for its back wall. I dine there tonight. Civilization comes to the wilderness.

Hawkwood reread his entry. He was becoming loquacious now that he no longer had to write of winds and courses and sailing arrangements. His log was turning into a journal.

At last we have dry powder, though keeping it so in this climate has tried the wits of every soldier among us. It was Bardolin who suggested sealing the powder-horns with wax. He has become a little odd, our resident mage. Murad regards him as the leader of the colonists, the scientific problem-solver, but also as something of a fraud. Whether this last attitude of his is assumed or not I do not know. Since his peasant lover turned out to be a shifter, Murad has been different—at once less sure of himself and more autocratic. But then who among us was not changed by that weird voyage and its horrors?

I would that Billerand were here, or Julius Albak, my shipmates of old. Our company is the poorer without them, and I am not entirely happy with Velasca as first mate. His navigation leaves a lot to be desired.

"Captain?" a voice said beyond the sailcloth flap that served as Hawkwood's door.

"Come in, Bardolin."

The mage entered, stooping. He looked older, Hawkwood thought. His carriage had always been so upright, his face so battered and grizzled that he seemed made out of some enduring stone; but the years were beginning to tell on him now. His forehead shone with sweat, and like everyone else's his neck and arms were blotched with insect bites. The imp that rode on his shoulder seemed as sprightly as ever, though. It leapt on to the crate which Hawkwood used as a desk and he had gently to pry the inkwell out of its tiny hands.

"What cheer, comrade wizard?" Hawkwood asked the old mage.

Bardolin collapsed on the heap of leaves and seacloak which had been piled into a bed.

"I have been purifying water for the invalids among us. I am tired, Captain."

Hawkwood produced a rotund bottle from behind his crate and offered it. "Drink?"

They both had a gulp straight from the neck, and spluttered over the good brandy.

"That calms the bones," Bardolin said appreciatively, and nodded towards the open log. "Writing for posterity?"

"Yes. The habit of a master-mariner's lifetime, though I am in danger of becoming a chronicler." Hawkwood shut the heavily bound book and rewrapped it in its oilcloth. "Ready for tomorrow?"

Bardolin rubbed the shadows under his eyes. "I suppose . . . How does it feel to be a lord?"

"I still sweat, the mosquitoes still feed off me. It is not so different."

Bardolin smiled. "What conceit we have, we men. We throw up a squalid camp like this and name it a colony. We distribute titles amongst ourselves, we lay claim to a country which has existed without us since time's dawn; we impose our rules upon things we are utterly ignorant of."

"It is how society is made," Hawkwood said.

"Yes. How did the Fimbrians feel, do you think, when they came together in their tribes nine centuries ago and made themselves into one people? Was there a shadow of their empire flickering about them, even then? History. Give it a hundred years and it will make heroes and villains out of every one of us—if it remembers us."

"The world rolls on. It is for us to make what we can of it."

The old mage stretched. "Of course. And tomorrow we will see a little more of it. Tomorrow the governor sets out to explore this place he has claimed."

"Would you rather be playing hide-and-seek with the Inceptines back in Abrusio?"

"Yes. Yes, I would. I am afraid, Captain, truly afraid. I am frightened of what we will find here in the west. But curious also. I would not stay behind tomorrow for all the world. It is man's insufferable curiosity which makes him set sail across unknown seas; it is a more potent force even than greed or ambition—you know that, I think, better than anyone."

"I'm as ambitious and greedy as the next man."

"But curiosity drove you here."

"That, and Murad's blackmail."

"Aha! Our noble governor again! He has brought us all into the tangle of his own machinations. We are flies trembling in his web. Well, even spiders have their predators. He is beginning to realize that, in spite of his bluster and arrogance."

"Do you hate him then?"

"I hate what he represents: the blind bigotry and pride of his caste. But he is not as bad as some; he is not stupid, nor does he wilfully ignore the truth, no matter what he says."

"You have too many new ideas, Bardolin, I too find it hard to accommodate some of them. Your hills which spout flames and ash—those I can believe. I have heard men talk of them before. But this *smell* of magic from the trees and soil; from the land itself. An earth which circles the sun. A moon bombarded by stones from beyond the sky . . . Everyone knows that our world is at the heart of God's creation, even the Merduks."

"That is the Church talking."

"I am no blind son of the Church, you know that."

"You are a product of its culture."

Hawkwood threw up his hands. Bardolin exasperated him, but he could not dislike the man. "Drink some more brandy, and stop trying to right the wrongs of society for a while."

Bardolin laughed, and complied.

THEY were to venture into the interior again in the morning, and Murad's dinner was both a social event and a planning conference. He had killed the last of the chickens, as if to prove to the world that he had no fears for the future, and one of the soldiers had shot a tiny deer, no bigger than a lamb, which was the centrepiece of the table. Bardolin examined its bones as if they were the stuff of an augury. Beside the meat courses there was the last of the dried fruit, nuts, pickled olives, and a tiny scrap of Hebrion sea cheese as hard as soap. They drank Candelarian which was as warm as blood in the humid night, and finished with Fimbrian brandy.

Hawkwood, Murad, Bardolin, Sequero and di Souza: the hierarchy of the colony. Murad's exclusive guestlist had antagonized half a dozen of the more prominent of the colonists, who felt they should have been drinking his brandy also.

The lucky few talked civilly enough amongst themselves, with the light of the precious ship's candles playing on their glistening faces. Sequero was mourning his horses; they were deteriorating fast in this foreign climate, and no fodder the men could find seemed to suit them. Not that a horse could bear a man anywhere in the jungle, Hawkwood thought; but from now on the nobility would walk like the meanest trooper. Perhaps that was what grieved the aristocratic young officer most.

Huge moths circled the candles, some as big as Hawk-wood's hand, and fizzling around them were the tinier insects which were nevertheless the more irritating. Despite the attempts Murad had made to make the gathering a gracious affair, with a couple of the female colonists as maidservants, the men around the rough board table and mould-spattered linen tablecloth were none too clean and tidy. Leather rotted here with incredible swiftness, they had found, and many of the soldiers were already securing their armour with twisted lengths of creeper or ship's rope. Soon they would be a crowd of savages dressed in rags.

The colonists were experimenting with the fruits which hung in profusion from almost every tree, Bardolin told them. Some were very good, others smelled like corruption the minute they were opened. A few birds had been trapped with greenlime smeared on branches. There was food here for all, if only they could learn how to use it, prepare it, recognize it.

"Food for savages," Sequero sneered. "I for one would prefer to trust to the ship's salt pork and biscuit."

"The ship's stores will not last for ever," Hawkwood said. "And most of them will have to be reserved for the homeward voyage. I have men trying to extract salt from the shallower pools on the shore, but we must assume that we have no way of preserving food. The barrelled stores must be kept intact."

"I agree," Murad said unexpectedly. "This is our country and we must learn to use it. From tomorrow onwards, the exploring party will be living off the land. It would be absurd to try and carry our food with us."

Sequero held up a glass of the ruby Candelarian. "We will miss many things ere long, I suppose. It is the price we pay for being pioneers. Sir, how long do you expect to be gone?" He was to be in command of the colony while Murad was away.

"A month or five weeks, not more. I expect progress

in my absence, Haptman. You can start clearing plots for those families with able-bodied men, and I want the coast surveyed up and down for several leagues and accurate charts made. Hawkwood's people will help you in that."

Sequero bowed slightly in his seat. He did not seem unduly burdened by his new responsibilities. Di Souza sat opposite him, his big red face expressionless. He was a noble only by adoption; he could not have hoped for Sequero's promotion. But he had hoped, all the same.

They lifted the sailcloth wall of Murad's residence to let air flow in and out. Around the fort the rude huts of the other colonists squatted, some of them lit by camp-fires, others illuminated by the bobbing globes of were-light kindled by those who knew some cantrimy. They were like outsized fireflies hovering fascinated in the darkness, an eldritch sight for the forest moths were circling them. Little flapping planets in erratic orbits about miniature suns, Hawkwood thought, remembering Bardolin's beliefs.

"They say that Ramusio tramped every road and track in Normannia in his spreading of the faith," Bardolin said quietly. "But the Saint's foot never trod this earth. It is a dark continent we have discovered. I wonder if we shall ever bring any light to it save for fire and werelight."

"And gunfire," Murad added. "That we have brought also. Where faith does not sustain us, arquebuses will. And the determination of men."

"Let us hope it is enough," the old wizard said, and swallowed the last of the wine.

TWELVE

THERE was a mist in the morning which hung no higher than a man's waist. It seemed to have seeped out of the very ground, and to those moving about the fort it was as if they were wading through a monochrome sea.

The expedition set off soon after dawn, Murad in the lead with Sergeant Mensurado at his side, followed by Hawkwood, Bardolin and two of the *Osprey*'s crew, the huge black helmsman Masudi and master's mate Mihal, a Gabrionese like Hawkwood himself. After them came twelve Hebrian soldiers in half-armour bearing arquebuses and swords, their helmets slung at their hips and clanking as they walked. The expedition sounded like a pedlar's caravan, Hawkwood thought irritably. He and Bardolin had tried to persuade Murad to leave the heavy body armour behind, but the lean nobleman had refused point-blank. So the sweating soldiers had an extra fifty pounds on their backs.

The remaining score or so of the demi-tercio turned

out to see them off, along with most of the colonists. They fired a volley in salute which sent the birds screaming and flapping for miles around and made Bardolin roll his eyes. Then Fort Abeleius was left behind, and the company was alone with the jungle.

They took a bearing with Hawkwood's bowl-compass, and set off as close as they could to due west. One of the soldiers was detailed to blaze a tree every hundred yards or so, though their path would have been easy to retrace since it looked like the blundering tunnel a stubborn bull might have made in the vegetation.

Slow going, the unceasing noise of hacking cutlasses, men gasping for breath, cursing the rabid undergrowth.

The day spun round, and they sheltered in the lee of the trees as the customary afternoon tempest battered down, making their surroundings into a dripping, sodden, steaming bathhouse. Then they crashed onwards again, nursing their dry gunpowder as though it were gold dust.

They found the rocky flank of the hill they had climbed on their first day, and at Murad's insistence they climbed it again with an agony of effort. Once at the top they paused to feel the freer air and have a look at a wider world. They divided into pairs and divested each other of the fat leeches which crept up their legs and down the back of their necks, then they started to parallel the contours of the hollow hill, following the line of the ridge round to the north-east, coming up almost to due north. It was a farther hike, but faster since they had no jungle to hack through.

Night came as they were finally on the descent, and they made a rough camp amid the rocks of the ridge, piling up stones into platforms to sleep upon. The mist came down to sour their tongues and bead the rocks, and the soldiers bickered over the lighting of the campfires until Mensurado silenced them. They stood watch three at a time, and it was about the middle of the graveyard watch when Hawkwood was roughly shaken awake by Murad.

"Look, down in the jungle. They've just appeared."

Hawkwood rubbed his swollen eyes and peered out into the noisy darkness below. Hard to see if he concentrated. Better to let his vision unfocus. There: a tiny blur of brightness far off in the night.

"Lights?"

"Yes, and they're not blasted glow-worms either."

"How far, do you think?" They were talking in whispers. The sentries were awake and alert, but Murad had woken no one else.

"Hard to say," the nobleman said. "Six or eight leagues, anyway. They must be above the trees. On the flank of one of these weird hills, perhaps."

"Above the trees, you say?"

"Keep your voice down. Yes, otherwise how could we see them? I noted no clearings within sight on the way down the ridge."

"What do we do?" Hawkwood asked.

"You get out your contraption and take a bearing on those lights. That is our route for tomorrow."

Hawkwood did as he was told, fumbling with bowl and water and needle in the firelight.

"North-west or thereabouts."

"Good. Now we have something to aim for. I was not happy at the thought of simply wandering into the interior until we struck that road."

"I don't suppose it's occurred to you that we were *meant* to see those lights, Murad?"

The nobleman's face twisted in a rictus-like smile. "Does it matter? Whatever dwells on this continent, we will have to confront it—or them—at some point. Better to do it sooner."

There was a strange light in Murad's eyes, an eagerness which was disquieting. Hawkwood felt as though he were on a rudderless ship with a lee shore foaming off the bow. That sensation of helplessness, of being manipulated by forces he could do nothing about.

"Go back to sleep," Murad told him in an undertone. "It is hours yet until the dawn. I will take your watch; there's no sleep left in me tonight."

He looked like a creature which no longer needed sleep anyway. He had always been sparely built, but now he appeared gaunt to the point of emaciation, a pale creature of sinew and bone held together by the will which blazed out of the too-bright eyes. The beginnings of fever? Hawkwood would bring it up with Bardolin tomorrow. With any luck, the bastard might even expire.

Hawkwood returned to his stony bed and shut his eyes to await his own sleep, that coveted oblivion.

THE sights of the night were not mentioned in the morning, and the party set off with rumbling stomachs. They had brought a little biscuit with them, but nothing else. If they were to live off the land, they would have to start doing so soon.

They left the crater-hill behind and plunged into dense forest once more, still descending. It was noon before the land levelled out, and the ground was boggy and wet with the run-off water from the ridge. Streams glittered everywhere, and the trees had put out great naked roots like buttresses from high on their trunks, so fantastical looking that it was hard to believe they had not been grafted on by some demented botanist. Masudi and Mensurado, slashing a path at the front, were sprayed with water when the creepers they sliced spouted like hoses.

They halted to rest, rubber-legged with fatigue and hunger. Bardolin and a few of the soldiers collected fruit from the surrounding branches, and the company sat down together to experiment. There was a buff-coloured circular fruit which when sliced open looked almost exactly like bread, and after a few cautious tastings the men wolfed it down, heedless of the old wizard's warnings.

They found also a huge kind of pear, and curved green objects growing in clusters which Hawkwood had encountered before in the jungles of Macassar. He showed the men how to peel off the outer skin and eat the sweet yellow fruit within. But despite the bounty the soldiers craved meat, and several walked with slow-match lit, ready to shoulder arms and fire at any animal they might encounter.

Another afternoon downpour. This time they continued trudging through it, though they were almost blinded by the stinging rain. Men held their water bottles up as they marched to collect the liquid, but it was full of the detritus of the canopy above, alive with moving things, and they had to empty out what they had collected in disgust.

They were imperceptibly beginning to slip into the routine of the jungle. They had tied off their breech legs with strips of leather and cord to prevent the leeches climbing inside them, and they accepted the daily rain as a normal occurrence. They became more adept at picking their way through the dense vegetation, and learned to avoid the low-hanging branches from which snakes occasionally dropped down. They knew what to eat and what not to eat—to some extent—though those who had gorged themselves on fruit were soon dropping out of the column to perform their necessary functions with greater and greater frequency. And the incessant noise, the screechings and warblings and wailings of the forest denizens soon became a scarcely registered thing. Only when it stopped sometimes, inexplicably, would they pause without saying a word, and stand like men turned to stone in the midst of that vast, unnerving silence.

The second night they lit their fires with snatches of gunpowder, since they had no dry tinder remaining, and built beds of leaves and ferns to try and keep something between their tired bodies and the vermin of the forest floor. Then the soldiers sat cleaning equipment and drying their arquebuses whilst Masudi and Mihal collected fruit for the evening meal. There was little talk. The lights of the night before were common knowledge, but the soldiers did not seem too disturbed by what they might imply. Where there were lights there was civilization of a sort, and they seemed to think that it was theirs to claim by the sword if they had to. They had yet to strike upon any sign of civilization, such as the road they had glimpsed from the ridge, however.

Masudi's shout brought them to their feet, and they pelted off towards it, grabbing burning faggots from the campfires and hurriedly setting them to the slow-match. The jungle was a wheeling chiaroscuro of shadow and flame, looming blacknesses, whipping leaves. They splashed through a shallow stream. The torch taken by the two fruit hunters rippled faintly ahead.

"What is it? What happened?" Murad demanded.

Masudi's black face glistened with sweat, but he did not seem very afraid. Behind him Mihal stood with a shirtful of fruit.

"There, sir," the giant helmsman said, raising his hissing torch. "Look what we found."

The company peered into the flame-etched night. Something else there, bulkier even than the trees. They could see a snarling face, a muzzle zigzagged with fangs and two long ears arcing back from a great skull. It was half-bearded with creepers.

"A statue," Bardolin's voice said calmly.

"It made me shout, coming across it like that. I nearly dropped the torch. I'm sorry, sir," Masudi said to the quivering Murad.

"It's a werewolf," Hawkwood told them, staring at the monolith. The thing was fifteen feet tall and snarling as though it longed to be free of the creepers which bound it. The body was almost hidden in spade-shaped leaves. One taloned paw lay on the ground at its feet. The jungle was slowly working the hewn stone apart, breaking it down and absorbing it.

"A good likeness," Murad said with a forced jocularity that fooled no one.

Bardolin had lit the cold glow of a werelight, and was investigating the statue more closely, though most of the soldiers had hung back, their arquebuses pointed at the surrounding darkness as though they were expecting flesh-and-blood doppel-gangers of the thing to leap into the torchlight.

A ripping of vegetation. The imp helped its master tear away the clinging leaves and stems.

"There's an inscription here I think I can read." The werelight sank down until it almost touched the wizard's lined forehead.

"It's in Normannic, but an archaic dialect."

"*Normannic?*" Murad spat out the word incredulously. "What does it say?"

The mage rubbed moss away with his hand. Around them the jungle noise had died and the night was almost silent.

> *Be with us in this Change of Dark and Life*
> *That we may see the heart of living man,*
> *And know in hunger that which binds us all*
> *To this wide world awaiting us again.*

"Gibberish," Murad growled.

The mage straightened. "I know this from somewhere."

"You've read it before?" Hawkwood asked.

"No. But something similar, perhaps."

"We'll discuss the historical implications later. Back to camp, everyone," Murad ordered. "You sailors, bring what fruit you've gathered. It will suffice for tonight."

THERE was little sleep for anyone that night, because the jungle remained as silent as a tomb for hours and the silence was more disquieting by far than any din of nocturnal bird or beast. The company built their fires despite the fact that the sweat was dripping off their very fingertips. They needed the light, the reassurance that their comrades were around them. The fires had a claustrophobic effect, however, making the towers of the trees press ever closer in on them, emphasizing the huge, restless jungle which pursued its own arcane business off in the darkness as it had for eons before them. They were mere nomadic parasites lost in the pelt of a creature which was as big as a turning world. That night they were not afraid of unknown beasts or strange natives, but of the land itself, for it seemed to pulse and murmur with a beating life of its own, alien, unknowable, and utterly indifferent to them.

THEY had another look at the statue when the sun rose. It seemed less impressive in daylight, more crudely sculpted than they had thought. Year by year, the jungle was comprehensively destroying it. They could only guess at its age.

Another day on the march. They followed the direction Hawkwood pointed out in the morning, keeping their route straight by checking and rechecking with the trail of blazed trees they left behind them. It was impossible to be sure, but Hawkwood reckoned that they had come some six leagues west of their first hill, the one Murad had named *Heyeran Spinero*. The soldiers quarrelled over this news, believing they had marched twice as far, but Hawkwood had averaged out his paces and even been generous in his reckoning. It seemed impossible that days of Herculean effort should have brought them such a small distance.

Murad alone seemed unconcerned, perhaps because he was counting on running into the natives of this country before they had trudged and hacked their way too many more miles.

Another hot night ensued, another pile of firewood to collect, another series of sweet, insubstantial fruits to wolf down in the light of the yellow flames. And then sleep. It came easy tonight, despite the heat and the marauding insects and the unknown things in the darkness.

BARDOLIN woke at some dead hour in the night to find that the fires had sunk into red glows and the sentries were asleep. The jungle was silent and still.

He listened to that vast quiet, the loudest sound the faint rush of his own heartbeat in his mouth. He had the strangest impression . . . that someone was calling him, someone he knew.

"Griella?" he whispered, the night air invading his head.

He got up, leaving his imp asleep and whimpering, and picked his way over the snoring forms of his comrades, oddly unalarmed.

Blackness like the inside of a wolf's throat surrounded and enfolded him. He walked on, his feet hardly touching the detritus of the forest floor, his eyes wide and unseeing. The jungle soared to tenebrous heights above him, the night stars invisible beyond the shrouding canopy of the trees. Leaves caressed his face, dripping warm water over him. Creepers slid across his body like hairy snakes, both rough and soft. He felt that he had sloughed away a thicker skin, and was left with each of his nerve endings naked and pulsing in the night, quivering to every waft of air and drop of water.

A deeper shadow before him, a shape blacker even than the witch-dark forest. In it two yellow lights burned and blinked in unison. Still, he was not afraid.

I'm dreaming, he told himself, and the merciful thought kept terror at bay.

The lights moved, and he was conscious of a warmth that had nothing to do with the night air. His skin crawled as it approached him, a black sunlight.

The lights were eyes, bright saffron and slitted with black like those of a vast cat. It was standing before him. There was a noise, a low susurration like a continuous growl but in a lower key. He felt the sound with his new skin as much as heard it.

And felt the fur of the thing, as soft as crushed velvet. A sensual, wholly pleasurable sensation which made him want to bury his palms deep in its softness.

The world spun, and the breath had been knocked out of him. He was on the ground, on his back, and two huge paws were on his shoulders. He felt the prickle of whiskers, sharp as needles, the thing's breath on his face.

It sank down on him as though it meant to mould itself to his body. His hands felt the thickly muscled ribs under the fur and brushed a line of nipples along the taut belly. He thought it groaned, an almost human sound. He was conscious of the throbbing warmth in his crotch, the heat of the thing as it pressed against him there.

And then it had reared up. A scratch of pain somewhere around his hipbone which made him cry out; his breeches were ripped off and it had plunged itself down on him, taking him inside.

A feverish heat and liquid grip of muscle. It pushed his buttocks into the moist humus, its head thrown back and the red mouth open so that he could see the long glint of fangs. He grabbed fistfuls of its fur as his climax came, and thought he screamed.

It was down on him again for a moment, and he could feel the teeth pressed against his neck. Then the crushing weight and heat were raised off him. He found himself sunk deep into the muck of the jungle floor, utterly spent.

He felt a kiss—a human kiss of laughing lips on his own. Then he knew he was alone again, back with his ageing body, the razor-awareness of everything gone. He wept like a struck child.

• • •

A ND woke up. Dawn had come, and the camp was stirring awake. The sour reek of old smoke hung heavy in the air.

Hawkwood handed him a waterbottle, looking ten years older in the grey morning, moss in his tawny beard.

"Another day, Bardolin. You look like you've had a hard night."

Bardolin swallowed a gulp of water. His mouth soaked it up and remained as dry as gunpowder. He swallowed more.

"Such a dream I had," he said. "Such a dream."

There were black hairs sweat-glued to his palms. He stared at them in curiosity, wondering where they could have come from.

T HE company broke camp in morose silence, the men moving slowly in the gathering heat. They shook out into their accustomed file, some gnawing fruit, others pulling up their breeches, their faces drawn by the chaos of their bowels. More and more of them were succumbing to the inadequacies of their strange diet. The surrounds of the camp stank of ordure. Hollow-eyed, they started off on the day's journey.

On the afternoon of this, the fourth day, the rain came down with its weary regularity, and they plodded on under it like cattle oblivious to the drover's stick. Masudi and Cortona, one of the strongest soldiers, were at the front chopping a path blindly with one hand shielding their eyes as though from too-brilliant sunlight. Behind them the rest of the soldiers staggered onwards, their once-bright armour now coral coloured in places, green in others. Their rotting boots sank deep into the leaf litter and muck and they were sometimes obliged to bend over and pull their feet free of the sucking mud with their hands.

Then the two point-men stopped. The heavy vegetation had given way like a breached wall and there was a clearing in front of them, the far side of it misted by the pouring rain.

"Sir!" Cortona shouted above the downpour, and Murad was shoving everyone out of the way to get to the head of the file.

A figure was sitting in the middle of the clearing, cross-legged and head bowed in the wet. As far as they could tell, it was a woman, her dark hair bound up, dressed in leather with bare arms and legs. She did not look up at the gaping explorers, nor did she acknowledge their presence in any way, but they knew she was aware of them. And there were odd flickerings of movement along the edge of the clearing behind her.

The company stood like men stunned, water pouring down their faces and into their open mouths unheeded. At last Murad drew his rapier, ignoring Bardolin's urgent hiss.

The woman in the clearing looked up, but at the sky above, not at them. For an instant her eyes seemed blank and white in the rain, lacking iris or pupil. Then the rain stopped as swiftly as it always did in this country. Their job done, the clouds began to break up and the sun to filter down.

The woman smiled, as though it were all her handiwork and she was proud of it. Then she looked straight at the crowd of men who stood opposite, swords drawn, arquebuses levelled.

She smiled again, this time showing white, sharp teeth like those of a cat. Her eyes were very dark, her face pointed and delicate. She rose from her sitting position in one sinuous movement that made the breath catch in the throat of every man who watched her. A bare midriff, lines of muscle on either side of the navel. Unshod feet, slender limbs the colour of honey.

"I am Kersik," she said in Normannic that had a slight burr to it, an old-fashioned slowness. "Greetings and welcome."

Murad recovered more quickly than any of them, and, aristocratic to his fingertips, he bowed with a flourish of the winking rapier.

"Lord Murad of Galiapeno at your service, lady." Hawkwood noted wryly that he did not introduce himself as his excellency the governor.

But the woman Kersik looked past him to where Bardolin stood with the imp perched, bedraggled and dripping, on his shoulder.

"And you, brother," she said. "You are doubly welcome. It is a long time since a Master of Disciplines came to our shores."

Bardolin merely nodded stiffly. For a moment they stared into each other's eyes, the battered old wizard and the slim young woman. Bardolin frowned, and she smiled as though in answer, eyes dancing.

There was a pause. The soldiers were drinking the woman in, but she seemed unperturbed by their hungry regard.

"You are bound for the city, I take it," she said lightly.

Murad and Hawkwood shared a glance, and the scarred nobleman bowed again. "Yes, lady, we are. But we are sadly puzzled as to how to get there."

"I thought as much. I will take you, then. It's a journey of many days."

"You have our thanks."

"Your men have been eating too much of the wrong kinds of fruit, Lord Murad of Galiapeno," Kersik said. "They have the air of the flux about them."

"We are unaccustomed as yet to your country and its ways, lady."

"Of course you are. Put your men into camp here in the clearing. I'll fetch them something to calm their stomachs. If they start the journey to Undi in this condition they might not finish it."

"*Undi*. Is that the name of your city?" Hawkwood asked. "What language might it be in?"

"In an old, forgotten language, Captain," the woman said. "This is an old continent. Man has been here a long time."

"And from whence did you come? I wonder," Hawkwood muttered, unsettled by being called "Captain." How had she known?

Kersik glanced at him sharply. She had heard his whispered comment.

"I'll return ere nightfall," she said then. And disappeared.

The men blinked. They had seen a tan blur across the clearing, nothing more.

"A witch, by Ramusio's beard," Murad growled.

"Not a witch," Bardolin told him. "A mage. The Dweomer is thick about her. And something else as well." He rubbed his face as though trying to scrub the weariness from it.

"Sorcery, always sorcery," Murad said bitterly. "Maybe she has gone to collect a few cohorts of her fellow warlocks. Well, I wonder what they'll make of Hebrian steel."

"Steel will do you no good here, Murad," Bardolin said.

"Maybe. But we have iron bullets for the arquebuses. That may give them pause for thought. Sergeant Mensurado!"

"Sir."

"We'll make camp, do as we're told. But I want the slow-match lit, and every weapon loaded. I want the men ready to repel any attack."

"Yes, sir."

AS the light died and the night swooped in once more, the company gathered about three campfires, each big enough to roast an ox over. The soldiers stood watch with powder-smoke from the glowing match eddying about their cuirasses, stamping their feet and whistling to keep awake, or slapping at the incessant probing of the insects.

"Will she come back, do you think?" Hawkwood asked, grimacing as he kneaded his bad shoulder.

Murad shrugged. "Why not ask our resident expert in all things occult?" He nodded at Bardolin.

The mage seemed on the verge of sleep, his imp lying wide-eyed and watchful in his lap. His head jerked, and the silver stubble on his chin glistened in the firelight.

"She'll be back. And she'll take us to this city of hers. They want us there, Murad. If they didn't, we'd be dead by now."

"I thought they'd prefer us sunk somewhere in the Western Ocean," Hawkwood said. "Like the caravel's crew."

"They did, yes. But now that we're here, I believe they are interested in us." *Or in me*, the thought came, alarming and unwelcome.

"And just who are *they*, Mage?" Murad demanded. "You speak as though you knew."

"*They* are Dweomer-folk of some kind, obviously. Descendants of previous voyagers, perhaps. Or indigenous peoples maybe. But I doubt that, for they speak Normannic. Something has happened here in the west. It has been going on for centuries whilst we've been fighting our wars and spreading our faith oblivious to it. Something different. I'm not sure what, not yet."

"You're as vague as a fake seer, Bardolin," said Murad in disgust.

"You want answers; I cannot give them to you. You will have to wait. I've a feeling we'll know more than we ever wanted to before this thing is done."

They settled into an uncomfortable silence, the three of them. The fires cracked and spat like angry felines, and the jungle raved deliriously to itself, a wall of dark and sound.

"What bright fires," a voice said. "One might almost think you folk were afraid of the dark."

Their heads snapped up, and the woman Kersik was standing before them. She carried a small hide bag which stank like rancid sap. The tiny hairs on her thighs were golden in the firelight. As her mouth smiled its corners arced up almost to her ears and her eyes were two light-filled slits.

Murad sprang to his feet and she stepped back, becoming human again. Mensurado was berating the sentries for having let her slip past them unseen.

"You do not need men to keep watch in the night," she said. "Not now I am here." She dumped the hide bag on the ground. "That is for those among you whose guts are churning. Eat a few of the leaves. They'll calm them."

"What are you, a forest apothecary?" Murad asked.

She regarded him, her head on one side. "I like this one. He has spirit." And while Murad considered this: "Best you should sleep. We will walk a long way tomorrow."

THEY set sentries, though she laughed at them for doing so. She sat cross-legged off at the edge of the firelight as she had been sitting when first they had seen her. Men made the Sign of the Saint when they thought she was not looking. They ate their meagre supper of gleaned fruit, not one of them trusting her enough to try the bag of leaves she had brought. Then they lay down on the wet ground with sword and arquebus close to hand.

Bardolin's imp could not settle. It would nestle against him in its accustomed sleeping position and then shift uneasily again and squirm out from beside him to take in the camp and the sleeping figures, the watchful sentries.

It nudged him awake some time before the dawn and in the half-sleeping state between unconsciousness and wakefulness he could have sworn that the camp was surrounded by a crowd of figures which stood motionless in the trees. But when he sat up, scraping at his gummed eyelids, they were gone and the Kersik woman was sitting cross-legged, not a particle of weariness in her appearance.

Murad sat with his back to a tree opposite, an arquebus in his hands with its slow-match burnt down almost to the wheel. His eyes were feverish with fatigue. He had watched her all night it seemed. The woman rose and stretched, the muscles rippling under her golden skin.

"Well rested for the travel ahead?" she asked.

The nobleman looked at her through sunken eyes.

"I'm ready for anything," he said.

THIRTEEN

Eighteen days they travelled through the unchanging jungle. Eighteen days of heat and rain and mosquitoes and leeches and mud and snakes.

Looking back on it, Hawkwood found it remarkable how quickly the men had been worn down. These were hardened campaigners who had seen battle in the dust-choked furnaces of the summer Hebros valleys. On board ship they had seemed swaggering veterans, hard men with rough appetites and constitutions of iron. Here they sickened like kittens.

They buried the first six days after they had met their new guide, the woman Kersik.

Glabrio Feridas, soldier of Hebrion. He had crouched shakily in the jungle to ease his overworked bowels, and it seemed to those who came across his corpse that he had voided all the blood that the mosquitoes and leeches had left in him.

After that, men ate the leaves that Kersik had brought for them. They avoided the fruits she told them to avoid,

and they boiled their water every evening in their rusting
helmets. There was no more flux, but many of them continued to feel feverish and soon the stronger men were
carrying the armour of those who could no longer support
its weight.

On the tenth day, Murad was finally prevailed upon
by Hawkwood and Bardolin to allow the soldiers to take
off the armour and cache it. The men piled it up and
covered it with fallen branches and leaves, blazed a dozen
trees around it and marched on the lighter by fifty
pounds, clad in their leather gambesons.

They made better time after that. Hawkwood calcu-
lated they were travelling roughly nor'-nor'-west, and
they were covering perhaps four leagues a day.

On the twelfth day Timo Ferenice was the second man
to die. A snake had sidled up to his ankle as he stood
nodding on sentry duty and bit quickly and efficiently
through boot, hose and skin. He had died in convulsions,
spraying foamy spittle and calling on God, Ramusio and
his mother.

The following day they hit upon a road, or track rather.
It was just wide enough for two men to walk abreast, a
tunnel of beaten earth and close-packed stones seemingly
well cared for, which led them farther to the north. They
had bypassed the cluster of lights Murad had seen from
the Spinero and were travelling almost parallel to the far-
off coast.

All the while they travelled, Kersik strode along easily
at the front of the column, frequently pausing to let the
gasping men behind her catch up. The land rose almost
imperceptibly, and Bardolin hazarded that they were
nearing the southern slopes of the great conelike mountain they had sighted on the first day of their landfall.

Their pace should have quickened upon hitting the
road, but it seemed to the members of the company that
their strength was ebbing. Lack of sleep and poor food
were taking their toll, as was the unrelenting heat. By the

seventeenth day, the twenty-first out of Fort Abeleius, the soldiers were stumbling along in linen undershirts, their leather gambesons too rotten and mouldering to be of any further use. And medicinal leaves or no, two of them were so far gone in fever they had to be carried in crudely thrown-together litters by their exhausted comrades.

"I believe I have yet to see her sweat," Hawkwood said to Bardolin as they sat in camp that night. Kersik was off to one side, her legs folded under her, face serene.

Bardolin had been nodding off. He started awake and caressed the chittering imp. The little creature ate better than any of them, for it happily gorged itself on all manner of crawling things it found in the leaf litter. It was just back from foraging and was contentedly grinning in Bardolin's lap, its belly as taut as a drum.

"Even wizards sweat," the old mage said, irritated because he had been on the verge of precious sleep.

"I know. That is why it's so odd. She doesn't seem real, somehow."

Bardolin lay back with a sigh. "None of it seems real. The dreams I have at night seem more real than this waking life."

"Good dreams?"

"Strange ones, unlike any I have known before. And yet there is an element of familiarity to them too. I keep feeling that everything here I have come across splices together somehow—that if I could but step back from it I would see the pattern in the whole. That inscription on the statue we found—it reminds me of something I once knew. The girl: she is Dweomer-folk, certainly, but there is something unknown at work in her also, something I cannot decipher. It is like trying to read a once-known book in too dim a light."

"Maybe there will be a brighter light for you once we hit upon this city. Tomorrow, she says, we'll arrive there. I wish I could say I was looking forward to it, but the discoverer in me has lost some of his relish for our expedition."

"*He* has not," Bardolin said, and he waved a hand to where Murad was doing his nightly rounds of the campfires, checking on his men.

"He cannot keep it up much longer," Hawkwood said. "I don't believe he's had more than an hour's sleep a night since we left the coast."

Murad looked less like an officer administering to his men than a ghoul preying on the sick. His lank hair fell in black strings across his face and the flesh had been pared away from nose and cheekbones and temples. His scar now seemed an extravagant curl of tissue, like an extra thin-lipped mouth on the side of his face. Even his fingers were skeletal.

"We have been ashore scarcely a month," Hawkwood said quietly. "We have buried five shipmates in that time—maybe more back at the fort by now—and the rest of us are close to breaking down. Do you really believe this land can ever be fit for civilized men, Bardolin?"

The mage shut his eyes and turned away. "I'll tell you after tomorrow."

THAT night the dream came to Bardolin again. But this time it was the woman Kersik who came to him in the night, nude, her skin a flawless bloom of honey. She was incandescently beautiful despite the two rows of nipples that lined her torso from pectoral to navel and the claws which curled at the tips of her fingers. Her eyes blazed like the sun behind leaves.

They made love on the yielding ground beyond the camp. This time Bardolin was atop her, grinding into her firm softness with the vigour of a young man. And all around the straining couple a masque of fantastic figures danced and capered madly, spindle-thin, cackling, with green slits for eyes and hornlike ears. Bardolin could feel their feet, light as leaves, dancing in the hollow of his back as he pushed into the woman below him.

But there was another presence there. He arched his head to see, despite the grip of her hand on the nape of his neck, a tall darkness towering above the frolics.

A shifter in wolf form.

NONE of them had slept well. Bardolin ached as though someone had been kicking him all night. The company dragged themselves erect, Sergeant Mensurado hauling men to their feet. Kersik looked on like an indulgent parent.

Murad appeared from the trees. He had shaved, the blood on his chin testimony to the effort it had cost him. His straggling hair had been tied back and he had changed into a clean shirt which was nonetheless dotted with mould. He looked almost fresh, despite the sunken glitter of his eyes.

"So we are to see this city of yours today," he said to Kersik.

The woman seemed amused at some private joke, as she often did. "Why yes, Lord Murad, if your comrades are fit to march."

"They're fit. They're Hebrian soldiers," Murad drawled, and he turned away from her with such languid contempt that Hawkwood actually found himself admiring him. The woman's smile took on a fixed quality for a second, and then became pure sunshine again.

They set off after a frugal meal of the inevitable fruit. It was weeks since any of them had tasted meat, and they were becoming nostalgic even at the thought of the ship's salt pork.

Another day of labour. Though they were tramping a passable road, they still had to take it in turns to carry the two delirious soldiers. Even Murad did his share.

There was more life in the jungle here, if that were possible. Not the squeakings and scurryings of before, but the crash and thump of larger beasts moving off in

the vegetation. Kersik appeared oblivious to them, but
the company travelled with loaded weapons and drawn
swords. They were aware of a subtle change in their surroundings. The trees were smaller, the canopy less dense.
Almost the forest here looked like secondary growth, a
reclaiming of land once cleared.

To reinforce this opinion they came across the remains
of huge stone-built buildings half hidden at the sides of
the narrow road. Bardolin wanted to pause and examine
them, for they seemed to be liberally dotted with carved
writing, but Kersik would not allow it. When he asked
her about them she seemed even more reluctant to give
out information than she had throughout the journey.

"They are *Undwa-Zantu*," she said at last, surrendering
to Bardolin's badgering.

"What does that mean?" the mage asked.

"They are *old*, from the earlier time, the first peoples."

With that one sentence she let loose a torrent of questions from both Bardolin and Hawkwood, but would answer none of them.

"You will learn more when we get to the city," was
all she would say.

THEY had reached the foot of the mountain to the
north of their anchorage. They could see it clearly,
even through the canopy overhead. It reared up like a
grey wall above the jungle, the forest struggling to maintain itself at its knees but gradually thinning and clearing
all the same.

"How far do you think we have come?" Bardolin
asked Hawkwood.

The mariner shrugged with one shoulder. He had taken
bearings as often as he could—Kersik had been inordi-
nately fascinated by the compass—and he'd had both
Masudi and big Cortona pacing to check his own count,
but in the day-to-day labour it was probable that major
inaccuracies had crept in.

"We're walking almost due north now," he said. "Since we met the girl, I'd say we've come some sixty leagues, but we've changed course several times."

They were far back in the file. Kersik was twenty yards in front, Murad striding beside her like her consort. Bardolin lowered his voice. Her hearing was better than a beast's.

"She slips past questions like a snake. She knows everything, I'm sure of it—perhaps the whole history of this land, Captain. For it has a history, you can be sure of that. These ruins look as ancient as the crumbling Fimbrian watchtowers you can see up in the Hebros passes, and they are six centuries old and more."

"Maybe we'll find answers in this city she keeps talking about, though where it might be I'm sure I don't know. The way she talks it must be on the slope of this damned mountain; but how could one build a city on slopes so steep?"

"I don't know. It may be that if there is a city there somewhere we'll find more answers in it than we bargained for."

The file halted. Murad called for them at its head and the wizard and the mariner hurried past the line of soldiers.

The way was blocked by a trio of figures so fantastic that even Murad had momentarily lost his poise.

Two were inhumanly tall, eight feet perhaps. They were black-skinned, a black so dark that it made Masudi's skin appear yellowish. Their limbs were bare and they wore simple loincloths, but where their heads should have been were incredible masks. One was of a leopard-like creature, only heavier and more muscular. The other had the head of a great mandrill, with bright blue patches of ridged flesh on either side of the flaring nose.

But the masks were not masks. The leopard-head licked its teeth and the eyes moved. The mandrill sniffed

the air, its nostrils quivering. In their human hands, the
two creatures carried bronze-bladed spears twice the
height of a man, wickedly barbed.

The third figure was tiny by comparison, shorter even
than Hawkwood. He seemed entirely human and his skin,
though deeply tanned, was as pale as a Ramusian's. He
wore a shapeless bag of supple hide for a hat, and white
linen robes which concealed his entire body except for
small, broad-fingered hands. His face was pouchy and
bejowled, eyes bright and black shining out of puffy
sockets. Were it not for the strange garments, he might
have passed for a well-to-do merchant of Abrusio with
too many rich meals and too much good wine under his
belt. His only ornament was a pendant of gold in the
shape of a five-pointed star which enclosed a circle. It
hung from his wattled neck on a gold chain whose links
were as thick as a child's finger.

"Gosa," Kersik said, and she bowed. "I have brought
the Oldworlders."

The leopard head growled deeply.

"Well done," the man in the linen robes said. "I
thought I'd provide you with an escort into Undi. And
my curiosity was consuming me. It's been a long time."
His glance strayed to the members of the company who
stood silent behind Kersik, even Murad at a loss for
words.

"Greetings, brother," Gosa said to Bardolin.

The mage blinked, but did not reply. His imp uttered
a single little yelp which sounded almost interrogative.
The leopard head growled again.

Murad stepped forward, clearly angered by being left
out of the exchanges. Immediately mandrill head levelled
the spear until it touched his chest, stalling him.

A series of clicks. Sergeant Mensurado, Cortona and
the other soldiers had their arquebuses in the shoulder,
the wheel-locks cocked back, the muzzles pointed
squarely at the exotic trio in the middle of the track.

Powder-smoke eddied about the company. Gosa sniffed at it, and smiled to show yellow teeth, canines from which the gums had retreated.

"Ah, the very essence of the Old World," he said, not at all put out by the weapons pointed at his ample belly. "Put up your weapons, gentlemen; you will not need them here. Ilkwa—for shame—can't you see the man is merely trying to introduce himself?"

The tall spear swung back to the vertical. Murad nodded at Mensurado and the arquebuses were uncocked, though the men kept their slow-match lit.

"Murad of Galiapeno at your service," the nobleman said wryly.

"Gosa of Undi at yours," the plump, berobed man said, bowing slightly. "Will you follow me into our humble city, Lord Murad? There are refreshments waiting, and those who wish to can bathe."

Murad bowed in his turn. Gosa, Kersik and the two outlandish beast-men led off. The company fell in behind them, still hauling the two litters with the fever-ridden soldiers.

The world changed in a twinkling.

The jungle disappeared. One moment they were walking under the shadowed shelter of the forest, and the next it had vanished. Uninterrupted sunshine blinded them. The borderline between the riotous vegetation and barren emptiness was as clear-cut as if a giant razor had shaved the mountainside clean of all living things.

Now they could see the true size of the peak which soared above them. Its head was lost in cloud, and though from a distance it had seemed perfectly symmetrical, closer up they could decipher broken places in its cone, ragged tears in the flanks of stone, petrified waterfalls where long-cold lava had once gushed forth. The place was a wilderness, a desert leached of colour, defined only in greys and blacks. There were dunes of what looked like ebony sand, weird bubbles of basalt, outwellings and

holes and the stumps of solidified geysers. A landscape,
Bardolin thought, like that which he had glimpsed
through Saffarac's viewing device long ago. Lunar, dead,
otherworldly.

The going was harder, and the men puffed and panted
as they laboured up the steep slopes. There was still a
road of sorts here, a crude pavement of tufa blocks.
Cairns marked its twistings and turnings as it zigzagged
up the face of the mountain. The men gasped in the withering heat, choking on volcanic dust, their faces becoming black with what looked like soot and tasted like ash.
It dried out their mouths and gritted between tongue and
teeth.

"I see no city," Murad rasped to Kersik and Gosa.
"Where are you taking us?"

"There is a city, trust me." Gosa beamed at him, a
benevolent gnome with obsidian shards for eyes. "Undi
is not so easily chanced across unless one is led there by
one of its inhabitants. And this is Undabane whose knees
we clamber across. The Sacred Mountain, heart of fire
whose rages have been tamed." He stopped. "Have patience, Lord Murad. It is not much farther."

The company became strung out despite all that Murad
and Mensurado could do. It was a line of antlike figures
struggling up the monstrous mountainside, the soldiers
pausing to catch their breaths, the litter-bearers changing
every hundred yards. So it was Hawkwood and Bardolin,
at the front, who saw it first.

A cleft in the mountain's conical top, a huge rent in
its perfect shape. The summit was still some six or seven
thousand feet above, but here they were working slowly
around its western face, and the cleft was invisible from
the northern approach. A glimpse of dark walls within
shooting to incredible heights, and something else.

At the base of the cleft was a monumental statue
weathered almost into shapelessness by the elements. It
was perhaps a hundred and twenty feet high, and vaguely

humanoid. A stump of a spear in one crumbling fist. Deep eyes visible in a face which had a snout for a nose. The impression of a powerful torso. The thing had been built out of tufa blocks bigger than the carrack's longboat and they were eroding at their joints so that it seemed to have a grid imposed upon it.

The rest of the party caught up as Gosa, Kersik and the two beast-men paused. There was only one litter.

"Forza died," Murad said to the questioning looks. "We don't know when—no one noticed. We built a cairn over him." He seemed angry with himself, as though it were his fault. "God curse this pestilent country."

Gosa pursed his lips disapprovingly, but did not comment. The company moved on again, the soldiers sullen and silent, even Mensurado cast down. The sick man's death seemed like an omen.

Rocks clattered under their feet, and their sodden boots were full of ash, blistering their heels and toes. They were down to their last swirl of water in the canteens, and Murad would let no one finish it.

Into the shade of the massive statue, their heads hardly reaching to its ankles.

The world contracted. They were trudging through a narrow place whose walls soared up hundreds, perhaps thousands, of feet on either side, a snake-thin gap in the wall of the mountain through which the wind whistled and hissed like a live thing. Water dripped down in glittering fringes from the gorge sides, and the men stood under the drips with their tongues out, begging. Flat, iron-tasting water full of grit, it nonetheless enabled their tongues to move about inside their mouths again.

The world opened once more, or rather exploded upon them. Like the change from jungle to ashen desert on the slopes of the mountain, the transition was abrupt and astonishing.

They found themselves on a shelf of rock, maybe a thousand feet up *inside* the mountain. Undabane was hollow, a vaster version of the crater which Murad had named the Spinero. They could look up and see the walls of the mountain rearing on all sides, sheer as cliffs, unscalable. The blue unclouded sky was a semicircle of pure colour above the rock.

And below there was a disc of brilliant jungle, as though someone had lifted it whole, a small, flat world of it, and placed it inside Undabane after knocking the summit off the hollow mountain. The view stupefied them. There was a dark curve across the crater floor, the shadow of the mountain's lip dragging in the wake of the sun. Looking at it, Bardolin understood in an instant the phases of the moon.

There were buildings down there amid the trees: pylons of black basalt monumental in size but dwarfed to insignificance by their setting, flat-roofed houses built entirely of stone, a stepped pyramid as tall as Carcasson's spires, the step faces painfully bright with gold. Avenues and roads. A city, indeed. A place utterly alien to anything they had seen before or imagined. It took speech out of their parched mouths and left them gaping. Even Murad could find nothing to say.

"Behold Undi," Gosa said with quiet satisfaction. "The Hidden City of the Zantu and the Arueyn, the Heart of Fire, the Ancient Place. Worth a trek, is it not?"

"Who built this?" Bardolin asked at last. "Who are these people you name?"

"All questions will be answered in the end. For now, we have but a little descent and then you will be able to rest. Word of your coming has gone ahead of you. There is food and drink waiting, and succour for the sick amongst you."

"Take us down there, then," Murad said with brutal directness. "I'll have no more of my men die in this hellhole because you stand there preening yourself."

Gosa's eyes flared with an odd light, though his face did not change. He inclined his head slightly and led the

party onwards, down a track which had been hewn out
of the side of the mountain. Kersik shot the nobleman a
look of pure venom, however.

They stumbled and stared and cursed their way down
to the floor of the crater, which by this time was nearly
all in shadow. There were dark clouds gathering in the
circle of sky thousands of feet above them, the beginning
of the daily downpour. They found themselves walking
along a wide, well-paved road which had rain gutters on
either side. It was a street of sorts, for there were more
of the flat-roofed buildings set back from it amid the
trees. As they hobbled deeper into the heart of the city
the trees grew sparser and the buildings closer together.
And there were people here.

They were tall, lean and black and were dressed in a
white linen-like cloth. They were delicately featured,
with sharply chiselled noses and thin lips. The women
were as tall and stately as queens, their breasts bare, gold
pendants ornamenting them. Many had their bodies decorated with some form of intricate ritual scarring which
swirled in circles and currents around their torsos and on
their cheeks. They regarded the company with interest,
and many pointed especially at Masudi, who was like
them and yet not like them. But they were restrained,
dignified. The company passed through what could only
be a market place, with stalls of fruit and meat set out,
but there was little hubbub. The people there halted to
stare at the ragged soldiers of Hebrion, and then went on
about their business. To Hawkwood, who knew the
crazed, chaotic bazaars of Ridawan and Calmar, the or-
derliness was unnerving. And there were no children anywhere to be seen. Neither were there any animals, not
even a stray dog or lounging cat—if they had such things
in this country.

The pyramid towered above the rest of the buildings,
its gold dulled now as the sun was hidden and the afternoon rain began to tumble down inside the mountain.

Gosa and his inhuman companions led the company to a
tall, square house off the market place and thumped upon
a hardwood door. It was opened by a tall old man whose
hair was as white as his face was black.

"I have brought them, Faku," Gosa said. "See they are
well cared for."

The old man bowed deeply, as inscrutable as a Merduk
grand vizier, and the company trooped into the house.

"Rest, eat, bathe. Do whatever you wish, but do not
leave the building," Gosa told them cheerfully. "I will be
back this evening, and tomorrow . . . tomorrow we will
see about answering some of those questions you have
been harbouring for so long."

He left. The old man clapped his hands and two
younger versions of himself appeared, shut the doors of
the room—which the company saw was a kind of foyer—
and stood expectantly.

Murad and his soldiers were glaring about them as if
they expected an armed host to rush out of the walls. It
was Hawkwood who smelled the cooking meat first. It
brought the water springing into his mouth.

Kersik said something to the old man, Faku, and he
clapped his hands again. His helpers swung open side
doors in the big room, and there was the gurgle of running water. Marble pools with fountains. Clean linen.
Earthenware bowls of fruit. Platters of steaming meat.

"Sweet Saints in heaven," Bardolin breathed. "A
bath!"

"It might be a trick," Murad snarled, though he was
swallowing painfully as the smell of the food obviously
tantalized him.

"There is no trick." Kersik laughed, darted into the
room and snatched a roasted rib of the meat, biting into
it so the juices ran down her chin. She came over to
Bardolin and stood close to him.

"Will you not try it, Brother Mage?" she asked, offering him the rib.

He hesitated, but she thrust it under his nose. That secret amusement was in her eyes. "Trust me," she said in a low voice, vixen grin on her face, mouth running with the meat juices. "Trust me, brother."

He bit into the rib, shredding meat from the bone. It seemed the most delicious thing he had ever tasted in his life.

She wiped the grease out of his silver beard, then spun from him. For an instant he could see her eyes in the air she had vacated, hanging as bright as solar after-images.

"You see?" she said, holding up the rib as though it were a trophy.

The men scattered, making for the piled platters and bowls. Faku and his colleagues stood impassively, looking on like sophisticates at a barbarian feast. Bardolin remained where he was. He swallowed the gobbet of meat and stared at Kersik as she danced about the gorging soldiers and laughed in Murad's livid face. Hawkwood remained also.

"What was it?" he asked Bardolin.

"What do you mean?"

"What kind of meat?"

Bardolin wiped his lips free of grease. "I don't know," he said. "I don't know." His ignorance suddenly seemed terrible to him.

"Well, I doubt they brought us this far to poison us." Hawkwood shrugged. "And by the Saints, it smells wholesome enough."

They gave in and joined the soldiers, wolfing down meat and slaking their thirst with pitchers of clear water. But they could not manage more than half a dozen mouthfuls ere their stomachs closed up. Bloated on nothing, they paused and saw that Kersik was gone. The heavy doors were shut and the attendants had disappeared.

Murad sprang up with a cry and threw himself at the doors. They creaked, but would not move.

"Locked! By the Saints, they've locked us in!"

The tiny windows high in the walls, though open to the outside, were too small for a man to worm through.

"The guests have become prisoners, it would seem," Bardolin said. He did not seem outraged.

"You had an idea this would happen," Murad accused him.

"Perhaps." Even to himself, Bardolin's calm seemed odd. He wondered privately if something had indeed been slipped into the food.

"Did you think they would leave us free to wander about the city like pilgrims?" Bardolin asked the nobleman. The meat was like a ball of stone in his stomach. He was no longer used to such rich fare. But there was something else, something in his head which disquieted him and at the same time stole away his unease. It was like being drunk; that feeling of invulnerability.

"Are you all right, Bardolin?" Hawkwood asked him, concerned.

"I—I—" Nothing. There was nothing to worry about. He was tired, was all, and needed to get himself some sleep.

"*Bardolin!*" they called. But he no longer heard them.

FOURTEEN

*W*HAT *is your name?*

"Bardolin, son of Carnolan, of Carreirida in the Kingdom of Hebrion." Was he speaking? It did not matter. He felt as safe as a babe in the womb. Nothing would touch him.

That's right. You will not be harmed. You are a rare bird, my boy. How many of the Disciplines?

"Four. Cantrimy, mindrhyming, feralism and true theurgy."

Is that what they call it now? Feralism—the ability to see into the hearts of beasts, and sometimes the craft to duplicate their like. You have mastered the most technical of the Seven Domains, my friend. You are to be congratulated. Many long hours in some wizard's tower poring over the manuals of Gramarye, eh? And yet you have none of the instinctive Disciplines—soothsaying, weather-working. Shifting.

A tiny prick in the bubble of well-being which enfolded Bardolin, like a sudden draught in a sturdy house, a breath of winter.

"Who are you?"

Kersik! She has much to learn of herbalism yet. Rest easy, brother of mine. All will come to light in the end. I find you interesting. There has not been much to seize my interest this last century and more. Did you know that when I was an apprentice there were nine disciplines? But that was a long time ago. Common witchery and herbalism. They were amalgamated, I believe, in the fifth century and brought under that umbrella term "true theurgy," to the profit of the Thaumaturgists' Guild and the loss of the lesser Dweomer-folk. But such is the way of things. You interest me greatly, Bardolin son of Carnolan. There is a smell about you that I know. Something there is of the beast in you. I find it intriguing . . . We will speak again. Rejoin your friends. They worry about you, worthy fellows that they are.

HE opened his eyes. He was on the floor and they were clustered around him with alarm on their faces, even Murad. He felt an insane urge to giggle, like a schoolboy caught out in some misdeed, but fought down the impulse.

A wave of relief. He felt it as a tactile thing. The imp clung to his shoulder whimpering and smiling at the same time. Of course. If he had been drugged it would have been left bereft, lost, the guiding light of his mind gone from it. He stroked it soothingly. He had put too much into his familiar, too much of himself. The things were meant to be expendable. He felt a thrill of fear as he caressed it and it clung to him. Much of his own life force had gone into the imp, giving it an existence beyond him. That might not be to the good any more.

Drugged? Where had that thought come from?

"What happened?" Hawkwood was asking. "Was it the food?"

It was an enormous effort to think, to speak with any sense.

"I—I don't know. Perhaps. How long was I gone?"

"A few minutes," Murad told him, frowning. "It happened to no one else."

"They are playing with us, I think," Bardolin said, getting to his feet rather unsteadily. Hawkwood supported him.

"Lock us up, drug one of us—what else do they have in store?" the mariner said.

The soldiers had retrieved their arms and lit their match; it stank out the room.

"We'll have that door down, and shoot our way out of here if we have to," Murad said grimly. "I'll not meet my end caught like some fox in a trap."

"No," Bardolin said. "If they are expecting anything, they are expecting that. We must do it another way."

"What? Await yonder wizard with a tercio of his beast-headed guards?"

"There is another way." Bardolin felt his heart sink as he said the words. He knew now what he would do. "The imp will go for us. It can get out of the window and see what is happening outside. It may even be able to open the door for us."

Murad appeared undecided for a moment; clearly, he had had his heart set on a fighting escape. He was still wound up too tightly; they all were. A spark would set them off and they would die here with the questions unanswered, and that was intolerable.

"All right, we'll let the imp go," Murad conceded at last.

Bardolin let out a sigh. He was utterly tired. He felt sometimes that this land had fastened on him like a succubus and would feed off him until there was nothing left but a withered husk that would blow away to ash in the wind. Soothsaying was not one of his Disciplines, and yet the presentiment had been upon him ever since they had made landfall that there was something deadly to the ship's company and to the world they had left behind, and it resided here, on this continent. If they escaped they would take it back to the old world with them like a disease which clung to their clothing and nestled in their blood. Like the rats which scurried in the darkness of the ship's hold.

He bent to the bewildered imp, stroking it.

"Time to go, my little friend." *Can you see the way out, up there in the wall? Up you go. Yes! That's it. Where the last of the daylight is coming through.*

The imp was peering through the narrow aperture in the wall. The entire company watched it in silence.

"I may leave you for some time," Bardolin told them. "But don't be alarmed. I am travelling with the imp. I will return. In the meantime, stand fast."

Murad said something in reply, but he was already gone. The world had become a vaster place in the wink of an eye, and the very quality of Bardolin's sight had changed. The imp's eyes operated in a different spectrum of colours: to it the world was a multivaried blend of greens and golds, some so bright they hurt to look at. Stone walls were not merely a blank façade, but their warmth and thickness produced different shadows, glowing outlines.

The imp looked back once, down at the silent room full of men, and then it was through the high, narrow window. It was hungry and would have liked to share in the meats that had been laid out for the company, but its master's will was working in it. It did as it was told.

Indeed, in some ways Bardolin *became* the imp. He felt its appetites and fears, he experienced the sensation of the rough tufa blocks under his hands and feet, he heard the noises of the city and the jungle with an enhanced clarity that was almost unbearable until he became used to it.

The rain had ended, and the city was a dripping, steam-shrouded place, fogged as a dawn riverbank. The light was dimmer than it should be; the crater sides would cut out much of the light in the later afternoon.

What to make of this hidden city? The volcanic stone of the buildings was dark and cold, but the lambent, upright figures of people were about—not many of them now—and a single crescent slice of sunshine glowed like molten silver way up on the side of the crater: the last of the departing sun. Soon night would settle. Best to wait a few minutes.

Something else, though. A . . . smell which seemed tantalizingly familiar.

The imp clambered down the side of the high wall like a fly, head-first. It reached the ground and scampered into a cooler place of deeper shadow, an alleyway it might have been called in Abrusio. There it crouched and breathed in the air of the dying day.

The daylight sank as though someone had slowly covered a great lamp somewhere beyond the horizon of the world. It was actually possible to see the growing of the night as a palpable thing. In minutes the city had sunk into darkness.

But not darkness to the imp. Its eyes began to glow in the murk of the alley and its vision grew sharper.

Still, that smell somewhere, hauntingly reminiscent of something from the past.

To our duty, my diminutive friend, Bardolin's mind gently prodded as the imp crouched puzzled and fascinated in the humid shadow.

It obeyed the urging of a mind that was moment by moment becoming one with it. Obediently it scuttled around the side of the house which imprisoned the company, looking for the front door, another window, any means of entry or egress.

There were things moving in the streets of the city. To the imp they were sudden dazzling brightnesses darting in and out of sight. It was the heat of their bodies that made them so luminous. The imp whimpered, wanted to

hide. Bardolin had to sink more of his will into it in order
to keep it under his command.

There—the door they had entered the place by. It was
closed, but there was no sign of Kersik, Gosa or the
beast-headed guards. The imp sidled over to it, listened
and heard Murad's voice within. It chuckled to itself with
an amusement that was part Bardolin's, and set one glowing eye to the crack at the door's foot. No lights, no
warmth of a waiting body.

Push at the door, Bardolin told it, but before it could
do as it was told it felt a growing heat behind it, the hot
breath of some living thing. It spun around in alarm.

A man might have seen a tall, bulking shadow looming
over him, with two yellow lights burning and blinking
like eyes. But the imp saw a brightness like the sun, the
effulgence of a huge, beating heart in the bony network
of the chest. It saw the heat rising off the thing in shimmering waves of light. And as the mouth opened, it
seemed to breathe fire, a smoking calefaction that
scorched the imp's clammy skin.

"Well met, Brother Mage," a voice said, distorted, bestial but nonetheless recognizable. "You are ingenious, but
predictable. I suppose you had no choice: that festering
pustulence of a nobleman would have left you no other
options."

The thing was a massively built ape, a mandrill, but it
spoke with the voice of Gosa.

"Come. We have kept you waiting long enough. Time
to meet the master."

A huge paw swept down and scooped up the imp even
as it leapt for freedom. The were-ape that was Gosa
laughed, a sound like the whooping beat of a monkey's
cry but with a rationality behind it that was horrible to
hear. The imp was crushed to the thing's shaggy breast,
choking at the vile heat, the stench of the shifter which
it had smelled but not quite recognized. It had been confused by memories of Griella, the girl who had been a

werewolf and who had died before they had set foot on this continent. It had not recognized the peril close by.

The were-ape limbered off at speed, its free hand bounding it forward whilst the short back legs pushed out, a rocking movement which seemed to gather momentum. Bardolin saw that his familiar was being taken towards the stepped pyramid at the heart of the city.

They passed other creatures in the streets: shifters of all kinds, nightmarish beasts that reeked of Dweomer, warped animals and men. Undi at night was a masque of travesties, a theatre of the grotesque and the unholy. Bardolin was reminded of the paintings in the little houses of worship in the Hebros, where the folk were still pagan at heart. Pictures of hell depicting the Devil as master of a monstrous circus, a carnival of the misshapen and the daemonic. The streets of Undi were full of capering fiends.

He should withdraw now, leave the imp to its fate and slip back into his own body, rejoin the others and warn them of what was waiting for them outside the walls of the house in which they were imprisoned. But somehow he could not, not yet. Two things kept him looking out of the imp's eyes and feeling its terror: one, he felt nothing but stark fear at the thought of abandoning his familiar, and with it a goodly portion of his own spirit and strength; the other was nothing more or less than sheer curiosity, which even in the midst of his fear kept him drinking in the sights of the nocturnal city through the imp's eyes. He was being taken to someone who perhaps knew all the answers, and as Murad hungered after power so Bardolin thirsted for information. He would remain in the imp's consciousness a little longer. He would see what was at the heart of this place. He would *know*.

"WHAT can he be at?" Murad demanded, pacing back and forth. The room was lit only by a few tiny earthenware lamps they had found among the platters and dishes, but the burning match of the soldiers glowed in tiny points and the place was heavy with the reek of the powder-smoke. Bardolin lay with his eyes open, unseeing, as immobile as the tomb carving of a nobleman on his sarcophagus.

"Two foot of match we've burnt, sir," Mensurado said. "That's half an hour. Not so long."

"When I want your opinion, Sergeant, I'll be sure to ask you for it," Murad said icily. Mensurado's eyes went as flat as flint.

"Yes, sir."

"It's dark out," Hawkwood said. "It could be he's waiting for the right moment. There are probably guards and it's only an imp, after all."

"Sorcerers! Imps!" Murad spat. "I've had a belly-full of the lot of them. *Brother* Mage indeed! For all we know he could be in league with his fellow necromancers, plotting to turn us over to them."

"For God's sake, Murad," Hawkwood said wearily.

But the nobleman wasn't listening. "We've waited long enough. Either the mage has betrayed us or his familiar has met with some mishap. We must get out of here unaided, by ourselves. Sergeant Mensurado—"

"Sir."

"—I want that door down. Two men to carry our slumbering wizard—Hawkwood, your seamen will do. We'll want as many arquebuses ready as possible."

"What about Gerrera, sir?" one of the soldiers spoke up, pointing to their fever-struck comrade who lay on his litter on the floor, his face an ivory mask of sweat and bone-taut skin.

"All right. Two more of you take him. Hawkwood, lend a hand there. That leaves us with seven arquebuses free. It'll have to do. Sergeant, the door."

Mensurado and Cortona, the biggest men in the company except perhaps for Masudi, squared up to the hardwood double doors as if they were an opponent in a fight ring. The two men looked at each other, nodded sombrely and then charged, leading with their right shoulders.

They rebounded like balls bounced off a wall, paused a second, and then charged again.

The doors creaked and cracked. A white splinter line appeared near the hinges of one.

Three more times they charged, changing shoulders each time, and on the fifth attempt the doors sagged and broke, the beam which had closed them smashed in two, their bronze hinges half dragged out of the wall.

The company hesitated a moment as the echo of the crash died away. Cortona and Mensurado were breathing heavily, rubbing their bruised shoulders. Finally Hawkwood raised one of the earthenware lamps and peered out into the gloom of the foyer beyond, in which they had met the old man Faku and his helpers. The place was deserted, the door to the street closed. The night seemed eerily silent after the jungle noise they were used to.

"There's no one here, it seems," he told Murad. He lifted the lamp this way and that. There was a stone staircase at the back of the big room. The running water of the pools had stopped except for an occasional drip. Shadows wheeled and flitted everywhere like restless ghosts.

"Now what?"

"We'll search the other rooms," Murad said. "Mensurado, see to it. It may be that the imp is lost somewhere upstairs or nearby. And that Kersik woman may still be around."

Mensurado led a trio of soldiers upstairs.

"I don't like it," Hawkwood said. "Why leave us unguarded? They must have guessed we were capable of breaking down the door."

"They are magicians and sorcerers, every one," Murad said. "Who knows how their minds work?"

They heard the boots of Mensurado and his comrades

clumping above their heads, then snatches of talk, and finally a cry, not of fear, more of surprise.

Hawkwood and Murad glanced at one another. There was a flurry of voices above, the thumping of feet and heavy things scraping across the floor.

Mensurado came running down the stairs. "Sir—take a look at this." He was holding a handful of coins.

Normannic gold crowns. On one side was a depiction of the spires of burnt Carcasson, on the other a crude, stylized map of the continent. Bank-minted money belonging to no kingdom in particular, but used in the great transactions between kings and governments. Coins such as this bribed princes, bought mercenaries, forged cannons.

"There are chests and chests of the damned stuff up there, sir," Mensurado was saying. "A king's ransom, the hoard of a dozen lifetimes."

Murad bit into one of the coins. "Real, by God. There's chests of the stuff you say, Sergeant?"

"Hundredweights, sir. I've never seen anything like it. The treasury of a kingdom could not hold more."

Murad threw aside the coin; it fell with a sweet kiss of metal on stone. "Everyone upstairs. Leave Gerrera and the mage here for the moment. I want every pouch and pocket filled. You shall each have your share, never fear."

He and Mensurado had a glitter in their eyes that Hawkwood had not seen before. As they left the room Hawkwood bent down beside the motionless Bardolin and shook him.

"Bardolin, for God's sake wake up. Where are you?"

No answer. The old mage's eyes remained wide open, his face as immobile as that of a corpse.

It sounded as though cascades of coins were being poured over the floor upstairs. Sharp blows as someone attacked a chest, splintering wood. Hawkwood felt no urge to join in the greedy festival. He loved gold as much as the next man, but there was a time and a place for it. As Mihal left his side to chance his luck upstairs, Hawkwood curtly ordered him back. Both Mihal and Masudi looked at him imploringly, but he shook his head.

"You'll see, lads. Nothing good will come of this gold. Me, I'll be happy to get out of here with my skin intact. That's riches enough."

Masudi grinned ruefully. "You can't run with your pockets full of gold, I'll warrant."

"Nor eat it, neither," Mihal added, resigned.

The soldiers began staggering downstairs, pockets bulging. They had even stuffed coins down the front of their shirts, giving themselves rattling paunches. Four of them were bearing two wooden chests between them. Murad descended last, holding up a lamp and seeming a little dazed.

"We'll come back," he was saying in a low voice. "We'll come back with a dozen tercios one day."

"I'd rather we had the tercios now," Hawkwood rasped. "If you want to leave this place, we'd best be going at once. There's no telling when that Gosa and his creatures will be back."

"I am not unaware of the need for urgency, Captain," Murad snapped. "What we carry away with us here could outfit an entire flotilla of ships, and can you imagine the backing I could call on when it became known that the Western Continent was stuffed with gold? We could bring an army here, and extirpate these monsters and sorcerers from the land for good."

"It's gold, yes, but minted in the form of Normannic crowns, Murad," Hawkwood said. "Did you think of that? What are they using it for, if not to spend in the Old World? We know nothing about what is going on in this land, or how it affects the Ramusian states at home."

"We'll find out another time," the nobleman said. "For now, all I want is to get clear of this place. Mensurado, the door. You men, pick up Gerrera."

Lumbering, rattling and clinking, the soldiers gathered themselves and prepared to leave.

But the door opened before Mensurado got to it. A black-skinned figure dressed in white stood there. The old man, Faku. His mouth opened.

A shot, amazingly loud in the confined space. Faku was hurled back out of the doorway.

"One less sorcerer," Mensurado snarled, and reloaded his arquebus with practised speed.

"We must move quickly," Murad said. "That shot will rouse the city. Out! Bring the chests."

What with the chests and the limp forms of Bardolin and Gerrera, only Mensurado and two other soldiers had their hands free. The company filed out into the hot night, stepping over Faku's body as though it were a pothole in the road. Hawkwood closed the old man's eyes, cursing under his breath.

"This way. Quickly," Murad said, leading off. The company followed him at a jog-trot, sweating and gasping ere they had gone a hundred yards. Coins slipped out of the soldiers' pockets to clink at the roadside.

The city seemed deserted. Not a light to be seen anywhere, not a living soul on the streets. But Hawkwood was continually aware of movement, like a flickering at the corner of his eye. The place was so dark that it was impossible to be certain. He looked up to see a disc of star-filled sky above the crater-rim, and was almost sure he saw things moving in that sky, wheeling darknesses which stood out against the stars. He had the uncomfortable notion that the city was not quiet and empty at all, but teeming with invisible, capering life.

The company paused to rest in a narrow side street, the soldiers who carried the heavy chests massaging their bloodless hands. They had come half a mile maybe from the house in which they had been imprisoned, and there was still no sign of a pursuit. Even Murad seemed uneasy.

"I thought the entire city would have been about our ears by now," he said to Hawkwood.

"I know," the mariner replied. "Everything is wrong, strange. What happened to Bardolin's imp, and to Bardolin himself? Why can't he come back to us? Are we being allowed to escape because—"

"Because what?"

"Perhaps because they have what they want."

Murad was silent for a long minute. At last he said: "It is a pity about the mage, but if you are right then we may yet get away unscathed. And after all, we bear him with us. His mind may yet return." He would not meet Hawkwood's eye, but scanned the massiveness of the buildings, the trees which were beginning to rear up in their midst; they were not far from the crater wall, and the narrow gorge which was their only exit.

"Time to move on."

The soldiers shouldered their burdens once more, and the company staggered onwards. The attack came so suddenly that they were surrounded before they had seen their assailants. The night was sprinkled with raging eyes, and huge forms charged them. The quiet was broken by roars and screams and wails from a hundred bestial throats. The men at the rear died before they could even drop the chests that weighed them down.

FIFTEEN

AT the top of Undi's pyramid was another building whose sides curved inwards towards its roof. The Gosa shifter took the imp inside, and then in a series of bounds it leapt up a narrow line of steps. They were on the roof of the structure, a square platform perhaps three fathoms to a side. There the imp was gently lowered to its feet, and the were-ape left. A grating of stone, and the opening in the platform closed behind it.

Bardolin looked up with the imp's eyes to see the encircling pitch-night of the crater walls, and above them a roundel of stars turning in the endless gyre of heaven. There were so many of them that they cast a faint, cold light down on the city. Many of them were recognizable—it was possible to glimpse Coranada's Scythe—but they seemed to be in the wrong positions. Even as Bardolin watched, a streak of silver lightninged across the welkin, a star dying in a last flare of beauty.

"Awe-inspiring, isn't it?" a voice said, and the imp jumped. Instinctively it looked for somewhere to hide, but the stone platform was stark and bare, and there was nothing beyond its edge but a long fall to the pyramid steps below.

Bardolin gripped the will of the creature in his own, steadied it, held it fast.

There was a man on the platform. He had come out of nowhere and stood with the starlight playing across his features. He seemed amused.

"An attractive little familiar. We in Undi do not use them any more. They are a weakness as well as an asset. Are they still as hard to cast through as I remember?"

Bardolin's voice issued out of the imp's mouth. The creature's eyes went dull as he dominated it completely.

"Hard enough, but we get by. Might I ask your name?"

The man bowed. "I am Aruan of Undi, formerly of Garmidalan in Astarac. You are Bardolin of Carreirida."

"Have we met before?"

"In a way. But here—let me spare your trembling familiar. Take my hand."

He extended one large, blunt-fingered hand to the imp. The creature took it and Aruan straightened, pulling. But the imp did not come with him. Instead a shimmering penumbra slid out of its tiny body as though he had dragged from it its soul. He was holding on to Bardolin's own hand, and Bardolin stood there on the platform, astonished, glimmering in the starlight like a phantom.

"What did you do?" he asked Aruan. The imp was blinking and rubbing its eyes.

"A simulacrum, nothing more. But it renders communication a little easier. You need not fear; your essence, or the bulk of it, is with your sleeping body down in the city."

Bardolin's shining image felt itself with trembling hands. "This is magic indeed."

"It is not so difficult, and it makes things more ... civilized."

Bardolin folded his imaginary arms. "Why am I here?"

"Can't you answer that yourself? You are a creature of free will, as are all God's creations."

"You know what I mean. What is it you want of me?"

The man named Aruan turned away, paced to the edge of the platform and stared out over the city of Undi. He was tall, and dressed in voluminous, archaic robes that a noble might have worn in the days of the Fimbrian Hegemony. He was bald but for a fringe of raven hair about the base of his skull, for all the world like a monk's tonsure. He had a beaked nose and deep-set eyes under bristling, fantastic brows, high, jutting cheekbones strangely at odds with the rest of his rather aristocratic face, as if someone had melded the features of a Kolchuk tribesman and a Perigrainian Landgrave. Hauteur and savagery, Bardolin noted them both.

"This is how I once looked," Aruan said. "Were you to see my true form now you might be repelled. I am old, Bardolin. I remember the days of empire, the Religious Wars. I have known men whose fathers spoke with the Blessed Saint. I have seen centuries of the world come and go."

"No man is immortal," Bardolin said, fascinated and apprehensive at the same time. "Not even the most powerful mage."

Aruan turned away from the dark city, smiling. "True, too true. But there are ways and means of staving off death's debt collectors. You ask what it is I want of you, and I am wandering around the answer. Let me explain something.

"In all the years I have been here, we have seen many ships arrive from the Old World—more than you could ever have imagined. Most of them carried cargoes of gold-hungry vultures who simply wanted to claim this, the Zantu-Country, and rape it. They were adventurers, would-be conquerors, sometimes zealots filled with missionary zeal. They died. But sometimes they were refugees, come fleeing the pyres of Normannia and the purges of the Inceptines. These people, for the most part, we welcomed. But we have never encountered an Old-worlder with your . . . potential."

"I don't understand," Bardolin said. "I am a common enough brand of mage."

"Technically, perhaps you are. But you possess a duality which no other mage who has come here from across the ocean has possessed, a duality which is the very key to our own thaumaturgical hierarchy here in the west."

Bardolin shook his head. "Your answers only provide the spur to further questions."

"Never mind. It will become plain enough in the time to come."

"I want you to tell me about this place—how you got here, how this began. What is happening."

Aruan laughed, a guffaw which made him sound like a hearty ruffian. "You want our history then, the centuries of it, laid before you like a woven tapestry for your eyes to drink in?"

"I want explanations."

"Oh—so little you think you are asking, eh? *Explanations*. Well, the night is fine. Give me your hand again, Brother Mage."

"A phantom hand."

"It will suffice. See? I can grasp it as though it were flesh and blood. In the other I will take your imp; it would not do to leave him alone here."

Something happened which Bardolin, for all his expertise in the field of Dweomer, could not quite catalogue. The platform disappeared, and they were thousands of feet up in the air and still rising. The air was cooler here, and a breeze ruffled Aruan's hair.

I can feel the breeze; I, a simulacrum, Bardolin thought with a start of fear. And then he realized that it was the imp's sensations he was feeling. Had to be. A simulacrum could not be given physical sensation.

Or could it? He could feel Aruan's hand in his own, warm and strong. Was that the sensation of the imp or himself?

They stopped rising. Bardolin could look down like a god. The moon had risen and was a bitten apple of silver which lit up the Western Ocean. The vault above Bardolin's head, strangely, did not feel any closer. The stars were clearer, but as far away as ever.

The incredible vastness of the world, night-dark and moon-silver, was staggering. The sky was a bright vault which spun endlessly above the sleeping earth, the Western Ocean a tissue of wrinkled silver strewn with the gossamer moonlight. And the Western Continent was a huge, bulking darkness in which only a few scattered lights burned. Bardolin could see the watchfires of Fort Abeleius on the coast, the tiny pricks of light that were the stern and masthead lanterns on the *Osprey* offshore, and inland red glows like scattered gleeds from an old fire.

"Restless forces of the world, at play amid the earth's foundations," Aruan said, sounding as though he were quoting something. "Volcanoes, Bardolin. This country is old and torn and troubled. It stirs uneasily in its sleep."

"The craters," Bardolin said.

"Yes. There was a great civilization here once, fully as sophisticated as that which exists upon Normannia. But the forces which create and destroy our world awoke here. They annihilated the works of the ancients, and created Undabane, the Holy Mountain, and a score of lesser cones. The *Undwa-Zantu* died in a welter of flame and ash, and the survivors of the cataclysm reverted to barbarism."

"The dark, tall people who inhabit your city."

"Yes. When first I came upon them, in the year of the Saint one hundred and nine, they were savages and only legends and ruins remained of the noble culture they had once possessed. They called themselves *Zantu*, which in their tongue signifies the Remnant, and their ancestors they called *Undwa-Zantu*, the Elder Remnant. Their mages—for they had been a mighty folk of magic—had degenerated into tribal shamans, but they preserved much that was worth knowing. They were a unique people, that elder race, possessed of singular gifts."

But Bardolin was gaping. "You've been here . . . how long? Four and a half centuries?"

Aruan grinned. "In the Old World I was a mage at the court of King Fontinac the Third of Astarac. I sailed into the west in a leaky little caravel called the *Godspeed*, whose captain was named Pinarro Albayero, may God rest his unhappy soul."

"But how—?"

"I told you: the shamans of the Zantu preserved some of the lore of their ancestors, theurgy of a potency to make what we called Dweomer in the Old World look like the pranks of a child. There is power in this country, Bardolin; you will have noticed it yourself. The mountains of fire spewed out raw theurgy as well as molten rock in their eruptions. And Undabane is the fountain-head, the source. The place is virtually alive. And the power can be tapped. It is why I am still here, when my poor frame should be dust and dry bone long since."

Bardolin could not speak. His mind was busy taking in the enormity of what Aruan was saying.

"I came here fleeing the purges of the High Pontiff Willardius—may he rot in a Ramusian hell for ever. With some of my comrades, I took ship with a desperate man, Albayero of Abrusio. He was nothing more or less than a common pirate, and he needed to quit the shore of Normannia as badly as we did." Aruan paused for a moment, and his eyes became vacant, as if looking back on that awful expanse of centuries, all gone to ash now.

"Every century or so," he went on, "there is a convulsion in the Faith of the Ramusians, and they must renew their beliefs. They do so with a festival of slaughter. And always their victims are the same.

"We fled one such bloodbath, my colleagues and I. Most of the Thaumaturgists' Guilds of Garmidalan and Cartigella became fugitives, for as I am sure you know, brother, the more prominent you are in our order, the less chance you have of being overlooked when the Ravens are wetting their beaks.

"So we took ship, some score of us with our families, those who had them, in the cranky little vessel of Pinarro Albayero.

"Albayero had intended to make landfall in the Brenn Isles, but a northerly hit us, taking us down to North Cape in the Hebrionese. We rounded the point with the help of the weather-workers amongst us, but not even they could help us make up our lost northing. The storms we rode would brook no interference, even from the master-mages amongst us. So we rode them out in our little ship, the weather-workers having to labour merely to keep us afloat. We were driven into the limitless wilderness of the Western Ocean, and there we despaired, thinking that we would topple off the edge of the world and plummet through the gaps between the stars.

"But we did not. We had hoped to find an uninhabited island among the archipelago of the Brenn Isles—for there were still such things, back in the second century—but now we had no idea where we might be cast ashore. The winds were too strong. It seemed almost as though God Himself had set His face against us, and was bent on driving us off the face of His creation.

"I know better now. God was at hand, watching over us, guiding our ship on the one true road to our salvation. We made landfall seventy-eight days after rounding North Cape, ninety-four after our departure from Cartigella.

"We landed on a continent which was utterly alien to anything we had experienced before. A place which was to become our home."

Aruan paused, chin sunk on breast. Bardolin could imagine the amazement, the joy and the fear which those first exiles must have felt upon walking up the blazing beach to see the impenetrable dark of the jungle beyond. For them there had never been any question of turning back.

"Half of us were dead within six months," Aruan went on, his voice flat, mechanical. "Albayero abandoned us, weighed anchor one night and was across the horizon before we had realized he was gone. He sold his knowledge to the nobility of Astarac, I afterwards found, enabling others to attempt the voyage in times of desperation. A good thing, as it turned out, for it meant that once or twice in the long, long years and decades and centuries following we had injections of new blood.

"We tamed the Zantu with feats of sorcery, and they came to serve and worship us. We lifted them out of savagery, made them into the more refined people you see today. But it was a long time before we truly appreciated their wisdom and learned to leave behind the prejudices of our Ramusian upbringing. We cleared Undi, which was an overgrown ruin lost in the belly of Undabane, and made it our capital. We made a life, a kingdom of sorts if you like, here in the wilderness. And we were not persecuted. You will never smell a pyre's stink in this country, Bardolin."

"But you did something, didn't you? I have seen manbeasts here, monstrosities of Dweomer and warped flesh."

"Experiments," Aruan retorted quickly. "The new power we discovered had to be explored and contained. A new set of rules had to be written. Before they were, there were some regrettable . . . accidents. Some of us went too far, it is true."

"And this no longer goes on?"

"Not if I do not wish it," Aruan said without looking at him.

Bardolin frowned. "A society glued together by the Dweomer. Part of me rejoices, but part of me recoils also. There is such scope for abuse, for—"

"For evil. Yes, I know. We have had our internal struggles over the years, our petty civil wars, if I can dignify them with that title. Why else do you think that out of all the founders of our country I alone remain?"

"Because you are the strongest," Bardolin said.

Aruan laughed his full, boisterous laugh again. "True enough! Yes, I was strongest. But I was also wisest, I think. I had a vision which the others lacked."

"And what do you see with this vision of yours? What is it you want out of the world?"

Aruan turned and looked Bardolin in the eye, the moonlight crannying his features, kindling the liquid sheen of his eyes. Something strange there, something at once odd and familiar.

"I want to see your people and mine take their rightful place in the world, Bardolin. I want the Dweomer-folk to rise up and cast away their fears, their habits of servitude. I want them to claim their birthright."

"Not all the Dweomer-folk are men of education and power," Bardolin said warily. "Would you have the herbalists and hedge-witches, the cantrimers and crazed soothsayers have their say in some kind of sorcerous hegemony? Is that your aim, Aruan?"

"Listen to me for a moment, Bardolin. Listen to me without that dogged conservatism which marks you. Is the social order which permeates Normannia so fine and noble that it is worth saving? Is it just? Of course not!"

"Would the social order which you would erect in its place be any more just or fair?" Bardolin asked. "You would substitute one tyranny for another."

"I would liberate an abused people, and remove the cancer of the religious orders from our lives."

"For someone who has spent the centuries here in the

wilderness you seem tolerably well informed," Bardolin told him.

"I have my sources, as every mage must. I keep a watch on the Old World, Bardolin; I always have. It is the home of my birth and childhood and young manhood. I have not given up on it yet."

"Are all your agents in Normannia shifters, then?"

"Ah, I wondered when we would get to that. Yes, Ortelius was one of mine, a valuable man."

"What was his mission?"

"To make you turn back, nothing more."

"Our ship carried the Dweomer-folk whom you would like to redeem; they were fleeing persecution, and yet you would have sent them back to the waiting pyres."

"Your ship also carried an official representative of the Hebrian crown, and a contingent of soldiers," Aruan said dryly. "They I could do without."

"And the other vessel, which ran aground and was wrecked on these very shores? Did you have a hand in that?"

"No, upon mine honour, Bardolin. They were simply unlucky. It was not part of my plan to massacre whole ship's companies. I thought that if I made the carrack, the ship with the leaders aboard, turn back the lesser vessel would follow."

"Am I then to thank you for your humanity, your restraint, when the beast you ordered aboard was responsible for the foul deaths of my shipmates?" Bardolin was angry now, but Aruan answered him calmly.

"The exigencies of the situation allowed no other recourse—and besides, Ortelius was outside my control. I regret unnecessary death as much as the next man, but I had to safeguard what we have built here."

"In that case, Aruan, you will have to make sure that none of the members of this current expedition ever leave this continent alive, won't you?"

There was a small silence.

"Circumstances have changed."

"In what way?"

"Perhaps we are no longer so concerned with secrecy. Perhaps other things occupy our minds."

"And who are *we*? Creatures such as your were-ape Gosa? Why must you always choose shifters as your minions? Are there no decent, proper mages left to you here in the west?"

"Why Bardolin, you sound almost indignant. You surprise me, you of all people."

"What do you mean?"

"I told you earlier."

"You've told me nothing, nothing of importance. What have you been doing here for all these centuries? Playing God to the primitives, indulging in petty power plays amongst yourselves?"

Aruan came close to the sparkling phantom that was Bardolin's presence.

"Let me show you what we have been doing over these lost years, Brother Mage, what tricks we have been learning out here in the western wilderness."

There was a change, as swift as breath misting a cold pane of glass. Aruan had disappeared, and in his place there loomed the hulking figure of a full-blooded shifter, a werewolf with lemon-bright eyes and a long muzzle glimmering with fangs. Bardolin's imp whimpered and hid behind his master's translucent simulacrum.

"It's not possible," Bardolin whispered.

"Did I not tell you, Bardolin, that we had found new and powerful wisdom among the inhabitants of this continent?" Aruan's voice said, the beast's muzzle contorting around the words, dripping ropes of saliva which glistened in the moonlight.

"It's an illusion," Bardolin said.

"Touch the illusion then, Brother Illusion."

Of course—Bardolin at this moment was no more than an apparition himself, a copy of his true self, conjured up by the incredible power of this man, this beast before him.

"I am no simulacrum, I assure you," Aruan's voice said.

"It is impossible. Sufferers of the black disease cannot learn any of the other six disciplines. It is against the very nature of things. Shifters cannot also be mages."

The Aruan shifter drew close. "They can here. We all are, friend Bardolin. We all partake of the beast in this country; and now so do you."

Something in Bardolin quailed before the werewolf's calm certainty.

"Not I."

"But you do. You have looked into the very heart and mind of a shifter at the moment of its transformation. More, you have loved one of our kind. I can read this in you as though it were inked across the parchment of your very soul." The beast laughed horribly.

"Griella."

"Yes—that was the name. The memory of that moment is burned within you. There is a part of you, deep in the black spaces of your heart, which would gladly have joined her in her suffering, could she but have loved you in return . . .

"Your imp is a poor sort of buffer against probing, Bardolin. Where you yourself might hold out against me, he is a free conduit to the heart of your fears and emotions. You are a book lying open to be read any time I have a desire to read."

"You monster!" Bardolin snarled, but fear was edging an icicle of dread into his flesh.

The werewolf came closer until the heat and stink of it were all around him and the great head blotted out the stars. They stood on the pyramid once more: Bardolin's image could feel the stone of it under its soles.

"Do you know how we make shifters in this country, Bardolin?"

"Tell me," Bardolin croaked. Unable to help himself, he retreated a step.

"For a person to be infected with the black disease, he must do two things. Firstly, he, or she, must have physical relations with a full-blooded shape-shifter. Secondly, he or she must eat a portion of that shifter's kill. It's that simple. We have not yet divined why certain people become certain beasts—that is a complex field which would reward more study. A question of personal style, perhaps. But the basic process is well known to us. We are a race of shape-shifters, Bardolin, and now you are one of us as you once secretly wished to be."

"No," Bardolin whispered, aghast. He remembered a kind of lovemaking, a sweating half-dreamt battle in the night. And he remembered Kersik offering him the rib of meat to bite into. "Oh, lord God, no!"

He felt a grip on his shoulder as he stood there with his hands covering his face, and Aruan the man was back again, the beast gone. His face was both kindly and triumphant.

"You belong to us, my friend. We are brothers in truth, bound together by the Dweomer and by the malady which lurks in our very flesh."

"To hell with you!" Bardolin cried. "My soul is my own."

"Not any more," Aruan said implacably. "You are mine, as much a creature in my keeping as Gosa or Kersik are. You will do my bidding even when you are unaware that the will which rules you is not your own. I have hundreds like you across the entire reach of the Old World. But you are special, Bardolin. You are a man who might in a former time have been a friend. For that reason I will leave you be for a while. Think on this at our parting: the race whose blood runs in you and me, in the veins of the herbalists and the hedge-witches and the petty cantrimers—it came from here, in the west. We are an ancient people, the oldest race in the world, and yet for centuries we have bled and died to satisfy the prejudices of lesser men. That will change. We will meet again, you and I, and when we do you will know me as your lord, and as your friend."

The wraith that was Bardolin began to fade. The imp screamed thinly and tried to run towards the spectre of its vanishing master, but Aruan caught it in his arms. It writhed there pitiably, but could not get free.

"You have no further need of your familiar, Brother Mage. He is a weakness you can do without, and I have already mapped the road from his mind to yours. Say goodbye."

With a flick of his powerful arms, Aruan wrenched round the imp's head on its slim neck. There was a sharp crack, and the little creature flopped lifelessly.

Bardolin shrieked in grief and agony, and it seemed to him as though the jungle night dissolved in a sunbrightness, a scalding holocaust which seared the interstices of his mind and soul. The world funnelled past him like a plummeting star, and he saw the city, the mountain, the black jungle of the Western Continent swoop away as though he were riding the molten halo of a blasted cannonball into the sky.

His shriek became the tail of the comet he had become. He fell to earth again, a raging meteor intent on burying itself at the heart of the world.

And struck, passing through a terrible burning and light into utter darkness.

SIXTEEN

THERE was at once too much and too little to take in. Hawkwood was absurdly reminded of a festival he had attended once in southern Torunna, when the effigies of the old gods had been displayed to public ridicule: huge constructions of wicker and cloth and wood in every grotesque shape and form dancing madly with the teams of men who lurked inside their colourful carcasses, until it was impossible to tell one warped form from another and they had dissolved into a whirling confusion of monstrous faces and limbs.

Here, it was dark. There were no colours, simply a monochrome nightmare. Shadows with blazing eyes which seemed to shoot up out of the very ground, the heat from their raging darknesses a palpable thing even in the depths of the night. Forms rather than bodies. A picture here of an animal's head set upon a bipedal frame, the warm splash of blood, the screaming. It passed with the vivid unreality of a dream. A dark mirage. But it was real.

The men at the rear screamed horribly, the chest they bore torn out of their hands. A crash, and then a shower of tinkling gold across the roadway. Shadows lifted the two men high in the air and then something happened too quickly to make out, and they were in pieces, their viscera ribboning out like flung streamers, their bodies become meat and shattered bone which were flung away.

As the shadows closed in, the men at the front fired their arquebuses, flashes and plumes of smoke. There were howls of pain, despairing wails from the approaching shapes.

The rest of the soldiers had dropped the other chest, and also their sick comrade, Gerrera. They bunched together and levelled their own weapons. Gerrera screamed as the shadows came upon him and he was engulfed, torn apart. A volley of arquebus fire, the iron bullets tearing into the ranks of the half-glimpsed foe and the night was clawed apart by their screams. Huge bodies could be seen decorating the roadway, immobile but at the same time subtly changing in bulk and shape.

The attackers drew off for a moment, and Murad's soldiers reloaded their firearms feverishly.

"We must make a run for it," the nobleman said, his narrow chest heaving and the sweat standing out on his face. "It's not that far to the gorge: some of us might make it. We'll all die here, else."

"What about Bardolin?" Hawkwood asked.

"He'll have to take his chances. We can't carry him. Maybe the creatures will recognize him for one of their own sorcerous folk—who knows?"

"Bastard!" Hawkwood spat, but he was not sure who he was speaking of.

The things came roaring out of the night again. Seven arquebuses went off, felling about half a dozen of them, but the rest kept coming. They were amongst the surviving soldiers, biting and clawing and bellowing: apes and jaguars and wolves, and one snake with arms which

Hawkwood slashed at viciously with his iron-bladed dirk
so that it thrashed to the ground screaming thinly, its head
becoming that of a beautiful woman even as its coils
lashed in its death throes.

Cortona was smashed to the ground by a great were-
ape and had his face ripped off with a twist of its fist.
Murad seized the dead man's arquebus, slid out the rammer and jammed it into the creature's reeking maw. The
iron of the rammer tore into the roof of its mouth and it
fell. Something came at him from behind and raked his
back with razor-sharp talons. He spun to find himself
facing a huge black cat, and stabbed the rammer into its
livid eye. He laughed as it shrieked and spun away, the
gun tool protruding from its punctured pupil.

One of the soldiers was hoisted into the air by two of
the beasts and torn asunder between them like a rotten
sack, his innards exploding to shower the fray with stinking gore, the gold which he had stuffed in his shirt and
pockets clinking out along with it. Another was pinioned
whilst a werewolf bit through the back of his neck, his
spine splintering in the tremendous jaws, his head lolling
on a tenuous connection of windpipe and skin.

Mensurado had followed Murad's example and was
stabbing out left and right with an iron arquebus rammer.
He was roaring in a kind of battle frenzy, shouting ob-
scenities and blasphemies, and the beasts actually made
way for him. All he had to do with his crude weapon
was break the skin, and the sorcery which maintained the
beast form of the shifter would be broken. The iron
would poison its system as surely as if a bullet had
pierced its vitals.

Hawkwood grabbed Masudi. "Take Bardolin. We're
going to run for it."

"Captain!" the big helmsman cried despairingly.

"Do as I say! Mihal, help him."

Masudi hoisted the unconscious mage on to his broad
shoulders whilst around him the dwindling company

fought for their lives. The three mariners had as secondary armament the cheaply made iron ship's knives which
were more tool than weapon, but which were more valuable than gold in the mêlée, more effective than a battery
of culverins could be. They slashed a way forward, the
iron blades snicking back and forth in their hands as
though they were threshing wheat. The beasts retreated
before them: they knew that one nick from the knives
meant death to them.

Behind the trio of desperate sailors the soldiers fought
on with rammers and gunstocks and knives. But they had
too many assailants. One by one they were enveloped,
brought down and torn to pieces. The road was littered
with gold coins and the fragments of bodies puddled with
gore and entrails. Murad, Mensurado and a couple of
others made a last effort, a combined charge. Hawkwood
risked a glance back at them, but he could only see a
crowd of monsters huddled together as if feeding at the
same trough. They broke apart as Murad, his shirt torn
from his back and his skin in strips, burst through them,
wielding a shard of an arquebus's wheel-lock. The nobleman sprinted away at unbelievable speed, a dozen
shifters in pursuit, and disappeared into the night.

Hawkwood's group shuffled onwards, turning and
spinning to keep their assailants at bay with lunges of
their dirks. The wall of the volcano towered above them
now and they were surrounded by trees and vegetation;
they had left the main part of the city. The cleft in the
crater wall could be seen as a wedge of stars ahead.

Mihal was too slow. As his arm snaked out to stab at
a shifter it caught his wrist. He was yanked off into a
scrum of snarling shadows and could not even scream
before they had finished him. One knocked Masudi down
from behind. Bardolin went sprawling and Hawkwood
staggered, his dagger flying out of his hand.

He scrabbled off on hands and knees into the bushes,
rolling and shoving himself forward into the vegetation

like a fox intent on going to earth. Then he lay, utterly
spent, the jungle teeming with howls, leaves brushing his
face. He tried to summon a prayer, a last thought, something coherent out of the terror which washed across his
brain, but his mind was blank. He lay there as dumb and
senseless as a cornered animal, waiting for death to come
ravening out of the darkness.

It came. He heard the bushes crackling, and there was
a sensation of heat beside him, the impression of a hulking presence.

Nothing happened.

He opened his eyes, his heartbeat a red light that went
on and off in his head, soughing through his throat like
the ebb and flow of an unquiet sea. And he saw the yellow eyes of the beast that lay beside him, its breath stirring his sweat-soaked forelock.

"Sweet God, get it over with," he croaked, fear
swamping him, robbing him of any last defiance.

The beast, an enormous werewolf, chuckled.

The sound was human, rational despite its author.

"Would I harm you, Captain, the navigator, the steerer
of ships? I think not. I think not."

It was gone. The night was silent, the utter silence of
the unquiet forest. Looking up, Hawkwood could see the
stars shining in between the limbs of the trees.

He waited for the beast to return and finish him, but
it did not. The night had become as peaceful as if the
carnage had been imagined, a fever dream vivid on waking. He sat up cautiously, heard a groan nearby and struggled drunkenly to his feet.

Nothing was working. His mind was immobilized in
shock, barely able to instruct the body which harboured
it. He staggered out on to the roadway and the first thing
he saw was the mocking sight of Masudi's head planted
on the paving like a fallen fruit, dark and shining.

Hawkwood gagged and threw up a thin soup of scalding bile. Other things lay on the road, but he did not care

to look at them. He heard the groan again and tottered over to its source.

Bardolin, moving feebly in a pool of Masudi's blood.

Hawkwood bent down to the mage and slapped the old man's face, hard. As if he were somehow to blame for the night's slaughter.

Bardolin opened his eyes.

"Captain."

Hawkwood could not speak, and he was shaking as though bitterly cold. He tried to help Bardolin up and slipped in the slick blood so that they were both lying in it like twins spat forth from some ruptured womb.

They lay there. Hawkwood felt that he had somehow lived through the end of the world. He could not be alive; he was in some manner of subtle hell.

Bardolin sat up rubbing his face, then fell back again. It took some minutes before finally they were both on their feet, looking like two intoxicated revellers who had splashed through a slaughterhouse. Bardolin saw Masudi's severed head and gaped.

"What is happening?"

But still Hawkwood could not speak. He dragged Bardolin away from the scene of the fighting, up the roadway to where the confining wall of the volcano reared up into the night cleft by its wedge of stars.

A S he walked, Hawkwood's strength returned and he was able to support the rubber-legged Bardolin. The mage was totally bewildered and did not seem to know where he was. He rambled on about pyramids and sea crossings and had philosophical arguments with himself about the Dweomer, reiterating its Seven Disciplines again and again until Hawkwood paused and shook him violently. That quietened him, but he seemed no less confused.

They reached the gorge which led outside the confining circle of the volcano's crater. In the darkness it was like the entrance to a primitive tomb, a megalithic burial place. It was unguarded, deserted. In fact, the entire circle of the city was dead and lightless, as though everything they had seen there had been delusion, the hallucinations of tired minds.

The pair stumbled through the cleft like sleepwalkers, tripping and rebounding off stone. They did not speak to one another, not even when they had finally come through to the other side and found themselves outside the hollow cone of Undabane with the barren slopes of the volcano stretching away below them in the moonlight, and beyond them the midnight sea of the jungle.

A shade rose out of the rocks before them and crunched through the tufa and ash until it was close enough to touch.

Murad.

Raw flesh glimmered over his naked torso, and sluggish blood welled from his wounds, black as tar. He was half bald where something had ripped his scalp from forehead to ear.

"Murad?" Hawkwood managed to ask. He could not believe that this human flotsam was the man he knew and detested.

"The very same. So they let you loose, did they? The mariner and the mage."

"We escaped," Hawkwood said, but knew that was a lie as the words passed his lips. The three of them stood as if they had not a care in the world, as if there were not a kingdom of monsters within the hollow mountain thirsting after their blood.

"They let us go," Murad said, his sneer still intact at least. "Or you, at any rate. Me I'm not so sure about. I may merely have been fortunate. How is the mage, anyway?"

"Alive."

"Alive." Suddenly Murad sagged. He had to squat down on his knees. "They killed them all," he whispered, "every last one. And such gold! Such . . . blood."

Hawkwood dragged him upright. "Come. We can't stay here. We've a long road ahead of us."

"We're walking dead men, Captain."

"No—we're alive. We were meant to stay alive, I believe, and at some point I want to find out why. Now take Bardolin's other arm. Take it, Murad."

The nobleman did as he was told. Together, the three of them stumbled down the slopes of the mountain, the ash burning in their wounds like salt.

By the time the dawn came lightening the sky they were almost at its foot, and the unchanging jungle whooped and wailed with weary familiarity before them. They plunged into it once more, becoming lost to the world of the dreaming trees, the shadowed twilight of the forest.

The hidden beast watched them as they disappeared, three wrecked pilgrims pursuing some cracked vision known only to themselves. Then it rose up out of its hiding place and followed them, as silent as a breath of air.

PART THREE

THE WARS OF THE FAITH

. . . Whensoever he made any ostyng, or inroad, into the enemies Countries, he killed manne, woman and child, and spoiled, wasted and burned, by the grounde, all that he might; leaving nothing of the enemies in saffetie, which he could possible waste or consume . . .

Chronicle of Sir Humphrey Gilbert, 1570

SEVENTEEN

CHARIBON was a prisoner of winter.

The heavy snows had come at last, in a series of blizzards which roared down out of the heights of the Cimbric Mountains and engulfed the monastery-city in a storm of white. On the Narian Hills the snow drifted fathoms deep, burying roads and villages, isolating whole towns. The fishing boats which normally plied the Sea of Tor had been beached long since, and the margins of the sea itself were frozen for half a league from the shore, the ice thick enough to bear a marching army.

In Charibon a small army of labourers fought to keep the cloisters clear of snow. They were assisted by hundreds of novices who shovelled and dug until they were pink-cheeked and steaming, and yet had the energy for snowball fights and skating and other horseplay afterwards. Unlike the poor folk of the surrounding countryside, they did not have to worry whether they would have enough food to see them through the winter. It was one of the bonuses of the religious life, at least as Charibon's clerics lived it.

The monastery-city went about its business regardless
of the weather, its rituals as changeless and predictable
as the seasons themselves. In the scriptoria and refectories the fires were lit, fed with the wood which had been
chopped and piled through the summer and autumn.
Salted and smoked meat made more of an appearance at
table, as did the contents of the vast root cellars. Enter-
prising ice fishermen hacked holes in the frozen sea to
provide the Pontiff and Vicar-General's tables with fresh
fish every now and again, but in the main Charibon was
like a hibernating bear, living off what it had stored away
throughout the preceding months and grumbling softly in
its sleep. Except for the odd Pontifical courier determined
(or well-paid) enough to brave the drifts and the blizzards, the city was cut off from the rest of Normannia,
and would remain so for several weeks until the temper-
ature dropped further and hardened the snow, making it
into a crackling white highway for mule-drawn sledges.

The wolves came down out of the mountains, as they
always did, and at night their melancholy moans could
be heard echoing about the cathedral and the cloisters. In
the worst of the weather they would sometimes even
prowl the streets of Charibon itself, making it dangerous
to walk them alone at night, and contingents of the Almarkan troops which garrisoned Charibon would peri-
odically patrol the city to clear the beasts from its
thoroughfares.

IT was after Compline. Vespers had been sung two
hours before, the monks had consumed their evening
meal and most of them were in their cells preparing for
bed. Charibon was settling down for the long midwinter
night, and a bitter wind was hurling flurries of snow
down from the Cimbrics, drowning out the howls of the
wolves. The streets of the city were deserted and even
the cathedral Justiciars were preparing for bed, having

trimmed the votive lamps and shut the great doors of Charibon's main place of worship.

Albrec's door was rapped softly and he opened it, shivering in the cold wind which he admitted.

"Ready, Albrec?" Avila stood there, muffled in hood and scarf.

"No one saw you leave?"

"The whole dormitory have their heads under their blankets. It's a bitter night."

"You brought a lamp? We'll need two."

"A good one. It won't be missed until Matins. Are you sure you want to go through with this?"

"Yes. Are you?"

Avila sighed. "No, but I'm in it up to my neck now. And besides, curiosity is a terrible thing to live with, like an itch which cannot be scratched."

"Here's hoping we can scratch your itch tonight, Avila. Here, take this." The little monk handed his Inceptine friend something hard and angular and heavy.

"A mattock! Where did you pilfer this from?"

"Call it a loan, for the greater glory of God. I got it from the gardens. Come—it's time we were on our way."

The pair of them left Albrec's cell and whispered along the wide corridors of the chapter-house where Albrec slept. Due to his position of Assistant Librarian, he had a cell to himself whereas Avila slept in a dormitory with a dozen other junior Inceptine clerics, for he had laid aside his novice's hood only three years before.

They crossed an arctic courtyard, their habits billowing in the biting wind. Scant minutes later, they found themselves outside the tall double doors of the Library of Saint Garaso. But Albrec led his friend around the side of the rime-white building, kicking his frozen, sandalled feet through piled snow and halting at a half-buried postern door. He poked his key into the hole and twisted it with a snap, then pushed the door open.

"More discreet here," he grunted, for the hinges were stiff. "No one will see us come and go."

But Avila was staring at the snowy ground about them. "Blast it, Albrec, what about our tracks? We've left a trail for the world to see."

"It can't be helped. With luck they'll be snowed over by morning. Come on, Avila."

Shaking his head the tall Inceptine followed his diminutive friend into the musty, old-smelling darkness of the library. Albrec locked the door behind them and they stood silent for a second, alarmed by the quiet of massive masonry and waiting books, the wind a mere groaning in the rafters.

Avila struck a light and their shadows leaped at them from the walls as the lamp caught. They threw back their hoods and shook snow from their shoulders.

"We are alone," Albrec said.

"How do you know?"

"I know this place, winter and summer. I can feel when the library is empty—or as empty as it ever becomes, with its memories."

"Don't talk like that, Albrec. I'm as jumpy as a springtime hare already."

"Let's go then, and stay close. And don't touch anything."

"All right, all right. Lead on, master librarian."

They navigated the many rooms and halls and corridors of the library in silence, tall cases of books and scrolls looming over them like walls. Then they began to descend, taking to narrow staircases which to Avila seemed to have been built into the very walls of the building. Finally they hauled up a trapdoor of iron-bound wood which had been concealed by a mat of threadbare hessian. Steep steps going down into uttermost dark. The catacombs.

They started down, the weight and bulk of the library hanging over and around them like a cloud. The fact that it was a winter-dark and wolf-haunted night outside should have made no difference to the darkness in here, but somehow it did. A sense of isolation stole over the pair as they stumbled through the accumulated rubbish in the catacombs and coughed at the dust they raised. It was as if they were two explorers who had somehow chanced upon the ruins of a dead city, and were creeping through its bowels like maggots in the belly of a corpse.

"Which wall is the north one?" Avila asked.

"The one to your left. It's damper than the others. Keep to the sides and don't trip up."

They felt their way along the walls, lifting the lamp to peer at the stonework. Chiselled granite, the very gutrock of the mountains hewn and sculpted as though it were clay.

"The Fimbrians must have been twenty years carving out this place," Avila breathed. "Solid stone, and never a trace of mortar."

"They were a strange people, the builders of empire," Albrec said. "They seemed to feel the need to leave a mark on the world. Wherever they went, they built to last. Half the public buildings of the Five Kingdoms date from the Fimbrian Hegemony, and no one has ever built on the same scale since. Old Gambio reckons it was pride brought the empire down as much as anything else. God humbled them because they thought they could order the world as they saw fit."

"And so they did, for three centuries or so," Avila said dryly.

"Hush, Avila. Here we are." Albrec ranged the lamp about the wall where there were mortared blocks instead of the solid stone of the rest of the place. The light showed the crevice in which Albrec's precious document had been discovered.

"Light the other lamp," the little Antillian said, and he reached into the crevice with a lack of hesitation which made Avila shudder. There might be anything in that hole.

"There's a room on the other side of this, no doubt about it. A substantial space, at any rate."

Avila found a staved-in cask amid the wreckage and rubbish. He set it on its end and placed the two lamps upon it. "What now? The mattock?"

"Yes. Give it here."

"No, Albrec. Valiant though you are, you haven't the build for it. Move aside, and keep a look out."

Avila hefted the heavy tool, eyed the wall for a second, and then swung the mattock in a short, savage arc against the poorly mortared stonework.

A sharp crack which seemed incredibly loud in their ears. Avila paused.

"Are you sure no one will hear this?"

"The library is deserted, and there are five floors of it above us. Trust me."

"Trust him," Avila said in a long-suffering voice. Then he began to swing the mattock in earnest.

The old mortar cracked and fell away in a shower. Avila hacked at the wall until the stones it held began to shift. He picked them out with the flat blade of the mattock and soon had a cavity perhaps six inches deep and two feet wide. He stopped and wiped his brow.

"Albrec, you are the only person I know who could cause me to break sweat in midwinter."

"Come on, Avila—you're nearly through!"

"All right, all right. Taskmaster."

A few more blows and then there was a sliding shower of stones and powder and dust which left them coughing in a cloud that swirled in the light of the lamps like a golden fog.

Albrec seized a lamp and got down on his knees, pushing the lamp into the hole which suddenly gaped there.

"Sweet Saints, Albrec!" Avila said in a horrified whisper. "Look what we've done. We'll never block up that hole again."

"We'll pile rubbish in front of it," Albrec said impatiently, and then, his voice suddenly hoarse: "Avila, we're through the wall. I can see what's on the other side."

"What—what is it?"

But Albrec was already crawling out of sight, his shoulders dislodging more stones and grit. He looked like a rotund rabbit burrowing its way into a hole too small for it.

H E was able to stand. Hardly aware of Avila's urgent enquiries on the other side of the wall, Albrec straightened and held up his lamp.

The room—for such it was—was high-ceilinged. Like the catacombs he had just left, its walls were solid rock. But this chamber had not been carved by the hand of man. There were stalactites spearing down from the roof and the walls were uneven, rough. It was not a room but a cave, Albrec realized with a shock. A subterranean cavern which had been discovered by men untold centuries ago and which at some time in more recent history had been blocked off.

The walls were covered with paintings.

Some were savage and primitive, depicting animals Albrec had heard of but never seen: marmorills with curving tusks and gimlet eyes, unicorns with squat horns and wolves, some of which ran on four legs, some on two.

The paintings were crude but powerful, the flowing lines which delineated the animals drawn with smooth confidence. There was a naturalism about them which was totally at odds with the stylized illustrations in most modern-day manuscripts. In the flickering lamplight one might almost think they were moving, coursing along the

walls in packs and herds and following long-lost migra-
tions.

All this Albrec took in at a glance. What claimed his
attention almost at once, however, was something different. A shape jumped out of the shadows at him and he
almost dropped his lamp, then made the Sign of the Saint
at his breast.

A statue, man high, standing at the far wall.

It was of a wolf-headed man, his arms raised, his
beast's mouth agape. Behind him on the stone of the wall
a pentagram within a circle had been etched and painted
so that the lamplight threw it into vivid relief. Before the
statue was a small altar, the surface of which had a deep
groove cut in it. The stone of the altar was discoloured,
stained as if by ancient, unforgivable sins.

There was a rattle of loose stone which made Albrec
utter a squeak of fear, and then Avila was in the room
brushing dust from his habit and looking both stern and
amazed.

"Saint's blood, Albrec, why wouldn't you answer
me?" And then: "Holy Father of us all! What is this?"

"A chapel," Albrec said, his voice as hoarse as a
frog's.

"What?"

"A place of worship, Avila. Men paid homage here
once, in some dark, lost time."

Avila was studying the hideous statue, holding his
lamp close to its snarling muzzle.

"Old stonework, this. Crude. Which of the old gods
might this one be, Albrec? It's not the Horned One, at
any rate."

"I'm not sure if it was meant to be a god, but sacrifices
were made here. Look at the altar."

"Blood, yes. Hell's teeth, Albrec, what about this?"
And Avila produced from his habit the pentagram dagger
they had found in their last visit to the catacombs.

"A sacrificial knife, probably. What made you bring it with you?"

Avila made a wry face. "To tell the truth I intended to lose it down here again. I don't want it anywhere near me."

"It might be important."

"It's more likely to be mischievous. And can you imagine me trying to explain it to the house Justiciar if it were found?"

"All right then." Albrec swung the lamp around to regard the other, darker corners of the cave. "We're forgetting what we came here for. Help me look for more of the document, Avila, and throw that thing away if you have to."

Avila tossed the dagger aside and helped Albrec sift through the rubbish which littered the floor of the cave. It seemed as if someone had tossed half the contents of a library down here a century ago and left it to rot. Their feet rested on the remains of manuscripts, and a jetsam of decaying vellum was piled against the walls like a tidemark. They knelt in it and brought the remnants to their noses, squinting at the faded and torn lettering in the light of the lamps.

"It's dry in here, or these would have been mushrooms long since," Avila said, discarding a page. "Strange—the wall beyond is damp, you said so yourself. What happened here, Albrec? What are these things, and why is this unholy chapel here in the bowels of Charibon?"

Albrec shrugged. "Men have lived on this site for thousands of years, rebuilding on the ruins of the settlements which went before them. It may be that this cave was nearer the surface once."

They found sections of texts written in the Merduk tongue with its graceful lettering and lack of illuminations. One group of pages had diagrams upon them which seemed to outline the courses of the stars. Another bore a line drawing of a human body, flayed so that the muscles and veins below the skin might be seen. The two monks made the Sign of the Saint as they stared at it.

"Heretical texts," Avila said. "Astrology, witchery. Now I know why they were walled up in here."

But Albrec was shaking his head. "Knowledge, Avila. They sealed up knowledge in here. They decided on behalf of all men what they might and might not know, and they destroyed anything which they disagreed with."

"Who are 'they,' Albrec?"

"Your brethren, my friend. The Inceptines."

"Maybe they acted for the best."

"Maybe. We will never know because the knowledge they destroyed is lost for ever. We will never be able to judge for ourselves."

"Not everyone is as learned as you, Albrec. Knowledge can be a dangerous thing in the hands of the ignorant."

Albrec smiled. "You sound like one of the monsignors, Avila."

Avila scowled. "You cannot change the way the world works, Albrec. No one man can. You can only do as you are told and make the best of it."

"I wonder if Ramusio would have agreed with that."

"And how many would-be Ramusios do you think they have sent to the pyre in the last five hundred years?" Avila said. "Striving to change the world seems to me to be a sure way of shortening one's tenure of it."

Albrec chuckled, then stiffened. "Avila! I think I have it!"

"Let me see."

Albrec was holding a few ragged pages, bound together by the remains of their cloth backing.

"The writing is the same, and the layout. And here's the title page!"

"Well? What does it say?"

Albrec paused, and finally spoke in a low, reverent

voice. " 'A true and faithful account of the life of the Blessed Saint Ramusio, as told by one who was his companion and his disciple from the earliest of days.' "

"Quite a title," Avila grunted. "But who wrote it?"

"It's by Honorius of Neyr, Avila. Saint Honorius."

"What? Like *The Book of Honorius*?"

"The very same. The man who inspired the Friar Mendicant Order, a founding father of the Church."

"Founding father of hallucinations," Avila muttered.

Albrec tucked the pages away in his habit. "Whatever. Let's get out of here. We've got what we came for."

They rose to their feet, brushing the detritus of the cave from their knees, and as they did there was a rattle of stone. They turned as one, the lamplight leaping in their hands, to find Brother Commodius appearing through the hole in the wall which led back to the catacombs.

The Senior Librarian dusted himself down much as Avila and Albrec had done whilst the pair stared at him in horror. The mattock they had left outside dangled from one of his huge hands. He smiled.

"We are well met, Albrec. And I see you have brought the beautiful Avila with you too. What joy."

"Brother, we—we were just—"

"No need, Albrec. We are beyond explanations. You have overreached yourself."

"We've done nothing wrong, Commodius," Avila said hotly. "No one is forbidden to come down here. You can't touch us."

"Be quiet, you young fool," Commodius snapped in return. "You understand nothing. Albrec does, though—don't you, my friend?" Commodius' face was hideous in its humour, the mien of a satisfied gargoyle, his ears seemingly too long to be real and his eyes reflecting the lamplight like those of a dog.

Albrec blinked as though trying to clear the dust from his eyes. Something in him seemed to calm, to accept the situation.

"You knew this was here," he said. "You've always known."

"Yes, I have always known, as have all the Senior Librarians, all the custodians of this place. We pass down the information as we do the keys of the doors. In time, Albrec, it might have been passed on to you."

"Why would I want it?"

"Don't be obtuse with me, Albrec. Do you think this is the only secret chamber in these levels? There are scores of them, and mouldering away in the dark and the silence is the vanished knowledge of a dead age, lost generations of accumulated lore deemed too harmful or heretical or dangerous for men to know. How would you like to have that at your fingertips, Albrec?"

The little monk wet his dry lips. "Why?" he asked.

"Why what?"

"Why are you so afraid of knowledge?"

The mattock twitched in Commodius' fist. "Power, Brother. Power lies in knowledge, but also in ignorance. The Inceptines control the world with the information they know and that which they withhold. You cannot give mankind the freedom to know anything it wants; that is the merest anarchy. Take that document you found down here, the one you have hidden so inadequately in your cell along with the other heretical books you have been concealing: your pitiful attempt to save a kernel from the cleansing fire."

Albrec was as white as a winding sheet. "You know of it too?"

"I have read others like it, all of which I have had destroyed. Why else do you think there are no contemporary accounts of the Saint's life extant today? In that one document resides greater power than in any king. The old pages you discovered hold within them the ability to overturn our world. That will not happen. At least, not yet."

"But it's the *truth*," Albrec cried, almost weeping. "We are men of God. It is our duty—"

"Our duty is to the Church and its shepherdship of mankind. What do you think men would do if they discovered that Ahrimuz and Ramusio were one and the same? Or that Ramusio was not assumed into heaven, but was last seen riding a mule into oblivion? The Church would be riven to its very foundations. The basic tenets of our belief would be questioned. Men might begin to doubt the existence of God Himself."

"You've told us why you are going to do what you are about to do, Commodius," Avila said with the drawl of the nobleman. "Perhaps now you'll be good enough to do it without wearying our ears further."

Commodius gazed at the tall Inceptine, as haughty as a prince before him. "Ah, Avila, you are always the aristocrat, are you not? Whereas I am merely the son of a tanner, as humbly born as Albrec there despite my black robe. How you would have graced our order. But it was not to be."

"What do you mean?" Albrec asked, and the tremor was back in his voice, fear rising over the grief.

"It's plain to see what has been happening here. Two clerics become victims of the unnatural urges which sometimes beset those of our calling. One lures the other into black magic, occult ritual"—Commodius gestured to the wolf-headed statue with the mattock—"and there is a falling-out, a fight. The lovers kill each other, their bodies laid out before the unholy altar which poisoned their minds. Not that the bodies will be found for a long time. I mean, who ever comes down here, and who will think to look beyond the rubble of a sealed wall?"

"Columbar knows we have been coming here—" Avila began.

"Alas, Brother Columbar died in his sleep this night, peacefully and in God's grace, his head resting on the pillow which stopped his breath."

"I don't believe you," Avila said, but his haughtiness was leaking away.

"It is immaterial to me what you choose to believe. You are carrion already, Brother."

"Take us both then," Avila said, setting down his lamp as though preparing for battle. "Come, Commodius: are you so doughty that you can kill the pair of us?"

Commodius' face widened into a grin which seemed to split it in twain and displayed every gleaming tooth in his head.

"I am doughty enough, I promise you."

The mattock clanked to the floor.

"The world is a strange place, Brothers," Commodius' voice said, but it sounded different, as though he were speaking into a glass. "There is more lurking under God's heaven than you have ever dreamed of, Albrec. I could have made you a glutton of knowledge. I could have sated your appetite and answered every question your mind ever had the wit to pose. It is your loss. And Avila—my sweet Avila—I could have enjoyed you and advanced you. Now it will have to be done a different way. Watch me, children, and experience the last and greatest revelation of all . . ."

Commodius had gone. In his place there loomed the brooding darkness of a great lycanthrope, a bright-eyed werewolf standing in a puddle of Inceptine robes.

"Make your peace with He who made you," the beast said. "I will show you the very face of God."

It leapt.

Albrec was shoved out of the way and hit the floor face-first. Avila had thrown himself to one side, scrabbling for the mattock. But the beast was too fast. It caught him in midair, its claws ripping his robe to shreds. A twist of its powerful arms, and Avila was flung across the cave, to strike the wall with a sickening slap of flesh. The werewolf laughed, and turned on Albrec.

"It will be quick, my little colleague, my tireless bookworm." It grasped Albrec by the neck and lifted him up as though he were made of straw. The vast jaws opened, bathing him in the stink of its breath.

But Avila was there again, his face a broken wound and something gleaming in his fist. He struck at the creature's back, trying to pierce the thick fur and failing. The beast spun round, dropping Albrec.

The Antillian watched in a daze as the werewolf that was Commodius smashed his friend across the breadth of the chamber once more. His own lamp had been broken and extinguished, and only Avila's light on the floor illuminated the struggle, making it seem a battle of shadowy titans amid the stalactites of the ceiling.

And kindling a glitter of something lying amid the detritus of the floor.

Albrec scrabbled over and grasped the pentagram dagger in his fist. He heard Avila give a last, despairing shout of defiance and hatred, and then he threw himself on the werewolf's back.

The creature straightened and the claws came reaching over its shoulders, raking the side of Albrec's neck. He felt no pain, no fear, only a clinical determination. He stabbed the pentagram dagger deep into the beast, the blade grating on the vertebrae as it shredded muscle and pierced the flesh up to its hilt.

The werewolf's head snapped back, its skull cracking against Albrec's own with a force to explode bloody lights in his head and make him release his hold and tumble to the floor like a stringless puppet.

The beast gave an odd, gargling moan. It was Commodius again, shrunken, naked, bewildered, the pentagram hilt of the dagger protruding obscenely from his back.

The Senior Librarian looked at Albrec in disbelief, shaking his head as though circumstances had baffled him, and then he crumpled on top of Albrec, a dead weight which crushed the air out of the little monk's lungs. Albrec passed out.

EIGHTEEN

THE blizzard struck as they were crossing the mountain divide. The pass disappeared in minutes and the world became a blank whiteness, featureless as a steamed-up window.

The column halted in confusion and the men fought to erect their crude canvas tents in the hammering wind. A numbing, aching time of struggle and pain, the fingers becoming blue and swollen as the blood inside them slowly crystallized, ice crackling in the nostrils and solidifying in men's beards. But at last Abeleyn and the remnant of his bodyguard were under shelter of a sort, the canvas cracking thunderously about their ears, the most accomplished fire starters amongst them striving to set light to the damp faggots they had carried all the way up from the lowlands.

It was a diminished band which accompanied the excommunicate King up into the Hebros. They had left the sailors and the wounded and the weaker of the soldiers behind to be tended by villagers in the foothills, along with an escort of unhurt veterans to guard them, for the folk in this part of the world, though Hebrian, were a hard, rapacious people who could not be trusted to treat helpless men with any charity. So it was with less than fifty men that Abeleyn had started the climb into the mountains that formed the backbone of his kingdom. He was afoot, like his subordinates, for he had put the lady Jemilla on the only horse which survived, and the dozen mules they had commandeered from the lowland villages were burdened with firewood and what meagre supplies they had been able to glean from the sullen population.

They had been eight days on the road. It was the eleventh day of Forgist, the darkest month of the year, and they were still twenty leagues from Abrusio.

THE lady Jemilla pulled her furs more closely about her and ordered her remaining maidservant to fetch her something to eat from one of the soldiers' fires. "And none of that accursed salt pork, either, or I'll have the hide flayed off you."

She was cold despite the fact that she had the best tent in the company and there was a fire burning by its entrance. She was beginning to regret her insistence that she accompany Abeleyn back to Abrusio, but she had been afraid to let the King out of her sight. She wondered what awaited them in the bawdy old city, which was under the sway of the Knights Militant and the nobles.

She bore Abeleyn's child—or so it would be believed. Were his attempt to reclaim his kingdom unsuccessful, her life would be forfeit. The present rulers of Hebrion could not allow a bastard heir of the former King to live. In carrying Abeleyn's issue she harboured her own death warrant within her very flesh.

If he failed.

He would not talk to her! Did he think that she was some empty-headed, high-born courtesan with no thoughts worth thinking beyond the bedroom? She had tried to wheedle information out of him, but he had remained as closed as an oyster.

The tattered raptor which was always coming and going was the familiar of the wizard, Golophin—everyone knew that. He was keeping the King informed as to events in his capital. But what were those events? Abeleyn was such a boy in many things—in sex most of all, perhaps—but he could suddenly go still and give that stare of his, as though he were awaiting an explanation for some offence. That was when the man, the King, came out, and Jemilla was afraid of him then, though she used all her skill at dissembling to conceal it. She dared not press him further than she already had, and the knowledge galled her immeasurably. She was as ignorant of his intentions as the basest soldier of his bodyguard.

Her thoughts wandered from the groove they had worn for themselves. The blizzard roared beyond the frail walls of the tent, and she found herself thinking of Richard Hawkwood, the mariner who had once been her lover and who had sailed away such a long time ago, it seemed. Where was he now, upon the sea or under it? Did he think of her as he paced his quarterdeck, or faced whatever perils he had to face in the unknown regions his ships had borne him to?

His child, this little presence in her belly, his son. He would have loved that: a son to carry on his name, something that whining bitch of a wife had never given him. But Jemilla had larger plans for this offspring of hers. He would not be the son of a sea captain, but the heir to a throne. She would one day be a king's mother.

If Abeleyn did not fail. If his betrothal to Astarac's princess could somehow be foiled. If.

Jemilla plotted on to herself, constructing a world of interconnecting conspiracies in her mind whilst the blizzard raged unheeded outside and the Hebros passes deepened with snow.

●　　●　　●

FOR two days Abeleyn and his entourage cowered under canvas, waiting for the blizzard to abate. Finally the wind died and the snow stopped falling. They emerged from the half-buried shelters to find a transformed world, white and blinding, drifts in which the mules might disappear, mountain peaks glaring and powder-plumed against a brilliant cobalt blue sky.

They slogged onwards. The strongest men were put to the front to clear a way for the others, wading through the drifts and bludgeoning a path forward.

Two more days they travelled in this manner, the weather holding clear and bitterly cold. Four of the mules died on their feet in the freezing star-bright nights and one sentry was found hunched stiff and rime-brittle at his post in the early morning, his arquebus frosted to his grey hand and his eyes two dead, glazed windows into nothing. But at last it seemed that the mountains were receding on either side of them. The pass was opening out, the ground descending beneath their feet. They had crossed the backbone of Hebrion and were travelling steadily down into the settled lands, the fiefs of the nobles and the wide farmlands with their olive groves and vineyards, their orchards and pastures. A kindlier world, where the people would welcome the coming of their rightful king. At least, such was Abeleyn's hope.

On their last night in the foothills they made camp and set to cooking the strips they had cut from the carcasses of the dead mules. There was still snow on the ground, but it was a thin, threadbare carpet beneath which sprouted tough clumps of brown upland grass which the surviving mules gorged themselves upon. Abeleyn climbed a nearby crag to look down on the bivouac, more the encampment of a band of refugees than the entourage of a king. He sat there in the cold wind to stare at this hard, sea-girt kingdom of his blooming out in the gathering twilight, the lights of the upland farms kindling below him spangling the tired earth.

A rustle of pinions, and Golophin's bird had landed nearby and stood preening itself, trying to sort its ragged feathers into some kind of order. Had it been a purely natural creature, it could not have flown in the state it was in, but the Dweomer of its master kept it breathing, kept it airborne to run his errands for him.

"What tidings, my friend?" Abeleyn asked it.

"News, much news, sire. Sastro di Carrera has struck some sort of deal with the Presbyter Quirion. It is rumoured that he is to be named the next King of Hebrion."

Abeleyn gave a low whistle. In his worn travelling clothes he resembled a young shepherd come to seek a herd of errant goats up here on the stony knees of the mountain—except that he had too much care written into the darknesses below his eyes, and there was a growing hardness to the lines which coursed on either side of his nose to the corners of his mouth. He looked as though he had lately become accustomed to frowning.

"Rovero and Mercado. What are they doing?"

"They barricaded off the western arm of the Lower City as you ordered, and there have been clashes with the Knights but no general engagement. The troops Mercado considers unreliable have been segregated from the rest, but we were unable to arrest Freiss. He was too quick for us, and is with his tercios."

"They don't amount to much anyway," Abeleyn grunted.

"More troops have been coming into the city though, sire. Almost a thousand, most of them in Carreridan livery."

"Sastro's personal retainers. I dare say their deployment was the price of his kingship. Is there anything official yet about his elevation to the throne?"

"No, lad. It is a court rumour. The Sequeros are infuriated, of course. Old Astolvo is barely able to hold his young bloods in check. The kingship should have been his since he is next in line outside the Hibrusids, but he did not want it. Sastro's gold, it is said, is being showered about the city like rice at a wedding."

"He'll beggar himself to get the throne. But what does that matter, when he will control the treasury afterwards? Any news from my fiefs?"

"They are quiet. Your retainers dare not do anything at the moment. The Knights and the men at arms of the other great houses are watching them closely. The slightest excuse, and they will be wiped out."

Abeleyn had a couple of elderly aunts and a doddering grand-uncle. The Hibrusid house had become thin on the ground of late. These relics of its past had left all intrigue behind and preferred to stay away from court and live their vague lives in the peace of the extensive Royal estates north of Abrusio.

"We'll leave them out of it, then. We can do it with what we have anyway. Get back to the city, Golophin. Tell Rovero and Mercado that I will be approaching the city in four days, if God is willing. I want them to have a ship waiting ten miles up the coast from the Outer Roads. There is a cove there: Pendero's Landing. They can pick me up, and we'll sail into Abrusio with all honours, openly. That will give the population something to think about."

"You will have no problems with the common folk, Abeleyn," Golophin's falcon said. "It is only the nobles who want your head on a pike."

"So much the better," the young King said grimly. "Go now, Golophin. I want this thing set in train as soon as possible."

The bird took off at once, leaping into the air, its pinions shedding feathers as they flailed frantically.

"Farewell, my King," Golophin's voice said. "When next we meet it will be in the harbour of your capital."

Then the bird was labouring away across the foothills, lost in the star-filled night sky.

• • •

THE company settled for the night, grateful for the fact that the worst of the winter weather had been left behind with the mountains. Abeleyn rolled himself in a boat-cloak and dozed by one of the soldiers' fires. He did not feel like sharing a tent with Jemilla tonight. It seemed somehow more wholesome to sleep under the stars with the firelight producing orange shadows beyond his tired eyelids.

He did not sleep for long, however. It was after midnight by the position of the Scythe when Sergeant Orsini shook him gently awake.

"Sire, pardon me, but there's something I think you should see."

Frowning, blinking, Abeleyn let himself be led out of the camp to the crag he had sat on earlier. Orsini, an efficient soldier, had placed a sentry there because it afforded a good view of the surrounding region. The sentry was there now, saluting quickly and then blowing on his cold hands.

"Well?" Abeleyn asked a little irritably.

Orsini pointed to the south-western horizon. "There, sir. What do you make of it?"

The world was dark, sleeping under its endless vault of stars. But there was something glowing at its edge. It might have been a mistimed sunset: the sky was red there, the clouds kindled with crimson light. A blush which lit up fully a quarter of the horizon glimmered silently.

"What do you think it is, sire?" Orsini asked.

Abeleyn watched the far-off flicker for a second. Finally he rubbed his eyes, squeezing the bridge of his nose as if trying to get rid of a bad dream.

"Abrusio is burning," he said.

ACROSS the breadth of Normannia, over the two great ranges of the Malvennors and the Cimbrics, down to the coast of the Kardian Sea and the city of Torunn, capital of Lofantyr's kingdom.

Here it was already dawn; the sun which would not light up Hebrion's shores for hours yet was huge over the rooftops of the city, and the streets were already busy with the morning life of the markets. Carts and waggons clogged the roadways as farmers brought their produce in to sell, and herds of sheep and cattle were being driven to the stockpens which nestled below the city wall to the west. And beyond the walls to the north the steam and reek of the vast refugee camps sprawled over the land like a rash, whilst Torunnan soldiers manned the gates in that direction, vetting every entrant into the city. Once-prosperous citizens of Aekir had turned to beggary and brigandage in the past weeks, and the more disreputable of the refugees were denied entrance to the walled centre of Torunn. Convoys of crown waggons laden with victuals were waiting to be hauled out to the camps to satisfy the immediate needs of the unfortunates, but Torunna was a country at war and had little enough to spare.

THE morning had started badly for Corfe. He was striding along the stone corridors of Torunn's Main Arsenal with Ensign Ebro hurrying to keep up beside him. The men of his new command had been grudgingly set aside a few barrack blocks for their quarters and were crammed into them like apples in a barrel. Ebro had seen to it that they were issued rations and clothes from the city stores, but as of yet not one sword or arquebus or scrap of mail had been forthcoming. And then, last night, a note had been brought to him from the Queen Dowager by a lady-in-waiting.

I have done what I could, it said. *The rest is up to you.*

So he was on his own.

He had applied to have more officers seconded to him; he and Ebro alone could not effectively command five hundred men. And he had had Ebro indent three times for armour and weapons to outfit his force, but to no avail. Worst of all was the rumour running about the Garrison Quarters that Lofantyr was going to set aside twenty tercios of the regular army for the job of subjugating the rebellious nobles in the south—the task Corfe had been entrusted with. Clearly, the King did not expect the Queen Dowager's protégé to accomplish anything beyond his own discrediting.

He hammered on the door of the Quartermaster's department, wearing again the ragged uniform he had worn at Aekir.

The Quartermaster's department of the Third Torunnan Field Army was housed in a vast string of warehouses close to the waterfront in the east of the city. The warehouses held everything from boots to waggonwheels, cannon barrels to belts. Everything needed to equip and sustain an army could be found in them, but they were giving Corfe's men nothing more than the clothes on their backs and he wanted to know why.

The Quartermaster-General was Colonel Passifal, a veteran with a short, snow-white beard and a wooden stump in place of the leg he had lost fighting Merduks along the Ostian river before Corfe was born. His office was as bare as a monk's cell, and the papers which covered his desk were set in neat piles. Requisition orders, inspection sheets, inventories. The Torunnan army had a highly organized system of paperwork which it had copied from its one-time overlord, Fimbria.

"What do you want?" Passifal barked, not looking up from the scraping nib of his quill.

"I indented for five hundred sets of half-armour, five hundred arquebuses, five hundred sabres and all the necessary accoutrements days ago. I would like to know why the requisition has not been filled," Corfe said.

Passifal looked up, his quill losing its flickering animation.

"Ah. Colonel Corfe Cear-Inaf, I take it."

Corfe nodded curtly.

"Well, there's nothing I can do for you, son. My orders are to release stores only to regular Torunnan troops for the duration—Martellus is crying out for equipment up at the dyke, you know—and that rabble the King has given you to play with are officially classed as auxiliary militia, which means that the Torunnan military is not responsible for their fitting-out. I've stretched things as it is, giving you uniforms and a place for them to lay their heads. So don't bother me any more."

Corfe leant over the broad desk, resting his knuckles on the rim. "So how am I supposed to arm my men, Colonel?"

Passifal shrugged. "Auxiliary units are usually equipped by the private individual who has raised them. Are you rich, Cear-Inaf?"

Corfe laughed shortly. "All I possess is what I stand up in."

Passifal gazed at the ragged uniform. "You got those rents at Aekir, I hear."

"And at Ormann Dyke."

"So you've smelled powder." Passifal scratched his white beard for a moment and then gestured with sudden peevishness. "Oh, take a seat, for God's sake, and stop trying to stand there on top of your dignity."

Corfe drew up a chair. Ebro remained standing by the door.

"I hear the King has played a joke on you, Colonel," Passifal said, grinning now. "He does that sometimes. The old woman rides him hard, and every so often he kicks at the traces."

"The Queen Dowager."

"Yes. What a beauty that woman was in her day. Not bad now, as a matter of fact. It's the witchery keeps her young, they say. But Lofantyr gets tired of being told which pot to piss in. He's outfitting an expedition to bring the south to heel—a proper one, infantry, cavalry and horse artillery—but he's going to let you go south and make an arse of it first to show his mother she shouldn't force her favourites on him."

"I thought as much," Corfe said calmly, though his fists clenched on his knees.

"Yes. My orders are not to let you have so much as a brass button from our stores. Those savages you style a command will have to fight with their fists and teeth alone. I'm sorry for it, Colonel, but that's the way it is."

"Thank you for explaining it to me," Corfe said in a flat voice. He rose to go.

Passifal stuck out a hand. "Not so fast! There's no hurry, is there? You served under Mogen, I take it."

"I did."

"So did I. I was a cavalryman in one of his flying columns in the days when we went out looking for the Merduks instead of waiting for them to march up to our walls."

"I also was cavalry," Corfe said, unbending a little. "But there was no need for horsemen in Aekir once the siege began."

"Yes, yes, I daresay . . . Old Mogen used to say that cavalry was the arm of the gentleman, and artillery the arm of the mechanic. How we used to love that cantankerous old bastard! He was the best man we've ever had . . ."

Passifal stared at Corfe for a long moment, as if weighing him up.

"There is a way to equip your men, after a fashion," he said at last.

"How?"

Passifal rose. "Come with me." His stump thumped hollowly on the floor as he came round from behind his desk and retrieved a set of keys from the hundreds hanging in rows along one wall of the office. "You won't like it, mind, and I'm not sure if it's right, but they're barbarians you're commanding so I doubt if they'll care.

And besides, the stuff isn't doing any good where it is, and technically it's not part of the regular military stores . . ."

Corfe and Ebro followed the one-legged Quartermaster out of the office, completely baffled.

THIS section of the Main Arsenal resembled nothing so much as the great market squares in the middle of Torunn. There were carts, waggons and limbers everywhere. Men were shifting stores from warehouses or into warehouses, culverins were being drawn by teams of oxen, and everywhere there was the squeal of pulleys and cries of labouring men. Down at the waterfront a trio of deep-hulled *nefs* had put in from the wide Torrin Estuary and were unloading cargoes of powder and pig-iron on to the quays, and a slim dispatch-runner had just docked, bearing news from the east, no doubt.

Passifal led them away from the hubbub to an older building which was set back from the waterfront. It was an ageing stone structure, windowless and somehow deserted-looking, as though it had been long forgotten.

The Quartermaster turned a key in the screeching lock and shouldered the heavy door open with a grunt.

"Stay close behind," he told Corfe and Ebro. "It's dark as a witch's tit in here. I'll strike a light."

The crack of flint on steel, and Passifal was blowing gently on the tinder-covered wick of an oil lamp. The light grew and he slapped shut the glass case on the lengthening flame, then held it up so that the radiance of it flushed the interior of the building.

"What in the world—?" Corfe said, startled despite himself.

The building was very long; it extended beyond the lamplight into darkness. And it was crowded.

Piles of armour lay all about, in places stacked until they almost reached the raftered ceiling. Helmets, gauntlets, breast- and back-plates, chainmail, vambraces, aventails, rusting and cobwebbed and dented by blows, holed by gunfire. Mixed in with the armour were weapons: scimitars, tulwars, rotten-shafted lances with remnants of silk still attached to their heads. Strange weapons, unlike any the Torunnans used—or any other western army, for that matter.

Corfe bent and picked up a helmet, turning it in his hands and wiping the dust away. It was high-crowned with a flaring neck-guard and long cheek-pieces. The helmet of one of the *Ferinai*, the elite cuirassiers of the Merduks.

"Merduk armour," he said as the realization smote him. "But what is it doing here?"

"Trophies of war," Passifal said. "Been here sixty years, since we threw back the Ostrabarian Merduks after they overran Ostiber. That was Gallican of Rone, if you remember your history. A good general. He beat them as they were approaching the Thurian Passes and sent twenty thousand of the black-hearted bastards to join their precious Prophet. The King staged a triumphal march for him here in Torunn, parades of prisoners and so on. And he shipped back a thousand sets of armour to display during it. When it was over they were dumped here and forgotten. Been here ever since. I had been meaning to get rid of them—we're pressed for warehouse space, you see . . ."

Corfe dropped the old helm with a clang. "You expect me to dress my men up as Merduks?"

"Seems to me you haven't a lot of choice, son. This is the best I can do. You'll not find a better offer in the city, unless you can persuade the Queen Dowager to stump up the necessary cash."

Corfe shook his head, thinking.

"It's not honourable, sir, dressing up as heathens," Ebro said passionately. "You should decline the command. It's what they want you to do."

"And what you want me to do also, Ensign?" Corfe asked without turning around.

"Sir, I—"

"We'll take the armour," Corfe said briskly to Passifal. "But we can't let the men wear it as it stands; folk will think we're the enemy. Have you any paint, Quartermaster?"

Passifal's white eyebrows shot up. "Paint? Aye, tons of it, but what for?"

Corfe retrieved the helm he had thrown down a moment before. "We'll paint this gear, to distinguish ourselves. Red, I think. Yes—a nice shade of scarlet so that the blood won't show. Excellent." He was smiling, but there was little humour in his face. "My men have no transport facilities. I'll have them here within the hour and they can pick out their armour themselves. Can you have the paint waiting by then, Quartermaster?"

Passifal looked as though he had been let in on an enormous joke. "Why not? Yes, Colonel, the paint will be here. It'll be worth it to see your five hundred savages dressed up in Merduk armour and splashed crimson."

Again, the mirthless smile. "Not only the savages, Quartermaster. Ebro and I will also be donning Merduk gear."

"But sir, we have our own," Ebro protested. "There's no need—"

"We'll wear what the men wear," Corfe interrupted him. "And I shall have to think up some sort of battle standard, since the regular Torunnan banners will, it seems, be denied to us. Good. All that remains now is to meet the General Staff and receive my specific orders. After that, we can begin to plan."

"No waggons or mules, no transport for our gear," Ensign Ebro said, a last-ditch effort.

Corfe grinned at him, unexpectedly good-humoured. "You forget, Ebro, that our command is composed of savage tribesmen from the mountains. What need have they of a baggage train? They can live off the country, and may God help the country."

Passifal was watching Corfe as though he had just that moment recognized him from somewhere. "I see you intend to pick up the King's gauntlet, Colonel."

"If I can, Quartermaster," Corfe said flatly, "I intend to throw it back in his face."

NINETEEN

"WHAT a pretty picture a burning city makes," Sastro di Carrera said, leaning on the iron balcony rail of the Royal palace. Abrusio spread out beyond his perch in a sea of buildings, ending almost two miles away downhill in the confusion of ships and buildings and docks which butted on to the true sea, the Western Ocean which girdled the known edges of the world. It was twilight, not because the day was near its long winter sleep, but because of the towers of smoke that shrouded the sun. Sastro's face was lit by the radiance of the burning, and he could hear it as a far thunder, the mutterings of the banished elder gods.

"May God forgive us," Presbyter Quirion said beside him, making the Sign of the Saint across his breastplate. Unlike Sastro, who was immaculately tailored, Quirion was grimed and filthy. He had lately come from the inferno below, in which men were fighting and dying by the thousand, their collective screaming drowned out by the hungry roar of the holocaust, the tearing rattles of volley-fire.

" 'And now,' " he said quietly, " 'is Hell come to earth, and in the ashes of its burning will totter all the schemes of greedy men. The Beast, in coming, will tread the cinders of their dreams.' "

"What in the world are you talking about, Quirion?" Sastro asked.

"I was quoting an old text which foretells the end of the world we know and the beginning of another."

"The end of the Hibrusid world, at any rate," Sastro said with satisfaction. "And think of the prime building land the fire will clear for us. It will be worth a fortune."

Quirion looked at his aristocratic companion with unconcealed contempt. "You are not King yet, my lord Carrera."

"I will be. Nothing will stop me or you now, Presbyter. Abrusio will be ours very soon."

"If there's anything left of it."

"The important parts will be left," Sastro said, grinning. "What a blessed thing a wind is, to blow the flames out to sea and take with it those heretical traitors and rebel peasants in the Lower City who defy us. God's hand at work, Quirion. Surely you can see that?"

"I do not like to ask God to intervene on my behalf; it smacks of hubris to assume that the Creator of the universe will think me, out of all His creations, worthy of attention. I merely try to further what I believe to be His divine will. In this instance, I needed two hundred barrels of pitch to set the Lower City alight."

"A practical kind of faith you Knights profess," Sastro said, raising his scented handkerchief to his face so that his mouth was concealed.

"I find it answers well enough."

The handkerchief was tucked back inside a snowy sleeve. "So how goes the fighting then, my practical Presbyter?"

Quirion rasped a palm over the stubble on his scalp. "Severe enough at times. Your retainers have been acquitting themselves well since I stiffened their tercios with contingents of Knights. The trained Hebrian troops are better, of course, but they are distracted by Freiss's men in their rear. He has three or four hundred arquebusiers holed up in the western arm of the Lower City cheek by jowl with the Arsenal, and they have had to tie up almost a thousand troops to keep him bottled in his bolthole."

"What of the navy? There was a lot of activity in the Inner Roads this morning."

"They were merely warping their ships off the docks; by now the fire will have swept down to the water's edge. They tried a few ranging shots at the palace this afternoon, but the distance is too far. We have a boom across the Great Harbour covered by the forts on the moles; it should suffice to keep the navy at bay, and their guns out of range of the Upper City. Abrusio was built to be defended from a seaborne attack as well as from a landward one. That works in our favour. And the confined nature of the battlefield means that our disadvantages in numbers are not so apparent."

"How far has the fire advanced?"

"As far as the Crown Wharves in the Inner Roads. It should almost be licking at the walls of the Arsenal itself. Mercado has had to set aside over three thousand men as firefighters, and another dozen tercios are overseeing the evacuation of the Lower City's population. He is as hamstrung as a bull caught half over a gate."

"His concern for the little people is laudable, but it will prove his undoing," Sastro said.

"The little people are fighting side by side with the city garrison, Lord Carrera," Quirion reminded him. "The population of the Upper City has remained neutral, but I would not place much faith in the nobles."

"Oh, they'll bend with the wind, as they always do. There's not a great house in Hebrion—even the Sequeros—who will tangle with us now. And the Merchants' Guild is being rapidly won over also. Gold is a marvellous comforter, I find, and the concessions that a future king can grant."

"Yes . . ."

The steady roar of the flames mixed with furious exchanges of arquebus fire made a collective wailing which at a distance seemed like Abrusio herself crying out in agony because of the inferno gnawing at her bowels. Warfare on this scale had not been seen west of the Cimbrics for twenty years, but now the Five Monarchies were being ripped apart by internal dissension and religious struggle: civil war in everything but name.

There were rumours that Astarac was going the way of Hebrion, the nobles fighting to depose the heretic King Mark and elect one of their own to the throne, helped, of course, by the Inceptine Order and the Knights Militant. And Torunna, as well as being menaced by the vast Merduk army which had lately been stalled at Ormann Dyke, had uprisings of its own to contend with. And Almark's king was dying—perhaps dead already—and was said to be intent on leaving his kingdom to the Church.

Quirion sighed. He was at heart a pious man, and a profoundly conservative one. Deeply convinced though he was that the Church was in the right and had to snuff out heresy wherever it took root—even were it to sprout in the palaces of kings—he did not like to see what he considered to be the natural order of things so disrupted and torn apart. Sastro now . . . he relished any anarchy which might further his own ambitions, but the Presbyter of the Knights in Abrusio would rather have been fighting heathens on the eastern frontiers than slaughtering folk who, at the end of the day, believed in the same God as he.

It was a feeling he kept to himself and scourged himself for at every opportunity, flying as it did in the face of the directives issued by the Pontiff in Charibon, God's direct representative on earth. He was here to obey orders which in the last analysis were equivalent to the will of God. There could be no shirking of such a burden.

THE fire hurtled through the narrow streets of Lower Abrusio like a wave, a bright tsunami which exploded the wooden buildings of this part of the city into kindling and ate out the interiors and the supporting wooden beams of those structures which were composed of yellow Hebrian stone until they toppled also. A dozen massed batteries of heavy culverins could not have bettered the destructive work, and the efforts of the soldiers-turned-firefighters in General Mercado's command to stem the onset of the flames seemed pointless, drops of maniac effort swamped in a sea of fire.

They were busy demolishing a wide avenue of houses southwest of the front of the conflagration, hoping thereby to form a firebreak which would starve the flames of sustenance. Engineers had laid charges at the cornerstones of all the buildings and were busy detonating them in a series of explosions which blasted the smoke into concentric rings, like the ripples of a stone-pocked lake.

While this went on, the fighting continued, the streets clogged with frantic, murderous scrums of armoured men who were being rained with cinders and burning timbers. Here and there companies and demi-tercios of arquebusiers had space to form up in lines and the opposing forces fired and reloaded and fired again only yards away from each other, the formations melting away under the withering barrage like solder in a furnace, to be replaced by reinforcements from their rear until one side broke and ran.

Wherever the regular Hebrian troops made a stand, the retainers of the Carreras and the Knights Militant who were with them could make no headway, though the Knights, their heavy armour some protection against bullets at all but the closest ranges, would form wedges of flesh and steel which would try to spear through the enemy lines by brute force. But they were not numerous enough. The firing lines opened to let them through after discharging a volley at point-blank range and those of the Knights who remained on their feet were swamped by scores of sword-and-buckler men to the rear.

And yet there was more to the battle than the mere contest between fighting men. Often in the middle of the carnage the combatants would cease their warring and as a body would seek shelter from the approaching holocaust. Men feared being burnt alive more than any other death, and would run into the enemy lines and be cut down quickly rather than remain to be consumed by the flames in their irresistible advance.

And civilians were there in the midst of the battling tercios and companies and demi-platoons. They fled their houses as the flames approached and died by the hundred as they ran through deadly crossfires or were caught by toppling buildings. Had anyone been in Abrusio who had also been at Aekir, he would have found the former more horrifying, for in Aekir men had been intent only on escape, on evading the enemy and the fire. Here they fought in the midst of the blaze, grappling with each other whilst the flames licked at their heads. Streets which were aflame from top to bottom but which were strategically valuable were defended to the last. The soldiers of Hebrion knew that by opposing the Knights they were labelling themselves heretics, the retainers of an excommunicate king, and that if they were captured, the pyre awaited them anyway. So no quarter was asked or given. The battle was more bitter than any struggle against the heathen, for the Merduks would at least take prisoners, intending them to swell the ranks of their slaves.

GOLOPHIN stood on the topmost column of Admiral's Tower, a walled platform which housed the iron framework of the signal beacon. With him was General Mercado, his half-silver face alight with the sliding crimson reflections of the burning city. On the stairs below a knot of aides was collected, ready to take orders out to the various bodies of soldiery about the Lower City.

A wall of flame hid the heights of Abrusio Hill, hid even the peaks of the Hebros beyond—a curtain whose topmost fringe dissolved into anvils and thunderheads of toiling smoke.

They started by burning books, Golophin thought. Then it was people, now it is the cities of the kingdoms themselves. They will consume the world ere they are done. And they do it in the name of God.

"I would curse them, but I have no Dweomer left," he said to Mercado. "All I had, I used to divert the fire from the waterfronts. I am as dry as a desert stone, General."

Mercado nodded. "Your work is appreciated, Golophin. You saved a score of the fleet's biggest ships."

"Much good they're doing us at the moment. When is Rovero to assault the boom?"

"Tonight. He will send in fireships to cover his gunboats, and the troopships last. With luck, by tomorrow he will be bombarding the Upper City."

"Bombarding our own city," Golophin said bitterly. His eyes had sunk so far into his head that they were mere glints which were answering the bloody light of the fire. His face was skull-like below the bald scalp. He had over-extended himself in his efforts to save the ships of the fleet, more than two dozen of which had been in dock when the flames had begun licking round the wharves. As it was, six of them had been destroyed and could be seen burning, alight from truck to waterline, black silhouettes of phantom ships surrounded by saffron light, their guns going off in chaotic sequence. Six great carracks with almost a thousand men on board, men who had been cut off from escape and had leaped into the

waters of the Inner Roads to drown like rats. Sailors did
not swim. It seemed ridiculous, farcical. Their bodies,
some ablaze, floated in the Inner Roads by the hundred.
Hundreds more were living yet, clinging to spare topmasts or anything else they had had the presence of mind
to fling overboard as the flames came ravening towards
their vessels. No one could get near them: the fires had
cut them off from land.

An unbearably bright flash, and seconds later the enormous boom of an explosion. The powder magazine of
one carrack had gone up and the ship, hundreds of tons
of wood and metal, had erupted into the air and was
raining its dismembered fragments down on the waters
of the harbour, starting fires on the other ships which had
managed to put off from the blazing wharves in time to
avoid its fate.

"If hell were a creation of man, it would be very like
that picture below us," Golophin said, awed by the spectacle.

"God has certainly no hand in it," Mercado said.

An aide came with a grubby parchment message. Mercado read it through, his lips muttering the words.

"Freiss's men have attempted to stage a break-out. The
fire is finally at the walls of the Arsenal. He is dead, and
most of his traitors with him."

"The Arsenal?" Golophin asked. "What of the stores
within it? My God, General—the powder and ammunition!"

"We've shifted maybe a quarter of it, but we cannot
get at the rest. First Freiss and then the fires have cut it
off."

"And if the fire detonates the powder stores?"

"The main stores are thirty feet below ground in stone
cellars. They have pipes in them which let out to the
harbour. If the worst comes to the worst I can order the
pipes opened and the powder magazines flooded. They
would take half the city with them when they went up.

Don't worry, Golophin—I won't let that happen. But it will mean destroying our powder and ammunition reserves, leaving only the naval stores here in the tower."

"Do it," Golophin said grimly. "Abrusio is hurt badly enough as it is. We must preserve something of her for Abeleyn to reclaim."

"Agreed." Mercado called an aide and began dictating the necessary orders.

"Rovero has taken a squadron to Pendero's Landing," the General went on when the aide had left. "Two carracks, some caravels and a trio of *nefs* in which are three thousand marines and arquebusiers of the garrison. He is going to try and convince the King that a land assault over the city walls will be more effective than attempting to carry the Great Harbour. If we can break the boom tonight, then in a couple of days we will be assaulting from both land and sea and another squadron can give supporting fire to the overland force if they attack the walls near the coast. That is Abeleyn's best bet, in my opinion. They have us pinned down here, by the fire itself and the guns they can bring to bear on us from Abrusio Hill. Also they are thin on the ground, and will be hard put to it to see off two attacks at once."

"Whatever seems best," Golophin said. "I am no general or admiral. I'll keep Abeleyn informed, though."

"Can that bird of yours bear a burden, Golophin?"

"A light one, perhaps. What is it?"

Mercado produced a heavily sealed scroll from his doublet. The galley-prow emblem of Astarac could be clearly seen, melted into the crimson wax which fastened it shut.

"This came today by special courier from Cartigella. It bears King Mark's personal seal and therefore can be opened only by another monarch. I think it may be urgent."

Golophin took the scroll. He itched to open it himself. "Good news, let us hope."

"I doubt it. Rumours have been coming in for days of an attempted coup in Cartigella, and of fighting through the streets of the city itself."

"The world goes mad," Golophin said quietly, stuffing the scroll into a pocket of his over-large robe.

"The world we knew is no more," Mercado said crisply. "Nothing will ever bring it back again now. If we are to fashion a new one, then we must build it on blood and gunpowder. And on faith."

"No," Golophin snapped. "Faith can have nothing to do with it. If we rear up something new, then let it be built upon reason and keep the clerics and the Pontiffs out of it. They have meddled for far too long: that is what this war of ours is about."

"A man must believe in something, Golophin."

"Then let him believe in himself, and leave God out of it!"

IN that winter of war and slaughter there were still a few kingdoms untouched by the chaos which was sweeping across Normannia. In Alstadt, capital of mighty Almark on the icy shores of the Hardic Sea, the trade and business of the city went on much as usual, with one difference: the banners of the Royal palace were at half-mast and wheeled traffic had been barred from the streets surrounding the palace. Alstadt was a sprawling, disorganized city, the youngest of the Ramusian capitals. It was unwalled save for the citadel which held the arsenals and the palace itself. Almark was a wide kingdom, a land of open steppes and rolling hills which extended from the Tulmian Gulf in the west to the River Saeroth which marked its border with Finnmark in the east. And to the south the kingdom extended to the snowy Narian Hills and the Sea of Tor, on whose shores nestled the monastery-city of Charibon. It was for this reason that Almark maintained a small garrison in Charibon to supplement the Knights Militant usually based there. Almark was a staunch ally of the Church which Charibon and its inhabitants represented, and its ailing monarch, Haukir VII, had always been a faithful son of that Church.

But Haukir was on his deathbed and he had no heir to succeed him, only a clutch of dissolute sister-sons whom the Almarkan people would not have trusted with the running of a baker's shop, let alone the mightiest kingdom north of the Malvennors and the Cimbrics. So the banners flew at half-mast, and the streets around the palace were quiet but for the screams of the scavenging gulls which swooped inland from the grey Hardic. And the dying King lay breathing his last surrounded by his counsellors and the Inceptine Prelate of the kingdom, Marat, who would oversee his departure from the world and close his tired eyes when his spirit fled.

The bedchamber of the King was dark and stuffy, full of the reek of old flesh. The King lay in the middle of the canopied bed like a castaway thrown up on a pale-sanded shore, one voyage ended and another about to begin. The Prelate, whom some said was his natural brother on the father's side, wiped the spittle which coursed in a line from one corner of Haukir's mouth into his slush-white beard. Some said it had been the fever, caught whilst journeying back from the Conclave of Kings in Vol Ephrir. Some said in whispers it was a stroke brought on by the King's outrage at the heresy of his fellow monarchs. Whatever had caused it, he lay withered and immobile in that wasteland of fine linen, his breath a stertorous whistle in his throat.

The King waved his hand at the assembled lawyers and courtiers and clerics, dismissing them from the room until all who remained were Prelate Marat, the Privy Minister and an inkwell- and parchment-laden Royal clerk, who looked distinctly uneasy at being alone in such august company.

The seagulls shrieked outside, and the hum of the living city was far off and distant, another world heard through a mirror. Haukir beckoned them closer.

"My end is here at last," he croaked in a poor mockery of his bellowing voice. "And I am not afraid. I go to meet He who made me, and the company of the living Saints, with the Blessed Ramusio at their head. But there is something I must do ere I leave this world. I must provide for the future welfare of my kingdom, and must ensure that it endures within the protection of the One True Faith after I am gone. Almark must remain firm in this era of heresy and war. I wish to alter my will . . ."

He closed his eyes and swallowed painfully. The clerk was nudged by the Privy Minister and hurriedly dipped his quill in the inkwell which dangled from one button-hole.

"The main provisions I made prior to this date I set aside. Only the secondary provisions of my previous will shall be honoured. I name Prelate Marat, Privy Minister Erland and—" He stopped and glared at the clerk. "What's your name, man?"

"F-Finnson of Glebir, if it please your majesty."

"And Finnson of Glebir as my witnesses on this fifteenth day of Forgist, in the year of the Blessed Saint five hundred and fifty-one."

The ragged breathing began to quicken. The King coughed up a mass of phlegm which Marat wiped away as tenderly as a nurse.

"Having no heirs of my blood which I consider suitable for bearing the burden of this crown, and seeing around me the world at this time falling ever farther into anarchy and heresy, I hereby leave the Almarkan crown to the stewardship of the Holy Church. I name my revered confessor, Prelate Marat, as regent of the realm until the High Pontiff, His Holiness Himerius of Hebrion, may see fit to make his own provisions for the ruling of the kingdom. As I entrust my soul to God, so I entrust my country to the bosom of God's representatives on earth, and I trust they will watch over Almark as the

Blessed Saint watches over my pilgrim spirit as it makes
its way into the glories of heaven . . ."

Haukir's head seemed to sink heavily into the pillow.
Sweat shone over his face and his lips were blue.

"Shrive me of my sins, Marat. Send me on my way,"
he whispered, and as the Prelate gave him the final blessing the Privy Minister turned to the scribbling clerk and
hissed in an undertone: "Did you get all that?"

The clerk nodded, still scribbling. Marat ended his
blessing and then paused.

"Goodnight, brother," he said softly. He closed the
staring eyes and laid the hands over the silent chest.

"The King is dead," he said.

"Are you sure?" the Privy Minister asked.

"Of course I'm sure! I've seen dead men before! Now
get that fool to make a copy of the revised will. I want
other copies of it made and posted in the market place.
And set out the black flags. You know what to do."

The Privy Minister stared at the cleric for a second,
some indefinable tension fizzling in the air between them.
Then he got down on one knee and kissed the Prelate's
ring. "I salute the new regent of Almark."

"And send me a courier, and another clerk. I must get
a dispatch off to Charibon at once."

"The snows—" the Privy Minister began.

"Damn the snows, just do as you're told. And get this
inky-fingered idiot out of here. I will meet the nobles and
the garrison commander in the audience chamber in one
hour."

"As you wish," the Privy Minister said tonelessly.

They exited, and the Prelate was left alone with the
dead King. Already he could hear the murmuring in the
chambers below which the appearance of the pair had
produced among the notables gathered there.

Marat bent his head and prayed in silence for a second,
the gulls still calling in their savage forlornness beyond
the shuttered windows of the chamber. Then he rose,

went to one of the windows and opened the shutters so that the keen sea air might rush in and freshen the death-smelling room.

Alstadt: broad, crude, thriving port-capital of the north. It opened out before him misted in drizzle, hazed by woodsmoke fires, alive with humanity in its tens of thousands. And beyond it, the wide kingdom of Almark with its horse-rich plains, its armies of cuirassiers. Himerius would be pleased: things could not have worked out better. And others would be pleased also.

Marat turned from the cold window to gaze down on the corpse of the King, and his eyes shone with a saffron light that had nothing human in it at all.

TWENTY

THEY were an unlikely looking crowd, Corfe had to admit to himself. They had never been taught to form ranks, present arms or stand at attention and they milled about in an amorphous mob, as unmilitary a formation as could be imagined.

They were clad in bruised, holed and rusty Merduk armour of every shape and type, but mostly they had picked out the war harness of the *Ferinai*, the heavy cuirassiers of the east, as it was the best quality. And perhaps it appealed to some savage sensibility within them, for it was the armour of horsemen and these men had once been horsemen. Their fathers and grandfathers had raided the coastal settlements of the Torunnans time out of mind, swooping out of the Cimbric foothills on their rangy black horses—horses which were the product of secret studs high in isolated valleys. Cavalry was what these men ought to be. Horse-soldiers. But Corfe could no more provide them with horses than he could with wings, so they must fight afoot in their outlandish armour.

Armour which had been rendered even more strange-looking by the liberal addition of red paint. The tribesmen seemed as happy as finger-painting children as they splashed it over their armour and hurled it at each other in gore-like gobbets. A crowd had gathered to watch, black-clad Torunnan soldiers lounging in the Quartermaster's yard and laughing fit to split their sides at the dressing up of the savages from the mountains, the ex-galley slaves.

As soon as the first Torunnan laughs were heard, however, the tribesmen went as silent as crags. A tulwar was scraped out of its threadbare scabbard and Corfe had to step in to prevent a fight which would quickly have turned into a full-scale battle. He called upon Marsch to calm his fellow tribesmen down and the hulking savage harangued his comrades in their own tongue. He was a frightening figure: somehow he had found a Merduk officer's helm which was decorated with a pair of back-sweeping horns and a beak-like nose-guard. Lathered with red paint, he looked like the apotheosis of some primitive god of slaughter come looking for acolytes.

"Someone to see you, sir," Ensign Ebro told Corfe as the latter doffed his heavy Merduk helm and wiped the sweat from his face. Ebro also wore the foreign harness, and he looked acutely uncomfortable in it.

"Who is it?" Corfe snapped, squeezing the acrid sweat from his eyes.

"Someone who has tasted gunsmoke with you, Colonel," another, familiar voice said. Corfe spun to find Andruw there, holding out a hand and grinning. He shouted aloud and pumped the proffered hand up and down. "Andruw! What in the hell are you doing here?"

"I ask myself the same question: what have I done to deserve this? But be that as it may, it would seem that I am to be your adjutant. For what misdeed I know not."

The pair of them laughed together while Ebro stood stiff and forgotten. Corfe mustered his manners.

"Ensign Ebro, permit me to introduce ... what rank have they showered upon you, Andruw?"

"Haptman, for my sins."

"There you are. Haptman Andruw Cear-Adurhal, late of the artillery, who commanded the Barbican Batteries of Ormann Dyke."

Ebro glanced at Andruw with rather more respect, and bowed. "I am honoured."

"Likewise."

"But what are you doing away from the Dyke?" Corfe asked Andruw. "I thought they'd need every gunner they could lay their hands on up there."

"I was sent to Torunn with dispatches. You have been seeking officers, I hear, driving the muster clerks mad with your enquiries. Apparently they decided that by seconding me to your command they could shut you up."

"And how goes it at the Dyke? Can they spare you?"

Andruw's bright humour faded a little. "They are short of everything, Corfe. Martellus is half out of his mind with worry, though as always he hides it well. We have had no reinforcements to replace our losses, no resupply for weeks. We are a forgotten army."

Andruw's gaze flicked to the weirdly garbed savages of Corfe's command as he spoke. Corfe noticed the look and said wryly: "And we are the army they would like to forget."

There was a pause. Finally Andruw asked: "Have you had your orders yet? Whither are we bound with our garish warrior band?"

"South," Corfe told him, disgust seeping into his voice. "I had best warn you now, Andruw, that the King expects us to end in some kind of debacle, fighting these rebels in the south. We are of small account in his plans."

"Hence the quaint war harness."

"It's all they would let me have."

Andruw forced a grin. "What is it they say? The longer

the odds, the greater the glory. We proved that at Ormann Dyke, Corfe. We'll do it again, by Ramusio's beard."

LATER that afternoon, Corfe reported to the Staff Headquarters for the detailed orders that were to send his command into its first battle. The place was busy with sashed officers and bustling aides. Couriers were coming and going and the King was closeted in conference with his senior advisors. No one seemed to recall any orders for Colonel Cear-Inaf and his command, and it was a maddening half-hour before a clerk finally found them. One unsealed roll of parchment with a scrawling, illegible signature at the bottom and a hasty impression of the Royal signet in a cracked blob of scarlet wax. It was in the stilted language of military orders not written in the field.

YOU *are hereby directed and obliged to take the troops under your command south to the town of Hedeby on the Kardian Sea, and there engage the retainers of the traitor Duke Ordinac in open battle, destroying them and restoring their master's fiefs to their rightful allegiance. You will march with due haste and prudence, and on accomplishing your mission you will occupy the town of Hedeby and await further orders.*

By command of the Torunnan war staff, for His Highness King Lofantyr.

THAT was all. No mention of supporting troops, timings, supplies, the hundred and one pieces of information which any military enterprise needed to function smoothly. Not even an estimate of the enemy's numbers or composition. Corfe crumpled the order into a ball and thrust it inside his breastplate. His look wiped the sniggers off the clerks' faces. No doubt they had heard about his strange soldiers and their stranger armour.

"I acknowledge receipt of my orders," he said, his

voice as cold as a winter peak. "Please inform the staff that my command will march at daybreak."

He turned to go, and one of the clerks let him get as far as the door before saying: "Sir—Colonel? Another message for you here. Not part of your orders, you understand. It was brought this afternoon by a lady-in-waiting."

He collected this second message without a word and left with it bunched in his fist. As he closed the door he heard the buzz of the clerks' talk and laughter, and his face gnarled into a grimace of fury.

The note was from the Queen Dowager requesting his presence in her chambers this evening at the eighth hour. So he must dance attendance upon a scheming woman whilst he was preparing to take an untried and ill-equipped command into the field. His first independent command. Dear God!

Better if I had died at Aekir, he thought. With honour and in comradeship with my countrymen. My Heria would have met me in the Saint's company and we would have shared eternity together.

Oh, dear God.

On an impulse, he veered away from the path back to the barracks where his men were stationed. He felt worn and tired, as if every step was a fight against something. He was too weary of the struggle to continue.

He wandered through the city for a while with no clear aim in mind, but something in him must have known whither he was bound for he found himself at the Abbey of the Orders as it was called, though once it had been the headquarters of the Inceptine Order alone. But that was before Macrobius had come into the city, and the black-clad Ravens had taken wing for Charibon rather than kiss the ring of a man they saw as an impostor, a heresiarch. This was now the palace of the High Pontiff, or one of them.

Corfe was admitted by a novice Antillian with white

hood and dun habit. When asked his business he replied
that he was here to see the Pontiff. The Antillian scurried
away.

An older monk of the same order popped out of a
nearby doorway soon after. He was a tall, lean man with
a sharp little beard and dirty bare feet slapping under his
habit.

"I am told you wish to see the Pontiff," he said, po-
litely enough. "Might I ask your business with him, soldier?"

Of course. Corfe could not expect to see the head of
the Church on demand. Much water had flowed under
many bridges since he and Macrobius had shared a turnip
on the nightmarish retreat from Aekir. Macrobius had
become one of the figureheads of the world since then.

"My name is Corfe," he said. "If you tell His Holiness
that Corfe is here, he will see me, I am sure."

The monk looked both taken aback and amused. "I will
see what I can do," he said. "Wait here." And off he
went.

Corfe was left just within the gate of the abbey, kicking his heels like a beggar awaiting charity. A dull anger
grew in him, a tired resentment that was becoming a familiar feeling.

The monk came back accompanied by an Inceptine, a
plump, well-robed figure who must have stayed to take
his chances with this new Pontiff when his fellows flew
the coop. He had a mouth like a moist rose and his fleshy
nose overhung it. His eyes were deep-set and dark-
ringed. The face of a debauchee, Corfe thought sourly.

"His Holiness is too busy at the moment to see anyone," the Inceptine said. "I am Monsignor Alembord,
head of the Pontifical household. If you have any peti-
tions you wish to place before the Holy Father then you
can place them through me. Now, what is your business?"

Corfe remembered a blind old man whose empty eye-sockets had been full of mud. A man whose life he had saved at risk to his own. He remembered sheltering under a wrecked cart and watching the rain pouring down on the displaced tens of thousands who walked the Western Road.

"Tell His Holiness that I hope he remembers the turnip."

The two clerics gaped at him, then closed their mouths and glared.

"Leave this place at once," Alembord said, his jowls quivering. "No one makes mockery of the head of the Holy Church. Leave or I shall call some Knights to eject you."

"Knights—so you are getting those together again, are you? The wheel comes round once more. Tell Macrobius that Corfe will not forget, and that he should never forget either."

The renegade Inceptine clapped his hands and shouted for the Knights, but Corfe had already turned on his heel and was walking through the gate, some small, odd sense of mourning twisting in him. Ridiculous though it was, it felt like the loss of a friend.

THE rest of his day was spent in the fog and mire of administrative matters, problems which he could get his teeth into and worry until they stopped kicking. It helped. It filled in the time, and kept his mind from thinking of other things.

Corfe managed alternately to bully and wheedle the Commissariat into issuing his men a week's rations for the march south. He divided his men into five understrength tercios, each under a man recommended by Marsch as a leader, or *rimarc* as it was named in their own language. Marsch he made into an ensign of sorts, to Ebro's glowering outrage, and Andruw as adjutant was entrusted with the rostering and organization of the command.

Twelve men had to be rejected as unfit; the galleys had broken them too completely for them ever to undertake active service again. These men Corfe sent on their way, giving them their rations and telling them to go home, back to the mountains. They were reluctant to leave because, Marsch said, they had sworn the oath along with the rest and would be bound by it until death. So Corfe asked them to act as recruiting agents once they regained their native valleys, and to send word of how many other tribesmen would be willing to take service under his banner when the spring came. He knew now that Lofantyr would never give him regular Torunnan troops. His command would have to be self-supporting.

As for the banner they would fight under, it took some thought. The tribesmen were pagan, and would baulk at fighting under the holy images which dominated the banners of the Ramusian armies, even if such banners were allowed to them. Corfe finally solved the problem in his own way, and had a seamstress in the garrison run up a suitable gonfalon. It was hastily done, and somewhat crude in conception as a result, but it stood out well atop its twelve-foot staff. Bright scarlet-dyed linen, the colour of sunset, and in sable at its heart the horned outline of the cathedral of Carcasson in Aekir. It was as Corfe had last seen it, a stark shadow against a burning sky, and the tribesmen were happy with it because to them it seemed the representation of Kerunnos, their horned god whom they worshipped above all others. Torunnan soldiers who saw the banner as it twisted lazily in the breeze saw only the outline of the cathedral, however, not its other, heretical, interpretation, and in time Corfe's men would be given a name because of that banner. They would be called the "Cathedrallers."

Now this last day in Torunn was wheeling to a close. The sun had disappeared behind the white summits of the Cimbrics in the west and Andruw was seeing to the last details of the command's organization. Corfe set off for the Royal palace and his audience with the Queen Dowager, and so preoccupied was he with the events of the day and the planning for tomorrow that he did not take off the scarlet Merduk armour, but wore it through the corridors of the Royal apartments to the bafflement and dismay of footmen and courtiers.

"LEAVE us," the Queen Dowager Odelia said sharply when Corfe was shown into her apartments by a gaping doorman.

They were not in the circular chamber this time, but in a broad hall-like room with a huge fireplace occupying one wall, logs the thickness of Corfe's thighs burning within it and iron firedogs silhouetted against the flames. The fire was the only light in the room. Corfe sensed rafters overhead, invisible with height. The walls were heavily curtained, as was the other end of the room. Rugs on the floor, soft under his boots after the stone of the palace corridors. The sweetness of a gleaming censer hanging by long chains from the ceiling. Crystal sparkling with firelight on a low table, comfortable divans drawn up to the fire. The place was how Corfe imagined a sultan's chambers might be, upholstered and draped and hidden, hardly any bare stonework visible. He took off his brutal helm and bowed to the golden-haired woman whose skin seemed to glow in the hearthlight.

"You look like a bogey-man destined for the terrifying of children, Corfe," Odelia said in that low tone of hers. A voice as dark as heather-honey, it could also cut like a switch.

"Take off the armour, for pity's sake. You need not fear assault here. Where in the world did you get it from anyway?"

"We must make do with what we can get, lady," Corfe said, frowning as his fingers sought the releasing straps and buckles. He was not yet familiar with the working of this harness, and he found himself twisting and turning in an effort to take it off.

The Queen Dowager began to laugh. "We had a contortionist come to amuse the court with his antics last spring. I swear, Colonel, you put him to shame. Here, let me help."

She rose to her feet with a whisper of skirts, and Corfe could have sworn he saw something black scuttle from beneath them into the shadows beyond the firelight. He paused in his struggles, but then Odelia was before him and her nimble fingers were searching his armour for the straps which would loosen it. She had his back-and breastplates off in a twinkling. They thumped dully on the rug, and after them in swift succession came the vambraces, the baldric which supported his sabre, his gorget, pauldrons, thigh-guards and gauntlets. He was left standing amid a pile of glinting metal, feeling oddly exposed. He realized he had enjoyed the sensation of her hands working about him and he was almost disappointed when she stepped back.

"There! Now you can sit and sup with me like a civilized man—if a badly dressed one. What happened to the fine clothes I had the tailor run up for you?"

"These are my campaigning clothes," Corfe said awkwardly. "I take my command out at dawn."

"Ah, I see. Have a seat then, and some wine. Stop standing there like a graven image."

She was different this time, almost coquettish, whereas before she had been intense, dangerous. In the kindly light of the fire she seemed a young woman, or would were it not for the veins thrown into vivid relief on the backs of her hands.

He sipped at the wine, hardly aware of it. The fire cracked and spat like a cat. He wondered if he dare ask her what he was doing here.

"The King knows of your . . . patronage," he said as she sat as if waiting for him to begin. Her gaze was alarmingly direct. It seemed to draw the words out of him. "I do not think he approves of it."

"Of course he does not. He resents what he sees as my interference in his affairs, though they were my affairs before he was born. I am not a figurehead or a cipher in this kingdom, Corfe, as you should know by now. But I am not the hidden power behind the throne, either. Lofantyr grows into his kingship at last, which is good. But he still needs someone to watch over his shoulder sometimes. That is the burden I have taken upon myself."

"You may have set me up for professional ruin, lady."

"Nonsense. I knew you would equip your men somehow, just as I know that you and your command will acquit yourselves admirably in the fighting to come. And if you do not, then you are not worth worrying about and I shall cast about until I find another promising soldier to bring under my eye."

"I see," Corfe said stiffly.

"We are all expendable, Corfe, even those of us who wear crowns. The good of Torunna, of the whole of the west, must come first. This kingdom needs capable officers, not sycophants who know how to nod at Lofantyr's every suggestion."

"I'm not sure exactly what I'll be able to accomplish with my five hundred savages in the south."

"You will do as you are told. Listen: Lofantyr has begun outfitting what he sees as the true expedition to bring the rebellious southern fiefs to heel. It will be under the command of one Colonel Aras and will march in a week or ten days. Two thousand foot, five hundred horse and a train of six guns."

Corfe scowled. "A goodly force."

"Yes. You are being sent to deal with Ordinac at Hedeby—not one of the most important rebels, but the king feels he will be more than capable of tying down your motley command; he can put over a thousand men into the field. By the time you have been trounced by him,

Colonel Aras and his command will have arrived on the scene to pick up the pieces, send you back to the capital in disgrace and get on with the real work of the campaign, the defeat of Duke Narfintyr at Staed."

"I see the King has everything planned in advance," Corfe said. "Is there any hope for my men and me, then?"

"I can only tell you this: you must defeat Ordinac speedily and move on to Staed. Colonel Aras does not outrank you and thus cannot give you orders. If you both arrive together at Staed, you will have to share the conduct of the campaign between you and thus there will be a greater chance of success for you and your men."

"What do you think of my chances, lady?"

She smiled. "I told you once before, Corfe: I think you are a man of luck. You will need all your luck if you are to prosper in this particular venture."

"Is this a test you've had the King set for me?"

She leaned closer. The firelight made a garden of shadows out of her features, started up green fires in her eyes. Corfe could feel her breath on his skin.

"It is a test, yes. I promise you, Corfe, if you pass it, you will move on to better things."

Abruptly she grasped his worn tunic and pulled him close. She kissed him full on the lips, softly at first and then with gathering pressure. Her eyes were open, laughing at his shock, and that suddenly angered him. He buried his fists in the gathered hair at her nape and crushed her mouth against his.

They were on the thickly carpeted floor, and he had ripped open the bosom of her dress while her laughter rang in his ears. Buttons flew through the air like startled crickets. The heavy brocade resisted even his hardened fists and she leapt up and down in his grasp as he sought to tear it off her.

Suddenly, the maniac absurdity of his position struck him, and he desisted. They crouched on the carpet facing each other. Odelia's breasts were bared, the round breasts of a woman who has given suck. Her dress had ripped to the navel and her hair was in banners about her shoulders, shining like spun gold. She grinned at him like a lynx. She looked incredibly young, vibrant, alive. He craved the feel of her again.

This time she came to him, sliding the gown from her body as easily as if it were a silken shawl. She was surprisingly wide-hipped, but her belly was taut and her skin when his hands met it was like satin, a thing to be savoured, a sensation he had almost forgotten in the recent burning turmoil of his life.

He explored the hardness of her bones, the softness of the flesh that clothed her, and when they finally coupled it was with great gentleness. Afterwards he lay with his head on her breast and wept, remembering, remembering.

She stroked his hair and said nothing, and her silence was a comfort to him, an island of quiet in the raging waters of the world.

SHE said not a word to him when he rose and dressed, pulling his tunic on and buckling the strange armour. Dawnsong had begun, though it was not yet light. His men would be waiting for him.

Naked, she stood and kissed him, pressed against the hard iron of his armour as he slipped the sword baldric over his head. She seemed old again, though, her forehead lined, fans of tiny wrinkles spreading from the corers of her eyes and the soft flesh hanging from the bones of her forearms. He wondered what magic had been in the night to make her appear so young, and she seemed to catch the thought for she smiled that feral grin of hers.

"Everyone needs a smidgen of comfort, the feel of another against them every so often, Corfe. Even Queens. Even old Queens."

"You're not so old," he said, and he meant it.

She patted his cheek as an aunt might a favoured nephew.

"Go. Go off to war and start earning a name for your-self."

He left her chambers feeling oddly rested, whole. As if she had plugged for a while the bleeding wounds he bore. When he strode his way down to the parade grounds he found his five hundred waiting for him be-neath their sombre banner, silent in the pre-dawn light, standing like ranks of iron statues with only the plumes of their breathing giving them life in the cold air.

"Move out," he said to Andruw, and the long files started out for the battlegrounds of the south.

TWENTY-ONE

THE squadron was a brave sight as it hove into view around the headland. War carracks with their banks of guns, *nefs* bristling with soldiers and marines, darting caravels with their wing-like lateen sails; and all flying the scarlet of the Hebrian flag at their mainmasts and the deeper burgundy of Admiral Rovero's pennant at the mizzens. As they caught sight of the party on the beach they started firing a salute. Twenty-six guns for the recognition of their king, every ship in the squadron surrounded with powder-smoke as the thunder of the broadsides boomed out. Abeleyn's throat tightened at the sight and sound. He was a king again, not a travelling vagabond or a hunted refugee. He still had subjects, and his word could still bring forth the bellowed anger of guns.

He and Rovero went below as soon as the longboats brought the King's party out to the ships. The squadron put about immediately, the ponderous carracks turning like stately floating castles in sequence, the smaller vessels clustering about them like anxious offspring.

Rovero went down on one knee as soon as he and Abeleyn were alone in the flagship's main cabin. Abeleyn raised him up.

"Don't worry about that, Rovero. If there's one thing I've learned in the past weeks, it's not to stand on ceremony. How long before we strike Abrusio?"

"Two days, sire, if this south-easter keeps up."

"I see. And what of the city when you left? How bad is it?"

"Sire, wouldn't you like to change and bathe? And I have a collation prepared—"

"No. Tell me of my kingdom, Rovero. What's been happening?"

The admiral looked grim, and hissed the words out of his lopsided mouth as though they were a curse uttered to someone behind him.

"I had a visit from Golophin's bird yesterday. The thing is almost destroyed. We have it in the hold as it cannot fly any more. It bore news of Abrusio, and this." The admiral handed Abeleyn a scroll with Astarac's Royal seal upon it. "It was meant for you, of course, sire, but the bird could go no farther."

Abeleyn held the scroll as gingerly as if it might burst into flame any second. "And Abrusio?"

"The Arsenal is burning. The powder magazines have been flooded, so there is no worry on that score. And Freiss is dead, his men taken, burned or fled into the Carreridan lines."

"That is something, I suppose. Go on, Rovero."

"We are holding our own against the traitors and the Knights Militant, but with the fire and the press of the population we cannot bring our full strength to bear. Fully two thirds of our men are fighting fire not traitors, or else they are conducting the evacuation of the Lower City. We may be able to save part of the western arm of Abrusio—engineers have been blasting a fire break clean across the city—but thousands of buildings are already in ash, including the fleet dry docks, the Arsenal, the naval storage yards and many of the emergency silos that were meant to feed the population in the event of a siege. Abrusio has become two cities, sire: the Lower, which is well-nigh destroyed and is, for what it's worth, in our hands, and the Upper, which is untouched and in the hands of the traitors."

Abeleyn thought of the teeming life of his capital in summer. The crowded, noisy, stinking vitality of the streets, the buildings and narrow alleys, the nooks and corners, the taverns and shops and market places of the Lower City. He had roved Abrusio's darker thorough-fares as a young man—or a younger one—out in search of adventure disguised as just another blade with money in his pocket. All gone now. All destroyed. It felt as though part of his life had been wiped away, only the memories retaining the picture of what once was.

"We'll discuss our plans later, Admiral," he said, his eyes unseeing, burning in their sockets as though they felt the heat of the inferno that was destroying his city. "Leave me for a while, if you please."

Rovero bowed and left.

He is older, the admiral thought as he closed the cabin door behind him. He has aged ten years in as many weeks. The boy in him is gone. There is something in his look which recalls the father. I would not cross him now for all the world.

He stomped out into the waist of the ship, his mouth a skewed scar in his face. That damned woman, the King's mistress, was on deck arguing about her quarters. She wanted more room, a window, fresher air. She looked green about the chops already, the meddlesome bitch. Well, older woman or no, she'd no longer be able to twist this king about her finger as it was rumoured she had in the past. Wasn't she getting rather stout, though?

●   ●   ●

T HE King of Hebrion stepped out of the cabin on to
the stern gallery of the flag carrack, which hung like
a long balcony above the foaming turmoil of the ship's
wake. He could see the other vessels of the squadron in
line before him scarcely two cables away, plain sail set,
their bows plunging up and down and spraying surf to
either side of their beakheads. It was a heart wrenching
sight, power and beauty allied into a terrible puissance.
Engines of war as awesome and glorious as man's hand
had the capacity to make them.

Man's hand, not God's.

He broke open King Mark's letter and stood on the
pitching gallery reading it.

> *My Dear Cousin,* it began. *This is written in haste
> and without ceremony—the dispatch galley waits
> in the harbour with her anchor aweigh. Her des-
> tination is Abrusio, for I know not where else you
> can be reached. Despite the terrible stories which
> are coming out of Hebrion, I believe that you will
> arrive back in your capital in the end and eject the
> traitors and Ravens who are intent on ruining the
> west.*
>
> *But I must tell you my news. My party was am-
> bushed in the foothills of the southern Malvennors
> by a sizable force of unknown origin, and we barely
> scraped through with our lives. An assassination
> attempt, of course, an effort to rid the world of yet
> another heretic. It can only have been arranged by
> Cadamost of Perigraine and the Inceptine Prelate
> of that kingdom. I fear other attempts have been
> made, on both you and Lofantyr, but obviously if
> you are scanning this missive you survived.*
>
> *The old laws which governed conduct and
> guided men's actions are destroyed. I have had an
> uprising of the nobles in Astarac to deal with, and
> it is only in the last few days that I have been able*

to call Cartigella my own capital again. But the traitors were ill-led and ill-equipped—and they had no Knights Militant to back them up. The army, which remained loyal in the most part, thank God, is now scouring Astarac for the remaining pockets of the rebels. But there are rumours that Perigraine is mobilizing and I must guard my eastern frontiers, else you would have Astaran reinforcements to help you in the sorry task of regaining your own kingdom.

My sister will wed you, and if she is as plain as a frog she is nonetheless a woman of sense and intelligence: More than ever we heretic kings must stand together, Abeleyn. Hebrion and Astarac shall be allied, for if we remain separate then we will fall alone. I will not waste time on pomp and ceremony. As soon as I hear from you that you are safe in Abrusio she shall be sent to your side, the living proof of our bond.

(Do you remember her, Abeleyn? Isolla. You pulled her plaits as a boy and mocked her crooked nose.)

From Torunna I have tidings much the same as here. Macrobius has been properly received as the true Pontiff, but according to my sources he is not seen much abroad and may be ailing, may God forfend. He is all that stands between us and utter anarchy. Lofantyr is directing the Merduk war personally, and yet Ormann Dyke seems to be neglected and the refugees surround Torunn by the hundred thousand. He is not a general, our cousin of Torunna. Sometimes I am not even sure if he is a soldier.

I must scrawl ever more hastily, as the tide will soon be on the turn. A Fimbrian army, it is said, is on the march. Its destination is reported to be the dyke, which may explain Lofantyr's neglect if *it does not excuse it. He has hired the old empire-builders to fight his wars for him, and thinks he can leave it at that. But the hound brought in over the threshold can prove to be a wolf if it is not watched and given discipline. I do not trust Fimbrian open-handedness.*

I end here. A pitiful missive, without grace or form to recommend it. My old rhetorics tutor will be grumbling in his grave. Maybe one day philosophers will once more have the time to dance angels on the heads of pins, but for now the world has too much need of soldiers and the quill must yield to the sword.

Fare thee well, cousin.

Mark

Abeleyn smiled as he finished reading. Mark had never been much of a one for polish. It was good to know that Hebrion did not stand alone in the world, and that Astarac seemed fairly on the road back to her proper order. The news of the Fimbrians was interesting, though. Did Lofantyr truly expect them to fight and die for Torunna in the east without wanting something more than coinage in exchange?

Isolla. They had all played together as children, at conferences and conclaves as their fathers changed the shape of the world. She was thin and russet-haired, with a freckled face and a bend to her nose that had been evident even then, when they were not yet into their teens. She was only a year or two younger than himself—quite old to be married for the first time. He remembered her as a quiet, long-suffering child who liked to be left alone.

Such memories were beside the point. The important thing was that the Hebro-Astaran alliance would be firmly cemented by this marriage, and personal feelings did not come into it.

(He thought of Jemilla and her swelling belly, and felt

a thrill of uneasy apprehension for a reason he could not fully understand.)

The feeling passed. He went inside and shouted for attendants to come and help him disrobe and wash. He poured himself a flagon of wine from the gimballed decanters on the cabin table, gulped it down, bit into a chunk of herb bread, gulped more wine.

The cabin door opened and his personal steward and valet were standing there, still in their castaway clothes, one chewing.

"Sire?"

He felt ashamed. He had forgotten that these men had been through whatever he had, and were as hungry and thirsty and tired and filthy as he was himself.

"It's all right. You are dismissed. Clean yourselves up and get yourselves as much food and wine as your bellies will hold. And kindly ask Admiral Rovero to step back in here when he has a moment."

"Yes, sire. The sailors have heated water for you in one of their coppers in the galley. Shall we have a bath prepared?"

A bath! Sweet heavens above. But he shook his head. "Let the lady Jemilla use the water. I will do well enough."

The men bowed and left. Abeleyn could smell himself above the usual shipboard smells of pitch and wood and old water, but it did not seem to matter. Jemilla was carrying his child, and she would appreciate a bath above all things at the moment. Let her have one—it would keep her away from him for a while.

He realized suddenly that he did not much like his mistress. As a lover she was superb, and she was as witty and intelligent as a man could want. But he trusted her no more than he would trust an adder which slithered across his boot in the woods. The knowledge surprised him somewhat. He was aware that something in him had changed, but he was not yet sure what it was.

A knock on the door. Admiral Rovero, his eyebrows high on his sea-dog face. "You wanted to see me, sire?"

"Yes, Admiral. Let us go through this plan you have concocted, you and Mercado, for the retaking of Abrusio. Now is as good a time as any."

There was to be no rest, no chance to sit and stare out at the foaming wake and the mighty ships which coursed along astern, tall pyramids of canvas and wood and gleaming guns. No time to turn away from the care and the responsibilities. And Abeleyn did not mind.

Perhaps that is what has changed, he thought. I am growing into my crown at last.

TWENTY-TWO

ALBREC'S head was full of blood, swollen and throbbing like a bone-pent heart. His face was rubbing against some form of material, cloth or the like, and his hands, also, felt swollen and full.

He was upside-down, he realized, dangling with his midriff being crushed by his own weight.

"Put me down," he gasped, feeling as though he might throw up if he did not straighten.

Avila set him down carefully. The young Inceptine had been carrying him slung over one broad shoulder. The pair of them were breathing heavily. Albrec's world dizzied and spun for a moment as the fluids of his body righted themselves. The lamp Avila had been carrying in his free hand guttered on the floor, almost out of oil.

"What are you doing?" Albrec managed at last. "Where are we?"

"In the catacombs. I couldn't bring you round, Albrec. You were dead to the world. So I piled up stone in front of the hole and tried to find a way out for us."

"Commodius!"

"Dead, and may his warped spirit howl the eons away in the pits of hell."

"His body, Avila. We can't just leave it down here."

"Why not? He was a creature of the lightless dark, a shape-shifter, and he tried to kill us both to protect his precious version of the truth. Let his corpse rot here unburied."

Albrec held his aching head in his hands. "Where are we?"

"I was following the north wall—the damp one, as you said—trying to find the stairs, but I must have missed them somehow."

"An easy thing to do. I will find them, don't worry. How long has it been since . . . ?"

"Maybe half an hour, not long."

"Great God, Avila, what are we going to do?"

"Do? I—I don't know, Albrec. I hadn't been thinking beyond getting out of this dungeon."

"We've killed the Senior Librarian."

"We've slain a werewolf."

"But he changed back into Commodius the librarian. It's the last thing I remember. Who will believe us? What signs are there on his body to tell anyone what he was in life?"

"What are you saying, Albrec? That we are in trouble for saving our own lives, for putting an end to that foul beast?"

"I don't know, I don't know what to think. How could it happen, Avila? How could a priest be a thing like that, all these years, all the years I have worked with him? It was he who haunted the library; I see that now. It was his unclean presence which gave it its atmosphere. Oh, lord God, what has been going on here?"

The pair were silent, their eyes fixed on the tiny lamp flame which did not have too many minutes of life left to it. But it did not seem important that they might soon

be left here in impenetrable darkness. The place seemed
different somehow. They had seen the true face of evil,
and nothing else could frighten them.

"They know," Albrec went on in a rasping whisper.
"Did you hear him? They know the truth of things, the
real story of the Saint and the Prophet, and they have
been suppressing it. The Church has been sitting on the
truth for centuries, Avila, keeping it from the world to
safeguard its own authority. Where is piety, where hu-
mility? They have behaved like princes determined to
hold on to their power no matter what the cost."

Avila fingered his black Inceptine robe thoughtfully.

"You have claw marks down the sides of your face,"
he told Albrec, as though he had only just seen them.

"There's blood on yours, too."

"We can't hide our hurts, Albrec. Think, man! What
are we to do? Columbar is dead at Commodius' hand
and Commodius is dead at ours. How will it look? We
cannot tell them we were trying to discover and preserve
the truth of things. They'll put us out of the way as
quickly as Commodius intended to."

"There are good men yet in the Church—there must
be."

"But we don't know who they are. Who will listen to
us or believe us? Sweet blood of the Blessed Saint, Albrec, we are finished."

The lamp guttered, flared, and then went out. The dark
swooped in on them and they were blind.

Avila's voice came thick with grief through the light-
lessness. "We must flee Charibon."

"No! Where would we go? How would we travel in
the depth of winter, in the snows? We would not last a
day."

"We'll not last much longer than that here once this
gets out. When Commodius is missed they'll search the
library. They'll find him in the end. And who is the only

other person who has the keys to the library? You, Albrec."

The little monk touched the torn skin of his face and neck, the lump on his forehead where the werewolf had knocked him. Avila was right. They would question him first, for he was Commodius' closest colleague, and when they saw his wounds the inquisition would begin.

"So what are we to do, Avila?" he asked, near to tears. He knew, but he had to let someone else say it.

"We'll have a day of grace. We'll stay out of sight and gather together what we can to help us on our journey."

"Journey to where? Where in the world are we to go? The Church rules Normannia, her Knights and clerics are in every city and town of the west. Where shall we run to?"

"We are heretics once this gets out," Avila said. "They will excommunicate us when they find the body in that unholy chapel and note our disappearance. But there are other heretics in the world, Albrec, and there is a heresiarch to lead them. The man some say is Macrobius has been set up as an anti-Pontiff in Torunn. Charibon's writ has no authority in that kingdom, and anyone hostile to the Himerian Church will be welcome there. The Macrobian kings will listen to us. We would be a powerful weapon in their armoury. And besides, Charibon seems now to me like a sink of corruption. If Commodius was a werewolf, could there not be others like him within the ranks of my order?"

"It does not bear thinking about."

"It must be thought about, Albrec, if we are to puzzle out a way to save our lives."

They stood awhile, not speaking, listening to the drip of water and the enfolding silence of the gutrock, the bowels of the mountains. Finally Avila moved. Albrec heard him groan from the pain of his hurts.

"My robe is ripped to threads, and I think I have some ribs broken. It is like a knife thrust into my side every time I draw breath. We must get back to our beds before Matins."

"You sleep in a dormitory, Avila. Won't your colleagues notice?"

"There is a bolster under my blankets doing service as a sleeping monk, and I stole out as quiet as a mouse. But I'll not be so quiet returning. Damnation!"

"You can't go back. You must come to my cell. We'll get some things together and hole up somewhere tomorrow—or today, as I suppose it must be—and leave tomorrow night."

Avila was gasping in short, agonizing pants. "I fear I will not be a swift traveller, my little Antillian comrade. Albrec, must we leave? Is there no way we can brazen it out?"

The decision had been made, but it terrified both of them. It would be so much easier to go on as if nothing had happened, to step back into the ancient routine of the monastery-city. Albrec might have done it, the inertia of fear tying him to the only life he had known. But Avila had painted things too clearly. The Antillian knew that their lives had changed without hope of recovery. They had stepped beyond the Church and were on the outside, looking in.

"Come," Albrec said, trying not to move his neck. "We've a lot to do before dawn. This thing has been thrust on us as Honorius' visions were thrust upon him, that poor, mad seeker after the truth. God has given us a burden as heavy as his to bear. We cannot shirk it."

He took Avila's arm and began leading him along the wall of the catacombs, touching its rough surface every now and then with his shaking palm.

"He died in the mountains, you know, died alone as a discredited hermit whom no one would listen to, a holy madman. I wonder now if it is not the Church which has been mad. Mad with pride, with the lust for power. Who is to say that it has not suppressed every holy truth-seeker who has arisen over the centuries? How many men have found out about Ramusio's true fate, and have paid for that knowledge with their lives? That is the pity of it. Take a lie and make it into belief, and it rots the rest of the faith like a bad apple in a barrel. No one knows what to believe any more. The Church totters on its foundations, no matter how much of its structure may be sound, and those good men who are in its service are tainted with its lies."

Avila groaned out a wrecked laugh. "You never change, Albrec. Still philosophizing, even at a time like this."

"Our fate has become as important as the downfall of nations," Albrec retorted humourlessly. "We carry our knowledge like a weapon of the Apocalypse, Avila. We are more potent than any army."

"I wish I felt so," Avila grated, "but I feel more like a wounded rat."

They found the stairs and began to ascend them as gingerly as two old men, hissing and grimacing at every step. It seemed an age before they reached the library proper, and for the last time in his life Albrec walked among the tiers of books and scrolls and breathed in the dry parchment smell. The title page of the old document crackled in the breast of his robe like a grizzling babe.

The air of the passing night was bitterly cold as they left the library, locking it behind them, and trudged through the wind-smoked snowdrifts to the cloisters. There were a few other monks abroad, preparing for Matins. Charibon was wrapped in pre-dawn peace, dark buildings and pale drifts, the warm gleam of candlelight at a few windows. It was different now. It no longer felt like home. Albrec was weeping silently as he helped Avila to his own cell. He knew that tonight whatever peace and happiness his plain life had known had been lost. Ahead lay nothing but struggle and danger and disputation, and a death which would occur beyond the ministrations of the Church. Death on a pyre perhaps, or in the snows, or in a strange land beyond all that was familiar.

He prayed to Ramusio, to Honorius the mad saint, to God Himself, but no light appeared before him, no voice spoke in his mind. His supplications withered into empty stillness, and try as he might he could not stop his faith from following them into that pit of loss. All he was left with was his knowledge of the truth, and there grew in him a resolve to see that truth spread and grow like a painful disease. He would infect the world with it ere he was done, and if the faith tottered under that affliction, then so be it.

CHARIBON came to life before the sun broke the black sky into slate-grey cloud. Matins was sung, and the monks went to their breakfasts; Lauds, and then Terce followed. The accumulated snows of the night were swept away and the city stirred, as did the fisher-villages down on the frozen shore of the Sea of Tor.

After Terce a group of scholars went to one of the Justiciars and complained that the library was not yet open. The matter was investigated, and it was found that the doors were locked and there were no lights within. The Senior Librarian could not be found, nor could his assistant. The matter was pursued further, and despite the frigid air a crowd of monks gathered around the main doors of the Library of Saint Garaso when at Sext they were broken open by a deacon of the Knights Militant and his men using a wooden beam as a battering ram whilst Betanza, the Vicar-General himself, looked on. The library was searched by parties of senior monks. By that time the body of Columbar had been discovered, and despite searches of the dormitories and cloisters the two librarians were still nowhere to be found. Charibon began to buzz with speculation.

Commodius' body was discovered just before Vespers,

after the upper levels of the library had been turned up-
side down. Monks searching the lower levels had come
upon a discarded oil lamp, and a pile of broken masonry
built up against a wall of the catacombs. It fell apart as
soon as they began to investigate it, and a monsignor
entered the little temple along with two armed Knights
to discover the corpse of the Senior Librarian stark and
staring, the silver pentagram dagger buried in its spine.

The circumstances of the discovery were not bruited
abroad, but the story made its way about the monastery-
city that the Senior Librarian had been foully murdered
in horrible surroundings somewhere deep in the foundations of his own library, and his assistant, along with a
young Inceptine who was known to be his special friend,
was missing.

Patrols of the Knights Militant and squads of the Almarkan garrison soldiers prowled the streets of Charibon,
and the monks at Vespers whispered up and down the
long pews when they were not singing to God's glory.
There was a murderer, or murderers, loose in Charibon.
Heretics, perhaps, come spreading fear in the city at the
behest of the heresiarch Macrobius who sat at the Devil's
right hand in Torunn. The senior Justiciars were forming
an investigative body to get to the bottom of the affair,
and the Pontiff himself was overseeing them.

But late that evening, in the white fury of yet another
snow-storm, two events went unremarked by the patrols
which were watching the perimeters of Charibon. One
was the arrival of a small party of men on foot, struggling
through the drifts with their black uniforms frosted white.
The other was the departure of two bent and labouring
monks bowed under heavy sacks, feeling their way
through the blizzard with stout pilgrim's staves and gasping in their pain and grief as they trudged along the frozen shores of the Sea of Tor, bypassing the bonfires of
the sentry-posts by hiking far out on the frozen surface
of the sea itself to where the pancake ice bunched and

rippled under the wind like the unquiet contents of a white cauldron. Albrec and Avila struggled on with the ice gathering on their swollen faces and the blood in their hands and feet slowly solidifying in the intense depth of the raging cold. The snowstorm cloaked them entirely, so that they were not challenged once in their fumbling progress. But it also seemed to be fairly on the way to killing them before their flight had even got under way.

THE party of black-clad men demanded admittance to the suites of the High Pontiff Himerius, and the startled guards and clerical attendants were spun into a frenzy by their unexpected appearance. Finally they were billeted in a warm, if austere, anteroom whilst the Pontiff was notified of their arrival. It was the first time in four centuries that Fimbrian soldiers had come to Charibon.

The Pontiff was being robed by two ageing monks in his private apartments when the Vicar-General of the Inceptine Order entered. The monks were dismissed and the two Churchmen stood looking at one another, Himerius still fastening his purple robe about his thickening middle.

"Well?" he asked.

Betanza took a seat and could not stifle a yawn: it was very late, and he had had a trying day.

"No luck. The two monks remain missing. They are either dead, if they are innocent, or fled if they are not."

Himerius grunted, regarding his own reflection in the full-length mirror which graced the sombre opulence of his dressing chamber.

"They are guilty, Betanza: I feel it. Commodius was trying to stop them from committing heresy, and he died for it." A spasm of indefinable emotion crossed the Pontiff's aquiline features and then was gone. "May God have mercy on him, he was a loyal servant of the Church."

"What makes you so sure that was the way of it, Ho-

liness?" Betanza asked, obviously curious. His big soldier's face was ruddy with the day he had spent, and
scarlet lines intagliated the whites of his eyes.

"I know," Himerius snapped. "You will send out
search parties of the Knights to find these two runaways
as soon as the weather permits. I want them brought back
to Charibon to undergo inquisition."

Betanza shrugged. "As you wish, Holiness. What of
these Fimbrians closeted below? Will you see them tonight?"

"Yes. We must know if their arrival here at this time
is a coincidence or part of a larger plan. I need not tell
you, Betanza, that the events of today must not leave the
city. No tales of murder in Charibon must trickle out to
the kingdoms. This place must be unbesmirched, pure,
unsullied by scandal or rumour."

"Of course, Holiness," Betanza said, at the same time
wondering how he was supposed to muzzle a city of
many thousands. Monks were worse than women for gos-
sip. Still, the weather would help.

"A courier arrived here this afternoon, while you were
occupied with other matters," Himerius said lightly, and
there was a different air about him suddenly, a glittering
triumph that he could not keep out of his eyes. The Pontiff turned and faced the Vicar-General squarely, his
hands clasped on his breast. It looked as though a wild
grin was fighting to break out over his face. For an instant, Betanza thought, he looked slightly mad.

"Good news, my friend," Himerius said, mastering
himself. He was once more the sober cleric, weighed
down with dignity and *gravitas*. "The courier came from
Alstadt. It would seem that our devoted son of the
Church, King Haukir of Almark, has died at last, may
the Saints receive his flitting soul into their bosoms. This
pious king, this paragon of dutiful faith, has left his kingdom to the Church."

Betanza gaped. "You're sure?"

"The courier carried a missive from Prelate Marat of Almark. He has been named regent of the kingdom until such time as I see fit to organize its governance. Almark is ours, Betanza."

"What of the nobles? Have they aught to say about it?"

"They will acquiesce. They must. Almark has a strong contingent of the Knights Militant in its capital, and the Royal armies are for the most part billeted further east, along the line of the Saeroth river. Almark is ours, truly."

"They say that events of moment are like nodes of history," Betanza mused. "Where one occurs, others are likely to happen at the same time, sometimes in the same place. You may face these Fimbrians with new confidence, Holiness. The timing could not have been more opportune."

"Precisely. It is why I will receive them now, though it is so late. I want the news to be a shock to them."

"What do you think they want?"

"What does anyone these days? The Church owns Almark, it controls Hebrion. It has become an empire. Accommodation must be sought with it. I have no doubt that these Fimbrians are come to test the waters of diplomatic exchange. The old imperial power is bending in the new wind. Come: we will go down and meet them together."

The Pontifical reception hall was full of shadows. Torches burned in cressets along the walls, and glowing braziers had been brought in to stand around the dais whereon rested the Pontiff's throne. Knights Militant stood like graven monuments every ten paces along the walls, blinking themselves awake and stiffening the moment the Pontiff entered and sat himself down. Betanza remained standing at his right hand, and a pair of scribes huddled in their dark robes like puddles of ebony ink at the foot of the dais, quills erect. To one side Rogien, the old Inceptine who was also the manager of the Pontifical court, stood ready, his bare scalp gleaming in the torch-light.

The Fimbrians had to walk the length of the flame-and-shadowed hall, their boots clumping on the basalt floor. Four of them, all in black, except for the scarlet sash that one wore about his waist.

Hard-faced men, wind-burn rouging their cheeks and foreheads, their hair cropped as short as the mane of a hogged horse. They bore no weapons, but the Knights who lined the walls on either side of them watched them intently and warily with fists clenched on sword-hilts.

"Barbius of Neyr, marshal and commander in the Fim-brian army," Rogien announced in a voice of brass.

Barbius inclined his head to Himerius. Fimbrians did not bend the knee to anyone save their emperor. Himerius knew this, yet the slight bow had so much of contempt in it that he shifted in his throne, his liver-spotted hands tightening on the armrests.

"Barbius of the electorate of Neyr, you are welcome in Charibon," the Pontiff said calmly. "The urgency of your errand is written in your face and those of your companions, and so we have deigned to grant you an audience despite the lateness of the hour. Quarters appropriate for your rank have been set aside for you and your comrades, and as soon as the audience is over there will be food and drink served to help sustain the flagging spirit."

Barbius made the slight bow again in acknowledge-ment of this graciousness. His voice when he spoke was the grate of sliding rock to Himerius' deep music.

"I thank His Holiness for his hospitality, but am grieved to say that I shall not be able to take advantage of it. I and my men are in haste: the main body of our force is encamped some five leagues from here and we hope to rejoin them ere the morning."

"Main body?" Himerius repeated.

"Yes, Holiness. I am here to reassure you that the

troops under my command bear the monastery-city nothing but goodwill, and you need not fear—nor need Almark fear—any rapine on their behalf. We are merely passing through, obeying the orders of the Electors."

"I don't understand. Are you not an embassy come from the electorates?" Himerius asked.

"No, Holiness. I am merely the commander of an eastwardbound Fimbrian army come to pay my respects."

The statement fell in the room like a thunderclap.

"A *Fimbrian army* is encamped five leagues from Charibon?" Betanza said, incredulous.

"Yes, excellency."

"Whither are you bound?" Himerius inquired, and the music was gone from his voice. He sounded as hoarse as an old crow.

"We are bound for the relief of Ormann Dyke."

"At whose behest?"

"I am ordered by my superiors, the Electors of Fimbria."

"But who has asked for your help? Lofantyr the heretic? It must be."

Barbius shrugged, his red-gold moustache concealing any expression his mouth might have conveyed. His eyes were as flat and hard as sea ice. "I am only following orders, Holiness. It is not for me to question the doings of high policy."

"Do you realize you are imperilling your immortal soul by succouring a heretic who has repudiated the validity of the holy Church?" Himerius snapped.

"As I said, Holiness, I am merely a soldier obeying orders. If I do not obey them my life is forfeit. I called in on you here as a courtesy, to ask your blessing."

"You march to the aid of he who shields the heresiarch of the west, and you ask my blessing?" Himerius said.

"My army marches east to stem the Merduk invasion. It is performing a service for every kingdom in the west, be they Himerian or Macrobian," Barbius said. "I ask you, Holiness, to look on it in that light. The dyke will fall in the spring if my forces do not reinforce it, and the Merduks will be hammering at the gates of Charibon within a year. It may be that King Lofantyr is paying our wages, but the service we render is of value to every free man in Normannia."

Himerius was silent, thinking. It was Betanza who spoke next.

"So you are mercenaries, you Fimbrians. You hire yourselves out to kings in need and fight for the gold in their coffers. What if the Merduk sultans offered you a greater wage than the western kings, Marshal? Would you then fight under the banners of the Prophet?"

For the first time, emotion crossed the face of the Fimbrian marshal. His eyes flared and he took one step forward, which made every guard in the chamber tense on the balls of his feet.

"Who built Charibon?" he asked. "Who founded Aekir and hollowed out Ormann Dyke and reared up the great moles of Abrusio Harbour? My people did. For centuries the Fimbrians were the buckler behind which the people of the west sheltered from the steppe hordes, the horse-tribes, the Merduk thousands. The Fimbrians *made* the western world what it is. You think we would betray the heritage of our forefathers, the legacy of our empire? Never! Once again we are in the foremost rank of those defending it. All we ask"—and here the marshal's tone softened—"is that you do not see our reinforcing of the dyke as an assault on the Himerian Church. We intend no heresy, and would keep on good terms with Charibon if we could."

Himerius rose and lifted his hand. The torchlight made his face into an eagle mask, eyes glittering blackly on either side of the aquiline nose.

"You have our blessing then, Marshal Barbius of Neyr. May your arms shine with glory, and may you hurl the Merduk heathen back from the gates of the west."

• • •

"WHY did you do it?" Betanza demanded. "Why did you legitimize the farming out of Fimbrian troops to heretics? It is senseless!"

He and the Pontiff were sweeping along one of Charibon's starlit cloisters, utterly deserted at this time of night. Their hands were hidden in their sleeves and they had their hoods drawn up against the biting cold, but the blizzards had ended and the night air was as clear as the bleb of an icicle, sharp as a shard of flint. Novices had swept the cloister clear of snow before retiring to bed and the two clerics were able to stride along without interruption.

"Why should I not do it? Had I refused the blessing, alienated the man, then I would have done the Church no favours and possibly a great deal of harm. We cannot argue with an army of Fimbrians. Think of that, Betanza! Fimbrians on the march again across the continent. The imperial tercios on the move. It is enough to make a man shudder with apprehension. We knew after the Conclave of Kings that something like this was in the wind—but so *soon*. Lofantyr has stolen a march on us, quite literally."

"But why bless his enterprise? It is giving tacit recognition of the Torunnan kingdom, which is no longer within the Church's fold."

"No. I merely blessed the Fimbrians: I did not wish Godspeed to heretics. If the old imperial power is once again stirring and taking an interest in the world, then it would be as well for us to keep it on our side. The Fimbrians are still a Himerian state, remember. They have never formally recognized the anti-Pontiff Macrobius, and therefore they are technically in our camp. Let us keep it that way. The Fimbrians themselves obviously want to keep the Church in their corner, else that brutish marshal would have marched past Charibon without a pause and we would be none the wiser of his passing.

No—despite the bequest of Almark we are not strong enough to antagonize the Electors."

Their sandals slapped on the frigid stone of the cloisters.

"I pity them, sleeping out on a night like this," Betanza said.

Himerius snorted. "They are soldiers, little better than animals. They hardly register any feeling except the most base. Let them shiver."

They took one more turn about the cloister, and then: "I will go to bed now, Holiness," Betanza said, oddly subdued. "My investigations into the death of Commodius will recommence at dawn. I wish to pray awhile."

"By all means. Good night, Betanza."

The Pontiff stood alone in the clear night, his eyes glittering under his hood. In his mind he was marshalling armies and putting the cities of the heretics to the torch. A second empire there would be on earth, and as mad Honorius had said it would rise in an age of fire and the sword.

I am tired, Himerius thought, his savage exaltation flickering out as the freezing wind searched his frame. I am old, and weary of the struggle. But soon my task will be fulfilled, and I will be able to rest. Someone else will take my place.

He padded off to his bed as silently as a cat.

"ALBREC. Wake up, Albrec!"

A blow on Albrec's cheekbone snapped his head to one side and tore the scab of ice from around his nose. He moaned as the cold air bit into the exposed flesh and fought open his eyes as someone shook him as though he were a rat being worried by a dog.

He lay half-buried in snow and a frost-white shape was pummelling him.

"All right, all right! I'm awake."

Avila collapsed in a heap beside him, the air sobbing

in and out of his fractured chest. "It's stopped snowing," he wheezed. "We should try to move on."

But they both remained prone in the drift which had come close to burying them. Their clothes had stiffened on their backs to the consistency of armour, and they no longer had any feeling left in their extremities. Worse, white patches of frostbite discoloured their faces and ears.

"We're finished," Albrec moaned. "God has abandoned us."

The wind had dropped, and they lay on their backs in the snow staring up at the vast vault of the star-crowded night sky. Beautiful and pitiless, the stars were so bright that they cast faint shadows, though the moon had not yet risen.

Far off the two clerics heard the forlorn howl of a solitary wolf, come down out of the terrible winter heights of the Cimbrics seeking food.

Another answered it, and then there were more. A pack of them off in the night, calling to one another in some unfathomable fellowship.

Albrec was strangely unafraid. I am dying, he thought, and it does not matter.

"Sailors believe that in oyvips live the souls of lost mariners who drowned in a state of sin," the little monk told Avila, remembering his childhood on the Hardic Sea.

"What's an oyvip?" Avila asked, his voice a light feather of a thing balanced on his lips, as though his lungs were too racked with pain to give it depth.

"A great, blunt-nosed fish with a kindly eye and a habit of following ships. A happy thing, always at play."

"Then I envy those lost souls," Avila breathed.

"And woodsmen," Albrec went on, his own voice becoming slurred and faint. "They believe that in wolves abide the souls of evil men, and, some think, of lost children. They think that in the heart of the wolf lies all the darkness and despair of mankind, which is why shifters usually manifest as wolves."

"You read too much, Albrec," Avila whispered. "Too many things. Wolves are animals, mindless and soulless. Man is the only true beast, because he has the capacity not to be."

They lay with the cold seeping into their bones like some slow, cancerous growth, staring up at the stark beauty of the stars. There was no longer any pain for them, or any hope of flight or life, but there was peace out here in the drifts, in the wild country of the Narian Hills where the Free Tribes had once roamed and worshipped their dark gods.

"No more philosophy," Albrec murmured. The stars were winking out one by one as his sight darkened.

"Good night, Avila."

But from his friend there was no reply.

THE Fimbrian patrol came across them an hour later, drawn by the shadowed figures of the wolves who were gathering around them. The soldiers kicked away the beasts and found two clerics of Charibon lying stiff and cold in the snow with their faces turned up to the stars and their hands clasped together like those of two lost children. The soldiers had to chip them free of the frozen drift with their swords. The pair had on their bodies the marks of violence and rough travel, but their faces were peaceful, as serene as the countenance of a sculpted saint.

The sergeant in charge of the patrol ordered them wrapped in cloaks and carried back to camp. The patrol followed his orders, picked up the bodies and started at the double back to where the campfires of the Fimbrian army glimmered red and yellow in the starlight, less than a mile away.

The wolves watched them go in silence.

TWENTY-THREE

THEY had made good time, marching sixty leagues in eleven days. Corfe had never seen anything quite like his motley little army of savage tatterdemalions. They were eager, talkative, fiercely good-humoured. On leaving Torunn they had changed completely, and their column often rang out with tribal songs, ribald laughter. It was as if the city had placed some kind of sombre restraint on them, but now that they were out in open country, marching with swords slapping at their thighs and lances in their hands, something in them took wing. They were undisciplined, yes, but they were more enthusiastic than any other soldiers Corfe had known. It was as if they thought they were marching south to take part in some manner of festival.

He put his views to Marsch one evening as they sat by the campfire, shivering in their threadbare blankets and watching flurries of snow lit up by the flames wheeling feather-like out of the darkness beyond. Almost a third of the men were barefoot, and many had no adequate covering to keep out the cold, but the bristling crowds about the other campfires were humming with low talk, like a summer garden alive with bees.

"Why do they seem so happy?" Corfe asked his newest ensign.

The huge tribesman wiped his nose on his blanket, shrugging. "They are free. Is that not enough to make a man happy?"

"But they are marching south to fight a battle which has nothing to do with them. Why do they seem so eager to do it?"

Marsch looked at his commander strangely. "How often do the causes for which men fight mean anything to them? For my people, the Felimbri, war is our life. It is the means by which a man advances himself in the esteem of his comrades. There is no other way."

Ensign Ebro, who was sitting close by with a fur cape clutched about his shoulders, snorted with contempt.

"That is the reasoning of a primitive," he said.

"We are all primitives, and always will be," Marsch said with unusual mildness. "If men were civilized truly, then they would not kill each other. We are animals. Something in us needs to fight in order to prove we are alive. My men have been chattels, beasts harnessed for brute labour. But now they bear the weapons of free men, and they are to fight like free men, in open contest. It matters not who they fight or where, or for what."

"The philosopher savage." Ebro laughed.

"So there is no cause needed," Corfe said.

"No. A man advances himself by making subject other men, either by killing them or so dominating them that they will not dare to challenge his word. Thus are kings made—among my people, at least."

"And what were you before the galleys claimed you, Marsch?" Corfe asked quietly.

The huge savage smiled. "I was what I still am, a prince of my people."

Ebro guffawed, but Marsch ignored him as if he did not exist.

"You could kill your Torunnan officers here and now, and leave for home. No one could stop you," Corfe said.

Marsch shook his head. "We have sworn an oath which we will not break. There is honour involved. And besides"—here he actually grinned at Corfe, showing square yellow teeth whose canines had been filed to sharp points—"we are interested to see how this colonel of ours will fare in open battle, with his Torunnan ways and his plain speaking."

Then it was Corfe's turn to laugh.

THERE was no chance of the column's approach remaining a secret. Their appearance was so outlandish and unique that entire villages turned out at the side of the mud-deep roads to stare at them as they trudged past. The last few days were spent on short commons, as the Quartermaster-issued rations had run out and the men had to subsist on what they could glean from the surrounding countryside. Several cattle were quietly appropriated from awe-struck owners, but in general Corfe prevented any large-scale foraging because this was Torunna they were marching through, his own country, and also he wanted to make the greatest speed he could.

The men were marvellously fast marchers. Though their time in the galleys had blunted the fine edge of their fitness, building brute strength up in place of stamina, they were able to crack along at a fearsome pace, unhindered by an artillery train or baggage of any kind. It was all the three Torunnan officers in the column could do to keep up with their subordinates as they strode along with their helms slung at their hips and their lances resting on their powerful shoulders. Corfe was privately amazed. He had been brought up to believe that the tribes of the Cimbrics were degenerate savages, hardly worthy of attention from civilized men except when they became a nuisance

with their raiding and brigandage. But now he was learning the truth of the affair, which was that they were
natural-born soldiers. All they needed was a little
discipline and leadership and he was sure they would
acquit themselves well against any foe in the world.

Andruw was similarly impressed. "Good men," he
said, as they sucked along through the rutted mud of the
winter roads towards Hedeby. "I don't think I've ever
seen a pack of fellows so keen for a fight. I'd give my
left ball for a good battery of culverins, though."

Corfe chuckled. Humour was coming with a strange
ease to him lately. Perhaps it was being free, in the field,
his own man. Perhaps it was the prospect of slaughter.
At any rate, he did not care to examine the reasons too
closely.

"They'd not get far in this mud, your culverins. Nor
would cavalry. I'm starting to think it's as well this force
of ours is all infantry. We may find it more mobile than
we supposed."

"They march fast enough, no doubt of that," Andruw
agreed ruefully. "I'll be a short man by the time we get
to Hedeby. I've walked at least an inch off each heel."

They were half a day's march from Hedeby when they
sighted a small group of armoured cavalry outlined
against the horizon ahead, watching them. Their banners
flapped in the cold wind that winnowed the hills on either
side of the road.

"Ordinac, I'll bet," Corfe said on sighting the
horsemen, "come to have a look at what he's up against.
Unfurl the banner, Andruw."

Andruw had their standard-bearer, a massive-thewed
tribesman named Kyrn, pull loose the cathedral banner
and let it snap out atop its twelve-foot staff, a point of
vivid colour in the monochrome winter afternoon. The
rest of the men gave out a cry at the sight, a five-hundred-
voiced inarticulate roar which made the skylined horses
flinch and toss their heads.

"Line of battle," Corfe said calmly. "He's having a look, so we might as well give him something to see. Andruw, take the fifth tercio forward and chase those riders away as soon as the others have shaken out."

Andruw's boyish face lit up. "With pleasure, sir."

The five tercios of Corfe's command got into line. Five men deep, the line extended for a hundred yards. As soon as it was in place, the standard flapping with the colour party in the centre, Andruw led one tercio up the hill towards the watching riders.

There were less than a score of horsemen there, though they wore the heavy three-quarter armour of the old nobility. When the tercio was within fifty paces they turned their horses and trotted away, not liking the odds. Andruw placed his men on the hilltop and soon a gasping runner was jogging down from his position. He handed Corfe a note.

Enemy camp half a league ahead, some three leagues out of town, it read. *Looks like they are beginning to deploy.*

"Your orders, sir?" Ensign Ebro asked. Like everyone else's, his scarlet armour was so liberally plastered with muck that it had become a rust-brown colour.

"We'll join Andruw's tercio," Corfe said. "After that, we'll see."

"Yes, sir." Ebro's voice was throbbing like the wing-beat of a trapped bird and his face was pale under its spattering of mud. "Is there anything wrong, Ensign?" Corfe asked him.

"No, sir. I—it's just that—I've never been in a battle before, sir."

Corfe stared at him for a moment, somehow liking him better for this admission. "You'll do all right, Ensign."

The rest of the formation joined Andruw's men on the hilltop and stared down to where the leather tents of the enemy camp dotted the land. Off to the left, perhaps a mile away, was the sea, as grey and solid as stone. Ordinac's castle at Hedeby could be made out as a dark pinnacle in the distance. Corfe examined the duke's men with a practised eye.

"A thousand maybe, as we were told. Perhaps a hundred cavalry, the duke's personal bodyguard and mostly pikemen apart from that. I can't see too many arquebusiers. These are second-rate troops, no match for the regular army. His guns—he has two, see? Light falcons—are not even unlimbered yet. Holy Saints, I do believe he's going to offer us battle at once."

"You mean today, sir?" Ebro asked.

"I mean right now, Ensign."

Andruw came over. "Time to fight, I believe. He'll come to us if we wait for him, though look at the mobs down there: he'll be half the day getting them into formation."

Crowds of men were collecting their stacked arms and milling about whilst gesticulating officers tried to sort them into some kind of order. The only organized group seemed to be that of the duke's bodyguard, who were drawn up in a two-deep line on their heavy horses ahead of the other troops, acting as a screen until their deployment was complete.

Corfe took in the situation in a moment. He was outnumbered: he was expected to fight a defensive battle. He occupied the high ground and thus had a good position. But his men had no firearms. The enemy could close to within firing range and blast away at him half the day whilst the cavalry threatened to cave in his flanks if he tried to close.

"We will attack," he said crisply. "Andruw, Ebro, go to your tercios. Marsch, inform the men that we are to charge the enemy at once and throw them into disorder before they have time to deploy."

"But the cavalry—" Ebro said.

"Obey your orders, Ensign. Marsch, peel off the rear

rank and keep it back as a tactical reserve. I'll call for it when it's needed. Understood?"

The big tribesman nodded and pushed his way through the men behind him.

"Are you sure about this, Corfe?" Andruw asked.

"I'm not going to sit here and wait for them, Andruw. This is our only chance. We must be quick. I want everything at the double. We have to catch them while they're trying to deploy."

"Half a league at the double in this armour?" Andruw said doubtfully.

"The men can do it. Come, let's get to work."

The colour party moved out first, whilst the ranks of men behind it retied their helmstrings and loosened their swords in the scabbards. Then the formation began to move. Corfe had taught them a few words of command in Normannic, and he shouted one now, emphasizing the order with a wave of his sabre.

"Double!"

The men broke into a lumbering trot, sounding like a moving ironmonger's stall. The formation began to co-alesce as they slogged downhill through the soft ground, tearing it into a morass as they went. Behind the main body, Marsch had his hundred of the reserve in a more compact mass following in the wake of their comrades.

Tearing effort, at first quite easy because of the down-hill slope, then getting harder as the feet began to drag, the lungs began to fight for air and the heavy armour crushed down on the shoulders. The men would be tired when they made contact, but the enemy would be dis-organized and in disarray. It was an exchange Corfe was willing to make.

Half a mile gone by, and the formation ground on in silence except for the suck of boots or bare feet in the mud, the clank and crash of iron, and laboured, gasping breathing. There was no energy to spare for battlecries.

Hard to fight the head up and make the brain work, to

keep thinking. But the furious thinking and planning kept the mind off the physical pain.

The screen of heavily armoured horsemen seemed at a loss. They had obviously not expected this move. A bugle call sounded, and the riders kicked their mounts into motion up the hill. The animals were heavily laden, moving in soft, mucky ground up a gradient. The best they could do was a fast trot, counting on their weight and momentum to break Corfe's formation; that, and the fear of coming to grips with lancers.

The tribesmen uttered a hoarse, tearing whoop as the two bodies of troops met with a ringing crash, the horses struggling uphill and the infantry running down to meet them. The line was staggered, the ranks intermingling as the horsemen drove wedges of iron and muscle into it. Corfe saw one of his men speared clean through by a lance, armour and all, and tossed aside like a gutted fish.

But the horsemen could not keep up their advance. Corfe's men seized their lances and dragged them out of the saddle, stabbed upwards into armpit and groin or slashed the tendons of the horses so the screaming creatures went down kicking madly, crushing their riders. And once a rider was on his back, it was impossible for him to get up again. The heavy armour kept him pinned in the muck until a gleeful tribesman ripped off his helm and cut his throat.

It was over quickly. The cavalry line was broken into knots of milling riders who were in turn engulfed and brought down. A score of pain-crazed horses galloped riderless down the hill along with a few lancers who had somehow kept in the saddle and flailed their mounts into a canter.

"Reform!" Corfe shouted. And his men paused in their looting of the dead to dress their ranks and straighten the line.

"Double!"

The formation jogged on again. Corfe had no idea how

many casualties his little army had suffered, but that did not matter. What was important was that they catch the rest of the rebel forces before they deployed.

His armour seemed light now. He had not struck a blow during the swift, brutal skirmish, too busy trying to direct things, to keep an eye out for the larger picture, to gauge the need for the reserve under Marsch. Now the battle energy was flowing in him, the cold strength that entered into every man at the imminent prospect of death. The tribesmen advanced downhill at a flat run, and this time Corfe heard them break out into the shrill, unearthly wail that was their battlecry.

A mob of men before them, some dressed in line, some crowded in a shapeless mass. There was the bristling array of a pike tercio, the long, wicked weapons swinging down to present a fence of spikes to the attackers. Corfe's command charged into the enemy.

The rebels were pushed into a tighter mass almost at once as the men at the forefront of the formation recoiled. Here and there a company got off a rattle of volley fire, but for the most part isolated arquebusiers were loading and firing at will. Maybe the duke had died in the cavalry battle, Corfe thought; there seemed to be no leadership beyond the officers of individual tercios.

Only the tercio of pikemen kept their ranks. The tribesmen beat down the long weapons with their swords and tried to pierce the formation and disrupt it, but rear ranks of the enemy brought their own pikes down over the shoulders of their comrades and impaled the impetuous attackers. Corfe's men were pushing back the disorganized mobs of rebels elsewhere, but were taking heavy losses against the pikes.

Corfe fought his way out of the scrum until he was at the rear of his men. Marsch was waiting there with the reserve, his eyes aflame with impatience.

"Come with me," Corfe shouted at them, and led them off at a sprint.

He took them along the back of the battlefront, around the enemy flank. They met a company of arquebusiers there, placed to guard against such a move, but they were among them before the enemy could let off a volley, hacking and stabbing like scarlet-clad fiends. The arquebusiers broke and fled into their camp. Corfe led his men onwards, through the outer tents of the rebel encampment, the tribesmen kicking through fires and slashing guy-ropes as they went.

They were in the enemy rear. Incredibly, no one had posted a reserve here. The pike phalanx bristled like a vast porcupine ahead of them, Corfe's men still throwing themselves on the pike points and striving to beat them down.

"Charge!" Corfe screamed, and led his hundred forward into the rear of the pikes.

The enemy had no chance. Impressive though pikemen might be in formation, once their ranks were broken they were impotent, their unwieldy weapons a handicap. Corfe's reserve tercio slaughtered them by the score, shredding their formation to pieces.

The battle was won. Corfe knew that even as the rebels were fighting to break away from this twofold assault. The rebel army had become a mob, losing any vestige of military organization. It was simply a crowd of men struggling to save themselves, with the scarlet demons of Corfe's warriors cutting them down like corn as they ran.

"I give you joy of your victory, Colonel," Andruw said, meeting Corfe in the midst of that mass of murder. "As pretty a move as I've ever seen, and these men of ours!" He grinned. "There must be a virtue in savagery."

Victory. It tasted sweet, even if it was over fellow-Torunnans. It was better than wine or women. It was an exaltation which burned away self-doubt.

"Keep up the scare," he told Andruw. "We'll pursue them all the way to Hedeby if we have to. They mustn't be given a rest, or a chance to reform. Keep at them, Andruw."

Andruw gestured to the howling, slaughtering tribes-men who were following the retreating army and turning their rout into a murderous nightmare.

"I don't think I could stop them if I tried, Corfe."

BY nightfall it was over. Hedeby's citadel had been surrendered by the town headsman, the nobility of the place having been killed in the battle. Corfe billeted his troops in the castle itself. The remains of Duke Or-dinac's forces were scattered refugees, lost somewhere in the surrounding countryside. Many had surrendered in the town square, too exhausted to flee any farther. These were imprisoned in the castle cells. The people of the town, in terror of the bloody, weirdly armoured barbari-ans in their midst, refused them nothing in the way of food, drink, or anything else they had a mind to take, though Corfe issued stark orders against any maltreat-ment of the citizens. He had seen too much of that at Aekir to countenance it from men under his own com-mand.

Four hundred of the duke's men had died on the field, and another tenscore were bleeding and screaming wounded, most of whom would follow their dead com-rades into eternity. Corfe's men had lost less than a hun-dred, most of the casualties being incurred by the tercio which had engaged the enemy pikes head on.

Ordinac kept a good larder, and there was a feast for those well enough to stomach it that night, the tribesmen drinking and eating at the long tables of the castle hall, waited on by terrified serving attendants—Corfe had seen to it that these were male—and recounting the stories of what they had personally done in the battle lately fought. It was like a scene from an earlier, cruder age, when men put glory in battle above all other things. Corfe did not greatly care for it, but he let the men have their fun. They had earned it. He was amused to see Ensign Ebro flushed and drinking in the midst of the rest, being slapped on the back and not resenting it. Clearly the relief of having seen out his first battle without disgrace had unbent him. He was roaring with laughter at jokes told in a language he could not understand.

Corfe went out of the smoky hall to stand on the old-fashioned battlements of Hedeby Castle and look down on the town and the land below, dark under the stars. Up on the hill overlooking the town there was a dull red glow. The townspeople had dragged the bodies of the slain there on Corfe's orders and made a pyre of them. There they lay, Torunnan men-at-arms and duke and Felimbric tribesmen, all burning together. Corfe thanked his luck that his men did not seem to require elaborate burial rites. As long as the corpse burned with a sword in its hand, they were happy. Such strange men; he had come close to loving them today as they followed him without question or hesitation. Such loyalty was beyond the fortunes of kings.

Footsteps behind him, and he found himself flanked by Andruw and Marsch, the tribesman clutching a flaccid wineskin.

"Drunk already?" Andruw asked, though he might have asked the same question of himself.

"I needed air," Corfe told him. "Why are you two out here missing the fun?"

"The men want to toast their commander," Marsch said gravely.

He had been drinking solidly the whole evening, but he was as steady as a rock. He offered the wineskin to his colonel, and Corfe took a squirt of the thin, acidic wine of southern Torunna into his mouth. The taste brought back memories of his youth. He had come from this part of the world, though he had been stationed so long in the east that he nearly forgot it. Had he not joined the army at a tender age he might have been burning on that pyre on the hilltop right now, fighting for his overlord in a war whose cause he knew little of and cared less for.

"Are the pickets posted?" he asked Andruw.

The younger officer blinked owlishly. "Yes, sir. Half a mile out of town, sober as monks, and mounted on the best horses the stables could provide. Corfe, Marsch and I have been meaning to talk to you." Andruw draped an arm about Corfe's shoulders. "Do you know what we've found here?"

"What?"

"Horses." It was Marsch who was speaking now. "We have found many horses, Colonel, big enough for destriers. It would seem that this duke of yours had a passion for breeding horses. There are over a thousand in studs scattered over the countryside to the south. Some of the castle attendants told us."

Corfe turned to look Marsch in the eye. "What are you saying, Ensign?"

"My people are natural born horsemen. It is the way we prefer to fight. And this armour we wear: most of it is the armour of heavy cavalrymen anyway . . ." Marsch trailed off, his eyebrows raised.

"Cavalry," Corfe breathed. "So that's it. I was a cavalry officer myself once."

Andruw was grinning at him. "The property of traitors is confiscate to the crown, you know. But I'm sure Lofantyr will not miss a few nags. He's been niggardly enough to us so far."

Corfe stared out at the fire-split night. The pyre of the slain was like a dull eye watching him.

"On horseback we'd have more mobility and striking power, but we'd also need a baggage train of sorts, a mobile forge, farriers."

"There are men among the tribe who can shoe horses and doctor them. The Felimbri value their horseflesh above their wives," Marsch said, with perfect seriousness.

Andruw choked on a mouthful of wine and collapsed into laughter.

"You're drunk, Adjutant," Corfe said to him.

Andruw saluted. "Yes, Colonel, I am. My apologies, Marsch. Have a drink."

The wineskin did the rounds between the three of them as they leaned against the battlements and narrowed their eyes against the chill of the wind that came off the sea.

"We will equip the men with horses then," Corfe said at last. "That's eight squadrons of cavalry we'll have, plus spares for every man and a baggage train for forage and the forge. Mules to carry the grain—there's plenty about the town. And then—"

"And then?" Andruw and Marsch asked together.

"Then we march on Duke Narfintyr at Staed, get there before Lofantyr's other column and see what we can do."

"I've heard folk in the town say that Narfintyr has three thousand men," Andruw said, momentarily sobered.

"Numbers mean nothing. If they're of the same calibre as the ones we fought today we've nothing to worry about."

The moon was rising, a thin sliver, a horned thing of silver which Marsch bowed to.

" 'Kerunnos' Face,' we call it," he said in answer to the questioning looks of the two Torunnans. "It is the light of the night, of the twilight, of a dwindling people. My tribe is almost finished. Of its warriors, who once numbered thousands, there are only we few hundred left and some boys and old men up in the mountains. We are the last."

"Our people have fought you for generations," Corfe said. "Before us it was the Fimbrians, and before that the Horse-Merduks."

"Yes. We have fought the world, we Felimbri, but our time is almost done. This is the right way to end it. It was a good fight, and there will be other good fights until the last of us dies a free man with sword in hand. We can ask for nothing more."

"You're wrong, you know," Andruw spoke up unexpectedly. "This isn't the end of things. Can't you feel it? The world is changing, Marsch. If we live to old age we will have seen it become something new, and what is more we will have been a part of the forces that did the changing of it. Today, in a small way, we began something which will one day be important . . ." He trailed off. "I'm drunk, friends. Best ignore me."

Corfe slapped him on the shoulder. "You're right in a way. This is just the beginning of things. There's a long road ahead of us, if we're strong enough to walk it. God knows where it'll take us."

"To the road ahead," Marsch said, raising the almost empty wineskin.

"To the road ahead."

And they drank from it one by one like brothers.

TWENTY-FOUR

THE reek of the burning hung about Abrusio like a
dark fog, stretching for miles out to sea. The great
fires had been contained, and were burning themselves
out in an area of the city which resembled the visionary's
worst images of hell. Deep in those bright, thundering
patches of holocaust some of the sturdier stone buildings
still stood, though roofless and gutted, but the poor clay
brick of the rest of the dwellings had crumbled at the
touch of the fire, and what had once been a series of
thriving, densely populated districts was now a wasteland
of rubble and ash over which the tides of flame swept
back and forth with the wind, seeking something new to
feed their hunger even as they began to die down for lack
of sustenance.

Fighting within the city had also died down, the pro-
tagonists having retreated to their respective quarters with
the fire-flattened expanses providing a clear-cut no-
man's-land between them. Many of the King's troops
were engaged in the business of conducting evacuees be-

yond the walls and yet others were still demolishing
swathes of the Lower City, street by street, lest the flames
flare up again and seek a new path down to the sea.

"We are holding our own rather nicely," Sastro di Carrera said with satisfaction. His perch on a balcony high
in the Royal palace afforded him a fine view of Lower
Abrusio, almost half of which lay in flickering ruin.

"I think we have exhausted the main effort of the enemy," Presbyter Quirion agreed. "But a part of the fleet,
a strong squadron, has not been in sight for days. Rovero
may have sent it off somewhere to create some devil-
ment, and the main part of Hebrion's navy is at anchor
beyond the Great Harbour. I fear they may assault the
booms soon."

"Let them," Sastro said airily. "The mole forts house
a score of heavy guns apiece. If Rovero sends in his ships
to force the entrance to the harbour they will be cut to
pieces by a deadly crossfire. No, I think we have them,
Quirion. This is the time to see whether they will consider a negotiated surrender."

Quirion shook his round, close-cropped head. "They're
in no mood for talking yet, unless I miss my guess. They
still have a goodly force left to them, and our own men
are thinly stretched. They will make another effort soon,
by ship perhaps. We must remain vigilant."

"As you wish. Now, what of my coronation plans? I
trust they are forging ahead?"

Quirion's face took on a look of twisted incredulity.
"We are in the middle of a half-fought war, Lord Carrera.
This is hardly the time to begin worrying about pomp
and ceremony."

"The coronation is more than that, my dear Presbyter.
Don't you think that the presence in Abrusio of an
anointed king, blessed by the Church, will be a factor in
persuading the rebels to lay down their arms?"

Quirion was silent for a moment. From the city below
came the odd crack of arquebus fire where pickets were

taking potshots at each other, but compared to the hellish chaos of the past days Abrusio seemed almost tranquil.

"There may be something in what you say," he admitted at last. "But we will not be able to stump up much in the way of pomp for a time yet. My men and yours are too busy fighting to keep what we have."

"Of course, but I ask you to bear it in mind. The sooner this vacuum is filled the better."

Quirion nodded and then turned away. He leaned on the balcony rail and stared out over the maimed city.

"They say that fifty thousand of the citizens perished in the fire, quite apart from the thousands who died in the fighting," he said. "I don't know about you, Lord Carrera, but for me that is a heavy load for conscience to bear."

"They were heretics, the scrapings of the sewers. Of no account," Sastro said scornfully. "Do not let your conscience grow tender on their behalf, Quirion. The state is better off without them."

"Perhaps.

"Well *perhaps* you would care to walk with me and show me your plans for the defence of the Upper City."

"Yes, Lord Carrera," Quirion said heavily. As he turned away from the balcony, however, he had a moment of agonizing doubt. What had he done here? What kind of creature was he making a king of?

The moment passed, and he followed Sastro into the planning chamber of the palace, where the senior officers of their forces were awaiting them.

THERE was no beauty in ships for the lady Jemilla. To her they were little more than complicated instruments of torture, set to float on an element which might have been designed specifically to cause her discomfort.

But there were times when she could dimly see some of the reasons why men held them in such awe and reverenced them so. They were impressive, if nothing else.

She was taking a turn about the poop-deck of the *Providence*, the flagship of Rovero and Abeleyn's squadron. If she did not spend too much time looking at the gentle rise and fall of the horizon and concentrated instead on the cold wind which fanned her pale cheeks, then she might almost enjoy the motion. In any case, she would rather die than be sick here on deck, in front of five hundred sailors and marines and soldiers, all of whom were stealing privy glances up at her as she paced heavily to and fro from one bulwark to the other.

The flagship was a magnificent two-decker mounting some fifty guns, four-masted and with high-built fore- and stern-castles. Seen from aft, with her gold ornament and long galleries hanging over her wake, she looked like nothing so much as some baroque church front. But her decks presented an entirely different aspect. They had already been strewn with sand so that when the time came the gunners and sailors would not slip in their own blood. The guns had been run out, the firetubs set around the mast butts, and the slow-match which would set off the guns already lit and spreading its acrid reek about the ship. They were cleared for action. Abrusio was just over a league away. The admiral had told her they were doing six knots, and would raise the city in less than half an hour. She would be confined when that happened in the dark below-decks, in the murky stench of bilge and close-packed humanity which was the particular hallmark of every warship. So she was making the most of the fresh air, preparing herself for the ordeal ahead.

Abeleyn joined her on the poop. He was in half-armour, black-lacquered steel chased with silver and with a scarlet sash about his middle. He looked every inch the sovereign as he stood there with one hand resting on his sword hilt and the other cradling the open-faced helm which he would wear into battle. Jemilla found herself curtseying to him without conscious volition. He seemed to have grown in stature somehow, and she noticed for

the first time the streaks of grey in his curly hair behind
the temples.

"I trust you are enjoying your last moments of freedom, lady," he said, and something in the way he said it
made her shiver.

"Yes, sire. I am no sailor, as you know. I would stay
up here throughout the battle if I could."

"I believe you would." Abeleyn smiled, his regal authority falling from him. He was a young man again. "I
have seen seasick marines lift their heads and forget
about their malady the moment the guns begin to roar.
Human nature is a strange thing. But I will feel better
knowing that you are safe below the waterline."

She bowed slightly. "I am selfish. I think only of myself, and sometimes forget the burden I bear, the King's
child." She could not resist reminding him, though she
knew he disliked her doing it.

Sure enough, his face hardened. The boy disappeared
again.

"You had best go below, lady. We will be within range
of the city batteries in less than half a glass."

"As you wish, sire," she said humbly, but as she started
for the companion ladder she paused and set her hand on
his. "Be careful, Abeleyn," she whispered.

He gripped her hand briefly and smiled with his mouth
alone. "I will."

The squadron went about, the sails on every ship flashing in and out as one, obedient to the signal pennants of
the flagship. They were around the last headland and
could see in the distance Abrusio Hill, the sprawl of the
city itself and the fleet which stood ready beyond its harbours.

The sight was a shock for Abeleyn, no matter that he
had tried to prepare himself for it. It seemed to him at
first glance that his capital was entirely in ruins. Swathes
of rubble-strewn wasteland stretched across the city, and
fires were burning here and there. Only the western wa-

terfront and the Upper City on the hillside seemed unchanged. But Old Abrusio was destroyed utterly.

As the squadron was sighted, the fleet began its salute, some four hundred vessels suddenly coming alive in clouds of smoke and flame, a thunder which echoed across the hills inland and carried for miles out to sea as the King was saluted and welcomed back to his kingdom. The salute was the signal for the battle to commence, and before its last echoes had died away the warships of Hebrion had unfurled their sails and were weighing anchor. The blank rounds of a moment before were replaced by real cannonballs, and the bombardment of the mole forts which protected the Great Harbour had begun.

The staggering noise of a fleet action was something which had to be experienced for anyone to believe it. Added to the guns of the ships now was the return fire of the batteries on the city walls and the harbour forts. As his squadron edged closer to the eastern half of the Lower City, where his forces would attempt their landing, Abeleyn saw the water about the leading squadrons of the fleet erupt in geysers of foam as the first rounds went home. Topmasts were shattered by high-ranging shells and came crashing down in tangles of rigging and wood and billowing canvas. The bulwarks of the leading ships were swept with deadly chain shot, splinters of oak spraying through the gun crews like charges of canister. But still the great ships in the vanguard sailed on, their chasers firing across their bows and producing puffs of rubble and flame from the casemates of the forts.

Abeleyn saw one tall carrack dismasted entirely, her towering yards shattered and crumpling over her side. She yawed as the fallen spars dragged her to one side and in a moment had collided with one of her sister-ships. But the battle for the mole forts and the boom was being obscured by rising clouds of pale powder-smoke. It seemed that the whole surface of Abrusio's Great Harbour, over a mile from one end of it to the other, was a

seething cauldron which bubbled steam, amid which the
masts of ships could be glimpsed as the smoke rolled and
toiled in vast thunderheads across the broken face of the
sea.

The *Providence*'s guns were roaring, softening up the
waterfront where the marines and soldiers of the squadron would make their landing. On the formation's vessels
the fighting men stood in unbroken ranks amidships, their
lips moving in prayer, their hands checking armour and
weapons one last time. Three thousand men to carry the
eastern half of Abrusio and hack a way up to the palace.
They seemed pitifully few to Abeleyn, but he had to remind himself that the fleet was doing its part in the Great
Harbour, and Mercado's men would be assaulting across
the burnt wasteland of the western city also. With luck,
his own forces should not have too many of the enemy
to contend with.

He could see the sea walls of eastern Abrusio now,
scarcely three cables away. The water was deep here,
seven fathoms at least, and even the carracks would be
able to run in close to the walls to support the landing
parties with point-blank fire.

The longboats and cutters of the squadron were already
on the booms, and sailors and marines were hauling together in sweating crowds to swing them out over the
ship's sides and down to the water so far below. All this
while the guns bellowed out broadside after broadside
and were answered by the wall batteries. Abeleyn had to
hold himself upright, unflinching, as rounds began to
whistle and crash home on the carrack. A longboat took
a direct hit and exploded in a spray of jagged wood and
gore, men flung in all directions, ropes flapping free. But
the work went on, and the small boats were lowered
down the sides of the ships one by one. There were
scores of them, enough to carry over a thousand men in
the first wave.

"Your boat is ready, sire," Admiral Rovero shouted

over the noise, his lopsided mouth seemingly built to concentrate the force of his voice. Abeleyn nodded. He felt a touch of warmth as Sergeant Orsini fell into step beside him, and took a moment to grip the man's shoulder. Then he put one leg over the bulwarks and began climbing down the rope ladder hanging there while a yard away on the other side of him the culverins exploded and were reloaded, running in and out like monsters let loose and then restrained.

He was in the boat, his heart almost as loud as the gunfire in his head. The vessel was already packed with men, struggling with oars and arquebuses and swords and ladders. Abeleyn stepped over them to the prow, where the laddermen were squatting ready. He waved his hand at the helmsman, and they cast off from the looming carrack along with half a dozen other crowded boats. The men's oars dipped, and they began to move over the shot-stitched water.

An agonizing time of simply sitting there while they crawled forward towards the walls. There were scores of boats in the water, a mass of close-packed humanity crammed into them, dotting the deadly space between the hulls of the warships and the sea walls of the city. But they took few casualties in that choppy approach. The broadsides of the carracks were smothering the wall batteries with fire like mother hens protecting their chicks. Abeleyn felt that if he stuck up a hand into the air he could catch a cannonball, so thick was the volume of shot screaming overhead. To his own alarm, he had a momentary urge to throw up. Several of the men in the boat had already done so. It was the waiting, the drawing tight of the nerves to unbearable tautness. Abeleyn swallowed a mouthful of vomit that was searing his throat. Kings could not afford to show such weaknesses.

They were at the wall, the boat's bow bumping against the weathered stone. Showers of rock were falling down on them as the shells from the carracks ploughed into the

defences above their heads. The naval gunners would el-
evate their fire at the last moment, giving their comrades
as much cover as possible in that murderous time of grappling with the ungainly ladders.

The laddermen stood up with their bulky charge—a
fifteen-foot ladder with hooks of steel at its top which
were clanging against the stone. They swayed and
lurched, their legs held steady by their comrades, until
finally the ladder had hooked on to an embrasure above.

Abeleyn pushed them out of the way and climbed first.
Golophin and Mercado would have railed at him for such
foolishness, but he felt there was nothing else to do. The
King must be seen to take the lead. If these men showed
their willingness to die for him, then he too must illus-
trate it in return.

So intent, so utterly concentrated were his thoughts,
that he did not even pause to wonder if any of the men
would follow him. The spectre of his death was something which hovered gleefully, cackling at his shoulder.
His feet were leaden in their boots. He pictured his precious body torn asunder, riddled with bullets, tossed
down into the bloody water below. His life ended, his
vision of the world, unique and unrecoverable, made ex-
tinct. The strain was so great that for a second the wall
in front of his nose seemed to turn slightly red, echoing
the thunder of blood through his booming arteries.

He drew his sword, awkward and heavy in his armour,
and climbed one-handed, gulping for air that would not
be sucked into his lungs fast enough.

A stone clanged off one shoulder, and he almost fell.
Looking up, he saw a wild-eyed Knight Militant looking
over the battlements at him. He froze, utterly helpless as
he stared into the man's raging countenance. But then the
Knight's face disintegrated as a volley of arquebus fire
from the boat below hammered into him, throwing him
back out of sight. Abeleyn climbed on.

He was at the top, on the walls. Men running, dismounted guns, rubble, gaping holes in the defences. Shot from the carracks whistling higher as the guns were elevated.

Someone running towards him. His own sword flicking out before he even thought of it, clashing aside the other man's blade. A boot to the midriff, and the man was gone, screaming off over the catwalk.

More of his own men behind him. They were clearing a stretch of wall, fighting the knots of the enemy who were rushing towards them, pushing them back. It was only then that Abeleyn realized how lightly the walls were defended.

I'm alive, he thought with keen surprise. I'm still here. We are doing this thing.

Something in him changed. Until now he had been so preoccupied by what he had to do, by the possibility of his own death or maiming, that he had been thinking like a private soldier obsessed with the precariousness of his own existence. But he was the King. These men were looking to him for orders. He had the responsibility.

He remembered the seaborne fight aboard Dietl's carrack, a hundred years ago it seemed. He remembered the delight in battle, the sheer excitement of it, and his own feeling of invincibility. And he realized in a tiny, flashing instant, that he would never feel that way again, not about this. That feeling had something to do with youth and exuberance and the joy at being alive. But he had seen his city burned to ashes. He had a child growing in a woman's belly. His crown had cost his people thousands of lives. He would never feel so untrammelled and unafraid again.

"Follow me!" he shouted to his men. The enemy were falling back off the walls as hundreds more of the landing forces struggled atop the battlements. He led his troops off the sea defences of Abrusio into the streets of the city itself and the bloody work which yet awaited them.

• • •

GOLOPHIN stared at the awesome spectacle. A city in torment, burned, bombarded and broken down. Perhaps in the east, with the fall of Aekir and the battles at Ormann Dyke, they could match this scale of destruction and carnage, but nothing he had ever seen before in his long life had prepared him for it.

He had seen the King's squadron assault the eastern sea walls as the main body of the fleet attacked the mole forts and the boom which protected Abrusio's widest harbour. But now he could see nothing, not even with his cantrips, for the entire enclosed trio of bays which formed the seaward side of the city was obscured by thundering smoke clouds. Three miles of shell-torn water from which a steady roar issued, as though some titanic, agonizing labour of birth were going on deep in that fog of war.

His familiar was dying somewhere aboard the King's flagship. He had worn it out with his errands and only a flicker of life remained within its breast, a last spark of the Dweomer he had created it with. He could feel the ebbing of its loyal, savage mind, and with it was fading his own strength. No light thing, the death of a familiar. It was like losing a child whose umbilical had never been cut. Golophin felt as old and frail as a brittle leaf, and the Dweomer had sunk in him to a dull glow. It would be a long time ere he was ready to perform miracles again.

And yet he chafed at being here, on the summit of Admiral's Tower, while the young man who was his lord and his friend fought for his birthright and the life of the city they both loved. The bastard traitors and Knights had ripped the bowels out of raucous Lower Abrusio. It would never be the same again, not in what remained of this old man's lifetime anyway.

General Mercado joined him, leaving the aides and staff officers and couriers who were clustered about the map-littered table on the other side of the tower.

"He is over the walls," the general said, one side of his face crannied with worry, the other silver perfection.

"Well, that is something. And the attack on the boom?"

"Too soon to say." An especially severe series of broadsides from the harbour tumult meant he had to raise his voice to be heard. "We've lost at least four great ships and there's no chance for the crews in that maelstrom. And those who make it ashore are being killed out of hand by the lackeys of the Carreras. At least two thousand men already."

"What of your land assault?"

"Slow progress there. They've thrown up breastworks along their front and my men are having to charge them across the wasteground. There will be no sudden breakthrough, not in this half of the city. We are merely pinning down his troops."

"So the main effort will be with Abeleyn?"

"Yes. His is the only assault which is presently getting anywhere. But with scarcely four thousand men the Presbyter cannot hold on to all his lines indefinitely. He will crack in the end. It only remains to be seen how much blood we must spill before he does."

"Great God, General, this will ruin the kingdom."

Golophin felt faint, worn, useless. The burly soldier steadied him with a hand on his thin arm.

"You should be resting, Golophin. We cannot spare men such as you, either now or in the future."

The old wizard smiled wanly. "My life is not of such great account, not any more. We are each of us expendable, save one. Nothing must happen to the King, Albio, or this is all for nothing. The King must be made to realize that."

"I'm sure he will be prudent. He is no fool, despite his youth."

"He is not such a youth any more, either."

• • •

THE enemy lines had broken, and those who could were retreating westwards, having spiked their guns and fired their magazines. The Carrera retainers led the rout, whilst the Knights Militant brought up the rear, fighting stubbornly the whole way. Abeleyn's men took heavy casualties as they followed up the retreat and stumbled into bitter hand-to-hand conflict with the Knights, who were well-trained and superbly armoured. It was only when the King halted the advance and reformed what men he could that the Knights were thrown back in disorder. Abeleyn's arquebusiers and sword-and-buckler men had become disorganized and intermingled. He separated them and led the advance with quick-firing ranks of arquebusiers alone, which cut down the stolid Knights Militant and sowed panic in the enemy forces. The streets were streaming with men, some intent on saving their own lives, others intent on cutting them down. It had become a running battle, one-sided and fast-moving.

A gasping courier found Abeleyn near the foot of Abrusio Hill, directing the pursuit of the fleeing traitors in person and jogging along with his advancing forces as he snapped out orders right and left. The courier had to tug at the King's arm before Abeleyn could be halted.

"What? What is it, damn it?"

"I am sent from General Rovero, sire," the man panted. "He presents his compliments—"

"Damn his compliments! What has he to say?"

"The fleet has broken the boom, sire. They're sailing into the Great Harbour and beginning to bombard the Upper City. They'll be landing their marines in minutes. Sire, the general and Golophin beg that you do not expose yourself unnecessarily."

"My thanks for their advice. Now run to the waterfront and hurry along those landing parties. I want the palace surrounded before the traitors can escape. Go!"

"Yes, your majesty." And Abeleyn had disappeared into the midst of his jubilant, advancing troops.

• • •

"IT is over," said Quirion.

Sastro's face was as pale as snow. "What do you mean, 'over'?"

They could hear the crackling of arquebus volleys as they stood in the high chambers of the palace's topmost tower. It and the thunder of heavy guns mingled with the crash and rumble of lacerated masonry. Shells were falling closer. Men's voices could be made out in individual screams rather than the far-off roar of battle which had been what they had heard from this eminence so far. A curtain of battle din was inexorably advancing towards them.

"Our lines are broken, Lord Carrera, and our forces—even my Knights—are in full retreat. The enemy ships have broken the boom and are in the Great Harbour trying the range for the palace. In a few minutes the bombardment of this very edifice will commence. We are defeated."

"But how is that possible? Only this morning we were ready to discuss terms with an exhausted enemy."

"You were ready. I never believed it would happen. Abeleyn is in the city as we speak, advancing on the palace. His men fight like fiends when he is at their head, and ours become discouraged. It may be we can draw together what troops of ours remain and make a stand here, perhaps sue for some terms other than those of unconditional surrender. I do not know. Your retainers are in utter rout, and even my people are much broken up. I have my senior officers in the streets trying to rally them, but I do not hold out much hope."

"Then we must escape," Sastro said in a strangled voice, his dreams and ambitions crumbling away before his eyes. But his life—it must be possible to survive. It was unthinkable that he would not.

"The palace is surrounded. There is no hope of escape, and especially not for you." Here a note of some subtle satisfaction crept into Quirion's voice. "If you are caught they will execute you out of hand for high treason. Myself and my men I believe they may let depart in peace—we are not Hebrionese, after all—but you and your men are traitors and will pay the ultimate penalty. I suggest, Lord Carrera, that to avoid public humiliation at the hands of Abeleyn's soldiery, you use this—" And here Quirion held out a long, wicked-looking knife.

"Suicide?" Sastro squawked. "Is that the only end for me? Take my own life?"

"It would be a kinder end than the one Abeleyn will permit you."

"And you—you will tamely submit to the dictates of a heretic king? What will the Pontiff think of that, Presbyter?"

"The Pontiff will not be pleased, naturally, but better that I bring him a thousand Knights out of this debacle than nothing. There is the future to think of. My men must live to fight again for the Church."

"The future," Sastro said bitterly. Tears were brimming in his eyes. "You must help me get away, Quirion. I am to be King of Hebrion. I am the only alternative to Abeleyn."

"You bought your nomination with your men's bodies," Quirion said harshly. "There are others whose blood is better. Make a good end of it, Lord Carrera. Show them that you died a man."

Sastro was weeping openly. "I cannot! How can I die, I, Sastro di Carrera? It cannot be. There must be something you can do." He clutched at Quirion's armoured shoulders as if he were a drowning man reaching for his rescuer. A spasm of disgust crossed the Presbyter's face.

"Help me, Quirion! I am rich—I can give you anything."

"You whining cur!" Quirion spat. "You would send a hundred thousand men to their deaths without a thought, and yet you cringe at the prospect of your own. Great

Gods, what a king you would have made for this unhappy realm! So you will give me anything?"

"Anything, for God's sake, man! Only name it."

"I will take your life, then," the Presbyter snarled, and he thrust the knife into the nobleman's stomach.

Sastro's eyes flared in disbelief. He staggered backwards.

"Sweet Saints," he gasped. "You have killed me."

"Aye," Quirion said shortly, "I have. Now get about your dying like a man. I go to surrender Abrusio to the heretic."

He turned on his heel and left the room without a backward glance.

Sastro fell to his knees, his face running with tears. *"Quirion!"*

He gripped the hilt of the knife and tried to pull it out of his belly, but only yelped at the pain of it, his fingers slipping on the slick blood. He fell to his side on the stone floor.

"Oh, sweet Blessed Saint, help me," he whispered. And then was silent. A bubble of blood formed over his open mouth, hovered, and finally popped as his spirit fled.

"THERE are white flags all over the city, sire," Sergeant Orsini told Abeleyn. "The enemy are throwing down their arms—even the Knights. Abrusio is ours!"

"Ours," Abeleyn repeated. He was bloody, grimed and exhausted. He and Orsini walked up the steep street to where the abbey of the Inceptines glowered sombre and high-spired on the skyline ahead. His men were around him, weapons still at the shoulder, but the glee of victory was brightening their faces. Shells were falling, but they were being fired by the ships in the harbour. The enemy batteries had been silenced. Men sank into crouches as a shell demolished the side of a house barely fifty yards away. Streamers of oily smoke were rising from the abbey as it burned from a dozen direct hits.

"Courier," Abeleyn croaked. His mouth felt as though someone had filled it full of gunpowder.

"Sire?"

"Run down to the waterfront. Get a message to Admiral Rovero. The bombardment of the Upper City is to cease at once. The enemy has surrendered."

"Gladly, sire." The courier sped off.

"I wish you joy of your victory, sire," Orsini said, grinning.

Abeleyn found himself smiling, though he did not know why. He held out his hand, and after a moment's surprise Orsini took it. They shook as though they had just sealed a bargain. The men cheered at the sight.

More Royal soldiers were congregating as the news spread. Soon there was a crowd of several hundred about Abeleyn, shaking their swords and arquebuses in the air and cheering, heedless of the cannonballs which were arcing down not far away. They picked up Abeleyn and carried him in crude triumphal procession towards the burning abbey and the shell-pocked palace which belonged to him again. Abrusio, broken and smouldering, had been restored to her rightful sovereign.

"Long live the King!" they shouted, a hoarse roar of triumph and delight, and Abeleyn, borne aloft by the shoulders and the approbation of the men who had fought with him and for him, thought that it was for this, this feeling, that men became conquerors. It was more precious than gold, more difficult to earn than any other form of love. It was the essence of kingship.

The shouting, parading troops were almost at the walls of the abbey, their numbers swelled to thousands, when the last salvo from the ships in the harbour came screaming down among them.

The street erupted around Abeleyn. One moment he was being borne along on the shoulders of a victorious army, and then the world became a heaving nightmare of bursting shells and screaming men. His bearers were scattered under him and he fell heavily to the cobbles, cracking his head on the stone. Someone—he thought it was Orsini—had thrown his body across him, but Abeleyn would have none of that. He would not cower behind other men like a frightened woman. He was a king.

Thus he was fighting to get to his feet in the panicked crush, pushing men aside to right and left, when the last shell in the salvo exploded not two yards away, and his world disappeared.

TWENTY-FIVE

THE woman was beautiful in the winter sunlight, tall and slim as a mountain birch, with something of the same starkness about her colouring. The officers on the galley quarterdeck directed quick, hungry glances at her as she stood by the starboard rail. She was veiled, of course, as all the Sultan's concubines were, but Aurungzeb was so proud of his Ramusian beauty that her veil was translucent, scandalous, as was her clothing. As the wind shifted the layered gauze about her body it was possible to see the momentary imprint of her nipples, the line of her thigh and calf. The stolen looks kept many of the Merduk sailors dreaming for weeks, while the slaves who toiled at the oars and who had once been free Ramusian citizens regarded her with pity and outrage. She was somehow more evocative of her people's enslavement than the chains that shackled them at wrist and ankle, a taunting display of Merduk prowess.

It seemed that she was staring out at one thing only, and saw nothing else: the monstrous central tower of what had once been the cathedral of Carcasson, horned, forbidding and black with the flames it had survived. It stood alone amid the rubble of what had once been the greatest city in the world and was now a desolated waste-land, save where the walls of the larger buildings stood like monuments to a lost people.

Aekir, the Holy City. Months had passed since its fall, but it was still a ruin. The Merduks had encamped by the thousand around the Square of Victories, where the statue of Myrnius Kuln stood yet, and their tents formed streets and villages in the middle of the desolation, but even their teeming thousands could not fill a tithe of the space within the broken circuit of the city's walls. They were like maggots come squirming in the long-dead corpse of a unicorn, and Carcasson was the dead beast's horn.

The woman called Ahara by her lord and master the Sultan Aurungzeb had once been someone else. A life-time, a millennium, a nightmare ago, she had been named Heria and had been married to an ensign of cavalry named Corfe. Until Aekir fell.

Now she was the bed toy of the greatest conqueror in the east. She was a trophy of war as much as ruined Aekir was, and she stared out at Carcasson's lonely spire as if in communion with it.

Her grasp of Merduk was very good now, but the Sul-tan did not know that. She had been careful to appear slow in comprehension and muddled in her own efforts at conversation. Not that there was much conversation required when Aurungzeb blew into the harem like a gale, calling for his favourite bedmate. One had to be willing and uncaring, and submit to whatever the Sultan had in mind.

She had no hope of deliverance: that dream had been knocked out of her long ago. And since her Corfe, who had been her life, was dead it did not seem to matter in what manner she spun out her existence. She was like a

ghost hovering on the fringe of life, with no expectations
and no prospect of change.

But she kept a little corner of her soul to herself. It
was for this reason that she pretended to be slow in learning the Merduk language. Aurungzeb would say things
in front of her, or hold discussions in her presence which
he was sure she could not understand. That was power
of a sort, a tiny gesture towards the maintenance of some
personality of her own.

And thus she stood here as the Sultan's galley was
rowed down the broad expanse of the Ostian river, with
ruined Aekir running along the banks on either side. And
she listened.

The commander of the main field army of Ostrabar,
Shahr Indun Johor, was deep in talk with the Sultan
whilst the staff officers kept to the port side of the quarterdeck. Heria, or Ahara, was able to eavesdrop on them
as the toiling slaves propelled the galley downriver towards the concentration of ships and men that waited
farther downstream.

"The Nalbenic transports have already docked, highness," Shahr Johor was saying. A tall, fine-featured
young man, he was the successor to Shahr Baraz, the old
khedive who had taken Aekir and made the first, fruitless
assaults on Ormann Dyke.

"Excellent." Aurungzeb had a white-toothed grin that
was somehow startling in the midst of that expanse of
beard, like suddenly glimpsing the bared canines of a
dark-furred dog. "And how soon will the fleet be ready
to sail?"

"Within two days, highness. The Prophet has blessed
us with mild winds. The transports will be in the Kardian
Gulf before the end of the week, and at their assigned
stations on the Torunnan coast three days after that. In
less than two sennights we will have an army on Torunnan soil south of the Searil river. We will have outflanked
Ormann Dyke."

"Ah, Shahr Johor, you gladden my heart." Aurungzeb's grin broadened. He was a hearty man with a thickening middle and eyes as black and bright as shards of jet. "Your excellency!" he called to the group of men on the other side of the quarterdeck. "I must congratulate your lord on his swift work. The treaty is only signed a week and already his galleys are at their station. I am most impressed."

One of the men came forward and bowed. He was of below medium height, dressed in rich embroidered silk and with a gold chain about his neck: the Merduk badge of an ambassador.

"My sultan, may he live for ever, will be gladdened by your confidence and pleasure, highness. Nalbeni has never wanted anything else but that it and Ostrabar might work together, as brothers would, for the propagation of the faith and the defeat of the unbelievers."

Aurungzeb laughed. His high spirits were spilling out of him. "We shall have a banquet tonight to toast this new cooperation between our states, and the confusion of the enemy who will no longer be able to defy the might of our armies behind walls of stone, but will have to come out into the field and fight like men."

Ahara was forgotten. The Sultan and his staff went below with the Nalbenic ambassador to pore over the maps they had already been poring over for days and fix the last details of their joint plans in place.

Ahara remained by the galley's rail. Aekir slid by, and the river became busier. There were hundreds of ships here, moored at the remnants of old wharves. A mighty fleet flying the Nalbenic flag, and an army encamped on the riverbank beside it. A hundred thousand men they said it numbered. Some had been withdrawn from before the dyke, others were fresh levies gathered throughout the winter from the farms and towns of Ostrabar and Nalbeni. Soon Torunna would be overwhelmed, the fortifications of Ormann Dyke rendered useless by the amphibious invasion. This panorama of men and ships was the death knell of the Ramusian west.

And it did not matter. The world Ahara had known had died here, in a welter of slaughter and rape and burning. She was numb to the possibility that the rest of the continent might soon fare similarly. She was only glad, in the small portion of her that remained her own, that she was allowed to stand here in the sunlight and listen to the seagulls and smell the salt air of the Ostian estuary. She gloried in her solitude.

But it ended, as it always did, and she was called below to attend upon the Sultan and his guests. Her dancing had come on apace, and Aurungzeb loved to have her perform for an audience. It whetted his appetite, he said.

The galley sailed on, the slaves bending at the oars, the vast armada of men and ships and munitions sliding past on each side. It seemed that the whole world had been picked up and reconfigured. It was a different place now, impervious to the wishes of the men who inhabited it. Some dreadful engine had begun to turn in the hot darkness of its vitals and could not be stopped any more than the sun could be halted in its path. The "force of history," a philosopher might call it, or a more practical man might simply name it "war." Whatever its epithet, it was about to break apart the world men had known, and fashion from the pieces something terrible and new.

Paul Kearney

<u>Hawkwood's</u>
<u>Voyage</u>

Book One of the Monarchies of God

0-441-00903-4/$6.50

Prices slightly higher in Canada

Payable by Visa, MC or AMEX only ($10.00 min.), No cash, checks or COD. Shipping & handling:
US/Can. $2.75 for one book, $1.00 for each add'l book; Int'l $5.00 for one book, $1.00 for each
add'l. Call (800) 788-6262 or (201) 933-9292, fax (201) 896-8569 or mail your orders to: